St

Anne Billson was born in 1954 in Southport, Lancs. She is the film critic of the *Sunday Telegraph* and a contributing editor of British *GQ*. Her published works are *Screen Lovers, Dream Demon* and *My Name is Michael Caine*. *Suckers* was 'Fresh Talent', W. H. Smith's choice of the best first novels, and it led to a place on *Granta*'s 'Best Young British Novelists' of 1993 for the author. *Suckers* is also available in Pan Books.

BY THE SAME AUTHOR

Suckers

ANNE BILLSON

Stiff Lips

PAN BOOKS

First published 1996 by Macmillan

This edition published 1997 by Pan Books
an imprint of Macmillan Publishers Ltd
25 Eccleston Place, London SW1W 9NF
and Basingstoke

Associated companies throughout the world

ISBN 0 330 34804 3

A CIP catalogue record for this book is available from
the British Library.

Typeset by CentraCet Limited, Cambridge
Printed and bound in Great Britain by
Mackays of Chatham plc, Chatham, Kent

'Being a woman is a terribly difficult trade since it consists principally of dealings with men.'

Joseph Conrad, *Chance*

'But there is no foundation for the statement, occasionally met with, that a vast lake underlies the district.'

Florence Gladstone,
Notting Hill in Bygone Days

'Stiff lips, stiff lips
Stiff lips, hey heat up a bit'

Sheena & the Rokkets, *Stiff Lips*

SPRING

ONE

AFTERWARDS, no one could remember what had got us started on ghosts. It wasn't the sort of thing we usually talked about. We all tolerated Daisy's tall stories, but it wasn't as though we egged her on. I'd never found any of that crap remotely interesting; I was aware that Susie always read her horoscope in the *Standard,* but she knew better than to read me mine.

Normally I might have pinned the blame on Ralph, who still retained a spotty adolescent appetite for the macabre. Ralph had seen all the horror movies ever made and could tell you within nanoseconds whether a picture of Christopher Lee with flashy dentures and red contact lenses had been lifted from *Dracula, Dracula Has Risen from the Grave,* or *Dracula Sucks,* but he'd learned long ago not to inflict his puerile Gothic fantasies on the rest of us.

But Ralph was recovering from the flu, and on that particular evening fell some way short of being his usual obnoxious self. Not only was he uncharacteristically subdued, but he had sloped off home to an early sickbed long before the conversation took its morbid turn.

I suppose it might have been Luke who set the ball rolling but, with everything that happened later, it's difficult to say for sure. But I remember his face as he spoke; all of a sudden, he was looking like a frightened little boy as he told us how once, as a child, he had been climbing the rickety old staircase in his aunt's farmhouse in Norfolk. He recalled how it had been cold enough for him to see his breath turn to vapour in the air, how he had started to shiver uncontrollably, and how he had looked up at the landing to see a grey lady waiting for him with arms outstretched and an expression on her face that was ineffably sad and, somehow, hungry.

Luke, sensibly recalling his parents' stern directive that he was never *ever* to talk to strangers, had promptly fled back downstairs to the warmth of the kitchen, and it was only later, when his aunt had strenuously denied the existence of any such person in the house, that he realized he had glimpsed someone who hadn't really been *there*.

Of course, that started Daisy off, and she launched into the one about the black cat that haunted her kitchen. I'd heard it before, but the story had snowballed. Previously, it had been a glimpse of movement, and faint disembodied miaowing. Now, though, it was cartons of milk disappearing from her kitchen table and entire packets of smoked salmon vanishing from the freezer. I told her it was more likely to be a gourmet burglar than a phantom feline, and wondered out loud how any animal, phantom or otherwise, could possibly get into one of those cardboard Tetrapacks when they reduced most humans to a state of gibbering frustration. Daisy accused me of not taking her seriously, which was fair enough, but then I made the mistake of replying that the only person who ever took Daisy seriously was Daisy herself, so then Luke and Susie and Miles jumped in and told us to shut up, but not before I'd got in one last cheap shot about our friend feeling her biological clock tick-tick-ticking away and fixing on her imaginary pet as a baby substitute.

I think it was Miles who steered the conversation back into calmer water by telling us how once, at school, he and his friends had spread a rumour about the science lab being haunted. It had started off as a prank, but before they knew it, boys who hadn't been in on the joke were claiming to have seen things. On three separate occasions, pupils fainted clean away in class. Chemistry experiments went spectacularly wrong – test-tubes exploding, acid burns and clouds of poison gas leading to more than one emergency evacuation. The last straw was when one particularly sensitive boy had a screaming fit and insisted the ghost had been trying to remove his trousers.

There were angry rumblings from parents. The Headmaster uttered grim threats in assembly. A Catholic priest was brought in to stalk the corridors and mutter in Latin. As far as Miles could remember, no actual exorcisms were performed, but the priestly presence seemed to do the trick, and there had been no further reports of paranormal activity.

None of us had met Clare before. She was a mousy little thing, altogether too pale and droopy for my taste, though I suppose she might have been quite attractive if she'd shed a couple of pounds, ditched the dowdy specs, and daubed on a bit of lipstick or whatever it is girls do to brighten themselves up. You can never tell with women. Some of them make themselves look drab on purpose.

The rest of us had been knocking around together for years, on and off, though Miles had been out of circulation for a while. We'd all assumed his absence had had something to do with his love life – it was a fair assumption with regard to Miles – but we were taken aback when he finally introduced us to Clare; she didn't seem his type at all. It must have been tricky for her as the sole stranger in our midst, but it wasn't as though she'd been trying very hard. Up until that point, she'd hardly opened her mouth, except to say please, thank you, and where's the bathroom?

Susie had just finished telling us about some American cousins whose house had been built on the site of a Sioux burial ground, and how, after being driven to distraction by nocturnal banging noises which seemed to be coming from *inside* the walls, they had torn out the plumbing and found, lodged within one of the pipes, a thick black snake.

'You see,' I said to Susie, 'there's always a logical explanation for everything.'

'Ah,' Susie replied, 'but who do you suppose had *persuaded* the snake to hide there in the first place?'

I was just telling her not to be so idiotic when we saw Miles nudge Clare. At any rate, it might have seemed like a nudge to him, but she flinched as though he'd slapped her across the face.

'Come on,' he was saying, 'aren't you going to tell them about Sophie?'

He'd been speaking *sotto voce*, but everyone heard, and we all looked expectantly at Clare. Her face flushed a gentle pink, and she whispered something into Miles's ear, apparently hoping the conversation would resume without her. We were all curious, but even so it might have stopped there, had it not been for Daisy.

'Sophie?' she piped up. 'Sophie *Macallan*? Oh, I'd give anything to know what *really* happened.'

Clare's face stopped being droopy and suddenly took on one or two sharp edges that hadn't been there before.

'This isn't a joke, you know,' she muttered, in a voice so low we all had to strain to hear it. 'I mean, you're all having a whale of a time here, wittering on about your grey ladies, and black cats, and little green men. You think it's *funny*, don't you? But what happened to Sophie wasn't funny at all. You can't expect me to talk about it as if it was just another of your amusing little anecdotes. I mean, Sophie was my *friend*. She was my *best* friend.'

But it was too late. Now we were sitting up and begging for it. Clare was obviously sitting on the ghost story to end all ghost stories.

'Come on, Clare,' urged Susie.

'Yes, come on, Clare,' said Luke. He picked up the bottle of wine and held it out to her. 'Have a top-up.'

'We really *want* to know,' said Daisy, and then added, rather spitefully, 'We won't let you go home until you've told us. Everyone's done their bit, except you.'

Clare was still looking for a way out. Her gaze fell on me. 'That's not true,' she said. 'What about *him*? He hasn't said anything yet.'

'Never mind about me,' I said. 'I go last. I always go last.'

In desperation, she turned to Miles. 'I don't want to. They can't make me.'

If she thought Miles was going to do the gentlemanly thing and take her part against the rest of us, she was wrong. He was pretending to be solicitous, but it was just a ploy to get her to do what he wanted; I recognized it because it was a technique I used as well. Miles obviously thought it would be a personal triumph for him if she could be persuaded to talk: he was the one who had brought her along, after all, and up until now she hadn't exactly been knocking us out of our socks with her social skills. Besides, I think he was getting a sadistic kick out of seeing her squirm. I know I was.

He draped his arm around her shoulders in a way that was more proprietorial than supportive, and I heard him say, 'Why not? Maybe it'll do you good to get it out of your system.'

Clare gave up. Her face lost its edge and went slack again. She looked at Miles one last time, but he was smiling in that supercilious way he has. I wondered why she put up with him. I wondered why she was putting up with *us*. Maybe, deep down, she was keen to spill the beans after all.

Then she seemed to make up her mind that, since she was being forced into it, she might as well do things properly. In an abandoned gesture, oddly out of keeping with the reserved front she'd been presenting up until now, she tipped her head back and drained her glass in one gulp. I found myself strangely moved by the sight of her exposed throat as she swallowed. I was beginning to find Clare rather intriguing.

'Oh, all right,' she said crossly, holding out the empty glass for a refill. 'You want to hear about Sophie? OK, I'll *tell* you about Sophie. I'll tell you *everything*. I'll tell you the *whole story*.'

And she did.

Afterwards, there were some of us who rather wished she hadn't.

TWO

SOPHIE hadn't spent more than a couple of nights in her new flat, so when she woke up at three o'clock one morning, it was some time before she was able to work out where she was.

The air was cold against her face. She lay in bed, staring in the half-light at the unfamiliar ceiling and shivering, until she realized that, if she wanted to get back to sleep, some sort of action would have to taken.

The curtains had been left by the previous occupier, and although they were not at all to Sophie's taste . . .

'Hang on a minute, said Luke. 'How do you know all this?'

'Sophie told me,' said Clare. 'She told me everything.'

'Yes, but how do you know what she was *thinking*?'

'Shut up and let her get on with it,' said Susie.

Clare sighed. 'You'll just have to trust me on this. I *know* what I'm talking about.'

'Yes, but . . .'

'Shut up and let her get on with it.'

The curtains had been left by the previous occupier, and although they were not to Sophie's taste, she hadn't yet had a chance to replace them. They were made out of some grubby man-made fibre which didn't flutter, or even flap, so much as *bulge*. They were bulging now, in the night breeze. Sophie slid out of bed and padded naked to the window with the intention of closing it.

It wasn't until she got there that she saw the window was already closed.

At the time, she never gave it a second thought. She rummaged around in the nearest suitcase until she found a big white shirt. She put it on, went back to bed and fell asleep almost immediately.

We'd been best friends since the age of twelve. I was one of two pupils assigned to look after Sophie when she arrived midway through term. For some reason I can't recall, she arrived very late at night, when the rest of us were already changed into our pyjamas. She stood there gravely, like a miniature grown-up, neatly buttoned up in non-regulation Burberry, clutching a small brown suitcase in one hand and a battered teddy-bear in the other. She told me later that the teddy-bear had once belonged to the Marquis of Montrose.

By that stage, most of the other girls in our class had paired off, or formed cliques, except for the dregs and the misfits, who were lumped together by default because no one else wanted to touch them. I lived in terror that someone would discover my secret – that I was a dreg and a misfit too – and had been searching in vain for someone to latch on to. And here, as if in answer to my prayers, was Sophie.

11

She was the prettiest girl I'd ever seen. She had long
fair hair that was usually tied back in a ponytail or
woven into a fat braid that hung neatly down her back.
She had perfectly even white teeth (with a slight gap
between the incisors), and skin that had a *café-au-lait*
glow to it, as though she had only just come back from
somewhere faraway, like Tahiti or the Bahamas. Even
her name was glamorous. *Sophie* – it made me think of
satin ballet shoes and velvet collars and whipped cream
and Belgian truffles and pancakes with maple syrup –
all the things I associated with the high life I had never
led.

And Sophie's home life seemed so much more
romantic and interesting than the drab mothballed
world of my grandparents. They had been my legal
guardians in the nine years since my parents had been
killed in a pile-up on the M42, leaving behind them just
enough money to put me through a relatively posh
school. But the M42! Even the road was wrong. Had it
been Sophie's parents, they would have got themselves
killed on the Via Veneto, or the Pacific Coast Highway,
or on one of those hairpin bends leading down to the
French Riviera.

We'd been told Sophie had missed half the term
because her mother had died, but it wasn't long before
she swore me to secrecy and whispered the truth. Selina
– Sophie always referred to her parents by their Chris-
tian names – had run off to Venezuela with a man
called Ramon who bred racehorses. In my eyes, of
course, this made her life seem even more exciting and
romantic; I'd known girls whose parents had split up,

but none whose parents had split up quite so emphatically.

Sophie detested her mother, but adored her father. As far as she was concerned, Hamish could do no wrong. In a rash moment, I once asked why, if he was such a fabulous father, had he not brought her up himself, instead of packing her off to boarding school?

'He travels abroad a lot,' said Sophie. 'A child would get in the way.' I remember thinking it peculiar, the way she referred to herself in the third person, as 'a child'.

'But why pick *this* school?'

'It's the best one, that's all.'

'Yes,' I persisted, 'but this is *Sussex*, and your father lives all the way up in *Scotland*.'

Maybe Sophie herself didn't know the answer. At any rate, that was the first time she ever told me to fuck off.

I was reminded of that as I came up the stairs and heard her shouting, 'Oh, for Christ's sake, I *told* you I needed this room finished before the fucking hallway!' She had to shout loudly to make herself heard above the noise from the radio.

Sophie didn't swear very often. Nor was it usual for her to raise her voice above her habitual breathy whisper; she usually didn't have to. People always craned forward to hang on her every word, whereas whenever I strained for the same effect they would always cup their hands around their ears and tell me not to mumble.

13

I'd started feeling apprehensive the second I turned the corner into Hampshire Place and laid eyes on number nine. It looked familar, though that wasn't surprising since it was standard-issue Victorian terrace, and it sometimes seemed as though I'd spent half my adult life wandering up and down these streets, gazing longingly at the windows and trying to divine what lay behind them.

I gazed longingly now, as I crossed the road, and saw someone standing in one of the upstairs windows, looking down. I couldn't see too clearly without spectacles, but I thought it might be Dirk. I waved, but he didn't wave back, and then a car came along, and I had to watch where I was going and lost sight of the window. I went up the front steps, found the door open, and went straight in.

My heart sank as I heard Sophie yelling. This was going to be embarrassing; Dirk and Lemmy were friends of mine, and it had been I who had suggested to Sophie that she hire them as decorators. I'd imagined I was doing everyone a favour, but it was turning out to be a disaster. Lemmy was artistic, but lacked ambition. Dirk occasionally knocked down walls for people; sometimes I wondered whether he did it with his head. But mostly they passed their time listening to Capital Radio, drinking Tennants Extra and smoking grass. Unfortunately, these activities were such an integral part of their lives that they continued to pursue them while working for Sophie.

The door to Sophie's flat was on the first landing, propped open with a paint can. I found myself looking straight into the bathroom, where Dirk, Lemmy and two stepladders were crammed between the toilet and the towel-rail amid a riot of Neapolitan ice-cream colour. They were slapping pale raspberry over even paler pistachio and singing tunelessly along to the radio, which was perched on the edge of the bath, making a sizzling noise like chips in a deep-fat fryer.

They broke off from their singing to greet me.

'Hi, Clare!' said Dirk.

'Kampuchea jambalaya manderlay *down the market*,' said Lemmy.

I mustered something non-committal in reply. It wasn't a speech impediment Lemmy had, not exactly, because you never had any trouble *hearing* what he said. It was just that very little of it ever made sense. He might as well have been jabbering in Cantonese, though Dirk always seemed to understand what he was talking about and would occasionally provide a loose translation.

The bathroom was next to the kitchen, which is where I found Sophie hunched over a steaming kettle with a pained expression on her face. Instead of saying hello, she said, 'I expect you want some coffee.'

I nodded assent, and she filled the cafetière with boiling water. 'They're imbeciles,' she said. 'They can't even tune the radio properly. No wonder they can't find full-time jobs.'

'Actually Lemmy's quite brainy,' I said. 'He did Biochemistry at university. At least, until he dropped out.'

'It might help if he learned to speak properly,' said

15

Sophie. 'I can't understand a word he says. It's embarrassing.'

'It is a bit of a problem with Lemmy,' I admitted.

'And would you believe they painted the bathroom the wrong colour? I told them to go over it again, but if they expect me to pay them twice they've got another think coming.'

She jammed the plunger down into the cafetière so violently that the worktop wobbled. 'Sorry to go on about it,' she said. 'It's not that I don't like them. It's just that they're not terribly competent.'

I was getting fed up with hearing her moaning. 'Maybe you should give them their marching orders,' I suggested.

Sophie shook her head. 'Oh, I couldn't do that. Wouldn't be fair. No, I'll manage.'

She unwrapped four coffee cups with matching saucers, fashioned from china so pale it was almost translucent, with handles so delicate there was barely anything to grip.

'I don't suppose you have any mugs?' I asked, already seeing Dirk's meaty fist accidentally mashing this doll's-house crockery into pearlized dust.

Sophie just didn't get it, 'There was nothing to drink from,' she explained patiently. 'I had to go out and *buy* these.' I thought plastic beakers from the local Qwik-Mart would have done just as well, but didn't say so. I knew what Sophie was like. 'Grenville's supposed to be bringing the rest of my stuff round tomorrow afternoon,' she added.

Grenville was a horrible little dwarf who lived not far

away, in Campden Hill Road, with Carolyn. Carolyn was, after me of course, probably Sophie's best friend.

'Want some help unpacking?' I asked her.

'Wouldn't say no.'

As she poured the coffee I said, as casually as I could, 'And will Miles be lending a hand?'

Sophie tensed. 'Not bloody likely. I believe he's off to Paris for the weekend.' She didn't say whether Miles was off to Paris on his own. She didn't have to; we both knew who would be accompanying him. I should have been relieved that I wasn't going to run into him after what I'd said on the phone, but instead I felt a keen disappointment.

'Do they take sugar?' asked Sophie, preparing to carry two cups of coffee next door to Lemmy and Dirk.

'Sure they do,' I said. To her credit, Sophie didn't make too much of a face as I told her exactly how much sugar they took, but she was forced to tip small quantities of coffee into the sink to make room for it. I didn't dare say they liked to drink it with milk, as well. They would just have to meet her half-way.

She went next door, and within seconds they were all three of them arguing, though I doubt whether anyone really knew what it was about, because Lemmy, as usual, was talking gibberish, and Dirk wasn't a whole lot more coherent. I heard him assuring Sophie that the living-room would be finished 'in a twinkling', which must have set off some free-flow association in his head because he then started to sing, 'Good Morning Starshine'. Lemmy joined in on the chorus with 'ooby dooby wabby, ooby wabby dabby' and together

17

they drowned out the radio, which was playing something by Bruce Springsteen.

Sophie came back with her arms wrapped around
her head, trying to block out the racket. Nothing in her
upbringing had prepared her for dealing with people
like Lemmy and Dirk. I asked for a guided tour of the
flat, hoping it would take her mind off them.

'You've seen the bathroom,' she said, leading me up
another short flight of stairs, 'and that was the kitchen,
and here we have ... the *bedroom*, which is the only
room they've managed to finish. I don't understand
why they keep starting on new rooms when they haven't
finished the old ones.'

'Oh, but this is nice,' I said quickly, and it was,
though I wasn't too keen on the colour – the walls had
been painted a watery buttermilk. White walls weren't
good enough for Sophie; nothing so reasonable, utili-
tarian or simple as *white*. No, it had to be white with a
twist – white with a dash of daffodil, or a whisper of
duck-egg, or a tinge of conjunctival pink.

There was a double bed, and a wickerwork chair,
and a vast wardrobe, and an old cheval mirror, and a
pile of about half a dozen suitcases, which I noticed
were either Globetrotter or Louis Vuitton or Mulberry.
For a long time now I'd been in the habit of checking
the labels on Sophie's possessions. You could always
rely on Sophie to ferret out the most stylish, the most
recherché, the most *expensive* product. It was always
worth rooting through the contents of her bathroom
cabinet, just to find out what kind of eyedrops she was
using, or what sort of vitamins were in vogue. Even her

toothpaste was a little-known brand that came in a plain white tube with navy lettering and cost twice as much as every other sort.

The bedroom floorboards were bare, but there were curtains up at the window. I assumed they had been left by the previous occupier and that she hadn't yet got round to replacing them, because they were not at all the sort of thing that Sophie would have chosen. But the window-sill was already crammed with Grape Ivy and other assorted houseplants.

'Were these here already?' I asked, meaning the curtains.

'No, I got them yesterday,' she said, meaning the plants. 'I needed some foliage for reference.' She went on to tell me she had been commissioned to design a calendar for a chain of nurseries. 'Four garden pictures, one for each season.'

She told me the name of the chain, but I had never been a gardener and it rang no bells. I assumed Sophie knew the people who owned it, or maybe they were affiliated to one of the dozens of companies with which her father had been associated in his lifetime. Sophie got most of her freelance commissions from friends, but even if she hadn't done, she would have found plenty of buyers. There was always a market for her precious floral doodlings; they went down well with mothers, or aunts, or, in my case, grannies, but for some reason they also went down well with picture editors on the more upmarket magazines. Sophie's idea of illustration was to fiddle away, delineating pernickety little details with a needle-nibbed Rapidograph. When

Sophie drew a flower, you could pick out each microscopic grain of pollen. You could make out the hairs on the backs of her leaves.

Up until now, I'd been thinking the flat was all right, but nothing special. The rooms were a decent size, but I would have expected Sophie to have gone for something grander, especially since price wasn't an issue. But as soon as we entered the living-room, I felt like weeping with envy. *Now* I understood what she saw in the place. The room was magnificently proportioned – parquet flooring, lofty ceilings – and rounded off by a pair of French windows which let the afternoon light stream in. There wasn't just space for a grand piano here; there was room for an entire chamber orchestra.

Even so, there was scope for improvement. The walls, for example, were brown. At first glance, I thought they had been coated with cappuccino paint in line with one of Sophie's *La Mia Casa*-inspired colour schemes, but on closer inspection it was obvious that Lemmy and Dirk hadn't been anywhere near them. I stretched out a hand and wiped a pale trail across the nearest wall with my fingers.

'Nice,' I said, wrinkling my nose at the smell of the sticky brown deposit on my fingertips.

'Don't mock,' said Sophie. 'It took fifty years of chain-smoking to achieve this subtle shade of tar.'

'Who lived here before? The Marlboro Man? I bet he died of lung cancer.'

'That's probably why the rent's so cheap,' said Sophie.

I turned to see if she was smiling. Cheap was not a word she used often. 'How cheap?'

She told me how much rent she was paying, and it wasn't what you'd call cheap at all, though it might have been a shade less than the going rate. I felt the pang I always felt when life was unfair, which these days seemed to be all too often.

'Look at this place,' I said, trying and failing to keep the resentment out of my voice. 'This room on its own is almost as big as my entire flat. And the location! You know I'd give anything to live round here.'

Sophie shrugged. It never occurred to her that other people couldn't live wherever they pleased. Some of us had to rely on hard-won housing trust accommodation at the unfashionable end of town.

'I'm not here for ever,' she said. 'Miles will sort himself out soon enough, and then maybe you can take over here when I move back.'

'Maybe,' I said. knowing full well I would never be able to afford rent like Sophie's. I couldn't even get on a council list in the area, unlike Dirk, who had inadvertently landed his and Lemmy's flat by passing out in the street after too many Diazepam and waking up to find himself at the head of a mile-long sleeping-bagged queue for high-rise housing.

In the meantime, I was stuck out in Hackney. Not through choice; it just happened to be where I'd ended up, and now I felt as though I'd never escape. Sophie had visited once, arriving with the air of someone who had just negotiated a sniper's alley in Sarajevo, and expressing horror that there wasn't a tube station in the vicinity, even though you probably could have counted on the fingers of one hand the occasions on which Sophie had travelled on the tube.

Getting from Hackney to Notting Hill was trial by public transport. It was a journey I made several times a week, and I had tried all the permutations, and there still wasn't a simple solution. You could go by bus and then tube, or by overland train and then tube, or – if you were feeling bold – by foot, bus and tube. Or you could go by taxi, of course, if you were either very, very rich, or very, very mad.

My obsession with Notting Hill was born on a Saturday night during those precious two years that I'd had to myself, when Sophie was off studying in Florence and I was left to my own devices in London. Freed from her influence for the very first time, I'd begun to make friends of my own, and one of these friends was going out with a man who knew someone who knew someone else who was giving a party one Saturday night, and so we decided to invite ourselves along. It wasn't the first time I'd been to Notting Hill, but it was the first time I realized it was *special*.

We wandered around the streets, weaving in and out of Portobello Road and Chepstow Villas and Ladbroke Grove and the roads between, laughing and giggling and going round in circles, stopping to gulp down a quick pint in every pub we passed, until finally we arrived, more or less by accident, at our destination.

It was the first truly grown-up non-student party I'd attended. Nobody snogged or danced or drank so much that they passed out in the middle of the floor. The other guests were older and wiser. They all had highly paid creative jobs, and sat around reeking of expensive perfume and smoking dope and discussing films and shows I'd barely heard of, let alone seen. I was introduced to a film-maker, and a couple of painters, and a chef, and a literary agent or two. They were all charming, shared their drugs, and included me in their conversations, but it was obvious I had nothing to say. I drank and smoke and blurted gaffe after gaffe, too drunk and stoned to care, and they were too kind to set me straight. For the first time in my life, I felt at home, I felt like *one of them*.

It was only afterwards I realized that, for one evening and one evening only, I had been granted a temporary visa to the promised land.

I never saw any of those people again, though they live on in my memory, suspended forever in a dazzling fragment of frozen time in which they will never wither or lose their sheen. Many times, I tried to retrace my footsteps to the house in which the party had taken place. I half-remembered passing a gatepost topped off by a sleeping lion, and pushing through the low-slung branches of an overgrown garden, and I combed every inch of west eleven, but I couldn't find the street, let alone the building.

Then Sophie's father died, and she came back from Italy to join me at art college and we ended up living together in a house in Parson's Green and I started to rely on her again and things went back to the way they'd been before, with me feeling as though she were somehow leaving me behind. It was then, in a last despairing bid for autonomy, that I dredged up the memory of that glittering evening – a memory in which Sophie had played no part – and attempted to rerun what was left of it in my head. By now the tape was warped by the passage of time, and parts of the recording were indistinct, or missing altogether, and I cursed myself for not having been more alert, for not having consciously committed more details to memory, and for having drunk too much, though I knew perfectly well that, had I been sober, I would have spent the entire evening languishing in the kitchen or on the stairs.

But that was how Notting Hill became the yardstick by which I was to judge all other areas of London, not to mention the rest of life. Notting Hill was my Shangri-La and El Dorado, my Mecca and Middle Earth. It gave off a warm glow I could feel all the way across town. It whispered seductively to me, it beckoned and teased, and I knew, I just knew, that if only I could move to an address with a west eleven postal code, everything in my life would be perfect.

Unfortunately I wasn't the only one who wanted to live in west eleven. Property was ridiculously expensive. Rents were sky-high. Council waiting-lists stretched off into infinity. In practical terms, it was out of the question.

But as soon as Sophie graduated, she and Miles decided to take out a joint mortgage on a garden flat in Holland Park – which didn't fool me because I knew it was simply another name for the posh end of Notting

Hill – and that was it. The jaws of the trap sprang shut, except that somehow I'd been trapped on the outside, looking in.

'I don't know why you're so keen on living round here anyway,' said Sophie. Only the other day, she told me, she'd been followed down the road by a one-legged man who'd called her a trollop.

'Trollop's rather a nice word, don't you think?' I mused.

Sophie looked at me oddly. 'Not when it's applied to you, it's not,' she said. 'I mean, I can think of things I'd rather be called.'

'You mean like pussycat?' This was below the belt. It was public knowledge that 'pussycat' was Miles's pet name for Sophie. We all knew that when your boyfriend started to call you 'pussycat' and other affectionate little pet names, it meant that your sex life was on the skids.

Sophie winced. 'I hate it when he calls me that. I really do.'

'And how *is* Miles?' I asked, straining once again to sound casual.

'Miles needs to work out what he wants,' she said firmly.

What Miles really wanted, I thought, was to have both Sophie *and* his bit of Czechoslovakian cheesecake grovelling at his feet, There didn't seem to be much room left for anyone else in the equation, and the thought depressed me.

'What about what *you* want, Soph? What about *you?*

'I know,' Sophie said in that tone which suggested she didn't know at all. She didn't know *anything*. In every other area of her life, Sophie was so completely in control that it sometimes took my breath away, but when it came to Miles, she had always let him walk all over her. When it came to Miles, she was the original please-wipe-your-feet-on-me doormat, and it made me mad.

I swallowed my rage and, before I could say something I might regret, marched over to inspect the French windows. I asked what kind of curtains she was going to have fitted.

'Oh, something flimsy. You can't have anything too heavy or they'll get in the way when you want to open the windows . . .'

Her voice trailed off. I turned round and saw her frowning, lost in thought. I asked what was up.

'I just remembered,' she said, and told me about how she'd woken in the middle of the night and had got up to close the bedroom window, only to find it already shut. It wasn't exactly a fascinating anecdote. I mumbled something vague in response and started walking the length of the room at a slow, measured pace, pretending it was my own place and fantasizing about where I would put my furniture.

'There was a dividing wall,' said Sophie, 'but your friend Dirk knocked it down. I didn't ask him to. He just went ahead and did it.'

'Oh, dear.'

'But it's probably for the best. It was one of those awful hardboard partitions. Now the place is more like it must have been originally. Before the house was divided into flats.'

I saw she was shivering slightly. 'Cold?'

'Maybe I should put the heating on.'

'But it's such a beautiful day,' I said.

'Does it feel damp in here to you?' asked Sophie.

I said it didn't feel damp at all, and suggested closing the open windows if she was cold.

'Not with the paint fumes,' Sophie said. 'In fact, I should probably have those other windows open as well.'

I opened the other set of French windows while Sophie went off to look for a sweater. The only thing standing between me and a direct drop into the basement level was an ornamental balustrade. It was warmer outside than in – one of those typical spring mornings, crisp and bright, full of promise. The sort of morning that inspired you to hunt frantically around for someone to fall in love with. I was in love already, of course, but I'd been putting Miles on hold in the light of recent events, and I was always open to offers. Actually, I was desperate for them.

I was leaning out even further, trying to get a look at the rest of the building, when Sophie came up, buttoning up a beige cashmere cardigan.

'Who else lives here?' I asked.

'For God's sake be careful,' she said, joining me at the balustrade. 'The railing's wobbly. I doubt it could stand too much weight.'

'Thanks a lot,' I said. She just *had* to keep reminding me that I wasn't stick-insect thin like her.

'Don't be so touchy,' said Sophie.

I stared fixedly out of the window so as not to see her smiling, though I knew she was. Below us, the steps down to the basement were fenced off from the street by a row of iron railings, though these hadn't done much to dissuade passers-by from using the tiny patio area as a dumping-ground for old crisp packets and crushed lager cans.

'The basement looks unoccupied,' I said hopefully.

'It's not,' said Sophie. 'There's a film director down there. Walter something. Walter *Cheeseman*.'

I felt a foolish flutter of excitement. A film director! 'Is he famous? What films has he made?'

'I haven't actually met him,' Sophie admitted. 'He's not often here. He's usually off somewhere making movies, Marsha says, but he occasionally comes back to pick up mail.'

'Marsha?'

'Marsha Carter-Brown. Ground floor. Big girl, nice and dependable. *Maître d'* at Cinghiale.'

My ears pricked up at the sound of that last name. Cinghiale was the swankiest Italian restaurant this side of town. It hadn't just been reviewed in the restuarant columns; photographs of the interior had been reproduced in the Sunday colour supplements, and the celebrity chef had appeared on Miles' arts programme, offering his opinion on the latest books and films. I confidently looked forward to Sophie getting matey with Marsha so we would be able to go to Cinghiale and sip dry Martinis at the bar and rub shoulders with TV personalities and fashion photographers and

Marsha would greet us by our first names and the celebrity chef would come out of the kitchen and sit down at our table, and I would feel at home.

'Perhaps we could have lunch at Cinghiale sometime?' I suggested.

'It's not that great,' said Sophie, with the insouciance of someone who had sampled the mixed green salad and mineral water at every restaurant in town.

I determined to get to know Marsha, none the less, and twisted my neck round, trying to get a look at the windows on the floor above us, though a decent view of them would have required putting more weight against the wobbly balustrade than was probably wise.

'What about up there?'

'Bloke called Robert,' said Sophie. 'Haven't met him either, but you can hear him bashing away on his typewriter.'

'You mean he's a writer?' A writer scored almost as many points as a film director. 'You live in a very creative house.'

'Sweetie, this is west eleven. Welcome to Bohemia.'

I felt that pang again. This was where *I* wanted to live, here in the throbbing heart of the city, in a cosmopolitan quarter full of fashionable bars and restaurants and galleries, where the cafés were crammed with movers and shakers discussing their latest novels and shows and films and exhibitions. I wanted to drink cappuccino and hatch creative projects in the company of creative people. I wanted to be a part of it. I wanted to participate. I wanted to contribute. I wanted to belong.

THREE

I'D ALWAYS considered Sophie my best friend, so when I discovered Miles was having an affair with someone who wasn't me, I felt I owed it to her to tell her what he was up to. It's what I would have expected of her if our roles had been reversed.

And because I was her best friend, she didn't hold it against me, though once or twice I got the impression she wished I'd kept my mouth shut. As though that would have made everything all right. As though it were better to live a lie. Maybe Sophie could live like that, but I couldn't.

We were having lunch. Crossing the city to eat out in the area was something I did regularly; it kept me sane. Sophie had discovered a brilliant little Thai café off Ladbroke Grove; Mick Jagger sometimes ate there, she said. This was only one of the reasons I had always wanted to live in that part of London. The only celebrities you were likely to encounter in Hackney were Labour MPs and they never actually *lived* there. I once read an interview with an alternative comedian who declared that he was proud to live in Hackney, but the next time I read about him he'd just bought a five-storey town house in Elgin Crescent.

The Thai café didn't have a licence, but you were

allowed to bring your own alcohol. I'd always left the choice of wine to Sophie ever since the time she and Miles had invited me to dinner and I'd recognized the wine they were cooking with as the bottle I'd left with them on my previous visit.

Our meeting got off on the wrong foot, as it were, when Sophie glanced down and said, 'What on earth have you got on your *feet?*'

'Loafers,' I said.

Those loafers meant a lot to me. I'd bought them only a few days previously, but the idea of them dated back several months, to when I'd glimpsed the advert in an American fashion magazine. It was an outdoorsy scene in which a smiling woman with rumpled blonde hair and country-casual clothes perched on a gate in front of a vista of fields and hills. The model was not uncommonly attractive, and yet she glowed with self-assurance. She had been born into a world infinitely better than mine. This was a woman who had never had to stand in the middle of Tesco's, totting up small change to see whether she had enough for an individual fruit pie to go with her jar of instant coffee. Come to think of it, individual fruit pie and instant coffee would never have passed her lips. She would have sipped only the choicest ground beans freshly brewed in a solid silver cafetière, nibbled only the costliest, most delicate pastries airlifted in from authentic Parisian patisseries.

That woman reminded me of Sophie. They had the same sort of golden aura. But at least Sophie had tasted instant coffee. I knew she had, because I had served it to her.

There was no item of clothing, no accessory in the advert that appealed to me directly, you understand, not even the loafers themselves. They were soft and tan and you could see the model's ankle-bones because she wasn't wearing socks. I had never owned a pair of shoes like that, nor had I ever wanted to, but now I found myself in the grip of a strange compulsion. I wanted those loafers. I *needed* those loafers. If I was going to lead the sort of life I wanted to be leading, those loafers had to be mine.

I studied loafer after loafer in shoe shop after shoe shop, but none measured up to the picture in my head. Until finally, I thought I'd found what I'd been searching for in the window of a humble Hackney cobbler's. I narrowed my eyes, I peered at them sideways – yes! They were as close as I would ever get.

And so, for the past few days, I'd been wearing them proudly. I teamed them with sea-island cotton socks and strode out with my hands thrust deep in trouser pockets, a golden aura radiating from my body, feeling brilliant and casual and supremely tasteful.

And then I'd met Sophie for lunch and she'd said, 'What on earth have you got on your *feet*?'

'Loafers,' I said.

'They look like Cornish Pasties,' said Sophie.

And so, with a mere few words from my so-called friend, my newly acquired golden aura was irredeemably soiled, and I'm prepared to admit I was feeling rather ratty over lunch that day. If it hadn't been for the Great Loafer Disaster, maybe, just maybe, I wouldn't have said what I said.

As usual, I was shovelling down nosh while Sophie picked her way fastidiously across her plate. Half-way through the pork dumplings with peanut sauce, conversation turned to the impending divorce of a couple we'd known for some time. Donna had been five months pregnant with their second child when she found out that Harvey was not on an extended business trip to the United States, as she'd been led to believe, but shacked up in Chelsea with a nineteen-year-old art student called Dorinda.

'What a bastard,' I said. 'But that's typical. That's what men are like.'

'Not all men,' said Sophie. 'Miles isn't like that.'

But you're wrong, I thought, Miles was *exactly* like that. All the time he and Sophie had been living together, he'd been conducting a string of extra-curricular relationships. I'd been the last but one.

And before I could catch myself, I was saying, 'Well, even if he *was* like that, you wouldn't want to know about it, would you.' I stated it as a fact, not a question. 'All successful partnerships require a degree of delusion on the part of one or both of the partners,' I said.

Sophie's fork froze in mid-air, and her slippery noodles plopped back on to the plate. She stared at me as though I'd kicked her in the stomach.

'What do you mean?'

'Nothing,' I said.

'*What do you mean?*'

'You wouldn't want to know.'

'Something's going on, isn't it?'

'Not really,' I said.

She put her fork down. 'If you don't tell me,' she said, 'I shall never speak to you again.'

So I was forced to tell her. She didn't leave me any choice. I told her the truth, which was that, for the past three months, Miles had been having an affair with a woman called Ligia. I didn't tell her about Holly, or Janie, or Carolyn, or any of the others, and I certainly didn't tell her about me.

'Ligia?' she echoed.

'As in *Tomb of*, but without the "e",' I explained.

'What a stupid name,' said Sophie.

'She's Czech,' I explained.

Sophie drained her glass and poured herself some more wine. She seemed quite calm. 'Damn,' she said. 'Now I can never listen to Dvořák again.'

'Just be thankful she wasn't French', I said, 'or you'd have to give up croissants.'

'Or Janáček or Smetana,' she added, looking down at the table and trying not to cry. Sophie was into classical music in a big way. She didn't like pop music at all. It was one of the things about her that I admired and tried to emulate, though I couldn't help listening to some of my old Madonna tapes when no one else was around.

'Are you all right?' I asked. Privately, I was a little disappointed she was taking it so well.

'Not really,' she said. 'I think I want to go home now.'

She slapped down a twenty pound note to pay for the meal, and stood up and left without another word.

I finished my food, paid up, and kept the change.

*

Within twenty-four hours, Sophie had moved out of the flat she shared with Miles. I felt rather hurt when we next met and she let slip she was sleeping on Carolyn and Grenville's sofabed.

'You could have moved in with me,' I said. I felt my ears burning. 'I have a spare bedroom.'

'It's terribly sweet of you,' she said, 'but I'd rather stick to west eleven. Everyone lives round here.'

'Everyone except me,' I muttered under my breath.

Miles was already begging her to move back, but she had been resolute. She'd been looking at flats with a view to renting. 'I'm going to let him stew for a couple of months,' she said. 'Then we'll see.'

'He's finished with Ligia, then?' I asked.

Her answer was cagey. I got the impression that Ligia was still very much part of the picture. This hadn't been what I'd hoped for, but I decided to make the best of it.

'It'll be good for you,' I said, 'living on your own for a bit.'

'Maybe,' said Sophie. She didn't sound too convinced.

'A girl doesn't know who she really is until she's lived on her own,' I said. Which made me the world expert on self-awareness.

I blame Schubert. If Schubert hadn't been such a gloomy bastard, I might never have wanted to change the record and none of this might have happened.

Then again, it might not have made the slightest bit of difference. It would still have happened, but in a different chronological order. It's like Miles once said: you can screw about with the schedules, but they're still made up of the same old programmes.

Dirk and Lemmy had taken Sunday off, but they'd finished the living-room at last.

'That didn't take so long,' I observed to Sophie.

'They were at it all night,' she said. 'I think they were on some sort of speed. And they were sloppy. Look here . . .' She pointed to a section of the wall where the nicotine stains were seeping through the white-with-a-soupçon-of-pistachio.

'It just needs another coat,' I said.

'They should have scrubbed before they started.'

Stains or no stains, the room looked wonderful now, as vast and airy as a ballet studio, and I told her so. It seemed to cheer her up a bit.

There were a couple of dozen tea-chests lined up against one of the walls. I couldn't wait to get stuck in and check out some more of Sophie's labels.

'Where can I start?' I asked.

Sophie rooted around in the nearest chest. 'Kitchen stuff,' she said. She tugged at the chest, but it wouldn't budge.

'How did you get them all the way up here?' I asked.

'Grenville and one of his friends,' said Sophie. 'I asked them to leave this one in the kitchen, but I guess we'll just have to unpack it here.'

I pried a lumpy package out of the box and peeled off layers of newspaper. Nestling in the middle was a plain white teacup. I turned it this way and that – it couldn't have been plainer or more perfect – and carefully placed it where it wasn't going to be stepped on. Being around Sophie's crockery made me paranoid. She had been collecting it for years, scouring the shops along Westbourne Grove and Portobello Road or, when she got tired of slumming it, going into Selfridges or Harrods and splashing out on some ordinary-looking piece of Minton or Royal Doulton or Clarice Cliff or Ming the Merciless which would cost more than most people's entire dinner services.

'Let's set up the stereo,' she suggested. 'Let's have music while we work.'

'Miles let you bring the sound system?'

'Everything except the CD player.'

'You mean he fobbed you off with the LPs? Sophie, *nobody* plays records any more.'

Sophie shrugged. 'Who needs CDs?'

Sophie pretended not to know what plugged in where, so I hooked up the stereo for her. She disliked portable phones and digital watches and just about anything that bleeped or flashed, though her technophobia appeared to be selective since as far as I know she had never had problems with her Moulinex.

'So where are the records?' I asked. Sophie pointed to a series of large carrier bags propped up against the wall. She extracted a record and placed it on the turntable.

I'd been expecting to groove on down, but I should have known better. The record turned out to be a bloke singing in German to gloomy piano accompaniment. It was the sort of thing you might play at a funeral if you wanted mourners to throw themselves into the open grave and sprawl sobbing on top of the coffin.

'Jesus,' I said. 'Couldn't we have something a little more cheerful?'

Sophie had a long-suffering look about her, and it occurred to me that I must have been sounding exactly like Miles. 'There's nothing wrong with Schubert,' she said.

'I wasn't suggesting there was. I just thought the unpacking might go with more of a swing if we had something a bit . . . *bouncier.*'

Sophie relaxed slightly. 'Put something else on, if you want, I don't care. Anything but Dvořák.'

I crouched down by the bags and began to flip through the first one. The records had been packed, with Sophie's customary fastidiousness, in alphabetical order. Some of the albums were so ancient they were mono. Perhaps she'd inherited them from Hamish. Perhaps that was why she was so reluctant to swap them for compact discs.

I recited the names as I went. 'Albinoni, Allegri, Auric. Who *are* all these guys? When are you going to join the rest of us in the twentieth century?'

'Auric *is* twentieth century,' Sophie said.

I kept stopping to marvel. The sleeves were fabulous: simple arrangements of classic typography, or glowing colour portraits of the artistes with spray-on Fifties hair-dos. Bach, Beethoven, Brahms. But it wasn't the sort of stuff I wanted to hear.

Then I reached a sparkling little oasis in the middle of the dry classical desert.

'Now we're talking,' I said. '*This* is more like it.'

Sophie didn't respond. She was busy unwrapping a primitive terracotta salad bowl which had probably been handwoven and spat upon by toothless Calabrian peasant women.

I said, 'I didn't know you were a closet Hendrix fan.'

That gave her a jolt. She looked up, and said, 'What?'

'*Are You Experienced?*'

'At what?'

'That's the title. *Are You Experienced?* by Jimi Hendrix.'

'What instrument does he play?'

She had to be doing it on purpose. Even I had heard of Jimi Hendrix. 'Dead hippy chap who played guitar with his teeth,' I reminded her. '*Purple Haze.*'

'Oh, yes,'she said, looking blank. 'It must be one of Miles's. I must've brought it along by mistake.'

I carried on flipping, and the further I flipped, the more obvious it became that these were not Sophie's records at all. For a start, they weren't in alphabetical order: Jefferson Airplane, Electric Prunes, Captain Beefheart, Pink Floyd . . . Some of the names rang bells, but not all. This was *way* before my time.

'Looks like you walked off with a bunch of them.'

'I don't see how,' said Sophie. Carefully she placed a small milk jug on top of one of the crates, and came over to conduct a closer examination.

'Look at that,' I said. I'd reached an album by a band so obscure its name failed even to pass the distant tinkle test.

ANNE BILLSON

Sophie crouched next to me. 'These are not my records,' she said.

'The covers are really tatty,' I said. 'Miles must have played them to death.' The fact that they could only belong to Miles made me all the more fascinated by them. He was about eight years older than me and Sophie, but I'd had no idea his musical tastes were so incredibly retro.

Sophie relieved me of the album I was holding, slid the disc half-way out and tutted. 'No inner sleeve. Look at all these scratches.'

She resheathed the record. I took it back from her to examine the psychedelic cover design, which looked as though it had been screen-printed in someone's kitchen. The colour scheme – shocking pink and electric purple and a lime green so acidic it etched itself on to the retinas – was so garish that my eyes picked up shimmering after-images when I moved my head. I found that if I stared hard enough, I could almost see faces.

The lettering was a cream-puff approximation of an Art Nouveau typeface. It was almost illegible.

'The Drunken Boots,' read Sophie.

'Boats,' I corrected her. 'The Drunken Boats.'

'They're a pop group?'

'It would seem so,' I said. 'They can't have been very famous.' I tried to unscramble the sleeve notes. 'Jeremy Idlewild, vocals. Hugo Baudelaire, vocals and lead guitar . . .'

Sophie started to laugh. 'Come *on*,' she spluttered. 'Hugo *Baudelaire*?'

40

Sophie's laugh was quite unlike the rest of her. When something struck her as particularly funny or absurd, when she really let rip, her laugh was big and bold and just the tiniest bit dirty. It was a very infectious laugh and one of the things I'd always liked about her. I had fond memories of us laughing ourselves silly, but such occasions had become rarer with the passage of years.

But, as always, now that Sophie had started, I couldn't help laughing too. 'That's what it says here,' I giggled. 'Hugo Baudelaire, vocals and lead guitar . . .'

'*Baudelaire* . . .' Sophie wheezed.

'Then it's Mark Humble, no, *Hamble*, bass guitar . . . and Ralph Ergstrom, drums,' I said. Each name brought a fresh gale of mirth from us both. 'I'll play it, shall I?'

Sophie instantly sobered up. '*Must* you?'

'Purely in the interests of research,' I said.

Sophie was in too good a mood to put up much of a fight. I placed the record on the turntable. As my friend had already observed, its owner had not taken a great deal of care of it, and it sounded that way – and not just because I had become accustomed to the background noiselessness of the CD experience. As soon as the needle landed on the surface there was an outbreak of crackling, like tyres on gravel, punctuated with a recurring *kerthump* as the stylus tripped over the same scratch on every circuit.

But these sound effects were endearing compared to the music itself: a booming drumbeat overlaid by twanging which sounded more like a Jew's Harp than an electric guitar. The vocals – the nasal droning of a public schoolboy trying to imitate a working-class

41

regional accent – added the final kiss of death. It was a noise which drilled right through to the centre of your head.

> *Down there down there down there*
> *Going down down down going down down down*
> *Down there down there down there*
> *When the lights are gone and the dark comes out*
> *We'll all be going down there down there*

'Goodness,' said Sophie. 'How eloquent.' She cracked up again. 'It's just *awful.*'

But I was intrigued. 'It's interesting. It's a social document. Look here, they've even got a track called *Notting Hell.*'

'It's not interesting at all,' said Sophie. 'It's deeply monotonous. Dum-dum-dum-dum-dum. Worse than Philip Glass.'

'Who *are* these guys?' I began to pore over the sleeve notes, but at that point there was an unspeakably clumsy change of key which made us both collapse. Sophie jammed her fingers in her ears. I plucked the needle from the surface of the vinyl and slid the record back into its sleeve.

'Take it away, Clare. I won't have it in the house.'

'But it belongs to Miles.'

'I don't believe it does,' she said. 'He must have borrowed it from someone. Look, I don't want any of this pop stuff. These are not my records and I'm never going to play them. Take them. Take them all.'

I was about to say I didn't want them because, like

everyone except Sophie, I'd graduated to CDs and no longer bothered with LPs. But then I realized they would provide an excellent excuse for getting in touch with Miles. It hadn't been so long ago that he'd told me to stop pestering him, but he could hardly object to me phoning now I had a legitimate reason.

FOUR

IRK AND Lemmy had been loafing around Notting
Hill since before the dawn of time. There was barely
a backroom in which they had not snorted illegal
substances, barely a stretch of pavement with which
they were not on intimate terms, barely a gutter into
which they had not puked at one time or another.
Shopkeepers and market stallholders would greet them
by name as they passed, and Dirk and Lemmy would
always greet the shopkeepers and market stallholders
right back, even though names and faces weren't their
forte and they would probably have greeted a ten-foot
gila monster if it had said hello to them first.

Dirk and Lemmy also happened to be the only
people I knew, apart from Sophie, who had resisted the
CD revolution and clung to their clunky old records. It
was not a conscious resistance, more of an all-round
vagueness in the face of implacable technological
advance, combined with continual lack of funds and
Dirk's apparent inability to comprehend that just
because compact discs were smaller than records didn't
mean there was any less playing time on them.

So it was to Dirk and Lemmy that I turned when I
decided to tape Miles' records before handing them
back to him, and they agreed to give me access to their

equipment for the afternoon in return for half a dozen cans of beer. They lived half-way up a Sixties tower block by the canal. This was in west ten, only a casual saunter away from trendy art gallery territory, but a world away from the heady glamour of my beloved west eleven; the lifts in their building smelled of urine, and each time I visited there was some vile new display of graffiti in which words ending in -uck, -ucker and -ock played a prominent part. But Dirk and Lemmy's flat had always come in useful when I'd needed to stop overnight and hadn't liked to impose upon Sophie, and the view from their fifteenth-floor balcony was breathtaking.

'Wow, man,' said Dirk. 'I haven't heard this since we did that light show at Looby Loo's.'

'One pill makes you larger,' sang Lemmy, 'and one pill makes you small.'

Ever since the needle had hit the first record, Dirk and Lemmy had been in hippy heaven. Dirk started babbling about the old days. Lemmy played an imaginary guitar with his teeth. They grooved all the way through Jimi Hendrix, Jefferson Airplane, Pink Floyd and the Thirteenth Floor Elevators. They even grooved all the way through the Drunken Boats.

'You've heard this before?' I asked.

'Down there down there down there,' sang Lemmy.

'Not since we ate those mushrooms at Marty's wedding,' said Dirk.

'Let's get this straight,' I said. 'You've *heard* of the Drunken Boats.'

ANNE BILLSON

'Havana kenyatta regatta dem *Boats*,' said Lemmy.

'Yeah, great band,' said Dirk. 'Didn't they used to live somewhere round here?'

'Did you ever meet them?'

'Who?'

'*The Drunken Boats*. You just said they used to live around here.'

'Bandung travolta yabba dabba *Sophie's pad*,' said Lemmy. 'Antonioni carboretta killer-shark.'

'What?'

'Lemmy says that a whole bunch of famous people have lived in Notting Hill at one time or another,' said Dirk. 'He says it's an area of great historical interest.'

'Did you ever run into Jeremy Idlewild?'

'Yeah, I met Jeremy,' said Dirk. 'Lots of times. But we called him Jimmy.'

'You did?' I felt the satisfying snap of connections clicking into place, and picked up the album cover. 'How about Hugo Baudelaire?'

'I remember Hugo. Nice bloke.'

'Benelux carvol uppity,' said Lemmy.

'I don't suppose Baudelaire was his real name,' I said.

'Nah,' said Dirk. 'He changed it.'

'What was he called really? Does he still live round here?'

Dirk and Lemmy looked at one another, looked back at me, and shook their heads. 'Nah,' said Lemmy.

'What about Mark Hamble? Ralph Ergstrom?'

'Arbogast banana boat-song vindaloo *down there*,' said Lemmy.

46

'Couldn't hope to meet a nicer crew,' said Dirk, lighting the latest in a series of spliffs.

I paused. Something wasn't quite right here. My initial crackle of excitement was fast giving way to the dull crump of disappointment.

I asked, 'How about Paul Verlaine and Arthur Rimbaud?'

'Paul and Arthur? Seems like only yesterday. Nice blokes they were.'

'I don't suppose you ever came across Gustave Flaubert.'

'Played great guitar, he did.'

I sat back and sighed. 'I expect you were best mates with the Beatles, as well.'

Dirk and Lemmy both made faces. 'The *Beatles*? Nah, we never met the *Beatles*. Wasn't rock 'n' roll was it? Not the *Beatles*.'

Dirk thought hard for a moment. 'Pink Floyd, now. They lived round here. Did Lemmy ever tell you he did a light show for Pink Floyd?'

FIVE

'I HEAR YOU'VE been a naughty boy,' I said to my friend Graham.

We were sitting in a basement bar just off St Martin's Lane. Graham pretended not to know what I was talking about. He peered warily at me over the top of his Mexican lager and asked, 'What do you mean?

'Sophie,' I said.

'Oh, yeah,' he said, looking suitably embarrassed. 'That,' he said.

'I told her I'd give you a good ticking-off. That was appalling behaviour. Dreadful.' I'd started off intending to strike a blow for my sex, but now I couldn't help sniggering, as though he and I were part of the same conspiracy. I was rather pleased about the way things had turned out.

Graham looked pained. 'I don't know what got into me. I know that's a terrible cliché, but it's true. I'm so embarrassed; I've never done anything like it before. I've always liked Sophie, and now she thinks I'm an asshole.'

'But she's right,' I said. 'You *are* an asshole.'

I hadn't expected to run into Sophie at that dinner-party. After her one disastrous expedition to my flat, I found it difficult to imagine her existing anywhere but in the restaurants and shops of her west eleven domain, with occasional excursions to Knightsbridge. As far as I knew, she wasn't even aware there *was* a south of the river. I felt slightly miffed when I saw her there. Clapham, evidently, had a cachet which Hackney lacked.

Our hosts, Larry and Berenice, were making strenuous efforts to matchmake Sophie with another guest, which annoyed me because they'd never seemed in the least bit anxious to modify my own single status. Not, of course, that I was in the least bit anxious about it myself. The guest they were trying to pair her off with was Graham.

Now I'd known Graham for years, and even though our relationship had never been anything other than platonic, I tended to feel a little possessive if he started paying too much attention to other women in my presence. In a sense, I'd always looked on him as my property, though of course there was no way I could possibly go out with a man who wore a brand of aftershave named after a small Mediterranean island, who wore sandals with grey socks and woolly tanktops knitted for him by his mother, or who combed his hair across his head to try and hide the fact that it was getting thinner by the second.

I liked Graham, but he was just a little too earnest, a little too *nice*. He didn't fit the picture of the sort of man I usually fancied, namely swaggering arrogant bastards like Miles. Graham simply hadn't been born with the sort of social ease I required from an escort –

he was far too obsequious to waiters and doormen, too
easily flummoxed by menus and wine lists, and he
always asked what *you* wanted to do, where *you* wanted
to go, instead of laying out his plans for the evening as
though they were *fait accompli.* Miles glided across the
dance-floor of life, whirling his partners into sub-
mission, while Graham trod on your toes and tried hard
not to lead.

Worst of all, Graham aspired towards political cor-
rectness, though this wasn't entirely his fault; he'd been
raised by devout Socialists. When I'd first met him, he'd
been deeply involved with an environmental conscious-
ness-raising group, and had once helped organize a
student sit-in on behalf of a species of otter. Graham
liked to complain that pornography was the instrument
by which women were subjugated not just sexually, but
socially and economically, or that a film in which men
with the acting ability of treetrunks beat each other to
a pulp with their bare fists was marred by its intensely
male ethos, or that choc-ice commercials were degrad-
ing to the viewer as well as to the Mexican peasants who
harvested the cacao trees.

Larry and Berenice didn't know Graham as well as I
did, or they would never have entertained the notion
that he might be a suitable partner for Sophie – *Sophie*
– who confidently expected that any suitor who dared
ask her out would be pulling in not less than sixty grand
per annum, would be equally at ease on the piste and
in the saddle, would be capable of telling the difference
between Sevruga and Beluga, and would know instinctively where to purchase amusing little gifts of tasteful

silk lingerie. Graham supplemented his income as a freelance illustrator by working as an office cleaner. His idea of a tasteful gift was a year's subscription to the *New Statesman*.

Sophie was seated next to Graham at the table and although she listened politely I could tell she was finding him tiresome. Her smile was a little too fixed, her responses a little too automatic. Like me, she preferred unreconstructed bastards like Miles, but her doormat tendencies were to the fore, and so she hung wide-eyed on Graham's every word. I noticed, though, that as the evening wore on she spent more and more time facing towards Larry, who was sitting on her other side.

The party broke up around midnight. I was one of several guests who ordered minicabs, and, since Hackney was way off everyone else's route, ended up being the first to leave, so I didn't hear about what happened next until a couple of days later, when Sophie and I met for lunch.

Sophie was especially partial to the stuffed prosciutto boules on a bed of crushed basmati, but it was a restaurant of which I too was fond, because it was always packed with faces familiar from television arts programmes: a rent-a-mob of flashers and scribblers who were invariably wheeled on whenever the producer wanted a tame talking-head to disgorge a steady trickle of sound-bites. I acted cool and pretended not to recognize anyone, even when Sophie hailed one or two celebrities she knew personally, but their very presence made me feel as though I were feeding directly from the trough of popular culture.

We placed our orders. Sophie was offhand and distracted, responding tersely to the usual conversation openers. I sensed she was angry, but hardly dared ask what about; I was tired of having to stick up for Dirk and Lemmy all the time.

Finally, I plucked up the courage to ask if she was all right.

'No, I am not,' she snapped. 'I'm still recovering from my close encounter with *your* friend.'

I had no idea what she was talking about. I racked my brains and couldn't come up with a single friend we had in common. She couldn't mean Dirk and Lemmy, because they were plural. And she couldn't possibly be talking about Miles. And though I'd met Carolyn and Grenville and Charlotte and Toby and Isabella on several occasions, they were still more her friends than mine. I was stumped.

'What do you mean?' I asked at last.

'That chap I was sitting next to the other night.'

'Oh, *Graham.*' I began to relax, feeling as though a catastrophe had just been averted, but was startled by the expression of loathing that flashed across Sophie's face at the mention of his name. My first instinct was to take it personally. First Lemmy and Dirk, and now Graham had been designated *persona non grata*. Was it my fault if I didn't hang out with Old Etonians and Oxbridge graduates?

'He's not that bad,' I said unconvincingly.

Sophie's face suddenly crumpled. 'Clare, it was *awful.*'

It was then that she brought me up to date on the post-Clapham party incident. David and Camilla had needed to get back to relieve their babysitter, so they'd taken the second minicab. And then there had been such a lengthy wait that Larry had finally been forced to phone the cab company to find out what had happened.

He had gone into his study to make the phone call, Sophie said, and emerged with the news that there had been a mix-up, and that now there wouldn't be another cab for at least an hour and a half. The next day, when she thought it through, she wondered whether he'd phoned at all. Perhaps there never had been another cab. Perhaps Larry and Berenice had planned what happened next, which was that Graham offered to run her home, and, in the absence of alternative transport, it seemed best to accept.

'Well, that's not so bad,' I said as the waitress plonked a plate of grilled feta pouffe down in front of me.

'Wait,' said Sophie. 'It gets worse.'

Graham lived off the North End Road, which in itself was enough to take him out of the running as far as Sophie was concerned. He had turned into Hampshire Place and dropped her off right outside number nine. She clambered out of his Y-registration Fiesta (another strike against him) and turned to peck him chastely on the cheek and thank him for the lift.

'I wonder if you'd mind waiting till I'm inside,' she

said. Sophie always said this to cab drivers, and they usually obliged. But Graham had said, 'I'll do better than that, *I'll escort you to your front door.*' And before she'd had time to protest that it wasn't really necessary, he was out of the car and leading her by the elbow up the front steps.

'Thank you,' she said, unlocking the door. She pecked him on the cheek again. Talking about it to me, she was adamant that she in no way encouraged him.

'I could do with a coffee,' he said.

Sophie was tired. The long and fruitless wait for a cab had been the last straw in a pointless evening. She felt like going straight to bed, but didn't want to seem ungrateful.

'Yes, of course,' she said. 'Come in.'

Graham came bounding up the stairs behind her and followed her into the living-room. It was as though he were the wrong scale, she said. He wasn't touching her or anything, but all of a sudden the room, big as it was, seemed crowded.

'Nice place you've got here,' he said.

She apologized for the state of it. Dirk and Lemmy were still painting the woodwork, and the floor was covered in dustsheets. They had upended some of the empty packing cases to use as makeshift chairs on their frequent cigarette breaks. Sophie picked up the brimming ashtray and the two dainty cups (one of which was already missing a handle) and prepared to whisk them down into the kitchen.

The only item of proper furniture was the new sofa, which was still covered in protective plastic. Graham arranged himself right in the middle of it and smiled a self-satisfied smile.

'How about a drink?' he said.

'Coffee coming up,' said Sophie.

'I mean a nightcap.'

'You're driving,' she reminded him.

'Just one.'

'There's only wine,' she said.

'Wine's fine.'

So she poured him a glass of Sauvignon. 'Aren't you having one?' he asked. She shook her head, and stood and watched over him as he gulped the wine. He peered at her over the rim of his glass. 'Why don't you sit down?' he asked, patting the sofa beside him with his free hand.

Sophie didn't know how to refuse without seeming paranoid. She didn't want him to sense her nervousness, so obligingly sat down, but as far away from him as the size of the sofa would allow. They made small talk – about the dinner, about the flat, about West London in general. After what seemed like a lifetime, Graham finished his wine and held out his glass and asked, 'How about another?'

Sophie shook her head. 'I'd like to go to bed now.'

He raised an eyebrow. 'Me too.'

'Well, then,' said Sophie. She hadn't been single for a long time. She couldn't quite remember the accepted etiquette for this type of situation.

'You know,' said Graham, tilting towards her, 'you're a very beautiful woman. His leg crept sideways until it was nestling against hers and she had to shift away to break the contact. *Oh God*, she thought, *here we go*, and decided on the direct approach, so there could be no misunderstanding.

'I think you're very nice,' she said, 'but I don't want to sleep with you.' Only the first part of the statement was a lie. She was conscious that her body language had locked into defensive mode: knees tightly together and pointing away from him, arms folded tightly across her chest, shoulders hunched, as though she were about to roll up like a hedgehog.

He smiled and placed his hand on her thigh. She smiled back and tried to prise it off, but it clung there like a limpet.

'I think you'd better leave,' she said.

'Hey,' he said. '*You* were the one who brought up the subject of sleeping together.'

'I want you to leave,' she said. '*Now.*'

And then he said something strange. 'Lady,' he said, 'I live here.'

It threw her off balance. 'I beg your pardon?'

'Look on this as a preliminary expedition,' he said, and then he was all over her, groping her breasts and thighs. It was so unreal that she didn't panic. She opened her mouth to protest, only to have it immediately stoppered by his tongue, which was bloated and slimy and seemed much too big.

This couldn't be happening. Only a couple of hours ago, this man had been wittering on about the rights of women and now here he was, forcing himself on to her. She plucked feebly at his hands, but there seemed to be more than two of them; it was like wrestling with an octopus.

At last, she managed to unplug her mouth. In the process of propelling herself away from him, out of range, she brought her knees up and, more by accident than design, one of them connected with his groin.

The breath whistled out of his chest – more breath than any one person should have had in his lungs. He brought his own knees up and rocked back and forth on the sofa, hissing angrily. The sound frightened her, but as soon as it stopped the silence frightened her even more. Perhaps she'd done him serious damage.

'Bastard tried to rape me,' Sophie said, shaking her head in disbelief at the memory, 'and there I was, worried in case he was *hurt*.'

She continued to back away and, to her horror, heard herself apologizing. What was the matter with her? Why should *she* have to apologize, for Heaven's sake? But eventually she managed to get her mouth around the words she'd been wanting to say all along. 'Get *out*!'

Graham was slumped forward. Slowly he raised his head and looked at her. His face had turned grey, and the whites of his eyes were tinged with red. 'So you want to play it the hard way,' he whispered.

'Get out,' she said again, but the command didn't sound quite so steady this time. Thinking she might burst into tears if she opened her mouth to say any more, she instead pointed firmly at the door, a gesture which struck her as absurdly melodramatic, like something more appropriate to a stern Victorian patriarch ordering a pregnant maidservant out into the snow.

Graham coughed, as though he'd been swallowing

seawater. Colour was seeping back into his face. 'Look,'
he spluttered, 'I was only trying to . . .'

That Graham was so obviously his usual weedy self
gave her fresh confidence. 'Out!' she yelled, 'or I'll call
the police!' Her words rang out through the night, and
she instantly regretted their loudness. What if the
neighbours had heard? Noisy arguments were such bad
form, and she knew the house was badly sound-proofed,
because sometimes she could hear the man upstairs on
his typewriter, or Marsha vacuuming in the flat below.
She prayed they weren't lying awake in their beds and
listening to her now.

But Graham's nerve had been booted out of him
along with his breath. He was smaller and frailer now;
she couldn't understand how someone only a couple of
inches taller than she had managed to be so intimidat-
ing. He hauled himself up and hobbled painfully
towards the door.

By now she was so tired and strung out that what he
did next might have been a trick of her imagination. In
the blink of an eye, he turned back towards her and
hissed, '*Cockteaser.*' And then added, in the very same
breath, 'I'm sorry, I don't know what got into me.'

At that stage she could cheerfully have pushed him
down the steps, but she allowed him to hobble down
at his own pace. On his way out of the flat, he turned,
as if wanting to apologize again, but she tumbled him
out onto the dark landing and slammed her door and
leant against it, weak with relief. She could hear him
stumbling down into the hallway. He was muttering
something to himself as he went. It sounded like,

'Down *there*, down *there*.' She thought he must be referring to that part of his anatomy on which she'd inflicted pain.

I'd polished off my feta. Sophie had been talking so much she'd made little headway with the prosciutto, but then she never did finish her food. I asked if she wanted it, and she shook her head and shovelled the rest of it on to my plate. *Tomorrow*, I thought, as I always did, *I'll go on a diet tomorrow.*

'I was *furious*,' said Sophie. 'It took *hours* for me to calm down enough to go to bed, and even then I lay awake half the night fuming.'

'We are talking about Graham?' I asked. 'Graham *Gilmore*?'

'Who else?'

'But he's a feminist,' I said.

Sophie snorted. 'Trying to put his hand up my skirt isn't *my* idea of sisterhood.'

'You must have sent out the wrong messages,' I said, feeling unreasonably angry with her, but even angrier with Graham. He'd *never* made a pass at me, not once in all the years I'd known him, even back in the early days, when I *knew* he'd fancied me. How *dared* Sophie come along with her long blonde hair and girly ways and lead him astray? It was the same old story; every time I thought I had a friend, I made the mistake of introducing him to Sophie. That was one reason I'd taken up with Miles. To get even. Though all it had done was leave me more dissatisfied than ever with my life.

And then I simmered down, because I knew I wasn't being fair. 'Forget what I just said,' I told Sophie. 'What Graham did was *awful*. It was practically date-rape. Ooh, I'll give him a telling-off for that.'

'I could have reported him to the police,' said Sophie.

I shook my head. 'You invited him in. He might have said you were leading him on.'

'But I wasn't.'

'Your word against his. Who's to know?'

'You think it was my fault?' said Sophie.

'Of course not,' I said, though it was difficult to suppress that part of me that thought it probably was. How could it not be? *Everything* was Sophie's fault.

Sophie sipped at her mineral water. 'You know what really pissed me off? The next morning he sent flowers. And a note, saying how sorry he was. He said he'd drunk too much, but I was sitting next to him at dinner, Clare, and he hardly touched a drop all evening. It wasn't the alcohol, it was *him*. He just went psycho on me.'

'Bloody men,' I said, shaking my head. 'They're all the same.'

And then I added, 'Dead or alive.'

I don't know why I said that. The words just popped into my head.

Graham was looking so glum that I felt sorry for him.

'I'd never have guessed you had it in you,' I said, trying to cheer him up. In truth, I was looking at him in a different way now – as slightly less of a geek and slightly more of a stud. I realized with a shock I was teetering on the verge of finding him attractive. This was *Graham* – whose idea of an amusing evening's entertainment was sitting alone in his flat, constructing model aeroplanes from Airfix kits.

'Don't,' he said. 'I feel bad about it, really *bad*, the kind of bad you feel when you know you've done something completely out of character, and it makes you wonder what else you might be capable of. You know, maybe I could murder someone.'

'Come *on*. You put your hand on her thigh. That's hardly a capital offence.'

'It is on some university campuses in America,' said Graham.

'You've just tapped into your primitive urges,' I said. I fished around a little, trying to get him to direct some of those urges towards me, but he showed no sign of wanting to, and so we finished our drink and went our separate ways.

Whatever primitive urges *I* might once have had, meanwhile, were submerged beneath a sea of step-by-step cookery illustrations. It went like this: the art director provided me with a set of photographs which I would then convert into neat little line drawings. In some cases, the photographs were so badly lit or framed or posed that I had to use my imagination, but it wasn't what you'd call creative *carte blanche*; I didn't spend my working hours conjuring up ceiling-high extravaganzas of whipped cream. I had to follow the rules; I knew from weary experience that even the tiniest of deviations from the formula would lead to nit-picking editorial consultations which would end with me having to start again from scratch. This was how I'd been making my living for the past two years, and this was probably how I was going to be making it for years to come. Each time we completed one book, a similar but slightly different one would pop up on the schedules, and the art director would ask if I wanted to continue, and of course the work was too well-paid for me to turn it down and clamber back on the freelance merry-go-round.

I couldn't complain, not when so many people were struggling to make ends meet, but it wasn't what I'd had in mind when I'd opted for illustration as a career. I'd envisioned a life of sitting around café tables, dashing off witty little caricatures in between sips of red wine, or welcoming fashion and media VIPs to private views of my latest etchings. The reality was much more prosaic, but there was rent to pay. There was always rent to pay.

My publishers and I had already disposed of French and Italian cuisine, and now we were steadily working our way through cakes and puddings. From a dietary point of view, this was a disaster; daily toil over the contours and texture of plum duff or rhubarb crumble was giving me an insatiable appetite for stodge. It wasn't as though I was obsessed with weight, but it was galling to realize I was probably the only one of Sophie's female friends with a dress size in double figures.

Ironically, it was the sort of finickety work Sophie

would have adored – all those sprinklings of Parmesan and powderings of icing sugar. But it wouldn't have been prestigious enough for her. It went nowhere, did nothing, and impressed absolutely no one.

SIX

I T WAS SOME weeks before I saw Sophie again. She
kept cancelling our lunches and going all coy on me
if I pressed her for reasons why. This was how she
behaved when there was a new man in her life, but
when I bumped into Carolyn or Charlotte or Isabella in
the market, or phoned Miles to wish him a happy
birthday, it was obvious they knew even less than I did
about the state of Sophie's love life.

Then, finally, I ran into her accidentally-on-purpose.
I'd spent a lunchtime swallowing lager in the Saddleback Arms with Dirk and Lemmy, which had left me
feeling bold enough to stroll past number nine on the
way to the tube. My timing was spot-on. As I was
approaching the house, I saw Sophie clambering out of
a black cab, so laden with Harvey Nichols carrier bags
that she had to deposit some of them on the pavement
so she could rummage in her purse.

She saw me coming and said without surprise, 'Clare,
sweetie, give me a hand, will you,' as though we'd just
spent an entire morning in each other's company. I
obediently picked up the nearest bag, catching a
glimpse of exquisite folds of beige silk interleaved with
whisper-thin layers of white tissue-paper. A subtle,
agreeable scent wafted up to my nostrils. There was a

whole atmosphere in there, and I wanted to bury my head in it.

'I see you're branching out into beige,' I said, picking up another two bags and threading them onto my arm with the first.

Sophie failed to spot the irony in my tone. 'It's not beige,' she said. 'It's *écru*.'

Sophie was the only person I'd ever known who could wear beige successfully, though she normally referred to it as *écru* or *taupe* or *oatmeal* or *stone* or *cream* or *mushroom* or *off-white* or *Chinese brown* or *camel*, whatever it was being called that season. She even wore beige lipstick and nail polish. On her it looked classy and French. On me it looked drab, as though I were too chicken to wear anything brighter.

'You're a shopaholic,' I said. 'You need help.'

'Actually, I think I'm agoraphobic,' Sophie said cheerfully, again forced to relinquish her grip on some of the shopping so she could hunt in her handbag for keys. 'I can only bear to leave the house when there's the prospect of a reward. If it weren't for the trophies at the end of the trek, I'd probably never go out.'

Once inside, she made it clear that she had things to do, but offered me a cup of tea for the road. 'By the way,' she said. 'Remember that record you found?'

I asked her to be more specific.

'The one with the psychedelic cover,' she said. 'The Drunken Boots.'

'Drunken *Boats*.'

'Do you still have it?'

I explained that the records were currently with Dirk

65

and Lemmy. 'You did say you didn't want them in the house,' I reminded her.

She looked as if she were about to say something else, then changed her mind. I tried to pump her for information, but she was still being mysterious. I also dropped a wagonload of hints about how it was time she had a housewarming, but it wasn't until a week or so later that she rang to issue an invitation, as though she'd been mulling over my suggestion and had at last decided it made sense.

Almost before I'd replaced the receiver, I was whooping with delight. There was nothing I liked better than to hobnob with members of Sophie's social circle. I was already looking forward to an evening spent trying to wangle invitations to weekend house-parties in the Cotswolds, or even to farmhouses in Languedoc or villas in Tuscany, though the only invitation I'd received to date had been a seat at the Contemporary Dance Centre for a transvestite production of *Swan Lake*.

I'd expected some flicker of activity to be visible from the street, but the first thing I noticed was that, though there were lights on above and below, Sophie's windows were dark. There was no sign of life, no indication at all that anyone was at home, or indeed living there at all.

But Sophie was in, because when I rang her bell and hollered into the entryphone she did something which released the lock on the front door. I pushed it open, stepped inside, and found myself face-to-face with

Sophie's downstairs neighbour – a big-boned, affable woman with tawny hair and a face that was slightly horsey, but in the nicest possible way. She would have been the sort of friendly pony you would pat on the fetlocks and feed with apple-cores and lumps of sugar.

I liked Marsha Carter-Brown from the outset, perhaps because it was obvious that our lives trundled along parallel tracks, which meant there would be no danger of one of us being crossed by the other. Marsha wanted nothing from me, nor did I want anything from her. Except of course for a table at Cinghiale.

She finished locking her door and scanned me approvingly. 'You look as though you're going somewhere nice.'

I nodded, but didn't elaborate. Marsha, swathed in a fake fur coat with zebra stripes, appeared to be on her way out for the evening. I didn't want to put my foot in it by suggesting there was a party on the premises to which she hadn't been invited.

'You must be Marsha,' I said. 'I'm Clare. Sophie's friend.'

Marsha Carter-Brown had a handshake that would have cracked walnuts. 'Nice to meet you, Clare. Sophie's settling in nicely, isn't she?'

I nodded. 'It's a nice house. Wish *I* lived here.'

'You do?' Marsha arched her eyebrows. 'Maybe you should have a word with our agents.'

Before I could react, she added, 'About number four.'

I did a quick mental calculation. 'Top floor?'

Marsha nodded. 'Robert's place. Ask the agents about it. Sophie'll have their number.'

'Is he moving out?' I asked, but she'd already opened the front door and didn't hear me. 'See you!' she shouted back over her shoulder. 'Have a nice time.'

Sophie greeted me at the top of the stairs. 'You met Marsha? She's nice, isn't she?'

'Very nice,' I said. One more *nice*, I decided, and I would need to have my stomach pumped. I had been intending to ask Sophie about the top flat, but as soon as I saw what she was wearing, the intention was replaced by a more pressing concern. I'd taken all afternoon to get ready. After hours of deliberation, I'd finally selected a simple black dress with tasteful sequin trim, spaghetti straps and a low-cut neckline. But as soon as I saw Sophie, I realized I'd got it wrong. Again. Sophie was in a plain white T-shirt and beige trousers. Her casual wear might have been the equivalent of another girl's Sunday best, but I still felt overdressed, even if underdressed might have been a more appropriate word for it – I was acutely conscious of having exposed far too much bare flesh.

'Uh-oh,' I said, sparkling party mood instantly reduced to ash. 'Don't tell me I got the wrong day.'

'Poor Clare,' said Sophie. 'No you got it right. Don't worry, it hots up later.'

I headed straight for the living-room, which was as dark and deserted as it had looked from the street, and empty of furniture apart from the plastic-wrapped sofa and the record player, though Dirk and Lemmy had left a rickety stepladder and some cans of paint.

'Perhaps if you run into your friends, you could remind them they haven't finished the picture rail,' Sophie said in a neutral tone. 'I really would like to make use of my living-room at some point.' I mumbled a reply, certain that Dirk and Lemmy thought they'd finished. Sophie suggested we move through into the bedroom, where it was cosier.

It wasn't particularly chilly, but my bare arms were covered in goose-pimples, so Sophie lent me something to cover up with. Her beige sweater made me look as though I were suffering from some form of liver malfunction, but I thought I could probably get away with it once the harsh glare from the overhead light had been replaced by the gentler glow of the bedside lamp.

Sophie poured wine, and we picked at bread and cheese and fruit, and I went on picking at the bread and cheese long after she had pushed her plate to one side, and then, because I was still hungry, I raided her kitchen and munched through a packet of Bath Olivers and a jar of peanut butter as well.

The bedroom was indeed cosy. Sophie had installed a small television at the foot of the bed. It was fine for the two of us, propped up against a mound of pillows, but I could see it was going to get uncomfortably cramped when everyone else had arrived.

'What time are you expecting the others?' I asked.

'There are no others,' said Sophie.

'*No others?*' I yelled.

'Not in the way you mean. We're on our own here, kiddo.'

I felt the blood rush to my head. I wanted to shake Sophie until she squealed. Two hours I'd spent on my make-up alone. But it wouldn't do to let her know how much I'd been looking forward to the evening, so instead I asked, rather lamely, 'So what are we supposed to do?'

'We have another drink.' Sophie upended the wine to collect the last few drops before fetching another bottle from the kitchen, and after a few more glasses, I'd stopped caring about whether or not I'd been deliberately misled. I asked if she'd seen anything of Miles, and she told me she was still waiting to hear what he'd thought of the camera she'd bought him for his birthday. Then the conversation turned to work and, out of politeness, I asked how she was getting on with the gardening calendar. Sophie got up and rummaged through her portfolio. I prepared to respond with the usual blandishments, but as soon as I laid eyes on the picture, I knew they wouldn't be necessary.

'That's weird,' I said, squinting in the half-light. 'Really spooky.'

This, from me, was a compliment, but it put Sophie's back up. 'It's a *garden*,' she retorted. 'It's springtime, bright and leafy, not spooky at all.'

I couldn't agree. Sophie's drawings were usually so inoffensive – all sweetness and light, butterflies and flowers – but this one was verging on the sinister. It was easily the most impressive thing she'd done, but this realization, instead of cheering me up, gave me the gloomy feeling that the best things in life were once again passing me by. Here was privileged, frivolous, superficial Sophie, sticking a pencil into her very soul while I was stuck churning out step-by-step jelly doughnuts.

It was just a garden: neatly trimmed lawn, tidy hedge, stone bird-bath, wooden shed, gnarled apple tree. But it reminded me of something, and for the life of me I couldn't think what, though I had the feeling that something awful had either just happened or was just about to happen there.

'This is the best thing you've done,' I said, trying not to sound too bitter.

'I'd like to think so,' said Sophie, gazing at it tenderly, almost maternally. She tried to take it from me, but I was reluctant to let go. My instinct was telling me there were people hiding in the hedge, or behind the tree, but that if I wanted to catch a glimpse of them I couldn't let the drawing out of my sight for an instant.

'Why are you looking at it like that?' asked Sophie, and in a flash, I realized what the scene reminded me of. The Drunken Boats album cover. Sophie had gone psychedelic on me.

I had to close my eyes then, because all of a sudden I was feeling dizzy.

'I like the faces,' I said, though I don't know why I said that, because I didn't like them at all. I could still see them, even with my eyes closed. They gave me a funny feeling, and it was funny peculiar, funny frightening, not funny ha-ha.

'What faces?' asked Sophie.

I opened my eyes and pointed them out.

'Those are leaves,' she said, quite crossly.

'Of course they're leaves. But if you scrunch your eyes up, they look like people. Except *this* one's got a bird's head. And *that* one's got ... something weird going on where its eyes should be. Look there.'

I jabbed at the board with my finger. Sophie snatched it away, as though I were about to leave mucky fingerprints all over her precious work.

'Maybe so,' she said, sounding doubtful.

I leant over for another look, but the faces had vanished, and I was no longer sure I'd seen them in the first place. Once again the hedge was an ordinary hedge, and the apple tree was an ordinary apple tree.

The shed, though – I hadn't taken much notice of it before, but now I saw the door was slightly ajar, as though someone had just gone in.

Or as if someone – or something – were about to emerge.

I shook my head, hard enough to make my teeth rattle, trying to jolt myself out of this whimsical thinking. Sophie was looking at me curiously. 'What on earth are you doing?'

'Just trying to shake sense into my brain,' I told her. 'Sometimes my imagination runs away with me.'

'I know exactly what you mean,' said Sophie, and I felt a twinge of irritation. How could she possibly know? Sophie was one of the least imaginative people I'd ever met. She couldn't even imagine what it would be like to go shopping without a walletful of credit cards.

'They're just leaves,' repeated Sophie.

'If you say so,' I said, and then added, a touch maliciously, 'Maybe breaking up with Miles has been good for your artistic development.'

Sophie's reply was instantaneous. 'We haven't broken up.'

'Come off it. He's been going round introducing this Ligia woman as his girlfriend.'

She winced. I was exaggerating, but only slightly, and the news hit her where it hurt. But she pulled herself together in a jiffy; it was impressive to see. 'It's *me* that doesn't want to see *him*,' she reminded me. 'There are things we need to sort out before I move back. Miles can go out with other people if he wants. Maybe he should go ahead and get it out of his system.'

At about eleven o'clock I realized I was going to miss the last train, but Sophie assured me I was welcome to stay with her, she'd assumed that had been the plan all along. As the minutes ticked away to midnight, I was surprised she made no effort to get ready for bed. This wasn't like her at all: Sophie was one of those irritating early birds who were normally tucked up well before twelve o'clock, which meant they would invariably be up in time to listen to *Farming Today*.

But tonight she wasn't in a hurry to get tucked up, and she wasn't even yawning. The level of noise from the street outside slipped down a level from evening to night, the occasional stirrings of movement from the man upstairs died away, and, when we switched on the television, the viewing had dwindled to a choice between Open University and an old American cop show starring a has-been British actor.

Eventually we dispensed with the television altogether, and ended up talking more than we'd talked in years. We laughed a lot, and even cried a little. Sophie tried to explain why she was so upset by Miles' behaviour – 'It's not the infidelity I mind, it's the *lying*' – and we discussed art and sex and gardens and decorating and, before I knew where I was, I found myself defending Dirk and Lemmy yet again.

'Dirk's actually a very responsible person,' I was saying. 'Once, just for fun, he smashed an empty bottle in the street, and then spent the next half-hour picking up every last sliver of glass so that passing dogs and cats wouldn't cut their paws on it.'

Which was when the music started.

Sophie sat up very straight, and said, '*Party time.*'

I call it 'music' though from where we were sitting it was more of a tuneless thudding, a booming bass which you felt in your entrails, rather than heard through the normal channels of the ear.

Ker-chunk ker-chunk ker-chunk ker-chunk ker-chunk ker-chunk ker-chunk

I looked up at the ceiling. The noise seemed to be coming from up there, but there was so much echo it was difficult to tell.

On Sophie's face there was a look of exhilaration which put me in mind of Joan of Arc. 'I thought they were playing hard to get,' she said, almost shouting to make herself heard. '*This* is why I asked you round. *This* is what I wanted you to hear.'

'It's *loud*,' I shouted back.

'Don't you recognize it?'

I tried making sense of the racket, and after a while caught a hint of vocals.

Down there down there down there down there

It was our old friends, the Drunken Boats.

I tried to repress the sneaky little thrill of satisfaction I was feeling. Sophie's new flat was not so marvellous after all. At least my place in Hackney was solid and purpose-built and I didn't have to listen to neighbours' music thudding through the walls.

'Have you complained?' I asked, gesturing towards the ceiling.

Sophie was watching me attentively. 'It isn't Robert,' she said.

'But it can't be Marsha. I saw her go out.'

Sophie shook her head again. 'It took me ages to work out where it was coming from.'

'And?'

'It's coming from right here,' she shouted. '*From my own flat.*'

I looked at her and without saying another word got up and made my way towards the living-room. Just outside, I paused, and sniffed.

Sophie was at my elbow. 'Smell it?'

I nodded. Sophie was the staunchest of non-smokers and had never stopped nagging Miles to give up, so I knew this had nothing to do with her. There were so many freshly painted surfaces that the smell of cigarettes should have been overwhelmed, but it wasn't; it hung in the air, like a poisonous mist. It was a smell that went well with the *ker-chunk ker-chunk ker-chunk*.

The music was definitely coming from the living-room. I went in, and she followed, watching intently for my reaction. The smell of smoke was stronger in here, and now there was an extra ingredient to it, something I couldn't quite identify.

I was half-way across the room when the music stopped just as suddenly as it had begun.

It was only now there was silence ringing in my ears that I started to feel a small flutter of nervousness. I could think of only one explanation; both the noise and the smell had something to do with Dirk and Lemmy. Perhaps they'd inadvertently rewired the room so it had turned into one big receiver for Capital Radio. Maybe they'd left a cigarette burning. I prowled around the room, searching for fag ends, checking behind the paint cans in the corner, lifting each can in turn. I rooted through the pockets of the paint-splattered overalls draped over the stepladder, but all I found was a steel tape-measure, a grotty paper tissue, and a small scale model of one of the Klingons from *Star Trek*.

Sophie tailed me down to the kitchen and bathroom. Then, as we were trotting back up to the upper level, she announced, 'There's something you have to see,' and steered me across to the living-room windows. I obediently looked out into the street, but apart from the usual parked cars, there was nothing to see.

'What?' I asked, turning back to her. '*What?*'

Sophie's face had fallen. Saint Joan's vision had not

materialized. 'It's not happening,' she said. 'They must know you're here.'

'*What* isn't happening?'

'Only the music tonight.'

'It must be the man upstairs,' I said. 'Who else could it be?'

'I already told you,' Sophie said. 'I *know* it's not him.'

I was getting tired of this guessing game. 'You've got hidden speakers?'

'Better than that,' said Sophie.

I bit the bullet. 'It's nothing to do with Dirk and Lemmy, is it?'

'Better than that,' said Sophie. 'Much *much* better.'

Her eyes were shining again. I began to wonder if she had a fever.

'I give up,' I said. 'You win.'

Sophie smiled triumphantly.

'I've got ghosts.'

SEVEN

OF COURSE there had to be some other explanation. But I let her babble on, because if she was going mad, I wanted to be the first to know about it so I could pass the news on to all our friends.

'In the beginning I blamed it all on the man upstairs,' said Sophie. 'The music was bad enough, but you know how I feel about smoking. How *dared* he let his habit drift downstairs to pollute my air, my own private air, the air in *my* flat, in my *lungs*? I only hoped he wasn't smoking in bed. That would have been all I needed – the whole house going up in flames and my worldly goods burnt to a crisp before I'd even finished unpacking them.'

'How can you be sure it's not him?' I asked.

'We met,' she said.

It was the look on her face that tipped me off. It was the expression of a cat that had got not just the cream but everything else on the milk float as well.

'I see,' I said, unable to keep the note of disapproval out of my voice. This was classic on-the-rebound stuff. I felt she'd moved with unseemly haste. 'What's he like?'

Sophie went ahead and told me, and in enormous great detail. I didn't know how much of it to believe.

Night after night, the music had woken her up.

Sometimes it lasted for only a few minutes, once it had kept her awake for nearly an hour, but only when it had stopped was she able to get back to sleep. Until this one night, she said. Up until then, the noise had been a nuisance, no more, and she'd been meaning to talk to the man upstairs about it, but on this particular night, something really dreadful had happened and she didn't know how to explain it at all.

Sophie wasn't used to sleeping on her own. At school, I would often creep into her bed after lights out, and we would sit there whispering and giggling and nibbling Chocolate Olivers out of the latest parcel of treats from Hamish – or, to be more accurate, from his housekeeper.

We were both plagued by nightmares. I dreamed repeatedly about a giant one-legged koala bear that hopped through the streets, thirsting for the blood of innocent children. I would have only a few minutes in which to find a safe hiding-place under the stairs or in the wardrobe, but once I'd found it, I'd have to listen trembling as the bear howled and sniffed the air and drooled and came closer, ever closer. *Hop . . . hop . . . hop . . .* It never found me, of course, though the tension was so unbearable that I sometimes wished it had.

Sophie, whose imagination was never quite in the same league, had been having recurring nightmares about squealing piglets being chased and stung on their fat pink bottoms by bumble bees. This didn't sound terribly alarming to me, but I always shuddered dutifully whenever Sophie told me about it. It seemed only fair – my stories about the one-legged bear, which I

79

tended to embellish with every retelling, would leave her quaking under the bedclothes with fright.

It was on one of these exchange-of-nightmare sessions that we both finally owned up to being afraid of the dark.

'I'm glad you're there when I wake up in the night,' I told her.

'Me too,' said Sophie. 'When I grow up, I'm going to get married, so there'll always be someone there when I wake from a bad dream.'

There was no one there this time. She dreamed she was drifting through the halls of the Brera gallery in Milan. It was one of her favourite galleries; after her last visit, she'd sent me a postcard of Mantegna's *Cristo Morto* – the painting famed for its dramatic foreshortening.

The gallery in the dream was like something by De Chirico, with deserted colonnades and unnaturally elongated shadows. There was something wrong about the paintings and it was making her feel uneasy. She had the uncomfortable feeling that all the virgins and bishops and saints were shifting their positions behind her back.

Past a Poussin landscape she drifted, past a Masaccio triptych, and Matisse's dancers and lots of other pictures which shouldn't really have been there, not all together in that particular gallery, until she found herself standing in front of Mantegna's Dead Christ. His crinkled soles pressed up against the foreground, as though He were actually there, lying in a glass-fronted recess. Sophie stared in horrified fascination at the jagged holes in His feet. The flesh was dead flesh, the colour and texture of old green cheese.

She became aware of a muffled rhythmic booming. It beat up through the floor and she couldn't work out why it was making her feel so panicky. *Ker-chunk ker-chunk ker-chunk.* It was coming closer, getting louder, echoing off the walls as it came. She knew she had to tear herself away from the painting before something dreadful happened, but she couldn't.

And now it was too late.

The booming grew louder until it filled her head. It was all around her, now inside her, and there was no escape.

Ker-chunk ker-chunk *ker-chunk*

In one swift and sudden movement, Christ sat upright on His slab. He fixed her with His blazing eyes, and stretched out His arms. Then, unable to reach her through the glass, He threw back His head, and His mouth opened so wide it gaped from ear to ear like a slit throat and you could see His oesophagus quivering on the vaulted ceiling of His larynx, and He let out a bloodcurdling shriek, the sound pitched so high it was barely human.

Sophie jerked awake. The room was cold, but her armpits were damp. She was filled with an overwhelming sense of dread, as though she'd been woken like that many times before, and something awful happened next. But she couldn't remember what it was. She didn't *want* to remember what it was.

Her head was enveloped in silence, but her ears were

still ringing with the shriek, and she realized with sickening certainty that it wasn't just inside her head, the sound was ricocheting off the walls of the room. It hadn't been a figment of her dream – it had been *real.*

She tried to get her senses sorted out. The sound had come from the direction of the living-room. More than anything else in the world, she wanted to snuggle down in bed and pull the duvet up around her ears. She wanted to sink into a dreamless sleep and not wake until it was daylight, when the birds would be chirruping and the other occupants of the house would be going about their everyday business, and she would hear their telephones ringing and their toilets flushing and the clickety-clack of Robert's typewriter and the gentle hum of Marsha's vacuum cleaner.

In the daylight, she knew, her fears would seem ridiculous.

But she also knew she couldn't go back to sleep, not now.

She got up. Something was pulling her towards the living-room. As soon as she opened the door, the music started up. She thought it had probably been there all along, but that for some reason she hadn't been hearing it.

Ker-chunk ker-chunk ker-chunk ker-chunk

It was much too loud, even louder than usual, and now it wasn't just the bass beat and an occasional hint of vocals – it was overlaid with screeching and twanging and droning, like a rock concert from hell, and she couldn't ·fool herself any longer into thinking it was coming from one of the other flats.

Going down down down
Down there down there

Perhaps she had been wrong not to resist the noise all those other times. Perhaps it had been taking advantage of her compliance to feed and grow stronger. She wanted it to stop, wanted desperately to switch it off, but how could she switch off something that hadn't been switched on in the first place?

Only now did she notice there was something different about the living-room. The walls were no longer freshly painted pistachio, but mottled with black and purple shadows, and sprinkled with gold and silver stars that glinted in the half-light. She moved in a dream towards the windows, which were draped with polyester velvet which was bulging like a schooner's sails in the draught.

Sophie stared at the windows. She knew she hadn't left them open. But they were open now.

Then she made the mistake of looking out.

The world outside was greenish, the colour of green cheese, the same colour as Mantegna's Christ, and to begin with, Sophie didn't notice the girl who was lying almost directly beneath her, two floors down. Her hair might have been red, but it was difficult to tell in the greenish light. At first Sophie thought she was just leaning awkwardly against the railings. Then she saw the girl's head was bent back in a position that was wholly unnatural – the neck had to be broken – and that protruding from the socket of her left eye was the tip of an iron spear. The other eye was wide open, and so was her mouth, though she made no sound. Only her fingers moved; they were flexing, opening and closing on empty air.

She was gazing up at the window through that wide-open eye, though Sophie wasn't sure if she could actually *see* anything.

Inside the room, the music pounded.

Ker-chunk ker-chunk ker-chunk

Something dark and wet was pooling on the pavement.

Sophie could only stand and stare. At that stage, what she was seeing didn't frighten her, because she knew it couldn't possibly be real. She was embroiled in another nightmare – an incredibly intricate one in which she had dreamed about waking but hadn't woken at all.

She wasn't really and truly afraid until she realized she wasn't alone. She had only to turn her head a fraction, and she would see someone standing just behind her shoulder. It was a *he*, of that she was sure. Already she could smell his familiar stale cigarette smell, mixed with alcohol, mixed with something else – something even more pungent and repulsive.

And, with a sensation not unlike that of stepping out of an aeroplane at forty thousand feet, she suddenly understood that it worked both ways. Whoever was standing there could see her too.

She turned, slowly.

The shadows shifted. And shifted once again.

She wasn't sure what she was seeing. There was more

than one of them: a man, maybe two men, or perhaps a man and a woman, perhaps a whole crowd of people, and she thought she heard someone giggle and say, 'Ooops'. She stood there for perhaps thirty seconds before her legs responded to the frantic signals from her brain. As soon as she could make them move, they carried her towards the door, and she didn't look back, because she was afraid of what she might see if she did.

She made it down to the landing outside her flat, only to realize that the idea of going anywhere near the railings outside made her feel faint with terror. So instead she headed up the next flight of stairs and hammered with her fists on Robert Jamieson's door.

And that was how Sophie finally met her upstairs neighbour.

It wasn't the way she would have planned it. She didn't get time to comb her hair or put on make-up or anything. She was wearing a nightshirt – her nipples and the shadow of her pubic hair were visible through the thin white cotton, and the neckline had slipped, exposing one of her shoulders in a saucy Nell Gwynn sort of way.

It was one hell of an entrance. She couldn't have staged it better if she'd tried.

There was the sound of the door being unlocked, and then she was looking up into the face of a tall, thin man with an open mouth. Sophie caught a whiff of dragon's breath before realizing she'd caught him in mid-yawn. He was in pressing need of a shave, but she didn't think she'd got him out of bed, because he was wearing jeans and a loose T-shirt which might have once been black but which was now a dusty grey.

He rubbed his eyes and muttered three words.

'Where's the fire?'

Sophie opened her mouth too, but the only sound that emerged was a pathetic little bleat, as if someone had pressed a button in her midriff when her batteries needed replacing.

The man stood and drank her in with his eyes, looking her up and down with a peculiar, rather self-satisfied little smile, and after a while he said, 'You'll do.'

She got mad at him then, and the anger helped snap her out of her shock. 'For Heaven's sake,' she snarled. 'Are you going to let me freeze to death?'

'Sorry,' he murmured, showing her in with an expression so tragic it was almost comical. 'And there I was, thinking I'd died and gone to heaven.'

He led her up to his living-room, and it was only when Sophie was shivering in the middle of it that she realized what a compromising situation she'd walked into. It wasn't so long since the unpleasantness with Graham, and now here she was, barely dressed, alone and defenceless in the company of a complete stranger. What if he turned out to be another creep?

But he was behaving like a gentleman, even if he didn't look like one. He found a musty army surplus overcoat and draped it around her shoulders before making her sit in an old brown armchair. He bent to light the rickety gas fire, mumbled something about a stiff drink and headed back down to the kitchen.

Sophie peered warily at his living-room. It was roughly the size of her own, but seemed smaller and darker, because the walls were lined floor-to-ceiling with books. All sorts of books: big ones, little ones, fat ones, thin ones, hardbacks, paperbacks, and ones without any backs at all. The only sort of books he didn't have were new ones; they all looked second-hand and well-thumbed, but at least that meant they weren't there just for show. And they looked dusty. Sophie stroked the mantelpiece with her finger and found it was also covered in dust. The whole place smelled of dirty laundry and unwashed dishes – this was evidently not someone who took his housework seriously.

The thought gave Sophie a warm glow of optimism in the middle of her anxiety. He couldn't possibly have a girlfriend, because a woman would never endure such squalor. It wasn't so much that Sophie felt like doing his washing-up for him, but perhaps he could be persuaded to hire her own Filippino cleaning-woman for a couple of hours each week.

Comforting sounds drifted up from the kitchen – the clink of glass, the gush of water from the tap. Sophie began to relax for the first time since she'd woken from the dream. She huddled beneath the greatcoat, staring half-mesmerized at the flicker of artificial gas flame.

It was only when her neighbour reappeared, carrying a couple of glasses of whisky, that she remembered with an unpleasant start that she ought to have been calling the emergency services. That poor girl. She shrugged the greatcoat aside and started to get up. 'I have to use the phone.'

He stepped so close that she was forced to sit down again. 'You look like you need a drink,' he said, towering over her as he handed her one of the glasses.

She breathed in the fumes, and coughed, before forcing herself to take a sip of amber liquid. It made her cough. But she liked the way he had taken control of the situation. After her past weeks of freedom, it was somehow reassuring to be told what to do.

She began to gabble, taking great gulps of air between words, and knowing all the while that little of what she was saying made sense. 'Outside ... on the railings ... girl ... window ... fallen out ...'

Her voice trailed away and she stared at him, a frightening new idea forming in her brain. What if the girl hadn't fallen out of the first floor window at all? What if she had fallen out of *the second floor window*?

Out of *this* flat?

What if this man had pushed her?

He gazed calmly back at her, and, as if reading her mind, shook his head. 'Come,' he ordered, holding out his hand. Meekly, she allowed him to help her up and lead her over to the window. It was smaller than hers, harder to fall out of, and not the sort of window through which someone could easily be pushed. He wrestled it open, letting in a current of cool night air which cut through the mustiness of the room.

'You saw someone out there?' he asked.

'There was a lot of blood,' Sophie said, hanging back, unwilling to look outside. 'She was . . . moving.'

'Shall we take another look?'

Sophie took a deep breath and risked it. Nothing stirred except a cat which suddenly darted across the road and beneath one of the parked cars that lined the street. There was no blood. No girl. There were just the railings, and the steps leading down to the basement flat, and the light out there wasn't greenish at all; it was the usual sodium orange.

The fear drained out of her like dirty bathwater, leaving her legs hollow and weak. He helped her back to the armchair. What an idiot she'd been. She didn't feel any better when she took a longer look at her upstairs neighbour and realized he was rather attractive, even though his breath was bad and his hair was sticking out at all sorts of odd angles and there were dark, puffy rings around his eyes. He was of a physical type similar to Miles. Not so well-groomed, obviously, but long-legged and gaunt, with a fetching air of fatigue.

But now he would think she was neurotic and she had totally ruined any chance she might have had.

Or maybe not. Maybe he didn't think she was an hysterical fool after all. He was nodding sympathetically.

'It could have been Ann-Marie,' he said to himself. 'It *was* Ann-Marie,' he repeated in a more confident tone.

He looked directly at Sophie and smiled. 'It was *Ann-Marie* you saw, am I right?'

'I thought I saw *something*,' Sophie said, hesitantly, because she wasn't sure his smile was the most appropriate response in the circumstances. 'But maybe I didn't. Maybe it was me.'

'Maybe it was,' he said. 'And maybe it wasn't. But I should finish your drink if I were you.'

She gulped down too large a mouthful and nearly choked. He patted her on the back until she'd finished coughing.

'Knock it back, and I'll get you another.'

Sophie could feel the whisky leaving a trail of warmth as it slid down into her stomach. She finished it quickly, and held out the empty glass. He told her to wait a second while he fetched the bottle.

She curled up in the chair again, already feeling more robust, and continued to survey her surroundings. The furniture was shabby, there were threadbare patches in the olive-green carpet, and only someone with severe cash-flow problems, she reasoned, would still be using a manual typewriter when everyone she knew had graduated to laptops; she spotted his Remington over on the table, surrounded by a chaos of books and papers. If he wrote for a living, she thought, then he obviously wasn't doing so well.

He came back with the bottle of whisky. 'Your name's Macallan? I saw it on your mail,' he said, pouring out two large measures before depositing the half-empty bottle on the mantelpiece.

'Sophie,' she said, transferring her glass to her left hand and extending the right for him to shake. He surprised her by lifting her fingers to his mouth and

kissing them. It was the gesture of a confirmed romantic, and she decided then and there to hit him with the
full version.

'Sophie Antigone Warbeck Macallan,' she rattled off.
'My mother had pretensions.'

He whistled. 'Some name. But it's a remarkable
coincidence. *My* name's Jamieson. Robert Dennis
Jamieson.'

Sophie chuckled, though she had no idea why. Now
that the fear had subsided, she was feeling lightheaded
and a little flirtatious, but if Robert had just made a
joke, she didn't get it.

'We have something in common,' he elaborated.
'We both share surnames with famous brands of whisky.
Jameson Irish, in my case, though I have an extra "i".
But you're *The* Macallan Single Highland Malt, and
that's spelt the same, isn't it? I don't suppose you're any
relation? You don't sound Scottish.'

'My father always said our ancestors hid in the hills
after Culloden,' Sophie said. 'But I don't think they
had anything to do with whisky.'

'Shame,' said Robert. 'What we're drinking, however, is neither The Macallan nor Jamesons.' He pinged
the side of the glass with his thumb and fingernail.
'This is Tesco's finest blended. But at least it's put some
colour back into your cheeks. When I first opened the
door, I thought you were a ghost.'

Their eyes met.

Sophie wasn't ready for intimate eyeball-to-eyeball
contact. She quickly looked away and laughed nervously. 'You're a writer?' she asked.

ANNE BILLSON

There was no reply, so she looked back. She'd
thought the question a straightforward one, but he
seemed perturbed by it. He was ruffling his already
untidy hair with one hand.

'Trying to be,' he said. 'But it's not easy when people
like Harry Fisher have got it in for you.'

'Who's Harry Fisher?' she asked.

Robert froze in mid-ruffle, as though only just
remembering he had company. 'Oh, just some scumbag
editor. But don't get me started on that. Tell me, how
are you settling in? Not sleeping so well? Music a little
too loud?'

Sophie stared into her whisky, embarrassed. 'I
thought it was coming from up here. Now I see that's
ridiculous.' She waved a hand at the only music-making
equipment she could see: an old radio.

Robert started to laugh. 'You thought it was *me*?
Playing that junk?'

'Yes, but it never really . . .'

He looked her straight in the eye again. 'Of course
it wasn't me.'

'Wasn't . . .?'

'It doesn't come from here.'

'Then where . . .?'

'Your place,' he said. 'Down there.'

A rush of air came out of her mouth, making a small,
soft noise which sounded like an 'oh'.

Robert took a packet of Marlboro from the table and
offered it to her. Sophie shrank back like a vampire
being offered garlic.

'I see you don't smoke,' he said, slipping a cigarette

92

out of the pack and lighting up. Sophie decided she had no right to object – she was on his turf, after all – but wondered whether he might be persuaded to kick the habit. It was his first major flaw. Apart from the bad breath, that is, and maybe the two things were connected.

He inhaled deeply, so deeply and intently that for a moment he seemed to be transported.

'The music . . .' Sophie reminded him.

'Basically it's all good unclean late-Sixties stuff. Hendrix, the Stones, Jefferson Airplane.'

Sophie wondered exactly how old he was. He was surely too young to have been a hippy, but there were fine lines etched into his face, and a sprinkling of grey in his hair.

'All I can hear is the . . . the Drunken Boots,' she said.

Robert's eyes narrowed. 'You mean Boats.'

'I found some records,' Sophie explained. 'Rock music records. In my flat, but they weren't mine. They were way before my time.'

He stared down at a worn patch on the carpet. 'You were bound to find out sooner or later. About the music, I mean. And about what you saw.'

'I'm beginning to think it was just a nightmare,' Sophie said.

'It was no nightmare,' he said, locking on to her gaze. 'I've seen it too.'

Sophie fought to stop her mouth falling open. 'You *did*?'

'Not tonight,' he said. 'Not recently. But I *have* seen it. I've seen other things, as well.'

'Other things?' Sophie sat up straight in her arm-chair. '*What other things?*'

Robert seemed to find this amusing. 'Put it this way,' he said with a bit of a snigger, 'I won't be looking in my bathroom mirror again in a hurry.'

Sophie couldn't believe he was laughing, but he sobered up instantly, and did the best possible thing in the circumstances: he leant over and kissed her. His lips were dry and tasted of stale tobacco, like his breath, but his technique was a marked improvement on Graham's sluglike intrusions. To Sophie's surprise, she found herself responding with some enthusiasm.

Just as she was getting into it, he pulled back.

'I'm sorry,' he said. 'I shouldn't have done that.'

'It's all right,' she said. 'Really.'

'I'm taking advantage.'

'No you're not.'

But he stood up, and said, 'Will you be all right now?'

'Don't know,' Sophie said, trying to make her face register apprehension in the hope that he would kiss it away.

'You won't be disturbed again tonight,' he said. 'I know this place. I know what it's capable of.'

'*Well*,' I said.

You had to hand it to Sophie. She would have turned Armageddon to her advantage. I couldn't help wondering how much she'd made up. An attractive unattached male in the flat upstairs; it sounded like wishful thinking to me.

94

'What happened then?'

'I went back to bed.'

'On your own?' I teased.

'He saw me downstairs. But that was it.' Sophie laughed her dirty laugh. 'Not on a first date, Clare.'

'Weren't you scared?'

'Not after that. He said that if anything else happened, I should yell, and he would come running. When I went back to bed, I could hear him moving about upstairs, and it was comforting. And I didn't really mind the idea of something else happening, not if it gave me an excuse to see him again. I even thought about screaming anyway, just to get him to come down.'

But the rest of the night passed without disturbance. For the first time since she'd moved in, Sophie found herself drifting off to sleep without thinking about Miles.

She was thinking about Robert Jamieson instead.

'Clare, he's fabulous.'

'But only five minutes ago you were saying it might not be over with Miles,' I pointed out. 'Don't you think you should wait? You've spent your entire adult life hopping from one man to another: from Hamish, to all those guys at college, to that Raymond bloke, to Miles. You've never been on your own. You don't even know what it's *like*.'

'Awful, isn't it?' Sophie admitted cheerfully. 'I really should try to be more independent. But I can't bear the idea of not having a man in my life, Clare. I don't feel like a complete person without one.'

I heard myself shouting. 'Of *course* you don't feel like a complete person! You've never given yourself the chance to *be* a complete person! You've never had an opportunity to find out who you really are!'

'Does anyone ever know that?' asked Sophie. 'Do *you* know who *you* really are, Clare?'

'Of course I do,' I said, but as soon as the words were out of my mouth, I felt a cold finger of doubt. Who was I? Who was I *really*?

'You saw him again, didn't you,' I said, feeling the cold spreading through my body. I was getting left behind again.

'Next morning he slipped a note under my door,' said Sophie, looking quite blissed out. 'Asking me to lunch.'

Now I understood why my own lunch dates with Sophie had gone down the drain. She took it for granted I would understand. I was expendable. Men came first. Men *always* came first.

'It wasn't exactly a date,' she said. 'More of a briefing. He said there were things I should know. And he said I should hear them while it was daylight.'

EIGHT

THE DOOR was open. The air was thick with the overripe smell of spaghetti sauce. She called 'Robert?' as loudly as she dared, and poked her head into the kitchen. It was nothing like her own gleaming workplace, but a vast cave which trickled with the fat of a thousand deep-fried breakfasts. Two aluminium pans sat quivering on the electric hotplates. She peeped into them to see what was cooking: one held a glutinous red liquid which bubbled and popped like molten lava, the other was three-quarters full of ferociously boiling water. Sophie wondered if Robert was aware that aluminium pans gave you Alzheimer's. She turned both hotplates down to a simmer and went on up to the living-room.

He was standing with his back to her, dressed in the same jeans and T-shirt as the night before, and struggling with something she couldn't see. She thought she heard him say, 'White women have eggs,' but immediately doubted her ears because it made no sense. He turned, and she saw he was tugging at a corkscrew wedged in the top of a wine bottle.

He seemed surprised to see her.

'The door was open,' she said by way of explanation.

'Frascati,' he said, indicating the bottle. 'I thought we'd go with an Italian theme.'

At long last, he managed to remove the cork and pour the wine. The glass he handed to Sophie was smeared, but she put her fastidiousness on hold and took a sip. The Frascati was warm, sweet, and not very pleasant.

'Something tells me you're more of a whisky drinker,' she said.

'Don't,' he groaned as though she'd hit a nerve. 'Not so much nowadays. Not nearly as much as I used to.'

Sophie set up a mental marker in her brain. Next time they had lunch – if there *was* a next time – she would be the one to choose the wine. There were certain areas in which Robert Jamieson needed educating. For example, he was lighting a cigarette now, and without even asking if she minded.

Robert caught her looking at him. 'You don't like the wine,' he said.

'Yes I do,' she lied.

'I'm skint,' he said, 'otherwise I would have taken you to a restaurant. I'm expecting a cheque right now. Payment for some poems I just had published.'

Sophie thought she could detect a slight puffing out of the chest as he said this, but the news didn't exactly fill her with enthusiasm. Poets, in her experience, were generally poor, pretentious and prospect-free.

He started down to the kitchen.

Sophie followed. 'You do journalism as well?'

'Here and there,' he said. 'I've written a novel too, but I'm still waiting to hear from my publisher.'

'Perhaps you'll let me read it,' she said.

'Maybe when I know you better,' he said. They

entered the kitchen and he turned the heat up under the saucepans. 'I'm not sure it's your sort of thing. It's rather unconventional – the language, and so forth.'

Sophie was mildly offended by the suggestion that she had conventional tastes. 'Do you have an agent?' she asked. 'I could introduce you to Grenville Hodge, if you like.'

Robert suddenly looked very haughty. 'I make it a rule never to associate with the offspring of famous parents.'

Sophie began to protest, but changed her mind. 'Have you got a title?'

'*Ways of Killing Women.*'

'Ways of . . .?'

'I might change it,' he said. 'It lacks cadence.'

Sophie nodded, though she thought lack of cadence was the least of its problems.

Robert jammed a fistful of dried spaghetti into the boiling water and stuck a wooden spoon into the glutinous red sauce, which responded with an eruption of sucking noises and renewed bursts of that overripe smell. Sophie watched in amazement as he cleared a small space on the edge of one of the work surfaces by sweeping everything – pieces of kitchen towel, onion skins, a flattened tube of tomato purée – onto the floor.

'Excuse the mess,' he said. 'I've never been too clever at housework.'

Sophie was beginning to wonder if she'd made a big mistake. Perhaps fear had acted as an aphrodisiac, because whatever spell he had cast over her the night before had lost its potency. Now she was finding him slightly irritating. He was like an overgrown undergraduate, eager to impress but devoid of the means by which to do it.

Sophie had to remind him about the spaghetti, which was already way past the *al dente* stage – any more boiling, and they would need to slurp it up with soup spoons. But Robert was aware he was approaching a critical stage in the food preparation; in a lighthearted manner, pretending to be an Italian dictator, he ordered her out of the kitchen.

It was turning into trial by taste bud.

'I'm not the world's most brilliant cook,' Robert admitted.

'It's delicious,' said Sophie, trying to swallow the pasta straight down, without letting the sauce come into contact with the inside of her mouth.

'Perhaps you'll cook for me sometime,' he said.

'I'd love to.' Sophie had managed to swallow about half her wine, sifting it through her teeth and trying not to let her mouth pucker, but before she could stop him, he'd picked up the bottle and refilled her glass to the brim.

'No, really,' she protested. 'I mustn't.'

'Yes, you must,' he said. 'You're going to be glad of that alcohol when you hear what I've got to tell you.'

She remembered the reason she was there. 'Fire ahead.'

He took her invitation literally and lit another cigarette, even though she hadn't finished eating. His fingernails were filthy and in need of a trim. 'Let's begin with what you know already,' he said. 'The house, as if you hadn't already guessed, is haunted.'

This was what Sophie had been expecting to hear, but all the same she giggled nervously. 'You're joking.'

'You wouldn't say that if we were sitting here in the dark. Everything seems normal now, doesn't it? But that's precisely why I asked you round during the day. If I'd said last night what I'm going to say now, you'd have wigged out.'

Sophie concentrated hard on not smiling. He was right. The daylight made a difference. 'So the girl on the railings was a ghost,' she said.

'In a manner of speaking.' Sophie blinked, and consequently almost missed seeing a number of expressions flit across Robert's face in rapid succession, so rapid that it was impossible to isolate any single one of them. The moment left her feeling slightly uneasy, as though a vital piece of information had been dangled in front of her nose before being snatched away and concealed.

'This is where it begins to get hairy,' said Robert.

'You mean it wasn't hairy before?'

'Thing is,' he said, '*she's not the only one.* Remember that pop group we were talking about?'

'The Drunken Boats?'

Robert got up and walked slowly to the window. 'Typical public-school hippies. High on dope or acid, most of the time. Jumping on every bandwagon that was going and then jumping off again, thinking they could fly. They managed to cobble that one album together, God knows how, and then self-destructed quite spectacularly. One of them – I think it was the singer – took an overdose. The lead guitarist covered himself in petrol and put a match to it. The drummer was decapitated in a car crash. All within days of one another. All in this house.'

'There was a car crash *here*?' asked Sophie, trying to picture it.

'Of course not.' He sounded impatient. 'I meant it all happened at once. But at least one of them died here, I'm certain. Which would explain why their spirits are unquiet.'

'And they're not likely to get any quieter so long as they insist on playing that awful music,' said Sophie.

'They were real no-hopers,' said Robert. 'I heard part of their album once, in Rough Trade. Customers trampled each other in the rush to get out of the shop.'

'And the girl was part of the group?'

Instead of replying, Robert gazed off into the middle-distance.

'Ann-Marie,' prompted Sophie.

Robert started to run his hand through his hair; it was a habit, she realized, which indicated he was giving serious consideration to something.

'Let's just say she was a superannuated groupie,' he said at last. 'Perhaps she was the one who introduced Jeremy Idlewild to the needle. That would make sense, wouldn't it? In fact,' his voice gathered conviction, 'I think it was Jeremy who oh-deed.'

'You seem to know a lot about them.'

'I did some research,' said Robert. 'It was my way of coping with the noise. Can you think of anything worse

102

than ghosts who play deafening rock music? Makes you long for the good old days when they just moaned and rattled chains.'

'What kind of research?' asked Sophie. 'How do you research a haunted house?'

'You look through back editions of the local paper,' said Robert. 'Or you frequent the pubs: Baldinger's, the Saddleback Arms, the Landrace Inn. Some of the oldsters can remember the juicy stuff – the axe murders and suicides and sex scandals. They have memories like attics, the ones whose brains haven't been scrambled with drugs and booze.'

'But what happened to Ann-Marie?'

Robert was now staring at a point in space somewhere beyond her left shoulder. She wondered if he were avoiding her gaze on purpose, or just having to concentrate in order to dredge up half-forgotten snippets.

'They had one acid party too many. She fell out of the window, and they were all so stoned no one noticed. She was found in the morning by a neighbour.'

Here Robert turned his big brown eyes on her and looked soulful. 'Poor Ann-Marie.'

'How awful.'

He became brisk. 'That's one version, anyway. There are others. Some people say it was murder, others that it was suicide. Ann-Marie threw herself out of the window to get away from whatever was going on inside the room. These guys, they were into some weird stuff.'

'You mean drugs?'

'I mean Devil worship. Amateurs, the lot of them,

but they really dug black magic, idolized people like Aleister Crowley. There were rumours about a hidden message on their album. Play it backwards, and you had a hotline to Satan.'

'And was there a message?'

Robert burst out laughing. 'Those boys didn't have a clue. They wouldn't have known Satan if he had come up and bitten them on the bum.'

'You can't possibly have ghosts,' I said to Sophie.

'Why not?'

I wanted to say, 'Because you're not creative enough.' But that would have been excessively cruel, so instead I told her she was too sensible.

'No, I'm not,' said Sophie. 'I *like* ghosts. They remind us there's a spiritual side to life, that death is not the end. We're all too hung up on material things.'

Look who's talking, I thought. Sophie was the original Material Girl. Her idea of a spiritual experience was walking through Harrods and being squirted by six different perfume saleswomen at once.

'They don't frighten you any more?'

'Not in the least,' said Sophie. 'They're noisy, but harmless.'

'How do you *know* they're harmless? That might be exactly what they *want* you to think. And then, just when you think it's safe to go back into the living-room . . .'

'These ghosts aren't capable of being devious,' Sophie said. 'They're stoned all the time, like your friends Dirk and Lemmy.'

'Pity you can't ask them to play something classical.'

'Don't be silly,' said Sophie. 'They're ghosts, not DJs.'

'You're so sure there's more than one of them?'

'Robert said it was the whole group. Plus poor old Ann-Marie.'

I counted them out loud on my fingers. One – the singer who oh-deed. Two – the drummer who lost his head in a car crash. Three – the guitarist who set fire to himself.

But that accounted for only three.

'What happened to the bass player?' I asked.

Sophie looked at me as though I'd gone mad. 'I haven't a clue. I never asked. I'm not a ghoul.'

'Maybe he's still alive,' I said. 'Maybe you could track him down.'

'Why would I want to do that?'

'Don't you want to find out everything you can?'

Sophie shook her head. 'He can't be alive, otherwise they wouldn't be haunting my flat, would they? Anyway, Robert's already done all the research that needs to be done.'

An interesting new thought occurred to me. 'Yes, tell me about *Robert*,' I said. 'How old did you say he was? Did he ever play in a rock band?'

'He's not a Drunken Boat, if that's what you're thinking,' Sophie said quickly. 'He thought they were awful. He sneered when I mentioned them.'

'Maybe that's just a front,' I said. Robert being an ex-Boat was altogether too neat an idea to be abandoned entirely.

'He's a writer,' Sophie reminded me. 'A poet.'

'So you said. Has he read you any of his poems?'

'It's only a matter of time.'

'I'm sure it is,' I said. 'I expect he'll compose an ode to your hair, or something.'

'Shut up,' said Sophie. But she was smiling.

It was nearly three o'clock in the morning when we finally slid beneath the duvet. Sophie had established a strict territorial line down the middle of the bed, as though she thought I was going to jump on her.

'Perhaps I should move in with you,' I hinted, without much hope of success. 'And then you wouldn't be on your own in the dark.'

Sophie reached out and turned off the bedside lamp. 'I don't think that will be necessary,' she said, and I could almost hear her smiling to herself. 'I'm *not* on my own any more.'

NINE

THE NEXT time I ran into Dirk and Lemmy, I mentioned Sophie's living-room. Dirk protested they'd been round three times that very week. They'd been painting radiators, and putting finishing touches to picture rails and skirting boards.

When I say 'ran into' Dirk and Lemmy, it had actually been the result of what amounted to a planned campaign on my part. Sophie had once again backed out of our latest lunch date, but I wasn't about to forgo my regular tastes of west eleven just because my best friend imagined she was in love, and so I tootled across town anyway and combed the local pubs looking for Lemmy and Dirk. It didn't take a great deal of combing to find them; as usual, they were in the Saddleback Arms.

I bought them drinks and packets of bacon-flavoured crisps. We sat next to the jukebox, which Lemmy fed continually with coins, though he never managed to hit the right combination of buttons. A German Shepherd sat on the floor nearby, chewing empty lager cans.

'Look at that dog, man,' said Dirk, impressed.

The dog cocked an ear, but carried on chewing.

'So,' I asked, 'have you met Robert yet?'

'Robert?' queried Dirk.

'Sophie's new boyfriend.'

'Oh, yeah,' said Dirk. 'We met Robert. Lots of times.'

I sighed. 'Just like you met the Drunken Boats.'

Lemmy thumped his glass rhythmically on the table. '*Down there*,' he sang, '*down there down there.*'

I tried again to get some sense out of them. 'Did you know the Boats used to live in Sophie's house?'

'Yeah, we knew that,' said Dirk. 'Course we knew that. It's historical, that house.'

'Middleton weimaraner archipelago,' said Lemmy. 'Acker pilkington *Sophie's pad.*'

I appealed to Dirk.

'Lemmy reckons that Sophie's house should have a Black Plaque on it,' Dirk said.

'What's a Black Plaque?' I asked.

'It's like a Blue Plaque,' Dirk explained. 'Only black.'

Over the next couple of weeks, I peppered Sophie's answering machine with messages. Occasionally, just occasionally, she deigned to call me back, but it was all rainchecks and do-you-mind-awfully-Clares and Robert this and Robert that. She couldn't talk about anything else. It seemed that his bad habits hadn't been sufficiently disagreeable to prevent her from going to bed with him. I was sick and tired of Robert Jamieson before I'd even met him.

But if Sophie really did have ghosts – and now I was no longer on the spot, hearing the music for myself, I was sceptical – then I thought she was neglecting them shamefully. She had no interest in investigating their origins, or finding out what made them tick, or asking whether their presence had a scientific or psychological basis. Whenever I tried to broach the subject on the phone, she would answer impatiently, as though the entire business were already ancient history. She seemed to regard the spectral infestation as little more than an unusual matchmaking device which, having performed its given task, was now redundant.

I couldn't help feeling bitter about it. It should have been me, not her. *I* should have been the haunted one. *I* was the one who had been through the gothic phase at college, until Sophie had persuaded me to knock all that nonsense on the head and strive for the beige ideal.

But some of us couldn't afford flats in the sort of houses where creative bohemian types had led interesting lives and died even more interesting deaths.

Some of us were still stuck on the wrong side of town.

Still, there was nothing to stop me from following up some of the leads. I played the Drunken Boats album again and again, and, if the sound quality didn't improve, at least I began to grasp an inkling of what they'd been getting at. The musicianship was crude. The lyrics were your basic schoolboyish take on decadence: torture, transvestism, necrophilia. But they had an energy and an appetite that made me feel almost jaded.

The disc had been cut before the practice of printing lyrics on the sleeve came into vogue, but the gist of the words was clear, and I was becoming expert at filling in the gaps with guesswork.

> *Long time since you went away*
> *And life is such a bore*
> *But that old refrain it lingers on*
> *L'amour toujours l'amour*

I was particularly fascinated by this last little riff, rewinding and replaying it so often that the tape stretched and I had to go back to Dirk and Lemmy's to record another. The more I listened, the more I became convinced that the last line wasn't 'L'amour toujours l'amour' at all.

It was 'La mort toujours la mort.'

I consulted every rock encyclopaedia I could lay my hands on, but the Drunken Boats were little more than a footnote, at most, in the more recherché margins of the late Sixties. I asked about them in Rough Trade, but I had even less success than Robert – the name drew a resounding blank.

I skimmed through some of the microfiches in Kensington Library, and I did stumble across a couple of interesting items, even if they weren't strictly what I'd been looking for. Up until the Fifties, I discovered, Hampshire Place had been known as Farrow Lane. It wasn't the only road in that area to receive a new identity; I learned that parts of Notting Hill had once been such a slum that some of the most notorious streets had been renamed in an effort to dissociate them from their sordid past. I tried to imagine Hampshire Place as a slum and failed. It was impossible to believe there had once been a cesspit of poverty and sleaze where now there was a fashionable winebar called The Barrio and a shop which sold ninety-nine different types of olive oil.

As for the unfortunate Ann-Marie, either I was looking in the wrong place, or the incident had not been deemed important enough to find its way into the local paper.

Poor Ann-Marie.

But there was another possibility, which was that Robert Jamieson had been talking a load of old bollocks. Sophie's bullshit detector tended to get stuck on a low setting whenever she fell in love. She would believe anything and everything said to her by a man who shared her bed.

Let me give you an example of Sophie's gullibility. A few days after I'd spent the night with her, we were talking on the telephone and she let slip that Robert had at last let her read some of his poetry.

'And?'

'He gave me a pamphlet,' she said. 'Hand-printed, I think.'

'Oh *do* read me one of his poems,' I said, using such a sarcastic tone that I wasn't expecting her to comply, but I heard the riffling of pages, and Sophie said, 'There's a short one here. It's called *The Gloomy Traveller.*'

There was a brief hush, and then she read in her best speech and drama voice:

The greenness of the midnight Nile
The waters foam-bedecked and vile
Like ooze from sleep-encrusted lids
Goes snaking past the pyramids.

I waited for her to go on, but there wasn't any more.

'That's it?' I said. 'That's the poem?'

'Robert says it's a haiku,' said Sophie.

'A what?'

'A haiku. A short Japanese . . .'

'I *know* what a haiku is; I read about it in a James Bond book. And what you have just read out is by no stretch of the imagination a haiku – not in any nuance, shape or form.'

I could almost hear the sound of air being displaced upwards as Sophie shrugged her shoulders. 'That's what Robert said,' she said, and I knew she was going to take his word for it over mine. He would only have to announce that giving head stopped you getting cancer, and she would be going down on him dozens of times a day.

I was keen to meet this Mr Jamieson, if only to expose him for the charlatan he undoubtedly was.

It was hard work, but I finally managed to lure Sophie away from her paramour and out on our long-overdue lunch date. Even though we arranged to meet in a restaurant less than ten minutes' stroll from her flat, she contrived to arrive twenty-five minutes late, which I thought was pushing it. By the time she rolled up, I had drunk one and a half kirs, bought a packet of cigarettes and smoked three of them even though I was generally a non-smoker, and passed all the way through anger, sadness and resignation into a state of Buddhalike serenity. So she couldn't be bothered to be punctual? See if *I* cared.

She rushed up breathless, wrinkled her nose dramatically when she spotted the cigarette in my hand, and threw herself into the vacant chair with the air of someone who had just passed the finishing post of the London marathon. I tried to work out why she was looking so different. Her lipstick was a shade plummier than usual, and her shirt looked as though it needed ironing, which was not something I would have noticed on anyone else though on Sophie it amounted to a major aberration. But the oddest thing, I realized after several minutes of scrutiny, was that she looked abnormally pale; even when Sophie hadn't just come back from holiday in the South of France or the Caribbean she usually managed to preserve her golden glow with self-tanning lotion or sunbed sessions. But I didn't mention it, because I knew she'd make some stupid crack about spending too much time in bed with the curtains drawn.

I did mention her weight loss, though. There hadn't been a lot of weight to lose in the first place. 'You're too skinny,' I said.

Sophie laughed delightedly, as though I had paid her a huge compliment. 'I *always* lose my appetite when I'm in love.'

'You don't have an appetite to start with,' I reminded her. As though to illustrate my point, she ordered pig's liver pâté with parsnips Beijing and then left most of it untouched.

'It was never like this with Miles,' she said.

'So you said on the phone.'

Sophie leaned forward and lowered her voice.

'Robert likes cellulite.'

'He *what?*'

'He likes cellulite. He says it turns him on.'

Sophie's credulity never ceased to amaze me. 'That's a hokey pick-up line if ever I heard one.'

'He says it reminds him of the flesh-tones in Titian and Reubens.'

'That's a load of tripe,' I said. 'Anyway, *you* don't have cellulite. There isn't an ounce of extraneous fat on you.'

It was true. But Sophie, like all the skinny girls I knew, imagined herself to be a repulsive blob of obesity. She insisted that, in the right light, and reflected in the right mirror, one could indeed see copious amounts of wobbly orange-peel around the tops of her thighs. And now Robert had succeeded in convincing her that this non-existent flab was seductive.

Robert was obviously skilled in telling people exactly what they wanted to hear.

'He sounds like a very unusual man,' I said, trying not to feel depressed. No one had ever said they liked *my* cellulite, which clung to my thighs like mottled jodphurs, and I doubted that anyone ever would.

'It's a shame he doesn't have more money,' said Sophie, suddenly looking sombre. Trust Sophie to face reality only where fiscal matters were concerned.

'Never mind,' I said. 'You've got enough dosh for the two of you.'

'It's not that,' said Sophie. 'It's just that money gives a man a sense of, I don't know, *self-respect*. If only he had a regular income, Robert would be perfect.'

'No such thing as a perfect man,' I warned her. 'He's like the free lunch – he doesn't exist.'

'You're such a killjoy,' said Sophie, 'always pouring cold water over everything I do.'

'I'm just trying to keep your feet on the ground.'

Sophie leaned all the way back in her chair and smiled and fluttered her lashes, even though the act was wasted on me. It wasn't difficult for her to forgive my petty comments. She was in a generous mood. She was *in love*. And she asked, 'Did it never occur to you that maybe I might want to *fly*?'

TEN

FOR THE next few days I was tied to my drawing-board by a batch of step-by-step muffin recipes so urgent and last-minute they were earning me double the normal rate. I didn't get time to phone Sophie, and of course it never occurred to her to phone me. But I often found myself brooding about her as I worked. I wondered whether Robert had developed an erotic fixation on her crow's feet, or her bunions, or on any of her other imaginary flaws. But I was getting fed up with leaving messages that were only rarely answered. By now, I reckoned, she would probably have moved into the flat upstairs on a more-or-less permanent basis. Sophie didn't waste much time where men were concerned.

One thing prevented me from consigning Sophie to the dustbin of dead friendship, which was where she deserved to be. If she had moved in with Robert, it would mean that her own flat was empty. I wouldn't be able to afford her rent, but perhaps she wouldn't object to me staying there now she wasn't using it.

It was then I remembered that Marsha had mentioned something about Robert moving out. Sophie had never referred to this, but perhaps Robert hadn't wanted to scupper his chances with her and had kept quiet about it. Or perhaps Marsha had got the wrong end of the stick, or perhaps I'd simply heard what I wanted to hear.

But I owed it to myself to find out. Robert's flat sounded a bit shabby, so perhaps his rent would be more reasonable than Sophie's.

One way or another, I was determined to make it to Notting Hill.

As soon as the muffins had been drawn and dispatched, I hatched a little plan and headed west. I was thinking of calling round at Sophie's on the pretext of looking for Lemmy and Dirk. I hadn't thought about what I was going to say or do after that, but as it happened, I didn't have to, because when I rang Sophie's doorbell, there was no answer. I stepped back into the road to gaze up at her windows, dazzling panels of reflected sunlight which gave nothing away, but I saw there were curtains now, pale muslin shrouds which, if anything, made the room look even less lived in than before.

I tried Sophie's bell again. Inserted into the adjoining space was the name Macallan, beautifully hand-lettered with a flourish on the capital M. Beneath that was Marsha's surname, printed clearly and neatly, no messing about. Only Robert had let the side down – 'Jamieson' was scrawled in faded Biro on an unevenly torn scrap of card. There was not even a bell for the basement flat; I assumed anyone visiting the film director had to go down to the basement and knock directly on his front door. If he was ever there to receive visitors, that is; when I'd last asked Sophie if she'd so much as got a glimpse of him in all the time she'd been living there, she'd said no. The mysterious Mr Cheeseman was still off making a film somewhere.

I was dithering on the doorstep, wondering whether to head for home or saunter along to the Saddleback Arms, when I heard a brisk footfall behind me. I turned to see Marsha Carter-Brown peering over the top of two large bags of shopping as she mounted the steps.

'Hello!' she shouted, even though there was no need for her to raise her voice. 'Looking for Sophie?'

There was no spark of recognition in her eyes, but she didn't seem to mind me helping her with the bags as she opened the door. 'We met a few weeks ago,' I reminded her. 'I'm Clare.'

'Friend of Sophie's, right?' said Marsha, still not appearing to recognize me.

'Sophie's out,' I said.

Marsha frowned at the idea of such an untidy social arrangement. 'Was she expecting you?'

'Not really. I was just passing, thought I'd pop in.'

Marsha checked her watch. 'Well, I'm dying for a cup of tea, so why don't you come in and keep me company. She might be back by the time we've finished.'

I said thank you, unused to such unconditional friendliness, and followed Marsha inside. Her flat seemed smaller than Sophie's, but perhaps this was just because the ceilings were lower and she'd had time to accumulate a lot more clutter. There were some richly patterned rugs, carved wooden heads, and a lot of other ethnic curios which looked as though they'd been picked up from a souk.

'You travel a lot?' I asked her.

'My father was a diplomat,' Marsha explained, 'so we moved around a lot when I was little. And yes, I still like exotic places. I love my job, but every so often I need to get right away from it. Keeps me sane.'

She made a pot of tea. The talk turned to restaurants, and I asked about Cinghiale.

'The food's good,' she said, 'but it's outrageously overpriced. And the clientele . . .' She made a face.

'What's wrong with them?'

'Oh, you know, assholes on expense accounts. Think they're the centre of the universe.'

'Maybe they are,' I said.

Marsha gave me a scornful look as she poured the tea.

'Of course it depends what universe you're talking about,' I added hurriedly.

'Try the real world,' she said.

I was about to say it was all very well, but sometimes the real world was negotiable only when you pretended you were at the centre of it, when there came a muffled thump from the flat upstairs, followed by a series of smaller, diminishing thuds.

We both looked up. It sounded as though a football had been dropped and had bounced lazily across the room. But Sophie was not a sports fan, hated football in particular, and only ten minutes previously had given all the signs of not being at home.

'I really did think she was out,' I said, blushing with embarrassment. Marsha would surely think I'd tricked my way into her home.

119

But Marsha wasn't the sort to waste time worrying about whether or not people had obtained cups of tea under false pretences. 'Sounds like she's fallen out of bed,' she said, her face tilted up towards the ceiling.

'Sophie's an early bird,' I said. 'She *never* sleeps late.'

Marsha's mouth fell open in surprise. 'Are we talking about the same person? Take it from someone who lives directly underneath, it's party all night, and lie in the following day. Lucky for her I don't have a nine-to-five job, or I'd be banging on my ceiling with a broom.'

There was another series of thumps. A slow, sly smile spread across Marsha's face.

'Tell you what, though. It sounds as if she's got a man up there.'

I had to agree. 'Probably Robert,' I said.

We both continued to gaze at the ceiling. We'd run out of things to say. After a while Marsha asked if Sophie and Robert had been together long.

'Not long,' I said.

'So what's he like?'

'Don't ask me,' I said. 'You've met him, I haven't.'

'I have?

I thought she was being unnecessarily thick. 'Robert. *You* know. Robert from upstairs.'

The penny still wasn't dropping. 'Robert from upstairs?'

'Robert Jamieson. Robert the writer. Robert the *poet*.'

When I said the word *poet*, Marsha's manner changed. All of a sudden the temperature plummeted as her warmth drained away, and her smile tapered off at the edges.

'Sure,' she said, but didn't sound sure at all.

'You must have met him,' I persisted. I couldn't understand what had gone wrong. Only a few seconds ago we'd been getting on like a house on fire, and now she was freezing me out. I was starting to feel very uncomfortable. *Uh-oh*, I thought. Maybe Robert and Marsha had had something on the go. Maybe I had just gone and put my foot in it.

'Oh, I met him all right,' she said.

'Sophie's been talking about him non-stop,' I said apologetically. 'She's besotted.'

But Marsha wasn't one to stand around gassing when there was action to be taken. She grabbed my wrist and pulled me towards the door. At first I thought she was throwing me out into the street, but out in the hallway she loosened her grip and started to climb the stairs.

'I don't know what she's been telling you,' she said, 'but we'd better make sure she's all right.'

'What if they're in bed?'

'They won't be.'

She knocked firmly on Sophie's door and, after a long silence, knocked again. Eventually, just as I was thinking about giving up and heading back to Hackney, we heard the sound of something heavy being dragged laboriously down the steps on the other side of the wall.

'What's she up to?'

'Sssh,' said Marsha.

There were more dragging sounds, followed by a scuffling, and the noise of a bolt being drawn and a latch lifted.

Then, nothing.

121

After a long pause, I tested the door with my shoulder. It swung inwards.

Sophie was kneeling in the kitchen doorway in her nightshirt, head down, the ends of her tangled hair brushing against the floor. The sight was so unexpected I could only stand and gawp. Marsha stepped past me.

'You OK?' she asked.

Sophie whispered something.

I crouched beside her. 'What's the matter?'

She whispered again.

I made out one of the words. *Hangover.*

'It's all right,' I said to Marsha. 'It's only a hangover,' but even as I said the words they sounded wrong. Sophie *never* suffered from hangovers, not since she'd knocked back too much champagne on her twenty-first birthday and had vowed never to overdo it again. As far as I knew, the vow had never been broken.

She didn't stir, not even when I bent over her, trying to gather her hair into a ponytail. But there was nothing to tie it back with, so I gave up and let it flop back down.

'You don't look so hot,' I said, trying not to feel too smug; it wasn't every day you could say something like that to Sophie, who was normally as well-groomed and glossy as an old-fashioned mannequin.

'Hrunk oough ouch,' she said. I couldn't tell whether this was, 'Drank too much,' or 'Thank you very much.' I could have done with Dirk there to translate.

Without another word she started to clamber up the steps to the upper level, using her hands and knees like a small child just learning to walk. Marsha and I stared at each other before tagging along behind her.

Sophie crawled into the living-room and curled into a foetal position in the middle of a new rug. Now her voice was coming over loud and clear.

'I think I'm going to throw up,' she said.

I watched, fascinated, as she drew herself up into a kneeling position. All I could think about was the rug, and how expensive it must have been, and what a shame it was going to get messed up. But Marsha had sprung into action. She thundered downstairs and, within seconds, was back with a plastic bucket, thrusting it under Sophie's chin like someone giving a nosebag to a horse. I couldn't help thinking this was the wrong way round – that it was *Marsha* who should have been given the nosebag.

Sophie stuck her head deep into the bucket. Her shoulders heaved and there was a sound like pearls from a broken necklace cascading onto a wooden floor. Marsha made soothing noises and with her spare hand massaged the upper part of Sophie's back. I wondered whether she'd learned the nursemaid act as part of her job-training to help her deal with Cinghiale's clientele when they overdid it on the alcohol front. Sophie uttered a low groan, feebly trying to keep her hair clear of the bucket, and heaved again.

I went down to the kitchen to fetch her a glass of water. I knew Sophie never drank tap-water; it had to be Evian or Badoit or, at the very least, Malvern. On my way past the bedroom, I peeked in to see if Robert was still around, but there was nothing but an unmade bed, clothes strewn all over the floor, and a strong odour of stale cigarettes.

Bed unmade. Clothes all over the floor. Smell like an old ashtray. This was not Sophie's style at all.

By the time I got back, she was sitting on the floor with her back against the base of the sofa, taking unnaturally deep breaths which threatened to turn into hiccups at any second. 'There now,' said Marsha, so capably that I almost wished I too were ill, so she could comfort me. 'Take it easy now.'

'What have you been doing to yourself?' I asked.

Sophie tilted her head back so I could see her pale, glistening face. I'd been wrong earlier when I decided she didn't look so hot. Now I realized the dark circles beneath the eyes made her look annoyingly ethereal, like an Arthur Rackham naiad.

'We drank too much,' she whispered. 'That's all.'

'We?' I asked. 'We?'

Sophie giggled weakly. 'You sound like the three little pigs.'

I felt like slapping her.

Marsha asked, 'Who's we?'

Sophie giggled again. 'Robert's a really bad influence.'

'Robert who?' asked Marsha. Once again, her manner had perceptibly cooled.

Sophie summoned enough energy to look scornful. How could Marsha be so obtuse? 'Robert *Jamieson*,' she said. 'You know – tall guy, dark hair, lives upstairs.'

'Robert Jamieson,' repeated Marsha.

I looked at her quizzically.

'Robert and me,' said Sophie. Her face had taken on that ecstatic look you see on the people who dance up and down Oxford Street banging tambourines. Marsha hunkered down so she was directly in front of Sophie and placed both hands on her shoulders, like a netball coach about to give a pep talk to an injured but vitally important player.

'That's *enough*,' she said. 'This has got to *stop*.'

I was beginning to wonder if Marsha harboured some peculiar puritanical objection to other tenants drinking and fornicating on the premises. Sophie was simply confused. 'What do you mean stop?' Damp hair dangled on either side of her face in ratty little tendrils. She giggled and asked, 'Do you want to hear this joke?'

I said to Marsha, 'They drank too much, that's all.'

'Robert's completely wicked,' Sophie murmured, trying to squirm away from Marsha so she could curl up on the floor again. 'Why do women have legs?'

Marsha gripped her even more firmly, and shook her. 'This isn't funny,' she hissed.

'But I haven't even got to the punchline,' said Sophie.

I thought Marsha was going a bit far. 'It's only a *hangover*,' I said.

'He's dead,' said Marsha.

Sophie started to cough. 'I *feel* like death,' she wheezed. 'I swear I'll never touch the stuff again.'

I was in need of a replay. I wasn't sure I'd understood correctly. 'He's what?' I asked Marsha. 'What did you just say?'

'Dead,' repeated Marsha. 'Robert Jamieson is *dead.*'

'Who's dead?' asked Sophie, as though she'd only just entered the conversation.

Marsha lost patience. '*Robert Jamieson!*' she yelled at the top of her voice. '*Robert Jamieson* is frigging *dead.*'

Sophie spluttered with laughter. 'That's not funny,' she gurgled.

'It's not meant to be,' said Marsha.

I was laughing too, until the room began to spin and I had to sit down heavily on the sofa.

'That's awful,' I said. I couldn't work out why I was feeling so guilty. Perhaps it was the way I'd been slagging Robert off to myself, and without ever having seen him. I'd heard so much about the man, and now he was dead, and I never would meet him. Poor Sophie. What rotten luck. Just as she was getting over Miles, as well.

Sophie hauled herself to her feet and stood there swaying. 'But I didn't even hear him go out!' she wailed.

'Take it easy,' said Marsha.

'He hasn't even left the house,' said Sophie.

'Ninety per cent of all accidents take place in the home,' I reminded her.

Marsha started to say something, but Sophie interrupted. 'Look, I *know* he's not dead. Let's go up and talk to him right now.'

'Which hospital did they take him to?' I asked.

'For Heaven's sake,' said Marsha, and I realized with a shudder of comprehension that we'd all been talking at cross-purposes.

'Listen to me,' Marsha said in her sensible schoolteacher voice. 'We're not talking about an accident. We're talking suicide. And we're not talking about this morning.'

'So what *are* we talking about?' I demanded.

'We're talking about a man who stood in front of his bathroom mirror and slit his throat from ear to ear.'

Now I knew why her manner had turned cold. I was feeling pretty chilly myself.

'You're lying,' said Sophie, but I knew instinctively that Marsha was telling the truth.

'Jesus Christ,' I said.

'And we're not talking about this morning,' said Marsha. 'Robert Jamieson has been dead for the past twelve years.'

SUMMER

ONE

'Y OU HAVE got to be kidding,' said Daisy. 'You mean Sophie Macallan was having it off with *a dead person?*'

I corrected her. 'She *thought* she was having it off with a dead person.'

'Either way it's creepy,' said Susie.

Miles was staring at the carpet. 'Sophie was going through a bad patch.'

'So how did you . . .?' Luke's voice trailed away. 'I'm sorry. None of our business.'

Miles shrugged. 'Doesn't matter. It's water under the bridge.'

'Things change,' Clare said darkly.

Some of her confessions had been a bit near the knuckle, I thought, especially considering Miles was present. Maybe she was trying to punish him for something, but she'd made the rest of us feel slightly uncomfortable as well. I addressed her directly and, I hoped, flippantly, trying to take some of the sting out of the evening.

'Quite a story,' I said.

She smiled at me. 'Wasn't it just,' she said.

I'm not usually slow, but a few beats passed before I realised her smile had been dripping with sarcasm.

'You women,' I said in retaliation. 'You all have such vivid imaginations.' The remark came out sounding a lot more vicious than I'd intended.

'Oh, piss off,' said Susie.

I tried to peck her affectionately on the cheek to show I was only joking, but she shied away with an expression of disgust. You didn't have to be Nostradamus to predict she was going to give me a hard time of it later on.

'But what about Sophie?' asked Daisy. 'What happened? I mean, I know what happened in the end, but there are so many different rumours about what led up to it.'

'So what did happen?' asked Luke.

'You mean you don't know?' Daisy asked. 'I thought *everybody* knew.'

'Maybe we should go,' Miles said to Clare. 'Maybe you've said enough.'

'You don't have to tell us the rest,' said Susie.

'I think we get the picture,' I added.

Clare looked me in the eye. It was as though she'd decided *I* was the enemy here.

'I don't think you get the picture at all,' she said. 'You wanted to know what happened, didn't you? Well there's more.'

Miles shifted uncomfortably in his seat. It served him right, I thought. He'd asked for it, and now he was getting it in spades.

'*Lots* more,' said Clare.

TWO

MILES WAS feeling sorry for himself. When I asked what the matter was, he explained with a certain degree of embarrassment that somebody had swiped his Mont Blanc in Kensington Church Street . . .

'Hang on,' said Luke. 'What happened to Sophie?'
    'All in good time,' said Clare.
    'You can't just leave it up in the air like that.'
    'Shut up and let her get on with it,' said Susie.
    'But she keeps jumping around,' protested Luke.
    'I'm telling it the way I remember it,' said Clare.
    'Yes, but . . .'
    '*Shut up and let her get on with it.*'

Miles explained that somebody had swiped his Mont Blanc in Kensington Church Street the night before. I'd dealt with step-by-step Mont Blanc preparation at an earlier stage of the cook book, and was about to ask him why he'd been wandering around Kensington Church Street with a chestnut cream dessert when he went on: 'Bastard swiped it out of my breast pocket while I was getting out of the car. Trendy new form of mugging, apparently. Quentin lost his Shaeffer the same way.'

ANNE BILLSON

And I realized, just in time, that he hadn't been referring to the edible type of Mont Blanc at all but to an incredibly expensive brand of fountain pen. Talk about a close shave; another few seconds, and I would have been nailing my ignorance to the masthead. 'Time to pack those puddings in,' I muttered.

I'd been talking to myself, but Miles overheard. 'You sound just like Sophie – always cutting out bread and potatoes or dairy products or whatever. It's a girl thing, isn't it? Always on some stupid diet.'

'I eat what I like,' I said, annoyed that Miles thought I might be one of those ditsy types with an eating disorder.

'Well, good for you,' he said in that faintly patronizing manner that never failed to make me grit my teeth. He spotted the waiter approaching. 'And what would you like to eat now?'

I ordered the shaggy parasols in white wine and parsley dressing followed by steamed quiff of wild boar with peeled grape polka-dots. Miles ordered a teensy spinach and bacon salad, and that was that. Now he'd made me feel like a glutton, and I accused him of having tricked me into ordering too much. He pleaded not guilty and explained that he had to leave room in his stomach for a dinner date later on.

I didn't have the heart to ask who the dinner date was with.

Cinghiale at lunchtime was packed with people whose faces were vaguely familiar. And here I was, right in the middle of the glittering throng – or a throng as glittering as any throng could be when everyone in it was dressed in shades of black and white and grey.

I had arrived ten minutes late, intending to impress Miles by publicly greeting Marsha by name, perhaps even bussing her lightly on the cheeks. But Miles, louche as ever, had trumped me by sauntering in ten minutes after that, by which time Marsha and I had completed our salutatory rituals, she had gone back to greeting customers, and I was firmly seated, bored with reading and re-reading the menu, and impatiently tapping my fingernails on the table. He was as bad as Sophie. They made a fine pair.

I stopped tapping when I saw him and got to my feet, thus enabling him to peck my cheek without having to stoop all the way down to my level. It was encouraging to see, out of the corner of my eye, that some of the vaguely familiar faces had swivelled in our direction, their owners trying to ascertain whether Miles or I fell into the need-to-know category.

One of the reasons I enjoyed being seen with Miles was that he was so extraordinarily good-looking. But whenever we ate out together I was forced to address myself, not to his face full-on, but to his patrician profile. I couldn't work out whether he presented this to me because he knew it was his best angle and wanted to share it, or because it allowed him to keep an eye on the rest of the room without having to crick his neck.

I didn't care; it was a pleasure to be seen in the company of features so flawless. I just wished my own didn't blend quite so successfully into the scenery.

*

135

The table next to ours was empty, but not for long. Midway through my shaggy parasols, I saw a couple being led up by one of the waiters. The new arrivals were small yet perfectly formed, so trim and laundered and shiny it was as though they had been assembled from a plastic construction kit. His hair was short – but not skinhead-constructivist-minimalist short. Her suit was fashionable – but not sharp-end-shopaholic fashionable. They carried His and Hers soft leather briefcases. They really were perfect – a model couple. I wanted to cut them out and keep them.

But it wasn't their appearance that impressed me so much as his impeccable manners. It was the way that he, and not the waiter, stood behind his partner as she sat down, gently easing her chair into position before trotting round the table and sitting down himself. I felt a slight ache. No man had ever pulled a chair out like that for me.

After that, I kept glancing over at them during lulls in our conversation, and there were plenty of lulls, because Miles was still fretting about his fountain-pen. Or maybe it wasn't just the pen. Whatever it was, though, his attention kept wandering, and I was getting fed up with having to talk about his work, his family, his Giorgio Armani jacket and his Paul Smith tie in an effort to keep him amused. I fancied talking about me for a change, but Miles didn't seem particularly interested when I made overtures in that direction. It was probably the way he yawned and looked somewhere else that gave the game away.

Meanwhile, the perfect young man at the next table

was pouncing on each word that dropped from his partner's lips and weighing it carefully as though it were a precious jewel. There had been a time, not so long ago, when Miles had treated *my* words and opinions as valuable gems. It wasn't as though I'd had a personality swap in the mean time. So what had gone wrong? Where was the problem? Why did I now get the impression he wished he were somewhere else?

'You're *sure* they're not your records?' I asked.

We had already established over the telephone they were not Miles's records, but the conversation was drying up again, and I was desperate to keep him from looking at his watch and saying, 'Well,' in that definitive way he had which was always a signal that he was about to get up and leave.

He was puffing angrily on a cigarette over a cup of espresso – angrily because he'd been trying for years to kick both habits, but never with any success. 'Of course they're not mine,' he snapped. 'I told you, I haven't played a record for years. I can't even listen to the bloody things; I can't stand all that hissing in the background. *No one* plays records now, no one except Sophie.'

'They're not hers.'

'How do you know?'

'She said so.'

Miles leaned across the table and spoke in a stage whisper. 'You know as well as I do that Sophie is not *with the programme* at the moment. She probably picked them up in the market and forgot.'

'I don't see why. She doesn't even like pop music.'

137

Miles, in his surprise, turned to face me full-on.

'She doesn't?'

'You've only been living with her for the past six years,' I pointed out.

For a few delicious seconds, he looked lost and confused, like a small boy whose mother is late arriving to pick him up from the school gates. I had the upper hand. But he rallied. Men like Miles always rallied. It was in their blood.

'All I know is they're not mine.'

'What am I supposed to do with them? I don't even have a turntable.' I didn't bother telling him the records were comfortably lodged with a couple of friends.

'Flog 'em,' said Miles, sounding like Captain Bligh. 'Take 'em to the Record and Tape Exchange.'

He called for the bill, we split it down the middle, and then he looked at his watch and said 'Well,' in that definitive way he had. As we got up to leave, he asked, as he always did, confident in the knowledge that I wouldn't take him up on it, 'Can I give you a lift to the nearest station?'

'You can do better than that,' I said. 'You can drop me off at my door.'

Miles instantly regretted his generous offer. I enjoyed watching him struggle not to let it show on his face.

'But you live in Stepney,' he said flatly. I could see his mind churning, trying to think of a way of backing down without seeming mean.

'It's *Hackney*,' I corrected him. 'But not any more. Now I live in Hampshire Place.'

Miles was visibly relieved at being let off the hook. Then what I'd just said sank in.

'Isn't that the same street as . . .?'

'The same *house* as Sophie,' I said. 'But you know she's not there right now.'

'Yes, of course,' said Miles. He showed no curiosity about the circumstances that had brought me to west eleven. Like Sophie, he simply assumed there was no obstacle to anyone living wherever they wanted. And the relief on his face grew ever more palpable as it dawned on him that my living in the same house as Sophie would absolve him of much of the responsibility he still felt towards her. Miles was not difficult to fathom.

We trotted out to his Peugeot – Sophie had a half-share in it, but didn't drive in town if she could help it. Miles, on the other hand, drove everywhere; it was a wonder his legs hadn't atrophied. Today he had driven all the way from Holland Park to White City and back, and now he was going to set out on that same journey all over again. You could have covered the distance by foot in half the time it took to inch through the traffic and find a parking space.

As we negotiated the one-way system into Hampshire Place, Miles politely declined my invitation to pop in and have another coffee. I wasn't going to let my disappointment show, even though I'd gone out and bought a cafetière and china cups and a packet of continental beans, just in case.

'You'll keep an eye on Sophie when she gets back, won't you,' he said, as I got out of the car.

And I assured him I would.

139

THREE

SOPHIE, confronted with the information that the man she loved had been pushing up daisies for more than a decade, had thrown a major hysterical fit and screamed 'I don't believe you!' over and over again. Between us, Marsha and I managed to steer her into bed and force-feed her with a couple of Marsha's sleeping pills.

And then Marsha led me upstairs, so that I could see for myself that flat number four was an ectoplasm-free environment. I followed numbly, feeling strangely bereaved. I'd listened to Sophie babbling on about Robert so much that it felt as though one of my own friends had just died.

The door was locked, but Marsha stuck her fingers under the edge of the hall carpet and groped around till she found a key.

Like Sophie's flat, this one was on two levels. On the first level, just inside the front door, was the kitchen. I stopped on the threshold and looked around, not wanting to soil my fingers by touching anything. It was the size of Sophie's kitchen and bathroom combined, but the fittings were cracked and antiquated, and spiders abseiled lazily down the dirty green walls. On the draining-board sat a single glass tumbler turned mossy and opaque with the encrustations of time, and the hob of the electric cooker was besmirched with rusty stains which might once have been tomato sauce.

We went up, without speaking, to the living-room. I'd imagined it as Sophie had described it – shabby but comfortable armchairs by the gas fire, walls lined with bookshelves, a donnish atmosphere – but it wasn't like that at all. There was no furniture, the floorboards were bare, and the dust so thick that here and there it had gathered into clumps, like ghostly tumbleweed. There was a dank smell, as though the windows hadn't been opened since the Stone Age. There were curtains, but the fabric looked frangible, as though it would crumble away if you tried to draw them.

'You see,' said Marsha. 'No one's lived here for years. Not really. Not since Robert . . .'

'What happened to his furniture?'

'He was always behind with the rent. All his stuff must have gone to the landlord. Not that it would have amounted to much.'

I wandered into the bedroom, and behind me the dust closed over my footsteps. There were signs of life in here, as though someone had made a half-hearted stab at cleaning up.

'So tell me,' I asked Marsha, 'why is it still empty?'

'I really don't know,' said Marsha. 'There's the suicide, of course, but I don't suppose that would put anyone off, not these days. I imagine there are some people who might even think it enhanced the value of the place.'

'I'm surprised no one's squatted,' I said.

141

Marsha made a non-committal face. 'Friends of mine sometimes put sleeping-bags down here. Mostly nomadic types who are just passing through and need a temporary base.'

'You give them the key?'

Marsha gave me a sidelong glance. 'Why? Do *you* want it?'

'Why not?' I said jokily, knowing she wasn't being serious.

We retraced our steps. The bathroom was wedged between the bedroom and living-room, as though squeezed in as an afterthought. We peered into the shadows. There was no natural light, and nothing happened when I yanked on the light cord, but we could just about see the cracked mirror over the washbasin, gleaming dully in the shadows.

'This was where he . . .?'

'In front of that very mirror,' Marsha said with a shudder that was not entirely devoid of pleasure. 'Just after my birthday, it was. The thirty-first of October. Hallowe'en. Can you believe it?'

We both stared hard at the floor. There was plenty of dust and grime, but I couldn't see anything that might have been bloodstains. Then again, you couldn't see much in that Stygian gloom.

'Why did he do it?' I asked.

Marsha shook her head. 'Why does anyone do any-thing? He was just depressed, I guess. Always was a bit of a misery.'

'Were you good friends?'

'No,' Marsha said quickly. 'We weren't friends at all.'

142

Something in her manner made me stop asking questions. Talking about Robert Jamieson was obviously making her uncomfortable.

We returned to the relative brightness of the living-room. 'The first time we ever met,' I said carefully, 'you said I should ask the agents about this flat. But that was when I thought poor old Robert was still in residence, so I never followed it up.'

I paused, hardly daring to breathe, and then asked, 'How much rent would they want?'

Marsha made a face. 'I wouldn't ask them,' she said. 'They'd charge you an arm and a kidney. *My* rent's pegged, but Sophie's paying through the nose.'

Another of my dreams evaporated. 'That's what I thought', I said, trying not to let the edges of my mouth droop.

Marsha suddenly cackled. 'But *Sophie* can afford to pay through the nose, can't she? Sophie's rolling in it.' She thrust her hands into the pockets of her suede trousers and did a peculiar little shuffling dance step, dislodging a great many clumps of dust. I watched silently, wondering if this were her normal behaviour or an aberration.

When Marsha had finished her soft shoe shuffle, she turned back to me with a mischievous gleam in her eyes and said, 'Why don't you just move in?'

I couldn't believe that I'd heard her right. I didn't dare say anything in case it broke the spell and she changed her mind.

'Why not?' Marsha went on. 'You want to live here, don't you? Who's going to know? Who's going to *care*?

I'm surprised no one's dossed down already, though I suppose you'd never guess from the street that the place is empty. I mean, what's the worst that can happen? The landlord can have you thrown out?'

I could think of worse things. I forced myself to address them now. 'Those friends of yours,' I said, straining to sound nonchalant, 'the ones who slept here. Did they ever, you know, complain ... about anything?'

'What do you mean?' Marsha asked briskly.

I struggled to find the best way of expressing it. 'Did they ever ... *hear* anything?'

She looked vacant for a moment before cottoning on. Then, very slowly and deliberately, shook her head.

I wasn't entirely convinced. 'How about you? Did you ever hear it?'

She folded her arms. 'Hear what exactly?'

'*Music*,' I said. 'Sophie kept hearing music which shouldn't have been there.'

'Clare,' said Marsha, 'I have lived here for almost sixteen years and never heard *anything* out of the ordinary. *There is no music.* The only time there has *been* any music is during August Bank Holiday and the Notting Hill Carnival, which I grant you is a bloody great pain in the arse.'

Her tone became gentler. 'Your friend is suffering from some sort of nervous collapse. She just split up with her boyfriend, right?' She tapped the side of her head. 'The poor girl needs a shrink, not an exorcist.'

*

Marsha went downstairs to check on Sophie, leaving me to wander around the empty flat and daydream. The idea of moving in there was seeming less preposterous and more of a practical proposition by the second. I was already imagining the walls painted white. I could already see shelves bowing gently beneath the weight of my books, which I would have arranged in alphabetical order by author, or title, or perhaps by subject, colour, or size – I hadn't yet decided. I could see Miles, with a Martini glass in his hand, and Larry and Berenice and all the other people to whom I owed dinners but had never had the nerve to invite to Hackney, because I knew they would have turned the invitation down. In my mind's eye, the rooms were already thronged with ghosts, but they were *my* ghosts, and it was *I* who had invited them there.

And so I achieved my heart's desire. I held on to the flat in Hackney, in case the new arrangement fell apart, but the rent was negligible, and I found a surprising number of short-term visitors to London who were only too willing to pay it for me, and not one of them complained about being stuck on the wrong side of town.

But at long last *I* was moving west. West to the land of silk and money, to the world of plenty, to the streets of gold where the cognoscenti roamed. West to the kind of life that, up until now, I'd only been able to dream about.

I began by tackling the queues and transfers of public

transport, but after only a couple of trips I'd had enough of lugging bags and cases onto trains crammed with people who scowled at me as though I were some hapless German backpacker. I rang Graham, and with a combination of cajolery and threat, talked him into spending his Saturday afternoon driving the rest of my essentials across town in his Fiesta.

Hampshire Place was already lined with cars, so we had to park some way down the road. As we staggered up to the house with my mattress, he groaned, and I thought he was balking at the prospect of carting the rest of my belongings all the way up to the second storey. I told him not to worry, he could dump the stuff in the hall if he liked, but it wasn't the climb that had been worrying him.

'I was just remembering the last time I was here,' he said. 'You know – that time with Sophie.'

I'd forgotten all about it until now. 'I'm only going to invite you in for coffee if you promise to molest me like you molested her,' I teased.

Graham chuckled politely. 'You don't feel threatened?'

I surveyed his scrawny frame, hung with an Aston Villa Supporters' Club T-shirt and baggy khaki shorts exposing pale kneecaps knobblier than a pair of Jerusalem artichokes. On his feet were short grey socks and grubby white plimsolls – not trainers, but *plimsolls*.

'I don't think so,' I said sadly.

Between us, we managed to drag the mattress up to the second floor. I hadn't finished cleaning, but the flat was starting to look habitable, and I'd managed to get rid of the musty smell by leaving the windows almost permanently open.

'It's a pretty good space,' Graham acknowledged.

I promised to invite him round for a meal there in the very near future.

According to Marsha, the water supply had never been cut off in the first place. The electricity board, only too happy to have another sucker on their books, didn't ask too many questions when we put in a request for it to be reconnected. The gas was still off, but I thought I could probably make do with an electric fire and some sensible clothes. If I lasted until winter without being chucked out on my ear, that is.

To begin with, the lack of a phone made me feel isolated, but as nearly all my freelance work came from the same source, I decided I could live with it. In the end, it turned out to be something of a relief to be freed from the heartache of constantly checking the answering machine for messages which were never there.

My place was never going to look as high-tone as Sophie's, but I was determined to get it sparkling clean, or at least clean enough for people not to feel they needed to pass through a decontamination chamber after each visit. And as I vacuumed and dusted and scrubbed, I sang. I started off singing along to tapes of old favourites from the Eighties, but found myself listening more and more to the recordings I'd made at Dirk and Lemmy's – Jimi Hendrix, Jefferson Airplane, and the Drunken Boats. Especially the Drunken Boats.

Down there down there down there. It seemed only appropriate. Sophie had been packed off to Provence for a
couple of weeks – Carolyn's parents had been talked
into letting her convalesce in their holiday home – but
I couldn't help thinking it was a shame she wasn't at
home to hear the sound of the Drunken Boats coming
through her ceiling. It would have been amusing to
think of her, down below, imagining she was having a
nervous breakdown all over again.

I'd almost forgotten I'd once heard the music myself.
But it was easy now to dismiss that memory as the result
of a drunken hallucination, or a party down the road,
or some of Sophie's hysteria rubbing off on me, or a
trick of the acoustics. You never could tell with these
old houses.

Naturally, I enlisted the services of Lemmy and Dirk.
My requirements were basic; I was quite content with
the same matt white silk finish on the woodwork as on
the walls. Unburdened with the intricacies of Sophie-
style colour schemes, they took only a few days to slap
white emulsion all over the living-room and bedroom
and most of each other. I'd decided not to bother with
the bathroom and kitchen until I could be sure my
occupancy was more secure, but I gave both rooms a
thorough hose down and scrubbed off years of accumu-
lated grime.

Marsha was right. Who was to know I was staying
there, other than a few friends? And who would give a
damn anyway? I sensed she herself was grateful to have
at least one other female in the building who was not a

fruitcake. I imagined that she, like Miles, felt my presence would absolve her of any responsibility towards Sophie. Poor Sophie. No one wanted to feel responsible for her.

After those few words from Marsha had unravelled her tidy little world, Sophie went to bed and stayed there for days on end. I was coming and going with boxes and bags, but once or twice popped in to see how she was doing. She didn't say much, but murmured thanks when I presented her with cartons of soup or salad from the delicatessen round the corner.

I did my bit, but mostly I left it to Carolyn or Charlotte. (Isabella would no doubt have chipped in, but she was on one of her visits to Mamma and Papa back in Milano.) It was in the nature of their respective upbringings that they would rise to occasions such as this, and between them they seemed to have worked out a subliminal rota system. Sometimes I would run into one of them on the stairs and we would exchange polite greetings, but even though we had spent entire evenings together in Sophie's company, I'm not sure they were able to recall exactly who I was.

I had the sense of brushing up against an exclusive little clique, but I didn't care. I'd finally arrived. I was where I'd always wanted to be, and, now I was there, the circle would just have to open up and let me in.

It was only a matter of time.

In the beginning, I have to admit, I was nervous about spending the night on my own – about spending it *there*, in that flat. I almost wished Marsha had kept her mouth shut about its history, but on the other hand, its history was one of the reasons it had been empty in the first place. In many respects, I owed it all to Robert Jamieson.

But that first Saturday, I stayed out until well after midnight, knocking back tequila in the Bar King with Dirk and Lemmy. They escorted me back to Hampshire Place, and I was tempted to ask them up for a nightcap, but that would have led to us staying up, drinking and talking, until daylight, which would have been postponing what I needed to do anyway, sooner or later, which was to make it all the way through the night on my own.

It was reassuring that the house didn't look the least bit ominous. The façade resembled a welcoming face, with windows in place of eyes. There were lights on in Sophie's flat (this was just before she'd been packed off to France), and lights on in Marsha's. And, quite unexpectedly, there were lights on in the basement as well.

So the mysterious Walter Cheeseman was at long last in residence. This was an excellent omen at the start of my new life. Not only could I now look forward to meeting another creative individual, but even his unseen presence boosted my confidence. Once I took my appointed place inside, it would be a full house, and I could relax in the knowledge that if anything horrible happened – and by now I was certain it wasn't going to – there would be plenty of neighbours on hand to provide me with protection and support.

Much as Robert Jamieson has provided protection and support for Sophie.

I waved that thought away. It was a bad one, and it gave me a bad moment. But I had good, strong, positive feelings about the flat. I couldn't say I was thrilled that a previous tenant had cut his throat there, but that was ancient history, and I had washed and scoured every room so thoroughly that every inch was now as familiar to me as parts of my own body. I knew there were no monsters lurking in the shadows, because there were no longer any shadows for them to lurk in. It was my territory. I had marked it with soap and water and paint. It was already beginning to feel like home.

Now I was feeling safe, I also allowed myself the luxury of feeling just a shade disappointed that the house was an ordinary house after all, a house like any other, with its history locked away where all history ought to be – in the past. It was obvious Sophie had been having a nervous breakdown, but I couldn't help wishing I were a little less well-balanced, a little more highly-strung, so that I too could hear music and see ghosts and people would bring me soup and force-feed me with Diazepam before arranging for me to fly off to their parents' holiday homes in the South of France.

Some people had all the luck.

And so I settled back on my mattress and watched something fuzzy and forgettable on my portable television (I had yet to find the best position for the indoor aerial) and started to read an article in *Cosmopolitan* entitled 'Men and Violence: Is it them or is it their

Hormones?' and then, before I knew it, I was waking up with the morning light streaming on to my face. It was too early to get up, but I lay there gazing contentedly at my new surroundings. Today was the first day of the rest of my life.

Now was the time to establish a new routine – a brisk new schedule in which I would be up with the lark and get my daily quota of step-by-step drawings out of the way before lunch, so I could spend the afternoon immersed in non-commercial but artistically challenging projects suitable for display in galleries or on the pages of magazines. My works of art would impress people and make them want to know me. And I would cut down on carbohydrates and ask Carolyn and Charlotte how much it cost to join the health club they visited twice a week. I would even ask my optician once again about switching to contact lenses, though I'd never had much success with them in the past, because my eyes were too dry. That's what the optician said anyway, though they looked watery enough to me. Maybe it was time to try again.

But I'd done it. My sleep had been dreamless and sweet. I'd proved there was nothing to be frightened of. I'd glimpsed nothing in the darkness but giddy new heights of career excellence and an exhilarating social life stretching into a glorious future.

It was what I truly wanted to believe. You can make yourself believe anything if you try hard enough.

FOUR

FOR THOSE first few weeks, I walked on air. I went swimming. I watched films at the Gate and the Coronet. When I wasn't slaving over a hot drawing-board, I wandered up and down Portobello Road, and though no one yelled hello to me the way they yelled hello to Dirk and Lemmy, I basked in the feeling of finally belonging. I did most of my food shopping at the market, and only got fobbed off with rotten fruit two or three times. I cut down on carbohydrates, and began to lose weight at a slow but steady rate.

During the long, light evenings, I sauntered up and down Kensington Park Road or Portland Road or Westbourne Grove, glancing furtively into Virginia's, or the Coppa Kettle, or the Bar None, all of them lit up like jazzy shop window displays and thronged with well-groomed people who had lovers to meet, money to spend, projects to discuss, esoteric brands of lager to drink.

And when I worked, I worked at the sort of desk I'd always dreamed about: an old oak table picked up for a song and hauled (with Dirk's help) up to my living-room, where it stood in front of the window, warmed by the afternoon sunlight, littered with bottles of ink and pencils and paints and sketchpads and jars full of brushes and rulers, and a cracked blue vase of tulips which had looked good while they were alive but which looked even better since they had drooped over the rim and gone crisp around the edges.

The acquisition of the vase had been a rite of passage – my very first purchase, as a local resident, from the market. It was an iridescent greeny-blue, like kingfisher plumage. If only it hadn't been cracked, it might have been worth something, but even with the crack it was an exquisite piece of pottery, the sort of thing that Sophie herself might have picked out. As soon as we were back on an intimate footing, I decided, I would give it to her as a token of our friendship. In my brave new world, I would need to reaffirm my friendship with Sophie and set aside all feelings of envy and spite.

I felt positively inspired by my new surroundings. I attacked the step-by-steps with gusto, sensing that even my routine work was attaining a new depth. Like Sophie's garden drawing, it had taken on a dark edge that made it stronger and more vital, less of a slavish rendering and more of a personal statement. In a certain light, I even thought I could make out sharp-featured faces peering out from between the layers of *mille feuilles*.

The table, and everything on top of it, offered irrefutable proof of artistic industry, but the most important quality, for me, was its location. Every few minutes I would glance up from the intricacies of jam roly-poly or spotted dick and out of the window on to Hampshire Place and the Victorian terrace on the other side of the street. The only eyesore was a Sixties block of flats a bit further down, but that was nearly obscured by the leafiness of the plane trees lining the street.

It wasn't heaven, but it was near enough.

The only blemish on my brand new life was a minor one, and I forced myself not to dwell on it. So long as I didn't dwell on it, it wouldn't be a problem.

The only blemish on my brand new life was neighbour noise, though I couldn't be certain which of my new neighbours was the culprit. Once or twice I had been woken up in the middle of the night by the *tap tap tippy tap tap* of distant typing. But it was very faint, and I soon learned to block it out.

About a week after I'd moved in, I came home to find Marsha chatting on the front doorstep to a tall fellow with a blond buzz-cut and dark glasses. He was clean-shaven and tanned, but with limbs that were way too long for his torso, and an unexpectedly sharp angle to his jaw that prevented him from being merely good-looking.

Lucky old Marsha, I thought.

'Here she is now,' she said as she spotted me. 'Clare, let me introduce you to our downstairs neighbour, Mr Walter O. Cheeseman. Take a good look at him while you can; it's not often he's around.'

Walter Cheeseman and I shook hands. He had the firm, dry, confident grip of someone who regularly pressed flesh for a living. 'Pleased to meet you,' he said. The accent was American.

I liked the look of him, and feeling playful and confident after one of my liquid lunches with Dirk and Lemmy, asked what the O stood for.

Walter Cheeseman grinned, displaying a set of preternaturally perfect teeth. 'An old cultural reference,' he said. 'Won't you guess my name?

'Oscar?'

He shook his head. 'A film reference.'

'Oliver . . .? Osbert . . .?'

He shook his head.

I'd run out of Os for the time being. 'So what is it?'

'Nothing,' he said.

'Go on,' I urged coquettishly. 'Tell me.'

'The O stands for nothing,' he repeated. 'Like Roger O. Thornhill in *North by Northwest.*'

In my lightly plastered state, I wasn't listening as closely as I should have been, but I knew I'd seen *North by Northwest.* It was a thriller by Alfred Hitchcock, who'd been one of my favourite film directors until Sophie had convinced me that thrillers were stupid and adolescent and couldn't hold a candle to arty costume dramas adapted from classic works of literature. I vaguely remembered a scene in which James Stewart dangled from the Statue of Liberty's torch, but I couldn't remember any names beginning with the letter O.

I asked Walter if his name was Ogden or Ozymandias. 'It's something too embarrassing to reveal in public, isn't it?'

Walter was very patient, though his grin had slipped a couple of notches. 'It's *nothing*,' he shouted, no doubt hoping that by raising his voice his words would penetrate my thick skull.

I jumped, and he lowered the volume apologetically. 'My mother thought middle names frivolous. She favoured a return to wholesome, apple-pie, middle-American nomenclature. But I was determined to be rich and famous. I was going to have monogrammed shirts, like the Great Gatsby, and I was damned if I was going to have them monogrammed with the letters WC.'

'Whereas with the O,' I pointed out, 'you're WOC.'

You could still see traces of that grin, but now it was more than a little frayed. 'Nice meeting you Clare,' he said in a resigned tone. He nodded farewell to Marsha and started down the steps to the basement.

I had no intention of letting it go at that, so I called after him, 'I understand you're a *film director*.'

Walter Cheeseman looked back, surprised and (I thought) a little pleased. He glanced at Marsha. 'You understand correctly.'

'I'd love to see some of your films,' I gushed. 'Can I get them on video?'

'I told you she'd be interested,' said Marsha.

'As a matter of fact, yes,' said Walter. 'They are all on VHS, though I'm afraid it's the American format, otherwise I'd certainly lend them to you.'

He frowned slightly, as though working out a complicated equation in his head. 'However, if you have an afternoon to spare, you're more than welcome to come down and watch them on *my* equipment.'

'I'd like that,' I said. I thought Walter O. Cheeseman

was a little bit weird, but quite dishy. Maybe he was just the ticket to help me get over Miles.

'Good,' he said. 'Better make it soon, though. I can't stick around too long.' He gave me one last grin, this time making no effort whatsoever to inject it with warmth, and clattered down the steps.

Marsha playfully whacked me between the shoulder blades as we went into the house. 'Go for it.'

'He's strange.'

'He's *American*,' said Marsha.

I wondered if Sophie had run into Walter before she'd been dispatched to the continent. Probably not; Sophie hadn't been out and about much after her breakdown, and now she wouldn't be back for another week. With a bit of luck, and some canny manoeuvring, I would have established a substantial head-start with Walter Cheeseman by the time she returned.

In the meantime, there were a few things that needed to be sorted out. One of them was the bathroom. I was having problems with it.

It didn't help that there wasn't a window. Now that Lemmy had fixed the wiring, it wasn't just the light that came on when you tugged the cord; it also started the death-rattle of an old extractor fan. It was so loud I'd almost had a heart attack the first time it had throbbed into action. It was so loud it drowned out the radio when I was in the bath.

But, in truth, the bathroom was so depressing with its chipped tiles and yellow walls and flourishing arachnid population that I spent as little time in there as possible. Lemmy had managed to get the ancient immersion heater working, but it was on its last legs, and though tubfuls of water were a possibility, they usually turned out more tepid than hot, and I had a horrid suspicion that the ventilation had been worked out by someone who thought carbon monoxide poisoning was something you got from chewing typewriter ribbons. Most of the time, I found it more convenient, not to mention safer, to use the showers after my sessions at the swimming pool.

It wasn't just the tiles in the bathroom that were cracked. There was also that crack in the mirror, an emphatic fissure that ran diagonally across the middle, so that it was impossible to look into it without seeing your face split into two halves which didn't quite match up at the edges. It could have been the cover design for a book about schizophrenia.

That mirror gave me the heebie-jeebies, and not just because it was impossible to forget what had once happened in front of it. One night, while I was brushing my teeth, I had the distinct impression that each half of my face was following its own separate game-plan. I'd already removed my glasses in readiness for bed, so I had to squint at the reflection to bring it vaguely into focus. One half of my face was drooling liquidised toothpaste over my chin like a rabid dog; the other was wreathed in yellowish shadow and scrutinizing me through brown eyes so dark and narrow they appeared almost black.

Normally, I wouldn't have worried. Except that my own eyes were blue.

It was a trick of the light, of course. The eyes in the mirror were not brown at all. How could I have thought that? I shifted on to my other foot and squinted even more, and – sure enough – the mirror reflected back eyes that were very definitely that insipid baby blue I despised so much.

After that, I tried to replace the cracked mirror with something more wholesome and flattering, but it had been fixed to the wall with some sort of superglue. I tried to pry it off with the corner of a metal ruler, but only succeeded in chipping one of the bevelled edges.

There was nothing for it but to let it stay there, though from then on I looked into it as little as possible. For putting on make-up, I switched to a magnified shaving mirror in the bedroom. And the market yielded a full-length looking-glass for the living-room; it was a scruffy old thing in need of resilvering, but it served its purpose.

They were useful, these new mirrors, and not at all frightening, but even so I didn't gaze into them any more than I had to, especially after dark.

One lunchtime I met up with Dirk and Lemmy and, even though I hadn't been intending to have the bathroom painted just yet, offered them another twenty-five quid to go over the yellow walls with a roller and some white paint. It wasn't a lot of work. They'd be able to knock it off in a day.

I was confident they would say yes, so it was something of a shock when they both stared mournfully at me and, in unison, shook their heads.

I couldn't understand it. They needed the money. Dirk and Lemmy *always* needed the money. 'Why not?' I asked, trying to keep the petulance out of my voice. I was feeling a little let down. If friends weren't willing to help out with the decorating, then what on earth was the point of them?

'Bad vibes, man,' said Dirk.

'Armani campanella viscose *dead men*,' said Lemmy.

I frowned at Lemmy, trying to catch his drift.

'Lemmy says that nothing on earth will get him to go back into that bathroom,' Dirk translated, though as usual it seemed as though he was intermingling Lemmy's observations with more than a few of his own. 'Just after we started on your living-room, he went for a slash and came out looking like he'd seen a ghost. You should have seen him, Clare. His face was whiter than a tab of Amytal, and I swear his hair was standing on end.'

Lemmy's hair was shoulder-length so this had to have been a sight worth seeing.

'After that,' Dirk said, 'whenever one of us wanted to take a leak, we came down here to the pub.'

I'd noticed they'd been spending as much time in the Saddleback Arms as in the room they were supposed to be painting, but since I'd been paying them by results rather than by the hour, there hadn't seemed much point in getting stroppy.

Dirk went to the bar to get more drinks. Forgetting for a minute that I needed him to act as interpreter, I leaned over to Lemmy and asked, 'What exactly was it about the bathroom that you didn't like?'

He looked straight at me and said, very slowly and clearly, 'Some guy cut his throat in front of the mirror.'

I jerked my head back as though he'd spat in my face.

Dirk came back to the table with the drinks. 'All right?' he asked brightly.

I managed to stammer, 'Wh-What did you say?' I could have sworn I hadn't mentioned Robert Jamieson's suicide to either of them.

'Deuteronomy costermonger mussolini,' replied Lemmy. 'Dick van dyke *bad vibes*.'

'Yeah,' said Dirk, nodding in agreement. '*Really bad vibes*, Clare.'

Robert Jamieson might have been dead, but evidently there were a lot of people in the world who were not yet apprised of the fact, because they kept on sending him mail.

'You'd think they'd have given up by now,' I remarked to Marsha one morning after we'd met in the hall to sort through the morning delivery. I was expecting a cheque, as well as half-hoping that someone somewhere would have sent me a postcard or invitation to a private view or launch party, but most of the post turned out to be for Marsha or Walter.

'What?' said Marsha, opening the latest of the many envelopes she received from all around the world. The picture on the stamp was of a red and yellow bird with an enormous fish sticking out of its beak. Marsha had friends in exotic places.

'That for Robert? Give it here.'

I handed the envelope over, a little reluctantly. The address was handwritten, and I was curious about the contents. 'What do you do with them?'

'With Robert's letters? I forward them. We're supposed to forward everything that isn't addressed to us.'

'What do you mean, *forward them*? Where on earth do you forward them to? The cemetery? The posthumous office? Isn't it all a bit *Twilight Zone*?'

'I send them to the agents,' said Marsha. 'Don't ask me what they do with them. Maybe everything's sent on to the family.'

'For a dead man, he certainly gets a lot of mail,' I observed, though I didn't say what was *really* exasperating, which was that he got more mail than I did.

'A fair amount,' agreed Marsha. 'But it's probably only junk. You live in any old house like this, especially one divided into flats, and you're bound to get loads of things addressed to people who don't live here any more. I mean, look . . .'

She picked up another envelope. 'Here's one for Arthur Mowbray. We've had quite a few for him, and he hasn't lived here for God knows how long. Before my time, anyway. And here's another one . . . for . . .*Nicholas Wisley Esquire*? Get a load of that fancy handwriting, will you? Oh well, this one's a first – I've never heard of anyone called Wisley.'

I looked wistfully at the rogue envelopes as Marsha rounded them up and tucked them into the pocket of her towelling bathrobe.

'Don't you ever feel like opening them?' I asked. 'Just out of curiosity?'

I'd shocked her. 'Clare! It's private! Anyway, what would be the point? It's not as though it's likely to be anything exciting. Besides, life's too short; I get quite enough letters as it is, and I don't want to have to read everyone else's as well.'

And with that, she gathered up her own correspondence, slapped me affectionately on the back, and marched back into her flat with a hearty slam of the door.

A few days later, when, as usual, the morning postal delivery failed to shower me in a cascade of exciting letters and invitations, I picked up the latest of Robert Jamieson's letters and took a long hard look at it. The address had been written in loopy Biro on blue Basildon Bond.

Damn it, I thought. *Why should he get more post than me?* And, not daring to stop and think, I slipped the letter down inside the waistband of my jeans.

I needn't have bothered with the subterfuge, because Marsha wasn't around. I thought she'd probably stayed overnight with her so-called boyfriend – a twice-divorced travel agent who lived in Fulham. But I felt guilty, and half-remembered reading somewhere that tampering with mail was one of the few crimes, like setting fire to Her Majesty's shipyards, that was still punishable by death. So I slunk back upstairs, ready to hide the protruding edge of the envelope with my arm, even though there was no one else around.

Not surprisingly, I made it back to my flat unobserved. I poured myself a mid-morning cup of coffee and settled down to read the letter, as comfortably and as naturally as though it had been addressed to me.

Dear Robert,
My lawyer advised me not to write to you, but I still think a personal appeal is more likely to succeed than a court order. As you must surely be aware, Ben is fast approaching his fifteenth birthday. His teachers tell me he is interested in foreign languages, and has some talent in that direction, but in order to develop his oral skills he needs to spend time in France and Germany. The chance of a school trip has come up, but unfortunately I am already stretched to the limit and cannot possibly take on any more work, what with the two part-time jobs and all the extra stuff I do at home.

I know you have probably been finding things as tough as I have, which is why I have never nagged you about the outstanding payments. But I was wondering if perhaps you could possibly scrape something together over the next couple of months? He is as much your son as mine, and even though you have never displayed the slightest interest in his welfare, I can't believe you are as indifferent as you want people to think.

All my love, Maggie
P.S. He has been asking about you. What should I tell him?
P.P.S. Please get in touch. Even if you can't send any money, I would love to hear how you're doing.

P.P.S. Do you still write poems? I've still got the one
you dedicated to me.

The letter was undated. I studied the postmark, but it
was nothing more than a smudged arc across a con-
glomeration of different coloured stamps in minor
denominations. I felt sorry for Maggie, whoever she
was. Surely someone should have written to tell her
what had happened, especially if there was a child
involved. But what kind of man would lose contact with
his son like that in the first place?

I would have written and told her myself, except that
there was no return address.

FIVE

I WAS WANDERING through an art gallery, searching for Sophie, convinced she had just passed this way. If only I could walk fast enough, I would catch up with her. I'd gone past some very famous paintings, such as Sunflowers and the Mona Lisa, before realizing I'd been here before. Or had I? Perhaps I'd only watched Sister Wendy talking about it in a television programme.

But then my ears tuned into a distant thudding, and I realized with a dull shock of dismay that the sound was coming nearer.

Ker-chunk ker-chunk ker-chunk

Coming closer, getting louder, echoing off the walls of the gallery as it came.

I found myself in front of Mantegna's *Cristo Morto*, the one with the famous foreshortening and the crinkled feet, the one on the postcard Sophie had sent me. The flesh was dead flesh, the colour and texture of mouldy green cheese, and I stared at it transfixed, unable to tear myself away even though I knew something dreadful was going to happen – I knew because it had happened before, and nothing I could do would prevent it from happening again. I couldn't move and now it was too late, because the booming filled my ears. It was all around and there was no escape.

In a single swift and sudden movement, Christ sat upright on His slab and extended His arms out towards me. I gazed on Him with awe. His hands were enveloped in fluffy green oven mitts. He was offering me a fluted white dish.

I went up on tiptoe to peer inside, and what I saw made me gasp in wonder and delight.

It was a baked chocolate soufflé, fresh out of the oven.

I had never before laid eyes on such an impeccable soufflé. It sat there, gently quivering. My mouth watered in anticipation of the first bite – the delicate crunch as my teeth sank into crust light as a cloud, its barely there essence dissolving into bittersweet nothingness on my taste buds.

And then, all of a sudden, the soufflé collapsed into itself, and was gone.

Christ grinned broadly, revealing supernaturally perfect teeth and gums, and said. 'What's taking you so long?'

'You just have to look at him to realize he's a complete bastard,' Marsha was saying. We'd run into each other in the hallway again, and now we were talking about someone I'd foolishly pretended I'd met when in fact I hadn't, not ever, and it was starting to get complicated; the conversation had taken an awkward turn and I was beginning to think I would be found out. Marsha had just started to say something else when from upstairs there came the crash of a door being flung open.

We broke off and looked at each other. This was the first indication we'd had that Sophie was back in town.

We stared in amazement as she came hurtling down

the stairs towards us. The French sun had restored a little colour to her complexion, but her hair was uncombed and her eyes were wild. She came storming down like a fury and charged right up to me until her face was inches from mine. I tried to step back, but the wall was in the way.

She exhaled sharply, a gasp of stupified outrage.

I cringed. She had *dragon's* breath.

'Hi, Sophie,' I said.

'Hello, Sophie,' called Marsha.

But Sophie took no notice of her. '*You've been seeing him, haven't you?*' she yelled into my face.

So the jig was up. She'd finally found out about Miles and me. The fact that our relationship was over didn't make it any less awkward or embarrassing to be rumbled now.

'I have no idea what you're talking about,' I said, giving her my best wide-eyed and candid look.

'You *are* seeing him!' she shouted. 'Don't try to pretend you're not! You *are*! And I thought you were my *friend*.'

'Look,' I said, 'Miles hasn't even been . . .'

I trailed off. She'd fallen back a few paces, the wildness in her eyes now softened by a mist of bewilderment.

'*Miles*?' she demanded. 'Why the hell would you want to see *Miles*?'

'I thought . . .'

'Don't you *dare* try to confuse me,' she said, but the stridency was gone. 'You know perfectly well who we're talking about.'

169

ANNE BILLSON

'I'm sorry,' I said. 'I don't.'

The bewilderment vanished and her eyes hardened into glittering slits. 'Bitch bitch bitch. You know perfectly well I'm talking about Robert.'

My first thought was that she was referring to the letter I'd opened. I felt an instant's guilt, and heard Marsha go 'uh-oh' under her breath, but I didn't get an opportunity to respond because in the very next instant I found myself lying flat on my back on the floor, trying to protect my face from Sophie's fingernails as she knelt on top of me, slashing and clawing and screaming unintelligible words.

It was fortunate she was such a delicate creature; I was more shocked than hurt, Marsha grabbed her by the armpits and hauled her off easily, saying, 'That will be quite enough of *that*.'

'I'll get you,' said Sophie.

'Lovely to see you too,' I said, getting to my feet and brushing myself down.

'Don't think I don't know what you're trying to do,' she said. 'You've always been jealous of me, *always*. Do you think I don't notice?'

It was true I'd felt the occasional pang of envy, but I glanced at Marsha as if to say, *What's going on here?* and Marsha returned the glance with interest.

Sophie broke out of Marsha's restraining grasp, but she was calmer now. Her eyes flashed one last poison dart at me before she flounced back upstairs.

We heard the door crash shut behind her.

'Jeez,' said Marsha. 'Doesn't look as if ten days in Provence was enough now, does it?'

170

There was something else bugging me. 'Did you notice anything peculiar about her? I mean apart from the behaviour. Something about the way she looked.'

Marsha shook her head.

'She wasn't wearing beige,' I said.

But Sophie was back in town, and, though that first meeting didn't go so well, I soon found myself with another bonding opportunity. One evening, I spotted her in the Landrace Inn as I walked past. The windows were fitted with faux-antique dimpled glass which made whatever was on the other side ripple, like one of those flashback effects you sometimes get in old black and white movies, but through the undulation I made out Sophie. She was sitting in the corner, head bowed in deep conversation with a dark-haired man who might have been good-looking if only the window hadn't been blurring his features into one of those portraits by Francis Bacon.

I'd had enough of hanging out in the sort of lowlife dives favoured by Dirk and Lemmy. It was time to get myself a taste of the glittering west eleven life I'd been hankering after for so long. I was prepared to forgive Sophie's bizarre behaviour and put our long-standing friendship to some practical use, and I thought I would make a start by muscling in on her cosy tête-à-tête. Besides, I needed to meet more men, since Miles was no longer in the running, and my promising relationship with Walter had yet to develop past a state of nodding acquaintance.

But first I had to get a drink and pretend I'd been

there all along, so Sophie would think I took places like the Landrace Inn in my stride. By the time I'd elbowed my way to the bar, attracted the attention of one of the Australians who was holding court behind it, shelled out vast sums of money for a bottle of authentic Japanese lager, and wormed my way through the crowd to where she was sitting, it was too late. Her companion had legged it, and she was on her own.

The first thing I noticed was that it hadn't been the dimpled window that had rippled Sophie's hair: she really had crimped it into Pre-Raphaelite waves. It was reassuring to see that she was taking care over her appearance again, but the style struck me as very un-Sophie, as did the dark smudges of Cleopatra-style kohl around her eyes.

But she looked a lot healthier. She was as skinny as ever, but had definitely turned some sort of corner. The spark that had died the day she'd learned the truth about Robert Jamieson had returned to light up her eyes.

If anything, she was now looking at me a little too brightly.

'Oh, hi,' she said, with rather too much enthusiasm.

I looked down at the cigarette end smouldering in the ashtray. 'Are you with someone?'

Sophie followed my gaze. 'Oh, he had to get back,' she said, flipping the stub over and crushing the last wisps of smoke out of it with her thumb.

I parked myself in the chair opposite. 'Then you don't mind if I sit here.'

For a moment, Sophie looked as if she was about to say she *did* mind, but instead she said, 'Sorry about the other day in the hall. I'd been, er, having a peculiar dream.'

'That's OK,' I said.

'Things have been a bit ... strange recently,' she said, smiling to herself.

'Tell me about it,' I said rhetorically. 'But you're looking a lot better.'

'I feel so embarrassed,' Sophie said, bending forward so the Pre-Raphaelite ripples cast lacy shadows across her face. 'I expect you thought I'd gone bonkers.'

'Not at all,' I lied. 'What did the doctor say?'

'He referred me to a therapist,' said Sophie. 'She blames it all on Miles, of course. And on Hamish.'

'Too right,' I said. 'Men are always to blame for everything.'

'There's some interesting stuff coming out. Heavy mental baggage I had no idea I was lugging around.'

I said how I'd always rather fancied being in therapy, because it would be nice to have someone really listen to me, but Sophie went on as though I hadn't spoken. 'I tell her my dreams,' she said. 'And she never gets bored.'

'I never got bored when you told me your dreams,' I protested. 'Even the one about the piglets and the bumblebees.'

'But you're not a professional,' said Sophie. 'You can't tell me what they mean. What? What's the matter?'

I'd been grimacing with the effort of trying to dredge up something I'd only just half-remembered. 'I had a dream about baked chocolate soufflé,' I told her.

'Lucky old you,' said Sophie, but expressed no interest in hearing more. As other scraps of the dream filtered slowly back into my brain, I realized I didn't want to describe it to her anyway. I didn't want Sophie thinking her influence over me was so enormous that I even followed in her footsteps in my sleep.

We strolled back to the house together. As we drew nearer to Hampshire Place, Sophie saw something up ahead and checked her pace.

'Don't look now,' she whispered. 'It's the ashoo boys.'

I assumed she was referring to some local Asian or West Indian family, but all I could see were a couple of skinny teenagers lollygagging around on a louvred installation which I gathered had something to do with the cable company that had left lumpy furrows in all the pavements. They were both wearing red anoraks with the hoods up, which made them look like mutant hybrids of Little Red Riding Hood and the homicidal dwarf from that thriller set in Venice, and they were kicking their heels in oversized sneakers from which the laces dangled loose. They were the sort of people I would normally have crossed the road to avoid.

As we approached them, Sophie explained, 'Couple of weeks ago they came up to me and said, *Ashoo*. So naturally I replied, *Bless you*.'

She paused, waiting for a reaction.

'I don't get it.'

Sophie sighed impatiently. 'I'd heard it wrong. It wasn't *ashoo*, it was *ash*. *Hash*. They were selling dope.'

I asked if she'd bought any.

Sophie said she never touched the stuff, but let out such a loud and dirty laugh that the teenagers looked up and saw us. Sophie greeted them cheerfully. 'Hey,' she said. 'Whassup.'

Whassup. I nearly died with embarrassment.

'Bless you today?' one of them shouted as we passed.

'Not today, thank you,' Sophie called back.

'I thought you said you never touched drugs,' I said.

'It's a standing joke,' said Sophie. 'After that business with the sneezing, they started calling me the Bless You Lady.'

I said they probably called her lots of other things too, when her back was turned.

SIX

IT WASN'T just Sophie's appearance that had changed, it was her entire manner. I was unable to put my finger on it until a long time afterwards, but it felt as though she had passed through the gate into a secret garden and had locked it securely behind her so that no one else could get in.

My only consolation was that I was certain she'd locked out Carolyn and Charlotte and Isabella as well. I'd managed to tag along with Sophie so often now that her friends were becoming accustomed to having me around. I'd perfected the art of timing my exits from the house – it involved hovering on the landing with my ears on full alert – so they coincided with Sophie's, which gave me an excuse to walk down the road with her. Whenever she paused outside the Barrio or the Bar Belle or wherever she would be meeting her chums, and said, 'See you later, then,' I would stand my ground and say something along the lines of, 'What a coincidence, I was just popping in here myself,' and then of course it would be easy to stick around for the rest of the evening, even if nobody took much notice of me. No one was going to say, 'Push off fatty.' Not to my face.

*

I'd considered inviting Carolyn and the others to my housewarming, but the idea of the invitation being turned down had struck me as so mortifying that I'd chickened out. Normally I would have asked Graham as well, but I didn't think it was wise to put him in the same room as Sophie, just as I thought it prudent to save Dirk and Lemmy for a separate occasion. Miles, I knew, was spending the weekend with his parents in Ottery St Mary (where he'd never dared take *me*, though Sophie had always looked on it as a second home, and I'd heard Ligia had already been made welcome there), but I had mixed feelings about the prospect of him and Sophie getting back together again and probably wouldn't have invited him anyway.

So in the end it was just me, Sophie and Marsha. All girls together, plus a bottle of Australian Chardonnay.

'Very nice,' Marsha said, when she saw what I'd done with a lick of paint, a few hand-woven rugs and a couple of floor cushions. 'You've made it quite habitable. I must say I wasn't happy about this place being empty all that time.'

'Surely you're not frightened by a few ghosts,' purred Sophie. *Purred* was the operative word here; I had detected a slight cattiness in her attitude to Marsha ever since the Robert Jamieson business. Sophie never passed up on an opportunity to compliment Marsha on what she was wearing, even if it was something with patchwork inserts, or sequins sewn into amusing patterns on mohair jumpers, or beasts of the jungle appliquéd in silver and gold – flourishes which I knew

Sophie would have swallowed strychnine before allowing into any wardrobe of hers.

It was obvious to me that she was being the bitch of all time, but Marsha either failed to notice or chose to ignore it. The more I saw of Marsha, the more apparent it became that she paid little heed to other people's opinions. She trotted good-naturedly along life's highway, glancing to neither left nor right, her blinkers lending her a truly enviable contentment.

'No such thing as ghosts,' she said jauntily.

'Who knows?' said Sophie.

Marsha obviously thought it was time to change the subject. 'It's just the three of us?'

'Who else is there?' I said, though as soon as I'd asked the question I realized it sounded wistful, rather than blasé, as I'd intended.

'I thought you might have invited your gentleman friend,' said Marsha.

I was perplexed by the twinkle in her eye. 'You mean Walter? He couldn't make it.'

'I meant the bloke you were with the other night.'

I had no idea what she was talking about, and said so.

'You *were* in the Duke of York on Friday?' asked Marsha.

I thought back. 'Yeees.' I remembered popping in to look for Dirk and Lemmy, and staying for a gin and tonic, though I hadn't run into anyone I knew.

'I thought as much,' said Marsha. 'I thought I'd seen you through the window.'

'You should have come in. I would have bought you a drink.'

'Didn't like to interrupt,' Marsha said with a funny little smile. 'The two of you were getting along so well.'

I scoured my memory again, and came up with a resounding blank. 'But I was on my own.'

'*Sure* you were,' said Marsha, winking broadly.

Sophie was looking from one of us to the other, like a Centre Court spectator.

'I was on my own,' I repeated. 'Honestly.'

'It's OK,' said Marsha, 'I won't tell anyone.'

'There's nothing to tell,' I said, getting a bit annoyed.

As soon as Sophie realized she wasn't privy to any gossip worth repeating, she lost all interest in our exchange and drifted over towards the window. She picked up the blue vase, turning it this way and that. Dead petals fell to the floor like stones. 'Your flowers are way past it,' she observed.

'I keep meaning to get fresh ones,' I said, crouching at her feet to collect the petals in my palm.

Sophie set the vase down with the words, 'And where on earth did you find this bit of tack?'

This bit of tack?

My eyes were opened. It was the loafers all over again. The blue vase was indeed a piece of tack, and I couldn't think how I'd ever imagined otherwise.

'Just something I picked up in the market.'

'It's *cracked*,' said Sophie. 'You should chuck it away. I can find you an empty jar, if you need something to put flowers in.'

It was Marsha's turn to scrutinize the vase. 'I'll have it if you don't want it,' she said. 'I've got a pair of trousers in exactly that shade of blue.'

'What a splendid idea,' Sophie said brightly. 'You can stick a handle on the top and use it as a novelty handbag.'

I scowled at her, but she studiously avoided my gaze. Marsha didn't notice. She was peering through the window. 'It's so different from up here,' she said. 'I've got the same view, but not nearly so leafy.'

'Yes,' said Sophie. 'You generally get more foliage at this level.'

I couldn't hold back any longer. 'What on earth is the matter with you? You suffering from PMT or something?'

Sophie looked at me through wide and innocent eyes. 'What do you mean?'

But it was as though Marsha was equipped with a filter that blocked out everything she didn't need to hear. She'd pounced on one of my sketchbooks and was now flicking through it, uttering complimentary little cooing noises as she did so. 'These are nice. You're so clever. Ooh, look at that. I wish *I* could draw.'

Sophie peered over her shoulder at my rough sketches of the dead tulips, Dirk staring into his beer, the view from the window, and the odd feeble attempt at self-portraiture.

'So what are you working on right now?' she asked.

For a microsecond I thought about lying. But it was no good. 'Puddings,' I said.

Sophie sniggered, and I realized she'd known the answer all along. She'd just wanted to hear me say it.

'Not still on the puddings! Poor puddingy Clare! You must be *so* sick of them.'

'They pay the rent,' I said.

'You're not paying rent,' Sophie pointed out.

'I'm still paying it in Hackney,' I said.

'What puddings?' asked Marsha.

I slid the latest batch of step-by-steps out of my folder and spread them out over the table-top with a certain amount of pride. The work might have been lacking in glamour, but it looked slick and professional. By following my illustrations, a person really could learn how to bake.

'Good Lord,' giggled Sophie, pointing to the nearest. 'What in heaven's name is that?'

'Victoria sponge,' I said.

'The well-known soap actress,' said Sophie.

I ignored her. 'And that one's *tarte au praline*.'

'You did all these?' squeaked Marsha. 'But they're so *neat*. You are *so* talented. I can't tell you how jealous I am.'

'It's nothing,' I said, wondering whether it might not be a smart move to swap my friendship with Sophie, long-standing as it was, for a more confidence-boosting association with Marsha.

'The things people eat,' said Sophie, staring with horrified fascination.

I picked up the *tarte au praline* sequence and stared intently at it. 'My style has changed, don't you think?'

Sophie asked, 'What do you mean?'

I ignored the warning note in her voice. 'Don't you think the drawings are getting darker, more intense?'

'You mean a darker, more intense kind of pudding?' Sophie scrunched up her face, trying to focus on the finer details. 'You've got better at hands,' she observed. 'Some of your earlier efforts looked like clumps of fish fingers.'

I felt disappointment welling up. 'You don't think they look at all sinister? Or surreal? As though something horrible might intrude into the frame at any moment?'

'This one's scary enough as it is,' said Sophie.

'I think they all look delicious,' said Marsha. 'You must give me the recipes.'

I offered to get her some of the cookery books that had already been published.

'You mean people actually *eat* junk like this?' asked Sophie.

'Not everybody suffers from a fashionable eating disorder,' I said, but she wasn't to be deflected.

'Why do you waste your time on this rubbish?' she demanded. Her tone had turned quite spiteful, with not even a pretence at humour. I wondered if she'd drunk too much, though there were several inches of wine still left in the bottle.

Marsha persevered, sunny as ever. 'Don't you ever cook, Sophie?' she asked.

'Yes, but proper food. Not crap like this.'

'This isn't crap,' said Marsha, without antagonism. 'They're traditional recipes, exactly the sort of thing we serve at Cinghiale, only English rather than Italian. Oh, but Clare – these drawings really *are* brilliant.'

I was dreading what Sophie would come out with next, but all of a sudden she was looking beaten, as though Marsha's implacable niceness had finally worn her down.

'Maybe you're right,' she muttered. 'I suppose there's nothing wrong with a bit of tradition.'

And I saw her drag the fingers of one hand through the roots of her hair, several times. It was a new habit, and she didn't seem aware she was doing it, but it left her hair in the most frightful tangle.

The more time Sophie and I spent together, the cattier she became, though I suppose the two things might not have been unrelated. I was also spending more time with Carolyn and Charlotte and Grenville and Toby and Isabella as well, and although I didn't feel altogether at ease in their company, they seemed to accept me as one of them. I told myself that anyone looking on from the outside would have been hard-pressed to spot the difference.

There *was* a difference, though, and I was constantly being made aware of it. One hot night in August, we all trooped off down the road in search of a bar with air conditioning.

'There's the Rhumba Bar,' I pointed out as we approached it. Sophie had been pointedly ignoring me, but I wasn't going to let her get me down.

'I can't go in there,' said Toby.

'Yes you can,' said Carolyn.

'No I can't,' said Toby. 'They banned me.'

By now we were gathered in the open doorway of the Rhumba Bar. An unnatural breeze caressed our overheated faces as we peered inside. It was crowded, but not too crowded.

'But tell you what,' said Toby. 'It was an awful long time ago.'

He swaggered in like a gunslinger entering a saloon. We followed in a pack. A man in a collarless shirt was pouring drinks behind the bar and glanced up as we entered, but didn't look as though he had enough energy to throw anybody out. Carolyn went up to him and ordered drinks.

'What do you mean, *banned*?' asked Isabella as we clustered behind Carolyn.

'They banned me for playing Social Whirligigs,' said Toby.

Everybody chortled, except me. I hadn't a clue what Social Whirligigs was, or how you played it.

'Social Whirligigs is a gas,' said Grenville. 'Man, I love it.'

Charlotte giggled and punched him playfully on the arm.

'Me too,' I said impulsively, desperate to join in.

They all stopped laughing and turned to me and stared. Sophie was suddenly paying me more attention than she'd paid me all evening. 'You play Social Whirligigs, Clare?' she asked.

'Well, not very often,' I said, regretting my recklessness and trying to back down a little. 'I mean, I haven't played it for years.'

Charlotte, Grenville and Toby looked at one another and burst out laughing. Isabella looked baffled, Carolyn a bit uncomfortable.

Sophie was smiling maliciously. 'Show us.'

'I beg your pardon?'

'Show us how you used to play Social Whirligigs. We'd all like to see how it's done.'

'That's enough,' said Carolyn, though she couldn't stop the edges of her mouth from curling up into a smile. 'Don't worry about it, Clare.'

Sophie pouted, playing to the gallery. 'But I was *so* looking forward to seeing Clare play Social Whirligigs.'

'*I'll* show you how to play Social Whirligigs!' shouted Toby, planting his legs apart. He unzipped his fly, took out his penis and waggled it around.

Isabella let out a spirited whoop.

'For God's sake, put it away,' Charlotte said in a been-there-seen-it voice.

There was a slow eddy of excitement as other customers saw what was going on. Not to be outdone, Grenville had unzipped his trousers and was now foraging purposefully in his boxer-shorts.

'Get your dick out, and we're finished,' hissed Carolyn. 'For *ever*.'

'Men are such children,' said Sophie, looking at me and smiling triumphantly. 'Don't you think so, Clare?'

'I must have got Social Whirligigs muddled up with something else,' I muttered.

'Yeah, like Trivial Pursuit,' said Charlotte.

The man in the collarless shirt came storming round the bar and tapped Toby authoritatively on the shoulder. 'Right you are. Zip it up and get the fuck out of here. You're banned.'

'Gotcha!' Toby guffawed, stuffing his penis back inside his pants. 'You can't ban me, because I'm banned *already*.'

'Too right, matey, banned for bloody life. Show your face in here again, and I'm calling the cops.'

'It's not his face that's the problem,' said Grenville.

'You too,' said Collarless Shirt.

'But I ordered drinks,' said Carolyn.

'You want me to call the cops *right now?*' asked Collarless Shirt.

We left, Toby laughing and joking with anyone who would listen, Sophie acting sniffy, the others a little more subdued but pretending not to care. I tried to look as inconspicuous as possible. It wasn't hard, though I suppose I might have attracted attention by default; onlookers might have asked themselves, 'What's that plump girl in the spectacles doing with that glittering flock of beautiful people?' But I didn't think so. With a bit of luck, I would be able to revisit the Rhumba Bar any time I liked and no one would know me from Eve.

As we reached the exit, Toby turned back and made a sweeping bow. There was a small scattered shower of applause.

We started off down the road in search of another air conditioner. Sophie stalked on ahead, apparently more miffed at me than ever, though I couldn't understand why since she was the one who had scored all the points. Every so often I caught her sneaking glances in my direction – strange glances, angry and pained, like the expression of a tiny child faced with an even tinier sibling who is grabbing all the attention – but as soon as she saw me looking back she would pretend to be engrossed in something else.

'Well,' said Charlotte, drawing abreast of Carolyn and me as we strolled. 'At least now we know whose is biggest.'

Isabella came up behind us and asked, 'And whose is that?'

Charlotte and Carolyn both looked at me and giggled.

'Lucky old Clare,' said Charlotte.

I cringed inwardly. At the time, I thought she was just being bitchy about my *faux pas*.

SEVEN

I'D TAKEN to keeping the bathroom door closed at all times of the day and night. It wasn't the mirror I was frightened of so much as the eight-legged population, which had miraculously continued to flourish even after I had vacuumed up strands of web from every last corner. I kept the door shut because I didn't want spiders scampering all over the rest of the flat. More particularly, I didn't want them crawling into my ear as I slept and laying billions of tiny spider eggs in my brain. Not that shutting them in would have stopped them if they'd really wanted to make a break for it; they could have limbo-danced under the door any time they wanted.

One night I woke up at about three o'clock to an unfamiliar sound: a faint rustling, which seemed to be coming from the direction of the bathroom. The sound reminded me of the swish of silk against skin.

Oh God, I thought, *the spiders are out of control.*

I wasn't in a hurry to get up and investigate. I felt around for my glasses, slipped something on to my feet, and walked softly across to the small landing outside the bathroom door.

I stood there, poised in the half-light coming through my filmy new bedroom curtains, and listened, ears straining for the faintest scurrying of spindly legs, the susurration of cobwebs being spun, the gentle scrunch of teensy jaws chomping down on crunchy insect torsos.

Silence.

Dead silence.

I placed my hand on the doorhandle, and the rustling started up again as though I'd pressed a button. It was louder now, and quite obviously had nothing to do with spiders, unless they had somehow learned amazing new communication skills. What I was listening to was the faint hum of conversation, so faint that the sound of my own breathing would probably have drowned it out.

But I was holding my breath. I had to remind myself to let it out and draw in a fresh supply of air. I did this very gradually. I didn't want to make a sound.

There were several possibilities here. Either I was dreaming and so, lurking on the other side of the door, ready to pounce, was a bloodthirsty one-legged koala bear. Or I had burglars. But what kind of burglars would shut themselves in my bathroom? There was nothing worth stealing in there, unless they were after a half-empty bottle of Chanel No 5 which I'd stopped using after Sophie had said that it made me smell as though I'd covered myself in baby powder.

No, this wasn't burglars.

This was something *worse*.

I pressed my ear up against the door.

There were definitely two of them, chattering quietly, a gentle whispering that went on and on, neither rising nor fading away. It was so faint that, under other circumstances, I might have dismissed it as a mild attack of tinnitus.

Part of me was tempted to run back to bed and burrow beneath the duvet till morning, when I could go about my business as though nothing had happened, as though I hadn't heard noises in the middle of the night at all.

But I knew, with a heart heavy as suet pudding, that I had to open the bathroom door *right now*, or I would never feel safe in that flat again. I would have to leave Notting Hill and run back to Hackney with my tail between my legs. Back to a boring, anonymous life in the boondocks.

No, I wasn't going to be beaten.

I gripped the handle, took a breath so deep the air filled my body all the way down into my feet, and opened the door.

The next morning I bought a bag of croissants filled with apricot jam and hammered on Sophie's door. Whole minutes passed before she opened up, yawning and complaining and rubbing the sleep out of her eyes with her knuckles.

'Breakfast,' I said, waving the bag, and before she'd had the chance to frame a reply I'd dodged past her into the kitchen and switched on the microwave.

'Mmmmm not hungry,' she mumbled, groping for the kettle.

'That's all right,' I said cheerily. 'I'm sure I can manage them all by myself.'

Sophie shivered and disappeared to look for something to put over her nightgown, leaving me to make the tea and watch over the croissants. When they were ready, I piled everything on to a tray and carried it up to the living-room.

'Sleep well?' I asked as Sophie emerged from her bedroom, knotting the belt of a delightfully simple little silk dressing-gown.

She paused in mid-knot, looking vaguely troubled. 'Not really, now you come to mention it. Bad dreams.'

I'll *bet*, I thought.

Sophie's eyes suddenly opened wide. '*You* were in one of them.'

'Thanks a bunch,' I said.

'You were trying to make me wear the most ghastly cardigan,' she said. 'And I wouldn't. So I ran away.'

It hadn't been quite like that. When I'd finally summoned enough nerve to open the bathroom door, what I'd found in the shadows beyond had not been burglars, nor spiders, nor even one-legged koala bears, but Sophie, perched on the edge of my bath in her white cotton nightdress. Her bare arms looked skinny and vulnerable. Even without the light on, I could see that her skin was tinged with blue.

She had caught up the hem of her nightdress in her hands and was scrunching it into a sweaty little wad, murmuring softly to herself as she did so, nodding earnestly, arching her eyebrows as though listening to a reply, half-smiling, casting her eyes down and fluttering her lashes. It was the perfect portrayal of a woman holding up her half of a flirtatious conversation.

But whoever she was flirting with was in her dreams.

It wasn't the first time I'd caught Sophie walking and talking in her sleep. Once, at school, I'd found her standing by the window, gazing out into the dark grounds with unseeing eyes and muttering, 'I'll get you, my pretty, and your little dog too . . .' I'd read somewhere it was dangerous to wake sleepwalkers, so I'd done nothing but watch and listen, and eventually she'd returned to bed of her own accord. The incident had alarmed me, but I'd never mentioned it to her or anyone else, and I'd never caught her doing it again.

Until now. She looked cold, so I nipped back into my bedroom, looking for something to drape around her shoulders. By the time I returned, carrying one of the chunky cardigans knitted for me by my gran, Sophie was on the move. For an anxious moment I thought we were going to collide in the bathroom doorway, but she swept past, oblivious, and started down the steps towards my front door, taking them so rapidly I had to scamper to catch up. I was just in time to see a flutter of white nightgown as she slipped out of my front door, leaving it wide open behind her.

I couldn't believe I'd gone to bed with the door unlocked, but there was no other way Sophie could have got in.

I didn't follow her down the stairs. I didn't need to. I knew she wouldn't be going far. I stood there listening to her soft diminishing footfall until I heard the door to her own flat slam shut behind her.

*

'You can't remember any more than the cardigan?' I asked.

'No, I told you,' she said, wrinkling her forehead. 'Wait a minute.' She was thinking hard. 'Something about a man in a mirror? No, I've lost it.'

I was midway through my second cup of tea, and Sophie had gone down to the bathroom to take a shower, when my attention was caught by the back of a drawing board propped against the wall of the living-room. I went over to check it out, and nearly choked on my croissant. The style was unmistakably Sophie's – all that pernickety detail – but I'd never seen her tackle subject matter like this; it appeared to be the aftermath of some sort of battle between humans and unearthly demons. The humans had evidently come off second-best.

I wondered whether Sophie had been drawing in her sleep, as well as walking and talking in it.

Men and women were sprawled broken and bleeding in the long grass as bird-headed monsters sawed at their limbs or foraged in their entrails with sharp-clawed instruments. Other humans dangled naked and help-less from apple trees as mincing skeletons sucked the marrow from their bones or thrust red-hot pokers into contorted mouths. In the background, herds of razor-backed pigs roamed freely while shadowy beasts capered and pranced around a blazing hut, casting long black shadows over the land.

And, right at the front, a twiglike creature was ramming a spear through the eye of a redheaded warrior.

'What in hell is this?' I asked Sophie when she came up from the bathroom, towelling her hair.

'Oh, that,' she said. 'It's my summer garden. The calendar I was doing.'

I looked at the picture in silence. There was a lot to look at. It almost – but not quite – put me off the rest of the croissants.

As I lay awake in bed that night, I couldn't help thinking about Sophie's garden – the men writhing impaled in thickets of thorns, or trapped up to their waists in quicksand while rats and vipers gnawed on their upper bodies – and worrying that I was going to find myself transported there the instant I dropped off to sleep.

But my sleep turned out to be blissfully undisturbed, and it didn't take long to shrug off the feeling of impending doom the drawing had left me with. I didn't find Sophie in my bathroom again, though a couple of nights later I came home late to find her slowly drifting up the stairs towards my front door. I gently turned her around and guided her back to bed.

She didn't seem to be aware of these nocturnal escapades, and I decided not to mention them when, a couple of evenings later, I contrived to string along with her to a trendy new café-bar called Prague. The others were there already, knocking back different flavoured vodkas as though prohibition was coming into force at midnight. Isabella, who had just returned from one of her trips abroad, was doling out duty free cigarettes. Grenville, Toby and a pink-eyed friend of theirs called Phineas were arguing about how much a reasonable man might be expected to pay for a one-night-stand with various film actresses and TV celebrities. Eavesdropping on this conversation was like observing the mating habits of a particularly repellent form of wildlife, but when the novelty wore off I turned to the girls, who were talking about their eating disorders. To be specific, they were talking about losing weight, though the only one of us with any excess in the flesh department was me. The others were as skinny as sliced prosciutto.

I wasn't going to be outdone by these stories of bingeing and purging and starving and ridiculous diets consisting of nothing but lettuce leaves and vitamin pills.

'I ate seven doughnuts last week,' I said. 'One after the other. It was exactly like bulimia, only without the throwing up.'

There was a long pause which stretched way beyond the merely pregnant. They regarded me with expressionless eyes. Then everyone started talking again, all at once.

'Don't let those bitches get you down,' said Carolyn, leaning towards me a little unsteadily. 'They're all neurotic as hell about their weight.'

Of Sophie's girlfriends, I had always preferred Carolyn to the others, even though she'd had a gratuitous nose job and her father was a Tory MP who bankrolled the PR company she and Charlotte pretended to run on the days they didn't spend hanging out at the health club or buying up half of Harvey Nichols or Hyperbole. At least Carolyn made an effort to be friendly. 'You should have brought your boyfriend along,' she was saying now in a voice that was slightly slurred.

I looked at her carefully, decided she wasn't taking the piss, and confessed that I didn't have a boyfriend, not at the moment.

Carolyn drained her glass and passed it to Grenville for a refill. Mine was still half-full; the Social Whirligigs fiasco had taught me to exercise caution in this company.

'I meant the bloke you were with the other night,' she said.

I thought back. 'Which one? There've been so many.'

Carolyn's eyebrows shot up. 'So many men?'

'So many nights,' I said.

'Last week at the Rhumba,' she said, as Toby came up with her refill.

'But I was with you lot,' I said.

Toby elbowed me in the ribs so heavily that I nearly fell over. 'Up to no good, eh?' he bellowed.

'Not that I can remember,' I wheezed, rubbing my bruised abdomen and beginning to wonder if I were going mad. This was the second time I'd apparently been paired off with someone who wasn't there.

'You're a strange bird,' said Carolyn, contemplating me with her head on one side. 'But then so was he. I'd say you two were perfectly matched.'

'He was all right,' said Toby in a wistful tone that suggested he was more than a little envious. 'He was a dab hand at Social Whirligigs.'

'Yeah,' giggled Carolyn. 'And at least now we know whose is biggest. Lucky old Clare.'

That night, I thought about the garden again and tried to stay awake as long as I could, but sleep finally overtook me. I sank into an inconsequential sort of dream until about three o'clock, when something yanked me awake.

There must have been some sort of noise – a car door slamming in the street? Marsha coming home from the restaurant? – but now there was only silence. I lay there, senses on full alert. It was a false silence, and I didn't trust it. After a while, when nothing else had happened, I got up and tiptoed down to check that I had remembered to lock the front door. As I reached the level of the kitchen, my ears picked up a gentle tapping sound.

Someone was knocking softly on the front door.

I had no intention of opening up. I said, 'Hello?'

There was no reply. The rapping continued, soft yet persistent. I wished I had a spyhole, like Marsha.

But then again, perhaps not. I wasn't sure I wanted to see who was outside.

Tap tap tap

I said, 'Sophie?'

The knocking ceased.

As I stared at the door, I saw the handle turn.

The door, of course, didn't open, because it was locked and bolted. I'd made sure of that. But I took a step back.

197

'You can't come in,' I said, firmly but not too loudly. I wasn't sure I wanted whoever it was to hear.

'Go back to bed, Sophie,' I said.

And, if it was Sophie, then she did as she was told.

EIGHT

I T WAS LIKE playing a game, daring myself to see how far I could go. Opening Robert Jamieson's mail was turning out to be more fun than I'd had in ages.

> Dear Robert,
> Loved the latest poem, but afraid I can't help out.
> You know what women are like – Katie swears she'll
> quit if I put it in the mag, and some of the girls in
> the office have threatened strike action. But then
> what do you expect from college-educated bimbos?
> Maybe you should pop round one afternoon and
> soothe them with some of your manly charm.
>   Hate to do this to you, but couldn't you pump up
> the bondage and go easy on the mutilation?
> Restraint doesn't necessarily mean compromise, you
> know.
>   As ever,
>   Percy
> P.S. How about that drink?

I thought it was safe to conclude that Robert Jamieson was not a feminist.

I was tickled to death by this letter. I was dying to show it to someone, though since I wasn't supposed to have opened it in the first place I had to keep my feelings about it bottled up. But Robert was beginning to grow on me. He sounded like an incorrigible chauvinist and a refreshing contrast to Graham.

I would sit and look at Sophie and wonder exactly what she imagined she'd got up to with him. Perhaps she had unwittingly glimpsed his photo somewhere, or, like me, she'd opened one of those letters that kept arriving, day after day, and it had been that, coupled with the bust-up with Miles, which had triggered off her elaborate fantasies.

It was too late to ask her about it now, of course. I didn't want to set her off again. And besides, we still weren't getting on too well. When she wasn't cutting me dead, she was running me down in front of her friends, and yet I noticed she never went so far as to avoid me. Indeed, it sometimes appeared as though she were actively seeking out my company, as though there were something she desperately wanted to talk to me about but couldn't bring herself to mention.

Which was why we'd somehow ended up together, one night in the Bar None, two inseparables locked in a love/hate relationship. Her new-look crinkle-cut hair was pulled back into a ponytail, and she was looking more feline than ever in a black velvet jacket I'd never seen before.

That wasn't the only change of habit. I watched in astonishment as she pulled out a packet of Silk Cut, extracted a cigarette, and began to smoke it with an expertise that suggested she'd been puffing away for years. But it was the first time I'd ever seen her with a

fag in her mouth, and I was foolish enough to say as
much. She almost bit my head off.

'So fucking what?'

I'd had enough. 'Why are you being such a bitch?'

'Hardly surprising, is it.'

'You used to be so well-mannered,' I said.

'*Well-mannered?*' Her tone of voice took the mickey
out of mine. '*To whom* am I not being *well-mannered?*'

Me for a start, I thought, but out loud I said,
'Marsha.'

Sophie roared so loudly that several heads turned.
'Marsha!' she exclaimed. '*Marsha!* The woman is a
joke.'

'I rather like her,' I said.

'She is *absurd*,' Sophie continued. 'How can you take
anyone who wears cowboy boots trimmed with tassles
seriously?'

I heard myself saying, 'Just because someone has bad
taste doesn't mean she's a worthless human being.' The
idea had crept up on me unawares. I had never
entertained a thought like that before. I ran it through
my head again and gave it serious consideration. *Just
because someone has bad taste doesn't mean she's a worthless
human being.*

Then I thought, *nah*. Sophie was right. Tassled
cowboy boots were irredeemably naff. I said as much
out loud, *con brio*.

'Thank God for that,' breathed Sophie. 'You had
me worried there, old girl. I thought we were going
to have to set the fashion police on to you, and you
don't want to end up in *their* custody, believe me,

forced to wear beige all the time like I used to. Another drink?'

I nodded, even though my glass was only half empty, hoping to take advantage of Sophie's sudden geniality. She was up and down so fast, it was like trying to ride a whirlwind. She snapped her fingers to attract the waiter's attention. I'd never seen her do that before, nor could I remember having ever seen her drink this much. Normally, she stuck to wine, but now she was knocking back Mexican lager as though it were Day of the Dead.

Then, all of a sudden, everything fell into place. It was so obvious, I couldn't understand why I hadn't seen it before. Sophie had always had a chameleon-like quality. She'd always had a tendency to adopt the mannerisms of the men she was going out with. I couldn't stop staring at her as she gave our order to the waiter. I stared so hard she felt my gaze boring a hole into her skull and turned to meet it head on.

'*What?*' she demanded.

'You know,' I said.

'No, I don't know. Why are you looking at me like that?'

I thought *what the hell*, and said aloud what I'd been thinking, even though I knew it would sound absurd.

I said, 'You're still seeing him, aren't you?'

Sophie's mouth moved, but no sound came out. At last she found her voice, and it was a bitter one. 'Jesus Christ! You've got a bloody *nerve*!'

'This has got to stop,' I said. 'You know it's not healthy.'

She was shaking her head disbelievingly. I decided it was time to give it to her straight.

'Sophie,' I said. '*You're shagging a dead man.*'

She recoiled as though I'd slapped her. 'How can you *say* that? You know I hate that word.'

'I'm sorry,' I sighed. 'Let me rephrase it. You're *conducting an intimate relationship* with a dead man.'

'I don't mean *shagging*,' said Sophie. 'I mean *dead*.'

I gawped at her. 'What do you expect me to say? Vitally challenged? *Terminally experienced?*'

Sophie pushed her chair back violently and leaped to her feet. 'You're a two-faced bitch, you really are. And I thought you were my friend.'

'I *am* your friend, I said. 'I'm worried about you, that's all. I mean, how much do you really know about Robert Jamieson? Who is he, really?'

'Why don't you ask *him*?' she blurted, shooting me one last venomous look before stumbling out of the bar. I saw her dabbing her eyes as she went.

The waiter brought our drinks, and I finished them both.

My encounter with Sophie had left me troubled. *Why don't you ask him?* What had she meant by that? I needed company, and I needed it now. I walked fast down Portobello Road, knowing Dirk and Lemmy would be in the Boar's Head, an unreconstructed saloon bar sandwiched between a tattoo parlour and a betting shop, because they'd been talking about meeting someone there earlier.

The place was packed. Most of the drinkers were

bellowing at a boxing match on the giant television screen in the corner. Dirk and Lemmy had found a small space by the fruit machine.

'Where's your friend?' I asked.

'Nutella,' said Lemmy. I took this to be confirmation he had not yet arrived.

I bought drinks, and we started talking about cinema, which was one of Dirk's favourite subjects. For about the billionth time, he told me how *Performance* had been filmed just around the corner in Powis Square, and how Mick had been in it, and did I know that John Reginald Christie had once been a projectionist at the Electric Cinema, and that Sarah Bernhardt had stomped one-legged across the stage of the Coronet, back in the days when it was a theatre?

And then my heart did a bungee jump without elastic, because over Lemmy's shoulder I saw Charlotte and Grenville walk into the bar. I had no idea what they were doing there together, without their respective other halves, and I didn't care. But this was not their sort of hang-out at all.

Charlotte's eyes locked on to mine and she smiled in recognition and raised her arm, jiggling it like someone hailing a taxi. I glanced behind me, thinking that perhaps she was greeting someone else in the vicinity, that this couldn't possibly be *Charlotte* acting in an outgoing friendly manner towards *me*, but a rapid scan established that I was the only plausible object of her attentions. Everyone knew Charlotte had taken up with a lot of unsuitable men in her time, but I doubted whether any of them had had greased ponytails, armfuls of tattoos or pierced nipples poking through the holes in their grubby string vests.

The reason for their friendly approach was obvious, if I'd only had time to think about it. Charlotte and Grenville were out of their element. They would rather have died than admit it, but they were feeling ill at ease. Charlotte, sensing instantly that I was more at home in this atmosphere than either she or Grenville, had decided I might come in useful as their own personal guide to society's festering underbelly.

They accordingly made a beeline for me. They didn't have to push. The crowd sensed members of the social élite in its midst and parted like the Red Sea under orders from Moses.

And I started to panic. Charlotte and Grenville were from one compartment of my life, Dirk and Lemmy from another. The last thing I wanted was for elements from the different compartments to start getting mixed up together. I didn't want Charlotte and Grenville finding out what sort of a person I really was, or what kind of people I normally hung out with. I didn't want them finding out I was a *fake*.

I must have looked like someone who'd been having an eyeball-to-eyeball with the Medusa, because Dirk asked if I was feeling OK.

'Sure,' I said, not daring to take my eyes off Charlotte.

'Rostropovich,' said Lemmy. 'Gastarbeit king wenceslas.'

'Uh-huh,' agreed Dirk. 'Beam me up, Scotty.'

'Hang on a sec,' I said to Dirk and Lemmy. 'Back in

a tick,' and, leaving them standing there, I wove through the crowd to head Charlotte and Grenville off at the pass. They greeted me with taut little air-kisses and muted chirrups of pleasure.

'This place!' said Grenville, looking round. 'Did you ever see anything like it?'

I wished he would keep his voice down. 'As a matter of fact I did,' I said. 'There are a lot of places like this.'

'Who *were* they?' asked Charlotte.

'Who were who?' I asked.

'Those fabulous lowlifes you were talking to.'

'The long-haired hippy with the moustache,' said Grenville. 'And the gorilla. You know who they remind me of? Asterix and Obelix.'

Charlotte chuckled. 'Typical examples of traditional Notting Hillbilly.'

'Just some guys,' I said.

'Amazing,' said Grenville, still gazing enraptured at Lemmy and Dirk. 'You can always tell, can't you, when people have been too long on the dole.'

Charlotte clutched my arm. 'Oh my God,' she gasped. 'Don't look now, Clare, but King Kong's coming over.'

I looked up with dread in my heart. Dirk was wading through the crowd with an expectant grin on his face, like a channel swimmer who had just felt shingle beneath his feet. I could just see it. He was bound to make some stupid remark about the Restaurant at the End of the Universe, or Buster Gonad and his Unfeasibly Large Testicles. I knew I had to get out of there *right that second* or I would die.

'Excuse me,' I said. 'I have to go and powder my nose.'

'Hang on,' began Charlotte, but the slimmest of instants before Dirk reached us, I plunged back into the milling crowd and dog-paddled towards the Ladies. I made it just in time. The door swung shut, but not before I'd glimpsed Dirk staring after me, his face crumpling into an expression of childlike bewilderment.

I locked myself into one of those foul-smelling cubicles for a full five minutes, then spent a further five staring into the mirror, fiddling uselessly with lipstick and mascara, and aching all over, as though I were about to collapse with flu. There was nothing for it. I would have to swallow my pride and introduce everyone. Maybe they'd all get along with each other after all. But by the time I'd scraped together the strength to go back into the bar, it was too late. Charlotte and Grenville were nowhere to be seen.

Dirk and Lemmy had vanished too.

I went straight back to the flat and lay on my mattress with my head pounding, feeling like a heel of the first magnitude and trying desperately to think of ways of justifying what had now been blown up, in my mind, into a perfidious act of betrayal.

It wasn't my fault. I couldn't help being bad at straddling social boundaries. Dirk and Lemmy belonged to one part of my life, Charlotte and Grenville to another. Mix them together, and there could be an explosion. But what kind of explosion were we talking about here? Wouldn't it be simply an explosion of social embarrassment – a minor fart at the most? And wasn't I the only one in danger of being embarrassed by it?

It didn't matter what I told myself. I still felt like the lowest form of pond life. I couldn't sleep. I could hear Sophie in the flat below, and I knew she hadn't brought anyone home with her, but she was whimpering and groaning and squealing with what sounded like non-stop orgasmic pleasure.

Ker-chunk ker-chunk ker-chunk

She was really partying on down. I didn't know where she'd got the tape from, but she had the Drunken Boats on loud.

And I realized at last that it didn't matter much whether her lover was real, or a ghost, or a figment of her fevered imagination. At least *she* had company. At least *she* was having fun. Not like me, stewing here alone in my misery.

Maybe Sophie had the right idea after all.

Maybe the only good man was a dead one.

NINE

FROM THE outside, the basement flat looked more than a trifle shabby. Despite the bars on the windows, there was an air of delapidation, as though whoever owned it couldn't possibly possess anything worth stealing. At the same time, it didn't appear to be a flat that was regularly left unoccupied for months on end. But if passing squatters, winos or drug dealers had tried to break in, they would have found themselves stumped by a formidable security system. The rickety-looking front door turned out to be made of steel and fitted with every type of deadlock known to man.

I'd finally managed to corner Walter Cheeseman and remind him of his promise to show me some of his films. He'd invited me down the very next day. 'Is that an alarm or a biscuit tin?' I asked as he opened the door, pointing to a discreet black box attached to the outside wall.

Walter said it was an alarm.

'So if someone tries to break in when you're not here, the police turn up?'

'Not exactly,' said Walter. 'Not the *police*.'

I never did get round to asking him who turned up if it wasn't the police. He'd made the place as impregnable as Fort Knox, and as soon as he let me in, I saw why. It had nothing to do with the decor and furnishings, which screamed *expensive*, though the effect wasn't one of which Sophie would have approved; there were glass-topped tables, and a three-piece suite in cream-coloured leather, and fluffy white rugs strewn across the shiny parquet like cotton-wool clouds.

But it was the walls that grabbed the attention. Or, to be precise, what was *on* the walls, because they themselves were hidden from view. Every last inch had been fitted with adjustable shelving. And the shelving was stacked with modern technology: video recorders in half a dozen different formats, screens of all shapes and sizes, loudspeakers and computers and keyboards and editing equipment and earphones, and little lights that winked on and off and hundreds of metal film cannisters and laser discs and video cassettes, each with its neatly typed label giving the title, director, year of release, and running-time of the contents.

The labels and their neatly typed, perfectly spaced print made me wonder whether perhaps Walter wasn't a little too anally retentive for comfort.

While my host disappeared into the kitchen to make coffee, I examined the labels on the nearest stack of cassettes. The director was Walter Cheeseman, and the titles – *Edward Scissordick*, *Big Dick Tracy*, *RoboDick* and *Muff-Diving Miss Daisy* – spoke eloquently of their subject matter. Walter said most of his work had gone 'straight to video', but even in video form, I gathered, it had never been released on my side of the Atlantic. Walter blamed the distribution system, which he said was 'loaded against the independent operator'.

'I didn't realise you made porno movies,' I said, trying to hide my disillusionment as he came back from the kitchen carrying a pot of coffee, two mugs, and a large bowl of buttered popcorn.

'That's just my day job,' he said. 'It helps finance the real stuff. Here, I'll show you.'

He bade me sit down on the sofa, slotted a cassette into one of the machines, and we began to watch something called *The Pig and the Pendulum*. It was set around the turn of the century and opened like an episode of *Upstairs, Downstairs* before veering off into darker territory, in which a stuffy accountant became possessed by the evil spirits lurking in the basement of the house where he lived with his wife and daughters. To begin with, he confined himself to drinking and gambling and wenching, but one night, during an unexpected blizzard, the evil spirits took over completely and made him hack his family to pieces with an axe. As an afterthought, he hacked the servants to pieces as well.

'Recognize that location?' asked Walter.

I suddenly realised why the setting looked so familiar; the establishing shots had been filmed outside number nine. I hadn't recognized it immediately because Hampshire Place had been emptied of cars, and the lighting made it look so much more sinister than it really was.

'The special effects are really good,' I said to Walter, as the axe-blade whistled through the air for the umpteenth time and bit deep into the skull of Mr Wisley's maidservant, a sprightly minx who up until then had been displaying lots of cleavage as well as a cheeky line in Marxist ideology. In fact the special effects were awful, but they were a lot better than the acting and the script, and I was trying hard to say something complimentary.

'Aren't they just,' Walter enthused. 'Amazing what you can achieve these days. You know how the Soviets used to doctor their photographs so that politicians who fell out of favour ceased to exist? Well, now you can do the opposite. You can bring dead people back to life.'

'Really,' I said.

'Yes you can,' said Walter, failing to register my lack of interest. 'If you can only get someone on film, it's as good as having a piece of their DNA. You can make them walk and talk. One of these days, Hollywood will be able to do away with live actors altogether; they'll be able to dial up Greta Garbo and Humphrey Bogart – the greats – and programme entire new performances from them.'

The layout of the basement flat was different to those of the flats upstairs. There was no logic to it. The interior had evidently been demolished and the walls rebuilt from scratch. The route to the bathroom took me through Walter's bedroom, so I naturally took a good squint around. He was fanatically tidy. The only item of clothing not tucked away into one of the drawers or fitted wardrobes was a Ralph Lauren sweat-shirt draped over the handlebars of a fearsome-looking home fitness machine. Like the video room, it was all very elegant, if a trifle anonymous. It was as though

Walter had bought his furniture from a mail-order catalogue for harassed executives too busy to care.

I paused to look out of the bedroom window. This was the first time I'd seen the garden from this level, but it looked almost exactly the same as it did from three storeys up – hopelessly choked with weeds and overshadowed by the surrounding buildings, although I could just about make out a heavily weathered statue which might once have been a lion.

It was in the bathroom, as I washed my hands, that I heard a familiar sound.

Tap tap tap – the sound of distant typing.

I froze. The water continued to gush out over my hands, but the surroundings were so shiny white and brilliantly lit it was impossible to feel as uneasy as I normally did when I heard noises in my own dingy bathroom. I turned off the tap and the typing stopped. I turned it on again and the typing restarted.

It wasn't a typewriter at all – it was the pipes.

You don't know how relieved this makes me feel, I said to myself in the mirror. *There is nothing to worry about. There never was anything to worry about.*

Oh, these old houses.

It had been the plumbing all along.

One of the most perplexing mysteries of my life had just been solved, but that didn't mean I was prepared to forego my customary investigation of the bathroom cabinet. Walter's was stocked with various Ralph Lauren and Calvin Klein aftershaves, American pharmaceuticals, and bottles of vitamins with names like Buzz-B,

Soar-C, and High-D-High. I spotted one small brown bottle without a label; thinking it might be a brand of aftershave or vitamin pill so exclusive it didn't even have a name, I unscrewed the cap and sniffed. The smell of old socks was so powerful that for a moment or two I felt quite dizzy and had to clutch the edge of the washbasin to steady myself.

Definitely not aftershave, I thought.

By the time I got back to Walter, he was fast-forwarding through yet another video. 'Thought you'd got lost,' he said off-handedly.

'What's this one?' I asked, trying to sound keen, though I was thankful *The Pig and the Pendulum* had ground to its grisly conclusion. The novelty of Walter's film director status had worn off. Now I was trying desperately to think of a way of getting out of there which wouldn't offend him or squelch any potential amorous activity between the two of us. Not that there had been anything in Walter's attitude or behaviour to suggest I might be in with a chance, but I wasn't going to burn my bridges before I'd even spotted their symbols on the map.

'This one's *The Pork Butcher*,' said Walter. '*Mondo Film* reckons it's my *chef d'oeuvre*.'

'Do I detect a porcine theme?' I asked, recalling *The Pig and the Pendulum*.

'I guess so,' said Walter, looking pleased as punch that I'd noticed. 'But I like pigs, don't you? Cute, snuffly little creatures with wiggly tails. Were you aware they used to be kept around here in the nineteenth century? This part of Notting Hill was known as the Piggeries.'

'What, real live porkers? Where we're sitting now?'

'Maybe not this *precise* spot. A bit further north-west, perhaps. The people who lived here would complain about the smell of fat being boiled at night.'

'Why would they boil fat at night?'

'I don't know,' said Walter. 'I don't eat meat.'

'But you said you liked pigs . . .'

'Not to *eat*.'

'. . . and there's such a lot of blood in your films.'

'Don't let the blood fool you,' said Walter. 'Don't forget Hitler was a vegetarian.'

I couldn't see what Hitler had to do with it.

There were pigs-a-plenty in *The Pork Butcher*, albeit dead ones, bloody great carcasses split down the middle and suspended from hooks in the ceiling. But this wasn't the Piggeries; it was somewhere in South London, and – by the look of the haircuts and the old double-decker that had been hired to drive past the camera again and again, each time displaying a different route number – sometime during the Fifties.

The butcher's assistant was a mild-mannered wea-kling called Arthur who finally hit back against his bullying employers by hacking them to death with a large cleaver. Death by hacking was obviously a recurring *motif* in Walter's *oeuvre*.

Once again, the special effects were rather shoddy, but round about the second murder I began to feel slightly queasy. When Arthur embarked upon the

ANNE BILLSON

arduous process of chopping his victims' corpses down into joints, lights and livers, and selling them to customers in the shop, I realized I'd had enough. I knew perfectly well that the meat being sliced and diced in such detail wasn't human, but I could still feel ominous rumblings in the pit of my stomach.

'I wonder if you'd mind . . .' I motioned towards the remote control in Walter's hand, wanting him to switch it off.

'What? Oh, you mean . . . Hey, you all right?'

I made it to the bathroom just in time. All the popcorn came up again. By the time I'd staggered back, feeling shaky and embarrassed, Walter had switched the television off and slotted the videos back into their places on the shelf. He strode towards me, enveloped me in his arms and kissed me noisily on both cheeks. A physical overture at last! Unfortunately, I wasn't feeling robust enough to respond.

'You puked?' he said in an awestruck tone. 'You actually *puked*? I can't *believe* you did that.'

I started to mutter an apology, but he cut me off.

'To think that a film of mine had that effect. I'm so proud. *This movie made me puke.* Can we quote you on the packaging?'

'Sure,' I said, not caring what he did so long as I could get out of there.

'Would you care to lie down?'

If I'd been more on the ball I might have leaped at this invitation as the chance I'd been waiting for. Instead, I mumbled something about having to go back upstairs. 'I haven't watched this sort of film for a long time, you see. There was too much blood. And that strobe effect gives me a headache.'

'Just as well I didn't show you the next one,' said Walter. 'Not much blood, but an awful lot of strobe.'

I tried to look interested. 'Another pig movie?'

'No pigs. But you really should take a look at it sometime. I filmed most of it here, in this house. Marsha's in it, too.'

'She *is*? When was this?'

Walter did some rapid mental calculations. 'Twelve, thirteen years ago. But it's set in the Sixties.'

I felt there was some connection here that I should have been making, but I was still being distracted by a certain amount of seismic activity in the region of my stomach. I was torn between retiring to bed with a bucket, and risking social disaster by lingering to find out more.

I opted for a compromise. 'Perhaps I could come down and watch it another time,' I said, gravitating towards the door.

Walter unlocked it for me. 'Sure,' he said. 'Don't wait too long, though. I'm gonna have to leave soon.'

'Just so long as it's not another axe murder.'

'Not at all,' said Walter. 'This one's a semi-documentary, really. About a degenerate hippy rock group.'

And he told me what the film was called, though the title didn't make an impression on me until much later, when my stomach had settled down, and I'd started to mull over what he'd said.

Then I remembered. He'd called it *Down There*.

TEN

I HADN'T SEEN Dirk and Lemmy since our meeting in the Boar's Head, and I wasn't sure I wanted to, so embarrassed did I feel about my failure to introduce them to Charlotte and Grenville. I saw Charlotte and Grenville, though, and neither of them referred to the encounter. Nor would they ever refer to it again. It was as though it had never taken place.

We were drinking champagne cocktails in the Crow Bar. Isabella had just got back from Milan and was showing everyone her new Prada handbag. Walter seemed very knowledgeable about Milan, but Isabella had never noticed the statue of a flayed saint that stood in the cathedral, nor was she aware that one of the gargoyles on the roof bore an uncanny resemblance to Donald Duck, as Walter claimed. Isabella was more familiar with the nightclubs and clothes shops than with the lesser-known jewels in the city's cultural crown.

Walter was a great hit, which cheered me up no end; I was the one who had brought him along, which meant I scored extra points. Being American, he got on with everyone so famously that I seriously considered adopting a foreign accent myself. Class barriers dissolved before his élan. Grenville offered to represent him, even though Walter hadn't written a novel and, as far as I was aware, had no intention of ever writing one. Toby slapped him on the back and bought him drinks and tried to explain the rules of cricket. Isabella was charmed by his anecdotes about hitching through Europe, while Charlotte and Carolyn vied with each other to flatter and tease. He would have enchanted Sophie too, had I not ensured there was always at least one other person – usually me – between them. Once or twice, though, I did catch Walter glancing in her direction.

'That's Sophie, is it?' he asked me at one point.

'Uh-huh,' I said.

'She needs to put on weight,' said Walter.

I could have hugged him.

Fortunately, Sophie seemed preoccupied. She looked drained, and I wasn't surprised. The noises from downstairs were becoming louder and more abandoned with every night that passed. Either my friend was the world's most enthusiastic masturbator, or her phantom lover had spent most of his time in the afterlife picking up tips from Don Juan and Casanova.

Midway through the evening, Walter further endeared himself to me by leaning over to whisper conspiratorially, 'Just who *are* all these people, and what do they think they're doing?'

'They think they're having fun,' I replied.

'Did they *all* go to Oxford or Cambridge?'

'Not Sophie,' I said. 'She went to art college, like me. She only hangs out with these people because of her boyfriend.'

'Which one is he?'

'He's not here. Sophie and he broke up.'

Walter's eyes glinted. 'Really?'

It was time to change the subject, and quickly. 'Where do you get the ideas for your films?'

Walter so loved talking about his work that he instantly forgot about Sophie. 'From life, of course. All my stories are based on life.'

'Even the gory ones?'

'*Especially* the gory ones,' said Walter. 'And you know, they're all set around Notting Hill.'

'Not that last one you showed me,' I said. 'That was . . . Streatham?'

'Balham. I based *The Pork Butcher* on a real-life murder case from the Fifties – the Butcher of Balham, they called him. I exaggerated, of course, by having him carve up lots more people. In real life, he killed only one person, though he did cut her up into lots of tiny little pieces.'

'Did they hang him?'

'Didn't have to. He knotted strips of his shirt together, and hanged himself in his cell before the law could exact the full penalty.'

Grenville chose this moment to barge drunkenly in. 'Penalty? You like English football?'

'We're talking about capital punishment,' said Walter.

'We had that at school,' said Grenville.

'Walter was telling me about the Butcher of Balham,' I said. 'What was his name again?'

'Arthur Mowbray.'

I frowned into my wine, wondering why the name

sounded so familiar. Probably from Walter's film, I decided.

'The funny thing is,' said Walter, 'the reason I got interested in the first place was that he used to live in Hampshire Place.'

'You're kidding.'

'Although it wasn't called Hampshire Place in those days. It was . . .'

'Farrow Lane,' I said.

'That's amazing,' Grenville said, looking from one of us to the other. 'How do you guys know all this stuff?'

'I've lived here a long time, on and off,' said Walter. 'You get to meet people.'

I asked if he'd ever met anyone who remembered Arthur Mowbray.

'I met people who *said* they remembered him,' said Walter, 'and I read eyewitness reports, though you have to take most of them with a pinch of salt. Mowbray lodged in Hampshire Place for a couple of months, at most, but to judge by the number of people who swore they'd been out drinking with him, you would have thought he'd been out partying every night for years.'

There was still something I needed to ask.

'Which house did he live in?'

Walter chuckled. 'You mean you didn't realize? Why do you think I chose to live at number nine in the first place?'

Sophie left the Crow Bar early, complaining of a headache, though I was pretty sure this was just an excuse for her to go home and cavort with someone whose status put a whole new slant on the term 'ex'. Walter watched her go with what could only be described as regret, but I didn't mind; she would be out of the picture for the rest of the evening.

It wasn't long before the others were out of the picture too. Isabella led them off to some fashionable new tapas bar. Walter and I were included in the invitation, but he made his excuses and stayed where he was, and I stayed with him. It never occurred to me that he might simply want to pump me for information. By now I was getting tipsy while he had switched to mineral water, so my responses weren't as guarded as they might have been.

'Tell me about Sophie Macallan,' he said.

'What is there to tell?'

'That girl has secrets,' Walter said.

I looked him straight in the eye, thought *why not*, and said, 'Sophie's got this thing about Robert Jamieson.'

Walter looked as though he wanted to smile but thought it might ruin everything. 'I wasn't aware they ever met.'

'They didn't,' I said. 'Not exactly. But Sophie's obsessed with the idea of him. She thinks he's the perfect man. *Was* the perfect man.'

Walter threw back his head and roared with laughter so uninhibited it almost fooled me into believing it was spontaneous.

'What's so funny?'

'The perfect man? What a joke. I knew the guy.'

'You did?' Of course Walter must have known Robert Jamieson, I thought. Why hadn't I realized that before?

'A first-class fuck-up,' said Walter. 'Miserable, misan-thropic, misogynistic: our man was all the misses. Failed as a writer, failed as a lover, failed as a human being. Suicide was the only thing he ever got right, and even then he messed up on the timing.'

His face took on an oddly tragic cast. 'Most of the time he just wallowed in misery, waiting to be rescued, hoping for some stupid little woman to come along and sort him out.'

Disconcerted by his vindictive tone, I said that I thought wanting to be rescued was more of a feminine trait.

Walter hoisted an eyebrow. 'You reckon? In my experience it's the other way round. Only women are willing to be sacrificed to someone else's needs at the cost of their own. They sit and watch as their souls are sucked out of their orifices.'

'You don't have a very high opinion of women,' I said, feeling a little upset, though I couldn't say exactly why.

Walter suddenly switched on his strange humour-less grin. 'But I *love* you all. You girls are endlessly fascinating creatures. Men, by comparison, are ... predictable.'

'Men lie,' I said, staring into the bottom of my empty wineglass and feeling tearful.

'Of course they do,' said Walter.

'*All* men lie,' I said, thinking of Miles.

Walter was still wearing his grin. 'Like I said, they're predictable.'

*

I was predictable, as well. I couldn't resist purloining another of Robert Jamieson's letters. I told myself sternly that this would be the last time, that I wasn't going to do it again, I would leave this fantasizing about dead people to Sophie and from now on would dutifully leave their mail to be collected and forwarded by Marsha.

But before that, I wanted just one more peek into the life and times of the 'first-class fuck-up'.

Walter Cheeseman had certainly been merciless in his appraisal of the late Mr Jamieson's character. So much so that I wondered if Walter had a hidden agenda of his own. Was there a hint of jealousy there, perhaps? Did Walter suspect that Robert Jamieson had succeeded in being the subversive, controversial, original artist that Walter, with his cheap porno slasher movies, knew he could never be?

Perhaps suicide had been a final act of defiance in a subversive, controversial, original life. Better to die than to compromise one's ideals.

This one was on headed notepaper.

DEFOREST PUBLISHING

A Division of Arbooks International

Dear Mr Jamieson,
Thank you for submitting your novel to us. I am afraid we do not consider *Ways of Killing Women* suitable for publication at this present time and it is therefore being returned to you under separate cover.

While the novel is well-written, we feel that
readers may find the subject matter distasteful, if
not offensive. If you are thinking of submitting it to
other publishing houses and are hoping for a more
favourable reception, may I suggest you tone down
or even cut some of the more extreme passages (in
particular the episode with the vacuum cleaner on
pages 39 to 48, the trip to Llandudno on pages 84
to 87, the poisonous snake and the sanitary tampon,
pages 108 to 123, the liquidizer incident on page
161, and just about everything on pages 179 to 232).

Should you decide to revise these sections and
make them more accessible to a general readership,
we would be delighted to take another look. I hope
you do not find these comments too discouraging,
as there is no question that you have talent;
unfortunately we feel it is currently being
misdirected.

> Yours sincerely
> Madeleine Curran
> (Senior Editor)

P.S. I should inform you that several of the girls on
our staff found themselves unable to progress
beyond page 17. In fact, two of them confessed that
your writing made them physically ill. Can this really
be the sort of effect you intended?

The letter was dated August the fourteenth, but someone had corrected the year by hand and the numbers
were no longer legible. I wondered if it had taken
Madeleine Curran all this time to read Robert's novel,

or whether she'd written her rejection letter ages ago and it had somehow been caught up in a backlog of paperwork and only just come to light.

To me, *Ways of Killing Women* sounded nothing short of a masterpiece, a bestseller at the very least; Madeleine Curran just hadn't understood it. I wondered if there were any copies still in circulation. If so, perhaps I could resubmit one of them for publication somewhere else. Perhaps Robert's posthumous literary reputation lay in my hands.

Perhaps that was why I couldn't stop thinking about him.

I kept a careful watch on the mail for the next couple of the weeks, in the hope of intercepting the manuscript Madeleine Curran had said she was returning, but nothing of that sort turned up.

Try as I might, I couldn't make any more headway with Walter. I'd nuzzled up to him on the way home from the Crow Bar, but although he'd neither cringed nor pushed me away, he hadn't responded with the sort of enthusiasm I might have hoped for.

But, as the summer slipped away, I grew accustomed to having him around. He was a useful companion – amusing, informative, passably debonair – and his presence seemed to have put a stop to that tiresome but mercifully short-lived Scott-of-the-Antarctic syndrome in which everyone kept imagining they'd seen someone standing just behind me.

But then, one Friday morning, these halcyon days came to an end. There was a buzz on my entryphone.

The bell part of it worked, but the intercom facility was broken, so I had to nip down to see who it was. I rounded the last bend in the stairs to find Walter standing below me in the hall, surrounded by suitcases. His chin was covered with a light golden fuzz that indicated he hadn't bothered to shave. As I drew nearer my nostrils were greeted by the sharp tang of his body odour. Grooming had obviously not been high on his list of priorities that morning.

'I'm off,' he said, momentarily pushing his sunglasses up in order to rub his eyelids. It was only the third or fourth time I'd seen his eyes; the irises were a surprisingly pale grey, and the sockets were smudged with fatigue. I wondered if he'd only just developed a slight twitch in the nerves of his jaw, or whether it had always been there and I hadn't noticed.

'I don't blame you,' I said. 'I'm going back to Hackney for the weekend. Anything to avoid the Carnival.'

'No,' said Walter. 'I mean I'm *really* off.'

'But I thought . . .'

'I told you I never stay long. I've already stayed longer than I should.'

'But I don't want you to go.'

Walter's face clouded over. 'Bad dreams,' he said. 'Real stinkers. And they've been getting worse. Always do, this time of year. Especially now, this stage of the cycle.'

Even his fake smile let him down; he tried to turn it on, but ended up looking like a man in pain.

'What cycle?'

Walter waved his hand. He couldn't be bothered to explain in full. 'Architectural equivalent of PMT. You know.'

I didn't know at all. 'You can't just go,' I said, feeling as though a golden opportunity was slithering through my fingers like a raw yolk. I hadn't even made it to bed with him. 'When can I see you again?'

'Couple of months, maybe. I've used up all my credit for now. But I'm going to leave you with this.'

He handed me a plain brown envelope with my name printed on it. There was something bulky inside. I looked at Walter enquiringly. The nerve in his jaw twitched again.

'Keys,' he explained. 'The spare set of keys to my flat.'

'But why?' This was just typical. There I'd been, waiting all those years for a place in west eleven, and now two came along at once.

'That other film,' said Walter. '*Down There*. I really think you should see it. I've left the tape out for you.'

It should have struck me as odd that a person with so much expensive equipment in his flat would leave a set of keys with someone he barely knew, but it didn't. I was too busy thinking about all the advantages. I'd been squinting at a ropey old portable fourteen-inch television, and now, at last, I had access to a screen as big as a football field, Nicam stereo, forty-five cable and satellite channels, six different types of video recorder, and hundreds of titles on cassette and laser disc. It would be like having my own private screening room. Not to mention a comfortable, king-size bed and *en*

228

suite bathroom with hot and cold running-water and no cracked mirrors to give me the willies.

'Why are you doing this?' I asked him.

Walter peered with his pale grey eyes over the top of his sunglasses. 'Can I be honest with you, Clare?'

'Of course.'

'I'm giving you these keys,' he said, 'because I need your help. I can't work out whether it's going to be you or Sophie, and I want to keep both options open.'

Talk about brazen. But I appreciated his frankness. I tried to look him in the eye, but those wretched sunglasses were in the way again. 'It's me,' I said. 'I *know* it's me.'

He looked as though he was about to say something else, but we heard the noise of a taxi pulling up outside. I helped Walter down the front steps with his suitcases while the cab driver loaded the boxes that Walter had stacked on the pavement in readiness. Walter kissed me on the lips and then got inside the taxi and pushed down the window. 'See ya, kid,' he said.

As the taxi drove off, I realized too late that I'd forgotten to ask him for his new address. Ah well, no doubt Marsha would have it. I turned to go back upstairs, fingering the shape of the keys through the envelope.

So it was between me and Sophie.

But Walter had given the keys to *me*. Sophie was already history. Sophie didn't stand a chance.

ELEVEN

WITH WALTER out of the picture, I had to fall back on my faithful standby – Graham. Perhaps I could yet mould him into the man of my dreams. Anyway, he was better than nothing. It was time to make good on my promise of dinner.

My plan was to ply him with food and drink before suggesting, ever so casually, that we descend into the basement for a viewing session in more comfortable surroundings. And then, maybe, we'd go to bed, and Graham would submit to my will and start shopping at Paul Smith. That's how I'd envisaged it.

But things didn't happen like that at all.

The evening got off to a rotten start when he staggered in over an hour late, stewed to the eyebrows. So, instead of my greeting him as planned – breathless and giggling, Marsha's stainless steel cocktail shaker in hand and groovy sounds issuing from the tapedeck – I opened the door in a filthy mood, perfume no longer fresh, and stomach stuffed full of the Japanese rice crackers I had previously decanted into little lacquer bowls and deposited at strategic locations around the room. In short, the crackers were gone and the hoped-for effect of chic yet effortless hospitality was utterly ruined.

Graham had absorbed enough alcohol to propel him beyond the borderland of the merely frisky into the realm of excessively careful pronunciation of vowel sounds. His reactions were not so much slow as wayward. When I tried to air-kiss him, he misread my intention and jerked his head round so clumsily that my lips mashed against his cheek and clung there, like suction cups. By the time I'd peeled them off and found the mirror, my Poppy Red was no longer precisely delineated but radiating from my mouth like an exploding nebula.

I slipped into the bathroom for repairs. Graham hovered in the doorway, apologizing for being late, oblivious to the streak of scarlet warpaint I'd left smeared across his face. He told me he'd bumped into an old chum, and that they'd gone for a quick drink in Cinnabar, but then one glass had turned into two, and . . . well, that was all there was to it.

I didn't think this was much cop as an excuse – he'd had a date with *me*, not with this old chum – but when I pressed further, he was reluctant to go into detail. I had a feeling the chum had been female.

I looked at my watch pointedly. 'You've still got time to go and rejoin your friend,' I said. 'We can have dinner another time.'

Graham failed to spot the sarcasm. 'Nah,' he said. 'I'm here now. Might as well stay.'

'Oh well,' I said. 'If you haven't got anything better to do . . .'

'I didn't mean it like that.'

I asked frostily if he wanted a drink and clumped

down to the kitchen to fix one. The ice I'd taken from Marsha's fridge had long since melted. I poured the watery Margharita mixture down the plughole and began to measure out a fresh batch. This one would be warm, but I was past caring.

Graham appeared in the doorway and watched me jiggling the cocktail-shaker for several seconds before asking, 'What's that?'

'Maraccas.'

'I get it. You're mixing cocktails.'

'Whatever gave you that idea?'

'No need to go to all that trouble,' Graham said, picking up the bottle of tequila. 'I'll drink straight from this.'

'You do that,' I said.

I'd known Graham for years, but only now did I realize how little I knew *about* him. I knew he was more of a feminist than I was – when he wasn't attempting to play forcible hunt-the-salami with Sophie, that is. I'd always assumed he was a vegetarian as well, so I'd lined up a mushroom risotto and – my *pudding de résistance* – blackcurrant lubitsch with sweet 'n' sour *crème fraiche*.

Graham shovelled it all down and duly complimented me on my cooking, but I might as well have dished up a bucketful of vindaloo. If it hadn't already been obvious that he was smashed, the fact that he chain-smoked all the way through the meal, fork in one hand, fag in the other, might have tipped me off. It might have been worse, had I not managed to prise the bottle of tequila from his grip before he had made appreciable inroads and replace it with a glass of wine. He gave no indication, other than a brief baffled pursing of his lips after the first sip, that his brain had registered the switch.

After dinner, we nestled down amongst the floor cushions to drink and talk and listen to tapes, and I began to feel grateful to the old chum who had got Graham half-cut before his arrival. It was ages since I'd seen him so relaxed.

'Haven't heard this one in *aeons*,' he said. 'Not since I was a hippy. This is really mellow, till they ruin it with the stupid screaming.'

'You were a hippy?' I asked. 'I didn't think you were old enough.'

If I was ever going to take action, I decided it might as well be now. Under the pretence of topping up Graham's glass, I changed position so I was sitting right next to him. Then I reached into my handbag and pulled out my trump card. Graham's eyes lit up like Christmas tree lights.

'Is that what I think it is?' He sniffed the contents of the bag. 'You're sure it's not Earl Grey?'

I told him of course it wasn't Earl Grey. I'd had to go to enormous trouble to get my hands on it, since I was no longer seeing Dirk and Lemmy, who had previously supplied me with everything I'd ever needed. But on the way back from the shops the day before, turning into Hampshire Place, I'd spotted two stunted figures in red anoraks kicking their heels on the louvred installation at the end of the street.

I did some quick mental arithmetic. I had just enough cash left. I shuffled level with the Ashoo Boys, lugging my shopping like a bag lady. They were engrossed in a Gameboy, the smaller one stabbing buttons like a 100 wpm typist.

'Hi, there,' I said.

They looked up. Two pairs of eyes widened.

I turned on my sunniest smile. 'Remember me?'

They continued to stare at me big-eyed while the untended Gameboy bleeped itself silly.

'You're shittin me,' said the older one.

'No listen . . .' I said.

But before I could say another word, they were off, like a couple of miniature Linford Christies on their way to Olympic Gold. In seconds, they were half-way down the road. Only once did one of them pause long enough to glance back, but whatever he saw made him turn and run even faster.

I forced a smile, in case anyone was watching – *those crazy kids* – and hauled my bags the remaining two hundred yards to number nine. But I was baffled, and slightly hurt. Did I look like a plain-clothes police-woman? I was brooding on it when I ran into Marsha in the hallway and told her what had happened.

'You want grass? No problem,' she said. 'I can get you some.'

And she did, and that was that, except I refused to dwell on the detail that had really been bugging me. The way those Ashoo Boys had run, you would have thought they'd mistaken me for a member of the narcotics squad. But what I didn't want to admit was that they hadn't been looking at me at all.

They'd been looking at something over my shoulder.

'Got any skins?'

For a minute, I thought Graham was talking about prophylactics. I had those all right; I'd stowed a packet of three beneath my pillow, just in case.

Graham said, 'Cigarette papers.'

'I forgot,' I confessed. 'But the garage up the road should still be open.'

'We can do without,' said Graham.

He placed one of my glossy magazines on his lap as a worktop, extracted a single Marlboro Light from his packet and, with the end of a match, extracted the tobacco and blended it with a pinch of grass before poking it back into the hollow tube and sealing it with a twist, like a tiny white sausage.

'Pink Floyd, floor cushions, Mary Jane,' he said, lighting the joint and sucking the smoke into his lungs. 'I feel like I'm caught in a time-warp.'

We sucked at one sausage after another. My ears started to pick out things in the music they'd never heard before. I waited for Graham to make a move, but he seemed happy to waffle on about his days as a neo-hippy, when he'd worn granny vests and flares and listened to *A Saucerful of Secrets* while everyone else in the class was into speed and safety pins and shredded T-shirts. Graham always had mistimed his enthusiasms. Even the feminism had surfaced many years after fashionable men had moved on to a more laddish outlook.

But it was time to move into Phase Two of my master-plan. I was terrified of rejection – so the trick would be for me to persuade Graham to come up with the idea to sleep with me all by himself. I'd made a compilation tape of all the pop music I could find which I thought might get the message across – *Let's Spend the Night Together, Tonight I'll Be Staying Here with You, Ring My Bell, Skweeze Me, Pleeze Me* and *Nobody in Town Can Bake a Sweet Jelly Roll Like Mine.* But all Graham did was tap out an irrelevant rhythm on his knee, occasionally join in with a chorus and, every so often, exclaim, 'Bugger me, haven't heard this one for *years.*'

I began to feel the black dog of depression nipping at my heels. Why would any man – even Graham – want to bother with me, with my spectacles and mousy hair and stubborn saddle-bags of cellulite? Especially if my Hackney roots were showing, as I was sure they were. Perhaps I was just a pathetic social climber with ideas above my station.

Then I realized I was being paranoid. It wasn't me, *it was the drug.* Wherever Marsha got her dope from, it was a lot stronger than the stuff I was used to smoking with Dirk and Lemmy. I instructed myself to calm down, announced to Graham I was going to the bath-room, and got unsteadily to my feet.

The walk across the room seemed endless. Wisps of smoke hung unmoving in the air like broken cobwebs. *Damn those spiders*, I thought. I hadn't even reached the bathroom, but already I could feel the tickle of tiny legs scampering across my hypersensitive flesh.

Once inside, I locked the door, emptied my bladder

and tried desperately to remember what Plan B had been. Or was it Plan C? Surely it couldn't have been something as simple as spritzing myself thoroughly with Chanel No 5 and imposing my will on Graham by sheer force of personal fragrance? I couldn't see him falling for that, somehow, but I spritzed myself anyway, even if it did make me smell of baby powder. Maybe I could appeal to his paternal instincts.

Then, in the absence of anything more constructive to do, I took off my spectacles and polished the lenses, squinted into the cracked mirror to examine my face, plucked a few eyebrows, and carefully retouched my lipstick.

At some point, above the rattle of the extractor fan, I thought I heard Graham knocking on the door and calling, 'Are you all right in there?', though I was certain only a few minutes had passed since I'd left him. I checked my watch, but as I couldn't remember what time it had been in the first place, the fact that the hands had now slipped past midnight was less than meaningful.

I stared hard into the mirror, trying to hypnotize myself into feeling like five feet six inches of unalloyed sex-bomb. How could Graham resist me? My eyes stared back at me sceptical and unblinking, so dark with dilated pupil there was not even a hint of the insipid blue I disliked so much. For a while, I amused myself by transferring my weight from one foot to the other, so that the crack in the mirror dissected my face at a wide variety of different angles. In rapid succession, I was the Elephant Man, someone with a learning dis-

237

ability, the Mona Lisa with toothache, a leering serial killer, Sybil the schizoid woman, and a grinning pirate visage divided by a cutlass slash as deep and oozy as the Mariana Trench, down in the nethermost abysses of the Pacific Ocean, where there was neither a current, nor a ripple to disturb water that had endured, unmoving, for many thousands of years. It was the deepest, darkest, coldest place on earth. And the most silent.

Except for one sound, a repetitive *tap tap tap tippety tap* which echoed eerily through the darkness.

The sound of typing.

My spectacles fell off the side of the basin and landed on the floor with a clatter, yanking me back into the real world. The sound wasn't typing at all – it was a gentle rapping on the door, barely audible over the extractor fan, which was still rattling away overhead. How had I ever thought myself hemmed in by silence? That bathroom was as noisy as a percussionists' convention.

'Be right out,' I called.

I felt as though I'd dragged myself up from a dream. How long had I been swimming around in the Mariana Trench? I had a guest outside, waiting for what had seemed like hours. It would serve me right if he'd given up and gone home.

I put my spectacles back on and glanced at the mirror one last time. Nothing I could do would disguise the way I looked. My eyes were back to their usual shallow blue, nothing like the deep dark ocean. In a burst of bravado, I took the glasses off again and left them on the shelf over the bath. I looked better in soft-focus. A *lot* better.

Finally, I opened the door, turned off the bathroom light, and stepped back into the living-room.

Jefferson Airplane was on the tape deck. I'd been playing it so often that I recognized it instantly.

> *The white knight is talking backwards*
> *And the red queen's lost her head*

How true, I thought. Sophie could be the red queen; she had certainly lost her head. But who was the white knight?

Graham was standing over by the window with his back to me.

'What are you up to?' I asked, trying to sound jovial, as though he might just overlook my having left him to his own devices for the past ten or twenty or thirty minutes, however long it had been. I had half a mind to sneak up behind him and give him a great big hug. It would have been one way of breaking the ice. If I felt him cringe, I'd still be able to back down with my dignity intact.

But something stopped me. Graham's shoulders were hunched as though he were reading something, but I couldn't see how or what because he had turned off the lamp and the room was lit only by the light from the street outside.

His shoulders were shaking.

I took a step forward and said 'Graham?', and he

turned, and I saw that he wasn't shaking, nor was he reading anything, and it wasn't Graham at all. I'm not sure how I could tell, but perhaps it had something to do with the way his outline rippled, like a person glimpsed through the dimpled window of the Landrace Inn. He was more shadow than solid person, a shape made up of shifting black smoke.

I opened my mouth to say something, but no sound emerged.

I was beginning to think that maybe I should have kept my glasses on after all.

The shadow crept forward until I found myself looking into a half-formed face.

Definitely not Graham.

The shadow spoke, just as the room began to tilt at an impossible angle, and I lost my footing and slid towards the dark lake that waited for me under the house.

From somewhere above, I heard the words, 'What took you so long?'

AUTUMN

ONE

I MISSED DIRK and Lemmy like mad. All those evenings in their company no longer seemed like pointless loitering in the waiting-room of life. I couldn't
imagine how I'd ever regarded them as no better than
second-rate stop-gaps for the kind of social calendar I'd
always thought I wanted. Instead, as the weeks passed, I
found myself looking back on the times we'd spent
together as a long-lost golden age. Dirk and Lemmy
hadn't been . . .

'Hang on a minute,' said Daisy.

. . . substitutes. They'd been the real thing. Once or
twice I'd glimpsed them from afar, shambling along
Portobello Road or . . .

'Hell-*o*,' said Daisy, cupping her hands into a mega-
phone. 'Earth calling Clare.'
   Clare stopped talking and folded her arms. 'What
now?'
   'Excuse *me*,' said Daisy. 'Correct me if I'm wrong,
but didn't we just come face to face with the dead guy?'
   'Maybe,' said Clare. She smiled to herself. 'Maybe
not.'

I tried to stay out of it, but the provocation was too great. 'That's *cheating*,' I said. 'You can't just leave it there.'

Once again, Clare seemed to be directing most of her rancour towards me. 'Who says I've left it any-where?' she demanded testily. 'Look, do you want me to go on with this, or don't you?'

'That's just it,' said Daisy. 'You're *not* going on with it.'

Clare leaped to her feet, 'Fine. Party's over. Let's go, Miles, we're out of here.'

'*No*,' wailed Luke.

'Sit *down*,' pleaded Daisy, tugging at Clare's skirt. Clare glared down at her contemptuously, as though she couldn't believe one of us had actually sunk to the skirt-tugging level.

'*Please* sit down,' Daisy begged.

I could tell that Clare was savouring the sensation of being in demand. Then she said, simply, 'No more interruptions then,' and sat down again. She was look-ing grim, like a girl on a mission.

'No more interruptions,' repeated Daisy. 'And that's a promise.'

Dirk and Lemmy had been the real thing. Once or twice I glimpsed them from afar, shambling along Portobello Road or moseying around the north end of Ladbroke Grove. Once I spotted Dirk staggering along Golborne Road with an enormous Art Deco cocktail cabinet strapped to his back. But neither he nor Lemmy ever gave any sign of having noticed me, and I didn't have the nerve to approach them. Instead I kept my head down. I had to face it: the Boar's Head had been my own personal Garden of Gethsemane. I had publicly disowned two of my closest friends. It would serve me right if they decided to cut me dead in their turn.

But how I needed them now. They might not have listened as I poured out my heart, it's true. Or they might have babbled some of their hippy garbage, but once you dug past the layers of fish-heads and mouldy old cabbage leaves, there was sometimes, wrapped in old newspaper at the centre of all that crap, a gleaming nugget of perspicacity.

But I needed someone to confide in. I needed to be convinced that I wasn't going mad, that it was *pure coincidence* that an unnervingly large number of rational individuals honestly believed they'd seen me in the company of someone who, for want of a better way of putting it, *wasn't there.*

Walter Cheeseman had acted as a sort of deterrent but as soon as he departed, my shadow had returned to hover at my shoulder, whisper into my ear – even buy me drinks, or so I was told. You have *no idea* how frustrating this was. I kept thinking of that line from *The Wasteland* – 'But who is that on the other side of you?'

Well, who was it? More to the point, *what* was it?

And who could I talk to? And who would understand?

It was ironic, I thought, that since I'd moved to the hub of the social universe, my circle of friends had not gone supernova, as I'd confidently anticipated, but had dwindled into something of a black hole. I hadn't seen Larry and Berenice since their dinner party. Rufus and Nadia and the others had fallen by the wayside, and I didn't feel up to phoning them now, out of the blue, to dump *this* all over them. I could still hear the sympathetic noises people had made about Sophie. I didn't want them making those same noises about me.

Walter Cheeseman, with his interest in local history, might have lent an ear without sniggering, but he had deserted me as pitilessly as any lover. As for Graham, just because we were now having regular sex didn't mean I was ready to empty all my innermost secrets into his ear. It would have sent the wrong sort of message entirely. He might have started thinking our relationship was *meaningful.*

'But what did he *look* like?' I asked Carolyn, after she had once again started talking about the person everyone referred to as simply 'my friend'.

'What I meant was,' I said, 'Did you think he was good-looking?' By now I knew better than to say, '*What* friend?'

Carolyn wrinkled her brow, but delicately, so as to lessen the risk of permanent frown lines. 'Kind of,' she said. 'Rather fond of black, though, isn't he? You should coax him out of that post-apocalyptic get-up and into something a bit more cheerful. I remember when Grenville went through his all-black phase. Everyone started calling him the Undertaker, and it really pissed him off.'

I wasn't one hundred per cent happy about the idea

of any undertaker – phantom or otherwise – loitering at my elbow, but how could I possibly feel menaced in the middle of a packed bar or crowded street? How could I be afraid of something I couldn't see or hear or feel? It wasn't as though the *flat* was haunted – that might really have worried me. It wasn't even as though I was hearing things going bump in the night any more; even the typing noises had turned out to have a logical explanation.

But if Marsha and Carolyn and Toby and the others thought I had a good-looking, attentive, trendily attired companion in tow, then why should I need to set them straight? At least it stopped me feeling like a gooseberry.

Of course, I had also to face the possibility that if there was an unseen presence hovering over me in public, it might also mean he was hovering there in private as well, the only difference being there was no third party to tell me about it. If I didn't know when he was there, then neither did I know when he wasn't.

So it was better safe than sorry. Whatever this presence was, I didn't want it thinking I was a slob. I started to take more trouble over my appearance. I endeavoured to hold my face in an alert, lively expression at all times. I stopped recycling smelly T-shirts from the laundry bag. Even on the days when I didn't go out – and they were getting more frequent now that summer was over – I made sure my hair was gleaming, mouth carefully lipsticked, clothes fresh and neatly pressed. I began to feel almost as well-groomed as Sophie.

*

247

It wasn't hard to work out what was going on. Robert Jamieson had taken a fancy to me. Sophie and the others had wilted beneath the scorching heat of his passion, but I hadn't even flinched – actually I hadn't even noticed him, though he wasn't to know that – and now he was regarding me as an intellectual equal rather than as a mere plaything. First-class fuck-up indeed. The Walters of this world just didn't get it. People like Robert were artists and prophets, men ahead of their time. History was peppered with them; in their lives, they were rejected, neglected, ridiculed. Even after death, their heads were heaped with scorn. Only another outsider could understand.

Only *I* could appreciate what he'd been going through.

I didn't open every single envelope addressed to Robert Jamieson, or Marsha would have begun to smell a rat, but the occasional letters I managed to smuggle past her were fanning my curiosity into something approaching obsession. I caught myself feeling outrage on Robert's behalf as lesser mortals rejected his offerings. Editors cowered in the face of his blazing talent. Women made unreasonable demands, while their parents disapproved of him and dispatched letters as pompous and misguided as this:

> Dear Mr Jamieson,
> I must insist you stop sending letters to my daughter Rowena. As you know only too well, she has been in an extremely delicate state of health since that nasty

business with the shears. Furthermore, she never quite recovered from your last visit.

My husband and I fear that any further communication from you – or indeed mention of your name – may undo all the progress we have made. If you persist in pestering either Rowena or any of the staff at Sunnyfields, we shall be forced to apply for a restraining order.

If you ask me, you were the one who should have been locked up.

Mrs Iris Bynchon

There was no return address, but Mrs Bynchon had put pen to paper on 16 September. Which was only a couple of days ago.

I didn't pretend to understand what was going on here. Somebody somewhere was playing a cruel trick on poor, addled Rowena. A jealous boyfriend, perhaps? Or a pathologically shy admirer? Perhaps it was a psychoanalyst who saw it as part of a revolutionary new therapy? Whoever it was, they couldn't have known that Robert Jamieson was dead, or they would never have embarked upon such an awful, tasteless, hilarious deception.

It did occur to me, of course, that it might be Robert Jamieson himself who had been writing to Rowena. Even now.

But if that were so, then I wished, how I wished he would start sending letters to me as well.

Graham and Robert had nothing in common, neither physically nor mentally. Robert had been tall, I imagined, whereas Graham was a runt. Robert would have been saturnine, whereas Graham was washed-out and sandy. Robert had usually worn black, whereas Graham wore hand-knitted tank-tops. Robert in his lifetime had been masterful and charismatic, whereas Graham was, let's face it, a bit of a saddie.

So I couldn't understand how I'd thought I'd seen Robert Jamieson when it had been Graham all along. Afterwards, he told me I'd spent so long in the bathroom that he'd started to worry. When I'd finally emerged, he said, I'd taken only a couple of steps into the room and passed out. He'd put me to bed before crashing out himself on the living-room cushions. That was his story, and he was sticking to it.

What *I* remembered was having sex. Wild drunken sex, with lots of squelching noises.

Graham denied it, of course. I knew he didn't want me thinking he'd abused my semi-comatose body; he was keen to repair the damage done to his New Man reputation by the incident with Sophie. All right, so he'd removed my clothes, he admitted when pushed, but he hadn't taken advantage of me at all. If anything, he said, it had been I who had taken advantage of *him.*

But we must have really gone at it, because in the morning I woke to find myself cocooned in soggy bedclothes. Graham had already departed, but had left a mug of tea by my pillow. I'd reached out for it thirstily, but it had turned out to be stone cold, with a skin on top.

For those precious few seconds, Graham Gilmore had shimmered with borrowed allure, and afterwards, I found myself not averse to spending more time with him, though obviously there was no question of our being seen together in public, and I knew there'd be one hell of a scene if Sophie ever spotted him on the premises. Fortunately, he didn't seem to mind being smuggled in and out, and he told me he had no desire to see Sophie again – he thought she was excessively bourgeois, and that even though she was pretty, it was a conventional, uninteresting sort of prettiness. Needless to say, I wasn't about to discourage such opinions.

And so we kept each other company, and we had sex, though it usually took three or four drinks before I began to find Graham remotely attractive. I had yet to sleep with him while sober; I wasn't sure I was capable of going *that* far.

Even when I was inebriated, the earth didn't always move, but on less than satisfactory occasions I would close my eyes and think about Miles. Sometimes I would think about Robert too, although for obvious reasons that required a little more effort.

TWO

I SORTED through the heap on the mat. There were a couple of letters for Sophie, several airmail envelopes and a bill for Marsha, an oddly shaped package for Walter Cheeseman, a small brown envelope addressed to Robert Jamieson, and nothing for me, not even a bill.

I stared at the small brown envelope for a very long time. If I'd had a letter of my own to open, things might have turned out very differently. Had Marsha emerged from her flat at that point, I would have been happy for her to have scooped up Robert's envelope along with her own mail and whisked it away to that mysterious forwarding-office where it would never trouble me again.

But the silence from Marsha's flat was deafening. So I carried on looking at the envelope, turning it this way and that, studying the handwriting (small, neat, round) and holding it up to the light, trying to catch an outline of whatever was inside.

What had started off as harmless fun was now turning into an addiction. With every new envelope, I vowed to hit it on the head and never again open anything that didn't have my name on the front. But curiosity always got the upper hand.

And I had to admit I'd become addicted to the idea of Robert, as well. I was avid for information about him. What had he been like? What about his hopes and fears? I'd formed my own theories, of course, but there were gaping holes. Perhaps this latest letter would fill them in.

I took a quick look around, though by now my ears had become attuned to the early morning sounds of the house, and it was obvious no one was coming. I picked up the envelope and slid it down, as far as it would go, into the pocket of my dressing-gown.

As I was going back upstairs, Sophie's door opened.

'Any post?' she mumbled, rubbing her eyes.

I felt like a sales assistant who'd been caught with her fingers in the till. 'Couple of things for you, I think.'

Sophie peered at me sleepily, but there were faint creases of amusement around her eyes, as though she knew exactly what I'd been up to, and wanted me to know she knew.

'Any letters for *Robert*?' she murmured and slipped past me, carrying on down the stairs without waiting for a reply. I fled up to the sanctuary of my flat. Did she know? How *could* she know? Still trembling, I made myself a cup of Earl Grey and sat down by the window, putting my feet up on the table as I slit the envelope open.

Dear Robert,
Much as I'd like never to hear from you again, I feel
I must remind you I still have several of your
notebooks, the third draft of your unpublished

novel, your fancy French edition of Edgar Allan
Poe, and that wretched sheep skull you picked up
on Dartmoor.

I realize these things probably have some sort of
warped sentimental value for you, and so
conscience prevents me from consigning them to
the dustbin where they belong, though serve you
right if I did, because you've never shown any such
consideration to me or the things I value. Anyway,
you know perfectly well what my feelings are, so
perhaps you could arrange for someone to collect
them. I would rather you didn't come in person, as
I really have no desire to see you again.

If I don't hear from you within two weeks, I shall
donate the Poe to Oxfam and bin the rest.

Adios, creep

Polly

I'd hit paydirt. Not only was there an address at the top
of the notepaper; there was also a phone number. Not
for the first time, I wished I'd gone to the trouble of
having a telephone installed; leaving the flat to make
calls was becoming more and more of a chore. But
later that morning, I nipped out to buy a phonecard
from the newsagent's and installed myself in the BT
booth by the church.

After about the sixth or seventh ring, someone
answered. A woman's voice said, quite peevishly, '*What?*'

I asked to speak to Polly.

'You've got a wrong number.'

'Oh,' I said, 'I'm . . .'

'Hang on . . .'

I hung on. My ear was tickled by a distant buzzing at the other end of the line. While I waited, I read the suggestive stickers plastered all over the perspex booth.

ALL YOUR DREAMS COME TRUE.
IF IT'S PAIN YOU WANT, IT'S AGONY
YOU'LL GET.
THE GATES OF HELL ARE NOW OPEN.

I stood there, reading the stickers and wondering why no one went in for simple pleasures any more, with the gathering conviction that someone was standing right behind me, staring with gimlet eyes at the back of my neck.

I turned to look, but of course there was no one there. There never was anyone there.

I was about to hang up and retreat to the safety of my flat when the voice at the other end of the line said, 'There *used* to be a Polly, years ago, but she didn't leave her new number, oh, apparently she *did* . . . but it was a long time ago and, uh, apparently we've lost it.'

'Thanks anyway,' I said, feeling almost relieved.

'Hang on,' said the woman.

I hung on again, and listened to the sound of strange subterranean creatures shifting deep within the bowels of the telephone system; it reminded me of the darkness at the bottom of the Mariana Trench. Again, I had the eerie sensation of being watched. I shuffled my feet, anxious for the call to come to an end so I could retreat to a less exposed location.

The woman had placed one hand over the mouthpiece, but sloppily, so that parts of the brief discussion she was having with her companion kept breaking through.

'*Omigod*,' she was saying. 'What happened?'

My ears picked out the word 'blood'.

I felt a cold draught on the back of my neck.

I was about to hang up when the woman at the other end of the line started to speak again, in a stop-start fashion, as someone dictated information to her. 'She used to work . . . Where? . . . in a dark room . . . oh, a photographic *darkroom* . . . Gravesend? . . . Oh, somewhere off the *Gray's Inn Road*.'

I asked if Polly was a photographer.

'A secretary,' the woman said.

'You mentioned something about blood.'

'She made a complete recovery,' the woman said. 'Didn't she, Robert?'

The name hit me with the force of a ten-ton truck. '*Robert?*'

'Huh?'

'You were talking to *Robert?*'

'Not Robert. *Robin.* I was talking to *Robin.*'

'Well, thank you very much,' I said, unnerved.

She hung up.

A few days later, I was forced to go to Covent Garden to drop off the latest batch of step-by-steps. These days, it took a real effort for me to venture outside Notting Hill. West eleven was fast getting to be the only place where I felt secure, but I made it across town with only

one or two unpleasant sensations and afterwards managed to hop almost lightheartedly on to a number 38
bus. I traipsed up and down Grays Inn Road, searching
for something resembling a darkroom as clouds rolled
across the sky and threatened rain. As I wearily made
enquiries in my umpteenth office block, a receptionist
took pity on me, consulted someone in her company's
art department, and informed me there was indeed a
photographic darkroom in the vicinity. Armed with an
address at last, I detoured beneath a bridge and finally
arrived at a place called Devo's.

The first spots of rain were spattering down as I
entered. The air reeked of artificial pine air-freshener.
A curly headed man was stuffing strips of negatives into
translucent envelopes. He barely looked at me as I
spoke.

'You mean Polly Wilson? She stopped working here
years ago. Had to, really, after what she did. Oh, and by
the way, it's no smoking in here.'

I had no intention of smoking, but instead of object-
ing to his high-handed manner, I asked, 'What *did* she
do?'

Curlytop set the negatives to one side and looked at
me properly for the first time, though his gaze kept
veering off to one side, as though I were diverting him
from other, more important tasks. It reminded me of
the way Miles habitually looked over my shoulder, as
though he were expecting somebody more amusing to
walk through the door at any second.

'You don't know?' asked Curlytop.

'Haven't seen her in years,' I said.

He looked pensive. 'Maybe she'd better do the explaining.'

'But *why?*'

'Like I said, you'd better listen to her side of it. There were some weird stories floating around.'

'But I really need to get in touch with her,' I said. 'It's a matter of life and death.'

Curlytop clammed up altogether, as though he'd suddenly caught himself blabbing state secrets to an enemy agent. 'Can't help you.'

'Where does she live now?'

'Haven't a clue.'

I turned to leave. As I opened the door, Curlytop shouted something after me, but his words were drowned out by the rumble of a passing van.

I looked back. 'What?'

'Just remembered. She opened a bicycle shop with the insurance.'

I shut the door and stepped back into the office.

'What insurance?'

'Can't help you there.'

'A *bicycle* shop?'

'Yeah, I remember now,' said Curlytop, nodding slowly to himself. 'Because bikes was the last thing in the world you'd have expected her to go in for. Considering what she did.'

'What *did* she do?' I tried again, but he wasn't going to be drawn any further. I tried another tack. 'Where was this shop?'

He scratched his head. 'Somewhere around King's

Road? Somewhere up west, anyway. Doesn't make much difference. Bound to have gone belly up in the recession.'

'Well,' I said, 'thanks.' I made a vague resolution to keep my eyes peeled for bicycle shops next time I was in the King's Road, but it didn't sound too promising a lead. Curlytop was right. The business probably had gone bust by now. Nearly everything else had.

I was half-way out of the door again when he remembered something else.

'*Bicycles*, the shop was called. No, snappier than that. *Cycles*. That was it. *Cycles*.'

'Oh, *very* snappy,' I said, and was stepping back out into the street, when Curly said something that had me glancing over my shoulder all the way back to west eleven.

'Didn't take any bloody notice, did he, that friend of yours,' he grumbled. 'I *told* him there was no smoking in here.'

THREE

SWEET LITTLE Ann-Marie met a super bloke in a coffee-bar. She was dressed in her best skinny-rib and her most bum-skimming mini and her kinkiest, slinkiest boots in white patent leather with fake ermine trim. The super bloke was wearing a turtle-necked sweater and flared velveteen hipsters and his name was Gordon. She told him she was up on a day-trip from Purley, and they exchanged sun signs, and he asked her if she'd ever considered becoming a model, and then he let slip, not altogether accidentally, that he was manager of a trendy pop group called the Drunken Boats.

'Oooh,' she breathed, impressed. 'The Drunken Boats? Drunken *Dreamboats,* I call them. That Jeremy Idlewild is really fab, though my friend Mandy much prefers Hugo.'

'Perhaps you'd like to meet them,' said Gordon with a cunning smile.

'Would I?' squealed Ann-Marie. 'The Drunken Boats! They're just the *grooviest.*'

Graham winced. 'All rather bogus, isn't it? The dialogue's wrong. And the clothes are iffy as well.'

'He was working on a shoestring budget,' I said. I

didn't know why I was being so defensive on Walter Cheeseman's behalf, though I had to try and justify having dragged Graham all the way down into the basement to watch *Down There* – the video. I'd already recognized the familiar *la mort toujours la mort* on the soundtrack, but Graham had never heard of the Drunken Boats, and was fidgeting.

'Hasn't your pal got any Clint Eastwood?' he asked. He scanned the nearest stack of videos, reading the titles aloud. '*The Naked Bun. The Cooch Trip. Beauty and the Breast.* These sound like good clean fun.'

'I want to carry on with *this*,' I said. 'Walter said Marsha was in it.'

'Who the hell's Marsha?'

'She lives here. Ground floor. Walter shot some of the film in *this very house.*'

'Why? Couldn't he afford a proper studio?'

'This is a location,' I said. 'It's got history. Things happened here. Someone said it should have a Black Plaque on it.'

'What's a Black Plaque?'

'It's like a Blue Plaque,' I said, 'only black.'

'Sounds more like something you scrub with a tooth-brush,' said Graham.

While Gordon lured sweet little Ann-Marie back to the house in Hampshire Place and gave her a cup of instant coffee into which he'd surreptitiously slipped several large sugarlumps soaked in LSD, I told Graham all I knew about the Butcher of Balham.

Graham didn't seem impressed. 'You mean he didn't even commit the murders here? Where's the fun in that? It's a statistical probability that half the houses in London have had murderers living in them at one time or another.'

I admitted the information on its own wasn't particularly impressive, but when one also took into account that a) a woman had plunged to her death from one of the upstairs windows, and b) a man had stood in front of my bathroom mirror and cut his throat, then one was forced to start looking at our surroundings in a whole new light.

'Maybe it's lunar,' I said. 'Or magnetic.'

'You mean like ley lines?' asked Graham, perking up for the first time that afternoon. 'You mean there are ancient and powerful interplanetary forces which intersect at this particular point in time and space?'

'Maybe,' I said. 'I see it as more of a San Andreas fault. Every so often the pressure builds up and there has to be a sort of *quake* to relieve it.'

I stopped and thought about what I'd just said. It made a crazy kind of sense. 'A quake of pure evil,' I added, pleased with the melodramatic ring of the phrase.

Graham wrinkled his nose. 'If that's the case, you'd better start working out when the next tremor's due, so we can stand well back.'

By now, Ann-Marie was slipping into a drug-induced fantasy sequence involving lots of wide-angle lens camerawork and strobe effects. The other guests were transformed into ghosts and skeletons and vampires. The frills on someone's floppy shirt turned into doves which fluttered up into the air and disappeared, and a man climbed into a sleeping-bag which metamorphosed into a caterpillar and wriggled across the floor, carrying its screaming occupant away with it.

Graham shielded his eyes and said he could feel a migraine coming on, but at least he was sitting up and taking an interest. It wasn't hard to see why. Many of the actresses had shed items of clothing and the screen was awobble with bare bosoms, some with flowers painted on them.

'This is more like it,' said Graham.

'Don't get too excited,' I said. 'We know what's going to happen.'

'We do?'

'Sweet little Ann-Marie is going to take a swan-dive out of that window and die horribly impaled on the railings underneath.'

'I thought you hadn't seen this before.'

'I haven't.'

'Then how do you know what happens?'

'Because that's what happened in real life.'

'You're telling me this is a *documentary*?'

'No, but Walter always based his films on real life.'

'You're telling me *The Cooch Trip* is based on real life?'

'I mean his serious films.'

'This is supposed to be serious?' asked Graham, his eyes bulging. On the screen in front of us, a tall, dark stranger clad in nothing but a magician's hat and cloak was daubing astrological signs in red paint over Ann-Marie's naked body. Meanwhile a voice on the sound-track wailed, 'Gonna get ha-ha-ha-ha-ha-high tonight,'

263

and the walls flashed from black to purple to scarlet and back to black again.

'I guess he used a certain amount of artistic licence,' I said.

'So when's she going to jump?' asked Graham, sitting back with his arms crossed expectantly.

'Not right this second,' I said, checking the label on the empty video box, 'because we've still got forty minutes to go.'

'Can't we fast-forward?'

'I'd rather not,' I said, and even as I said the words I caught sight of a familiar face. 'It's *Marsha*!' I roared triumphantly. 'There she is, at the back.'

'Her tits are enormous,' observed Graham.

'She is a big girl,' I agreed.

'And in all the right places.'

Then I spotted someone else, someone who made me grab the remote control handset from Graham and drop to my knees right in front of the screen, like a handmaiden worshipping the great god Television. Graham, feeling less of a man now he no longer had control of the handset, began to whinge.

'I'm just going to run through that bit again,' I said.

'Must you?' said Graham. 'This is not exactly Match of the Day.'

'Thought I saw someone,' I said. I rewound, reran it, and punched the pause button. '*Look*!' I said, jabbing the flickering image with my finger so that the screen crackled softly. 'It's *Lemmy*! The one with the moustache.'

'You mean Lemmy who can't speak English?' asked

Graham, who had met Lemmy and Dirk on a couple of occasions. 'Lives round here, doesn't he? I bet all these extras live round here. I bet Cheeseballs invited them to this shindig and got them stoned so he could make use of them for free.'

I scanned the extras in earnest, hoping to catch sight of Dirk as well, but none of the other bopping figures scored on my recognition chart, and I didn't see Lemmy again. Marsha made a couple of further appearances and said one line – 'Who's got the butter?' – as the action degenerated into one big orgy of softcore groping.

The film ground on. A couple of unfunny comic subplots reached their unfunny denouements, and Ann-Marie gained carnal knowledge of most of the men, women and sleeping bags around the room, but the windows to eternity remained firmly shut.

Graham yawned. 'Isn't it time she took the plunge?'

I checked my watch. 'Any minute now.'

But Ann-Marie stayed away from the windows.

'Jump,' urged Graham. '*Jump.*'

But she didn't.

We watched it to the bitter end. As the cold light of dawn crept into the sky outside, the extras stood up and, one by one, got dressed and tiptoed home. But Ann-Marie, naked and pale except for the astrological signs on her body, stayed slumped and unmoving where she was. The tall, dark stranger who had been wearing the wizard's hat but who was now dressed in a plain black suit bent down to shake her by the shoulder. Ann-Marie's head flopped forward on to her chest. He

265

shook her again, lifted her eyelids with his thumb, took
her pulse.

Nothing.

'My God,' he announced in a flat accent. 'She's
dead.'

'Dead?' I yelled. '*Dead?*'

'Not possible!' shouted Graham. 'You can't overdose
on acid. It's a well-known fact!'

'What about the *windows*?' I yelled. 'And what happened to the *Drunken Boats*?'

'We want our money back!' shouted Graham, thump-
ing the glass-topped table so violently I feared it would
crack.

'But Ann-Marie *didn't* die like . . .' I started to say,
and then my voice trailed away, because the man in the
black suit turned towards the camera and, in what
appeared to be an improvised move, raised his eyebrows. Just before the screen faded to black, his face
cracked open in a smile, though I couldn't for the life
of me see what the joke was. It was a smile that was not
easily forgotten. Nor was it in the least bit reassuring.

'Not exactly Martin Scorsese, is he, your friend Mr
Cheeseboard,' Graham called after me as I went into
the kitchen to rinse out our wine glasses.

'He doesn't have Hollywood budgets,' I reminded
him, but by the time I emerged, he'd disappeared. I
could hear constipated grunting from the bedroom,
where I found him strapped into the fitness machine,
face turning beetroot as he tugged with all his puny
strength on one of the bars.

'You're supposed to *push*,' I told him.

'Old Cheesewire must be a masochist,' puffed Graham.

'I wish you'd stop calling him silly names,' I said, perching on the edge of the bed. Graham disentangled himself from the machine, strolled over to the wardrobe, and slid one of its doors open.

'What are you *doing*?'

'Just looking,' said Graham. 'Don't worry, won't touch.'

'You might set off an alarm.'

'Thought you switched that off when we came in.'

'There might be others. Walter Cheeseman's security-mad. He might have *man-traps*.'

'If he was going to protect anything, it would be all that equipment in the next room,' Graham pointed out reasonably. 'Jeez, look at these suits.'

Despite my misgivings, I got up for a closer look. The rails were hung with several hundred thousand dollars' worth of Giorgio Armani and Hugo Boss. All of a sudden, the wardrobe being fitted with its own burglar alarm didn't seem like such a far-fetched idea after all.

'Old Cheesebob's a conservative dresser, isn't he,' said Graham. 'This is all rather *bourgeois*, don't you think? Rather *straight*? Like a bank manager or a politician.'

'More like one of the actors on *LA Law*,' I said. It was typical of Graham not to recognize class when he saw it.

'That's what I said. *Boring*. Hasn't he got any Hawaiian shirts, or camouflage jackets splattered with

Vietcong blood? Doesn't he wear a baseball cap? He *is* American, isn't he?'

He slid the door closed, and, before I could stop him, had the adjoining one open. Plain white shirts, T-shirts and undershorts were crisply folded and stacked in neat piles on the shelving within.

'Talk about poncey,' said Graham, whose own white T-shirts had been boiled down into a uniformly unappetizing greyish-white.

'Hey, what's this?' He slid the door even further open. 'More video tapes,' he said, disappointed.

'That's Walter's job,' I pointed out. 'That's what he makes.'

'But why would he keep them hidden in the wardrobe?'

'Don't ask me,' I said. 'Maybe it's porn.'

Graham made a face. 'You're saying that *Beauty and the Breast* is family entertainment?'

'Can you see the titles?'

Graham bobbed down to get a closer look. '*Nicholas...*' he read. '*Daniel... Robert... Arthur...*'

He straightened up and turned to make a face at me. 'And I bet it's not the one with Dudley Moore in it. Well, well.'

'Well what?'

'Our host is gay.'

I couldn't help bristling. I had nothing against homosexuals, but the notion that *Walter Cheeseman* might be gay struck me as absurd. Would he have lent me keys to his flat if he hadn't been attracted to me?

'That's not possible,' I said.

'Use your head,' said Graham. 'I bet this is gay porn. Maybe our director even shot it himself.'

'He is definitely not gay,' I insisted.

Graham extracted one of the tapes. 'We can soon find out. Let's run this through the VCR.'

'Put it back,' I said, suddenly panicked. 'We can't watch it; it's private.'

'I'm not suggesting you *tell* him we watched it.'

'It's a matter of trust,' I said. 'Walter didn't lend me keys to his flat so I could poke around in his private possessions. Go on, put it *back*.'

Reluctantly, Graham did as he was told. 'Now we'll never know,' he said tantalizingly, but the truth was, I preferred *not* to know. The idea that I'd been entertaining intimate sexual fantasies about someone who wasn't remotely interested made me feel very foolish indeed. Perhaps Walter *had* been gay all along, and everyone had known except me. What if Charlotte or Grenville or Carolyn or Isabella or – heaven forbid – *Sophie* had seen me making goo-goo eyes at him? What if they'd been laughing about me behind my back? *Poor old Clare. Tries hard, but doesn't have a clue. Remember Social Whirligigs?*

The idea that I might have made such a gaffe made me grind my teeth with anxiety.

'There's no need to look like that,' said Graham as he closed the wardrobe door. 'Your friend will never know we've been here. Relax.'

He moved within range, and I pulled him down on to the bed. 'Let's do it,' I said, slipping my arm around his waist. 'Let's do it *right here*.' I'd had less than half a bottle of wine, but I knew that if I closed my eyes and thought about Robert, everything would be fine.

'Do what?' asked Graham.

'You *know*,' I said. 'Wouldn't you like a proper king-size bed for once, instead of that grotty old mattress?'

Graham sprang to his feet as though he'd sat on a wasp. 'I'd rather not,' he said primly. 'Not here. Not right now.'

'Upstairs then,' I suggested.

He was looking unaccountably anxious. 'I should be getting back,' he said.

I reminded him about the bag of groceries he'd left in my flat.

'Oh, yes,' Graham said, and mopped his brow. I couldn't understand why he was getting so flustered. It wasn't as though I was sulking about not getting what I wanted, the way a man would have done. On our way out, I patted him affectionately on the backside, just to show there were no hard feelings.

'Clare,' he said. 'I wish you wouldn't.'

'It's all right,' I assured him. 'No one's looking.'

We toiled up the stairs in silence. I wondered if I'd offended him. It was impossible to tell with men; when you *asked* if they were offended, they always denied it.

We had just reached the landing on the first floor when, without warning, the door to Sophie's flat flew open, and she stood there, framed in the doorway with her Mulberry shopping bag. So much for subterfuge. At best, I thought, she would make a scene and accuse me of consorting with a rapist. At worst, she would snigger and tell everyone I was dating a nerd.

But to my surprise, she did neither of these things. She coolly looked us up and down. I tried to forestall her, assuming this was the calm before the storm.

'Hi,' I said, attempting to push Graham up the stairs ahead of me, but he'd taken root on the landing. 'You've met, um, Graham,' I said, swallowing his name in the forlorn hope she wouldn't immediately place him.

But Graham piped up, 'Hi, Sophie.' I tensed, waiting for Hurricane Sophie to smash us into smithereens.

Sophie took a step forward. 'How dare you,' she said to Graham.

I wanted to curl up and die.

Then I heard her say, 'How *dare* you come and see Clare without looking in on me.' And she was smiling and saying warmly, 'Hello, how *are* you?' and air-kissing him and he was atmosphere-snogging her back as though they were best mates who hadn't seen each other since before the dawn of time.

'Don't be a stranger,' Sophie said as she started down the stairs. 'Promise you'll pop round.'

'Of course,' said Graham, apparently still in a state of shock, and no doubt as surprised as I was that she'd made no attempt to rip his head off.

'Toodle-pip,' she said, and disappeared downstairs.

'*Well*,' I said, as we continued upward. 'What's got into *her*?'

'I'm not sure what you mean,' said Graham, who was

mulling over something, shunting it around his brain with a sheep-like expression. 'She's all right really,' he said as I unlocked my front door.

'What do you mean, *all right really*?' I demanded. 'I thought you said she was bourgeois.'

Graham went on as though he hadn't heard me. 'And you've got to admit she's attractive.'

I felt like slamming the door in his face, but first I had to give him time to pick up his shopping. Our meeting with Sophie had completely put me off the idea of sex, which was just as well, since Graham obviously hadn't been in the mood in the first place.

But if Graham wasn't good for sex, what *was* he good for?

I was going to have to find myself another man.

FOUR

I DIDN'T HAVE a snowball's chance in hell of tracing Polly Wilson, but I'd combed all the relevant Yellow Pages, just in case. I'd found a bicycle shop called, quite simply, *Bicycles*, and another called *Bikes*. I'd tried both numbers, but one place had gone out of business and the person who answered the phone at the other informed me, with a certain degree of pride, that his company had only ever employed men.

I didn't know what I'd been expecting. What could Polly Wilson have told me that I didn't already know? That Robert Jamieson had been a bit of a bounder? That he wrote poetry? That he liked a drink?

But I couldn't help it; I felt compelled to find out everything I could. I owed it to myself, particularly since Robert and I were, in a manner of speaking, stepping out together. Was he or was he not good for my image? Did he complement the lifestyle I was trying to lead?

Because, if he did, I honestly couldn't see there was any barrier to our becoming more closely involved. The fact that I couldn't actually *see* him, I decided, I could live with. It might even be an advantage; all the indications were that he dressed quite tastefully, but because I couldn't actually *see* him, he could have had Garfield T-shirts and shiny purple shell-suits coming out of his ears and it wouldn't have bothered me. Deep in my heart, though, I knew that Robert wasn't the Garfield or shell-suit type. I felt as though I knew him already, and up to a point, I suppose, I did.

Marsha hadn't been much help. She'd known Robert Jamieson, had actually lived in the same house as him, but whenever I mentioned his name, her normally sunny manner would grow quite overcast. One afternoon in mid-September, when she'd invited me down to her flat to help her finish a big bowl of *tiramisu* she'd brought back from the restaurant, I tried for the trillionth time to pump her for information.

'Nobody wants to talk about him,' I grumbled.

'Why should they?' asked Marsha, 'The man is dead and buried. Thank God.'

'But you *knew* him.'

'Only by sight,' she said.

'What was he like?'

Marsha shrugged. 'Can't remember. It was so long ago.'

It was as though she were hiding something, but I couldn't imagine Marsha being devious. I wondered if there had indeed been romantic complications, as I'd once suspected, but concluded not; by now, I empathized with Robert well enough to know he would have found Marsha as dull as ditchwater.

But it was hard to understand her attitude. If someone I'd known even vaguely had cut his throat in an upstairs room, I would have made it my business to find out everything there was to know. I would have grilled everyone who had known the deceased and concocted theories about what had driven him to it. I would have found out what he'd had to eat on that last fateful day, what phone calls he'd made, whether he'd left a note, what he'd been wearing. I would have fantasized about getting there just in time to save him, about nursing him back to health and being rewarded with his undying devotion.

I would have made quite a good detective, if not a good nurse, but Marsha was not the curious type. Sometimes I found myself exasperated by her cud-chewing contentment, by the way it never occurred to her to dig beneath the surface of things. Sometimes I could see why she drove Sophie up the wall.

The best way of finding something is to stop looking for it. The best way of finding something is to stop looking for it and to start looking for something else.

Carolyn's birthday was coming up, and I was on the prowl for a present. I wanted something chic and witty, something that would stop everyone in their tracks and reflect glory on to me, the giver. I wanted something so unusual and astounding that everyone would realize I was a rare and valuable individual who would at all costs have to be invited to *their* birthday celebrations, too.

There was a catch, though. Whatever I decided on, it would have to be something not too expensive. My publishers had sworn there was a cheque on its way, but in the meantime I was having minor cash-flow problems.

I'd headed straight for Hyperbole – Carolyn's favourite store. It was also the favourite shop of Sophie and

Charlotte and, when she was in town, Isabella. But Hyperbole always left me flummoxed. I just didn't *get* it. Everything, to me, looked tacky and overpriced. And you needed unlimited self-confidence – or perhaps it was simply decades of training in an upper-class assault-course – even to hold your ground on the shop-floor. Spanish tourists dripping with gold jewellery elbowed me out of the way as I tried to examine the sunglasses. Arab women in designer yashmaks barged in front of me on the escalator. As I browsed in the shoe department, lanky American debs chattered to one another over the top of my head as though I didn't exist.

All the time I was there, I felt as though I were being watched, but this was a sensation different from the one I'd been having around Notting Hill. This time I could feel my neck burning beneath the concentrated glare of salesgirls and store detectives who automatically suspected pitiable lowlifes like me of slipping wispy £200 scarves into their £20 tote-bags while no one was looking. I tried to hold my face in an expression of imperturbable all-seeing shopping wisdom, but my features were growing saggier by the minute. I wondered if Robert were with me now. I hoped not. I didn't want him seeing me like this.

On the other hand, I knew that Robert wouldn't have given a fig for those snotty salesgirls and store detectives. Robert, I imagined, would have strolled brazenly out of the store with the ends of a dozen wispy £200 scarves trailing from his pockets. The thought made me chuckle softly to myself. Whatever anyone said about him, the man had been a maverick. Still chuckling, I escaped on to Brompton Road and headed south-west.

So it was that I found myself wandering the back-streets of Chelsea, peering up at buildings and into windows and wondering whether to transfer my territorial allegiance to south west three, even though these streets didn't have the magic of my beloved west eleven. It was a scant sixty minutes since I'd left the Hill, but already I was experiencing bittersweet pangs of nostalgia. And so it was that, without any warning, and wishing like mad I were back in the only territory that now felt like home, I stumbled across *exactly* what I'd been searching for all along.

It was one of those shops that look out of place, as though they've been converted from the front rooms of private houses. I shaded my eyes to cut down on reflection and tried to peer into the shadowy interior, wondering if there might be some undiscovered little gem of an antique buried beneath the dross. Through the window I made out a tangled pile of tortoiseshell spectacle frames, an old Leica or two, antique microscopes, and a telescope with a barrel the size of a cannon. In short, there was nothing here that was likely to make Carolyn wet herself with excitement. I would have trotted on down the road and never looked back had I not caught sight of the shop's name, painted in wobbly gilt Gothic on a glass pane in the door.

For a pulse-quickening moment, I thought it said *Cycles.*

Silly me, it was *Cyclops.*

I was surprised by the depth of my disappointment; I

hadn't realized just how much I'd been counting on finding Polly Wilson. I dithered by the door. Just a coincidence, surely; there was not a bicycle to be seen. But supposing I'd heard it wrong, supposing Curlytops had said *Cyclops*, and not *Cycles*? Or supposing he'd heard it wrong in the first place?

I pushed open the door, and stepped inside.

And stepped into another dimension, made of dark wood and suspended dust. It smelt like the drawer where my grandmother kept her serviettes.

I hovered near the door, trying to get my bearings as my eyes adjusted to the gloom. The near wall was covered with creepy-looking masks, their surfaces coated with flaking enamel in the colours of putrefaction, or scatterings of silver glitter which glinted like slime in the half-light. Some of the faces were made even creepier by grotesque attachments: outbreaks of fungi or baby goat-horns or broad flesh-wounds oozing with deep red lacquer. The expressions were greedy, suspicious and desperate, but there were beady little spaces where the eyes should have been.

I'd seen faces like these before – on the demons in Sophie's summer garden.

For a crazy couple of seconds, I toyed with the idea of buying a mask for Carolyn – it was a foolproof way of making everyone sit up and take notice – but common sense got the better of me. I wanted everyone to think I was interesting and unusual; I didn't want them thinking I was sick.

I turned my back on the sharp noses and foxy chins and, weaving my way through the rows of rickety wood and glass instruments, suddenly spotted a dim figure gliding towards me through the sea of junk. I'd already opened my mouth to say something when I realized I was about to address my own image reflected in a mirror on the other side of the shop. For a while there, I hadn't recognized myself at all. I waved, to make sure it really was me. The reflection waved back. I lowered my arm.

And the reflection carried on waving.

I looked round, but of course there was no one else there. There never was anyone there. I snorted out loud at my stupidity, but only ended up feeling even more stupid when someone asked, 'Can I help you?'

So there had been someone there after all.

'Just looking,' I said, turning towards the voice's owner as she emerged from behind a rack of antique surgical instruments. At first sight, I might have mistaken her for Sophie, except that her hair was a darker shade of blonde and she was wearing a shade of candy-pink lipstick that would have been a touch too bright for Sophie's taste. In the old days, that is, before she'd abandoned her all-beige ethos.

But these details were peripheral, because what struck me immediately was that, like Walter Cheeseman, she wore sunglasses, even though the shop was dark. Ray-Bans, I noted.

'Polly?' I asked.

Even though I couldn't see her eyes, I knew she was sizing me up, and it seemed like an age before she replied.

'Actually it's Lucinda.'

'You don't know a Polly Wilson, do you?'

There was no reply. I waited for what seemed like another age before saying, 'Well, sorry to bother you,' and turning to leave.

'Wait,' she said.

I waited.

'I was lying,' she said. 'I am Polly Wilson.'

I carried on waiting.

'What do you want?' she asked.

It spilled out of me in a rush. 'IwonderifI-couldtalktoyouaboutRobertJamieson.'

Her pink lips pursed in surprise. 'How did you find me?'

'The letter.'

'What letter?'

'Addressed to Robert. I opened it by mistake.'

'To *Robert*?' There was another long silence.

'Hello?' I asked at last.

'I haven't written to Robert Jamieson for, oh, twelve, thirteen years. Why *would* I write to him? He's dead.'

'I was wondering if you'd heard about that.'

'Oh, I heard all about it.' There was a sharp edge to her voice. 'The police went into enormous detail.'

'I'm sorry,' I said.

'What did you want to know?'

'Anything,' I said, feeling unprepared. What *did* I want to know? 'I'd like to know what kind of person he was. I'm living in his flat, you see.'

Polly Wilson was outwardly calm, but I could hear her breathing hard. 'Let me see,' she said. 'Let me see what I can tell you about Robert.'

'If it's too painful . . .' I began, though frankly I didn't care whether it was painful or not.

'No, no,' she said. 'It's just that I wouldn't want you getting the . . . wrong impression.'

Thanks to Marsha's reticence, I hadn't been getting any impression at all, but I didn't say that. I said, 'Yes, I'd appreciate it if you could set the record straight.'

Polly Wilson moved towards the front door. I thought for a second she'd changed her mind and was showing me out, but instead she reversed the sign so it would read CLOSED to passers-by.

'You might as well come through,' she said, and led me through the shop to a doorway hung with a heavy brocade curtain. As she held it up and I ducked beneath it, I felt as though I were visiting a gypsy fortune-teller; I almost expected to see a crystal ball, but the room beyond the curtain was a shabby parlour with no distinguishing features other than a window which opened on to a backyard the size of a postage stamp.

It was almost as dark in here as it had been in the shop. 'Let us cast a little light on this situation,' said Polly, turning on the bare light bulb that dangled from the middle of the ceiling. The room brightened a little, but not by much. I shivered, feeling vulnerable and far from home. My hostess turned her sunglasses on me. 'Did you bring it with you? The letter?'

I shook my head. 'This visit wasn't planned. I found you by accident.'

'I doubt that anything to do with Robert is an accident,' said Polly Wilson. 'What did it say, this letter of mine?'

281

I told her what I could remember, which, because I'd read it so often, was nearly all of it. She chewed her lip, and some of the pink lipstick came off on her teeth. 'I remember writing something like that, years ago.'

'How come it only just arrived?'

'Don't ask me,' she said. 'Anything's possible where that mad-bastard-son-of-a-bitch is concerned.'

To hear Robert described in those terms gave me an odd little flutter of excitement. 'You think he was mad?'

'I *know* he was mad, but that was no excuse; I also think he knew exactly what he was doing. Let me show you.'

Polly Wilson tipped her head back until I could see a bare light bulb reflected in each of the Ray-Ban lenses. Then, with the well-rehearsed flourish of a professional stripper – or perhaps a professional magician – she whipped the sunglasses off.

'*This*,' she said.

I stared at her stupidly. Only one of Polly Wilson's eyes looked back at me, but the other wasn't closed, not exactly. The lid had a lazy, almost concave appearance, as though the nerves had collapsed in on themselves.

At first, I thought she must have had a stroke. I fumbled for words. How sorry I was, how difficult it must be, how brave she must have been.

'Let us not be coy,' said Polly. 'I might as well give you the full works.'

The eyelid had no will of its own, and she had to force it up with her forefinger. Once the lid was propped open, it became apparent there was no *eye*

282

behind it. In its place was a strange new orifice – moist, pink, and cushiony, like a sphincter waiting to be probed. I was overcome by shock and embarrassment, as though I'd just watched Polly Wilson drop her knickers and open her legs.

All of a sudden I didn't feel up to standing. By the time I'd flopped into the nearest armchair and steeled myself for another look, Polly Wilson had let the eyelid sag back into its natural lazy droop.

'I'm sorry,' I said. 'I had no idea.'

I was relieved when she put her sunglasses back on. 'Of course not,' she said.

'How did it happen?'

Polly Wilson uttered a chilly laugh. 'How do you *think* it happened?'

My brain was still reeling. 'A car accident? When you were a child?'

She sighed, as though she couldn't believe how dense I was being. 'Why did you come here to talk to me?'

'To find out about Robert,' I said.

And then I said, 'Oh no. He *didn't.*'

'I'm afraid he did.'

A wave of nausea had begun to spread slowly but relentlessly out from my stomach.

'I had no idea,' I said again.

Polly Wilson surveyed me calmly, apparently more than satisfied with the effect she was having on her audience of one. 'You're right,' she said. 'You have *no idea.*'

I said, 'So perhaps you'd better enlighten me.'

FIVE

POLLY RELATED the details in a monotone, like an actress running through her cues for the benefit of a lighting technician. Robert had been going through a bad patch, she said. Sometimes she wondered whether Robert's entire life wasn't one long bad patch. Luck had nothing to do with it; Robert *made* things bad.

Ways of Killing Women had racked up yet another rejection slip. He'd had a letter from *Automatic Quarterly* complaining that his latest poems were so offensive they were unpublishable – 'I am not normally an advocate of censorship,' the editor had written, 'but I strongly believe this filth should be flushed down the nearest toilet.' And Robert had interviewed a distinguished lady novelist for the books pages of a national newspaper, but the finished article had been so vitriolic in its misogyny – the term 'dried-up old slag' was repeated more than once – that his editor had been forced to spike it. It was like that all the time with Robert, said Polly. Opportunities came his way, but he invariably screwed them up: he would miss deadlines, or write articles so libellous they had to be suppressed, or get into fistfights with his editors, who would end up vowing through bloodied noses never to commission him again.

Sometimes she suspected him of doing it deliberately.

On top of that, Polly said, he'd been having nightmares so bad he would wake up screaming in the middle of the night, and nothing she could say would calm him down; he'd have to drink half a bottle of Scotch before he could go back to bed. Once or twice, she'd woken to find him in the bathroom, leaning against the washbasin and staring into the mirror with wide open but unseeing eyes.

He'd always had a tendency towards paranoia, but lately it was worse than usual. He was convinced *they* were out to get him. *They* were all the editors and publishers in town, who had formed themselves into a sort of masonic consortium which would stop at nothing to bring him down, because his work was subversive and threatened the status quo. He couldn't go out of the flat without being followed, but now he wasn't even safe indoors, because *they* had bugged the rooms and were spying on him through two-way mirrors. Now *they* were even transmitting subliminal messages in an attempt to brainwash him. When Polly had asked what kind of messages, he'd described the horrible things he'd seen in the bathroom mirror: black-eyed demons, faces sweating blood and pus, and, worst of all, a man slowly drawing a razor across his throat, grinning all the while.

'That really spooked me,' said Polly. 'And then one day, I made the mistake of asking a question – oh, something perfectly innocuous, such as *Would you like a beer?* – which distracted him from his work. The thing was, it was impossible to *tell* when Robert was working, because most of the time he just sat in his armchair and stared at the wall. But this time, apparently, he wasn't just sitting and staring, he was *thinking*, and I'd ruined his concentration just as he'd been teetering on the brink of a radical insight that would change our understanding of the nature of the universe. So he flew into a rage and slapped me.

'In a way, it was a relief. Many times before I'd thought he was going to hit me, but this was the first time he'd actually made contact. I packed my bags and went back to the flat I'd been sharing with my sister before I'd moved in with him.

'My room was just as I'd left it, and there were still traces of Robert there, things I'd found eccentric and endearing before I'd got to know him better. I should have chucked them straight in the bin, but instead I made the mistake of sending that letter, the one you read, though I have no idea why anyone should send it to you now. What kind of sick bastard would do something like that?'

What kind of sick bastard indeed? I had my theories, but didn't like to interrupt Polly Wilson's stream of consciousness.

'I expected an apology, at the very least,' she said, 'but there wasn't so much as a peep from him until the day he turned up at the darkroom, bang in the middle of the afternoon, and invited me to dinner. It would be an occasion, he said, that would mark the end of our romance but signal the beginning of a deep and lasting friendship.

'He was drunk, of course, which put me in an awkward position; I knew it would take only a careless word from me, and his amiability would tip over into a childish tantrum, and if he threw one of those in the darkroom, it would end with me being given my marching orders. His manner was too loud for our surroundings as it was; he was already attracting glances from some of my workmates. He kept pulling a hip flask from one of his jacket pockets and slurping out of it with exaggerated lip-smacking noises, wiping his mouth with the back of his hand. He offered it to me, then to some of my colleagues, who shook their heads and went about their work with frozen smiles.

'I didn't want to go to dinner with him and said so, but he began to pace up and down, sighing ostentatiously, until I recognized the warning signs and asked when he wanted me to go round. He said *right now* and, when I said that wouldn't be possible, his eyes began to bulge, and for a moment I thought he was going to explode. But then he sort of simmered down and said OK in a surprisingly calm manner.'

Polly looked pensive. 'I should have told him to get out, but I wanted everyone to stop staring at us, and I wanted him to leave without making a scene. I should never have agreed to go round, but I walked straight into the trap. I walked into it through fear of losing my job. I walked into it out of *embarrassment*.'

Polly was staring down at her hands, studying her fingernails with the concentration of someone who was trying to decide whether it would be better to varnish them or, what the hell, pull them out with pliers. She might as well have been talking to herself, but I didn't care. If she wanted to pretend I wasn't there, that was fine with me.

'So I went back,' she said, 'just for that one evening.'

'Worst decision I ever made in my life,' she added.

'The fundamental fault of the female character is that it has no sense of humour,' declared Robert.

Polly didn't bother to reply. He was just trying to wind her up. Just because she hadn't laughed at his joke. Why do women have legs? She'd tried to smile politely, but it hadn't been funny. In fact, she'd found it offensive.

On the way to Hampshire Place that evening, she'd cursed herself for having been suckered into this unnecessary ordeal. Had there been any way of backing out, she would have taken it, but she didn't relish the prospect of Robert making another of his unannounced visits to the darkroom and flying into a rage.

Even so, the rages were preferable to his other ploy, which was breaking down into loud blubbery tears and threatening to kill himself. Polly would always give in, not because she believed he would actually carry out his threats, but because she couldn't bear being witness to such unseemly displays of emotion. Afterwards, when the police asked if he'd ever talked about suicide she'd had to say yes. She'd tried to explain it meant nothing, it had had no connection with what had ultimately happened – which was of a different order altogether – but the police had failed to grasp the distinction.

That evening, though, he'd started out on his best

behaviour. The flat was unusually tidy, and he'd gone to some trouble with his appearance; he smelled of freshly applied aftershave, and his shirt, though rumpled (Polly was no longer there to do his ironing), was clean. It was a white shirt, too, making a pleasant change from the usual funereal attire.

He'd tried hard with the food as well, though cooking had never been one of his strong points. He'd prepared spaghetti with bolognese sauce, and though the pasta was overdone and the sauce similar in texture to a sucking bog, Polly had tucked into it with appreciative comments, because she knew what an effort it was for him to apply his high-flying talents to such menial tasks as the preparation of meals. The wine was truly disgusting – Polly had a theory he'd burned out his tastebuds with too much cheap whisky – but she held her breath and thought of how wonderful life was going to be without him every time she took a sip.

To begin with, he couldn't have been more charming, encouraging her to talk, fetching her things and telling funny, pointed little stories about himself. If only he were like that more often, she thought, there would be no problem. He was adorable when he was like that.

But then it had started to go wrong. Robert drank so much that he became unnaturally merry. As the evening wore on, his anecdotes became less coherent, his delivery louder and more slurred, and his jokes degenerated into crude quips about women and sex, domestic pets and sex, bottle-nosed dolphins and sex, and not a single one of them funny, especially since the punchlines were mostly inaudible through his chortling. Polly realized it was just like before, only worse, and that if she objected to anything he said or did, the furniture would start to fly.

So it wasn't long before she found herself humouring him – something she had vowed never to do again. She giggled politely at the awful jokes, listened rapt to the pointless anecdotes, nodded sagely as he ranted about the nationwide conspiracy that was preventing him from taking his rightful position in the pantheon of literary fame.

Then he'd asked it. *Why do women have legs?*

'No idea,' she said.

'Go on,' he said. 'Take a guess. Why *do* women have legs?'

'So they can walk?'

'*Wrong!*'

Polly shook her head. She neither knew nor cared. She just wanted the evening to end so she could go home and never have to see him again.

Robert got up and leaned over the table towards her. His shirt had come untucked and the bottom corner trailed in his spaghetti sauce. His grin became so wide and goofy it was within a whisker of splitting his face from ear to ear.

'Why *do* women have legs?'

Polly shook her head listlessly.

'I'll tell you why,' said Robert.

He paused for dramatic effort, cocking his head.

'Ever seen the mess a *snail* makes?'

He shouted 'Boom *boom!*' and started to laugh so

maniacally she thought he might choke. She rather hoped he would. She couldn't even fake a smile.

'That's revolting,' she said.

Robert stopped laughing. 'The truth is often revolting,' he said. 'That's why artists are shunned by society. Because we tell the truth. That's what that tawdry pathetic little twerp couldn't understand.'

'Is *that* what this is about?' asked Polly, getting to her feet, ready to leave. 'You're still pissed off because Harry Fisher spiked your piece?'

Robert turned his head to one side, fixing her with one unwavering basilisk eye. 'Why are you sticking up for him?'

'I'm not,' she said.

And then, before she realized what was happening, he'd swept his arm across the top of the table. Plates, glasses, cutlery hit the floor like timpani. She stared at the strands of spaghetti coiled amongst the wreckage and thought *Thank God*, at least she wouldn't have to swallow any more of *that*.

'Isn't it fucking *typical*,' said Robert. 'Each time a man reaches for the stars, there's one of you castrating bitches trying to drag him back and cut off his nuts.'

'No, there isn't,' she said reasonably, but already he was coming round the table towards her, fists clenched, approaching fast. She backed away. 'Don't you *dare*,' she said in a low voice. 'Don't you *dare* hit me again. If you so much as touch me I'll call the police.'

He stopped, and grinned again, so affably that she was left feeling foolish. 'Who said anything about hitting you?'

He dipped down and she thought he was going to clear up the mess on the floor. She started forward, ready to help, but already he'd straightened up again. Now he was holding a knife and fork.

'I'm not going to hit you,' he said 'I've got a better idea. I'm going to cut you up and *eat* you.'

Polly laughed nervously. His grin didn't seem so amiable now.

Robert carefully wiped the knife and fork on the front of his shirt, leaving it streaked with orange stains. 'You heard about the Japanese student who loved his girlfriend so much he chopped her into pieces? He stored them in his freezer, and then, piece by piece, he *ate* her.'

'That's not funny,' said Polly.

'Of course it's not funny, you stupid fucking cunt,' said Robert. 'It's not *meant* to be funny. It's fucking tragic.'

'Don't call me a cunt,' Polly said, tight-lipped and trembling.

'Why not? You should be flattered. It's a quote from the great Chicago playwright David Mamet, but of course you're too ignorant to know something like that.'

'That's *it*,' said Polly. 'I've had *enough*.'

'Where do you think you're going?'

'Anywhere but here.'

'But we haven't had dessert. I've prepared a nice Instant Whip. Butterscotch flavour. Your favourite.'

'I *hate* Instant Whip,' said Polly.

'Basically, my love, I can't let you go. Not. Just. Yet.'

'You can't keep me here,' said Polly.

Robert looked at his watch. 'Just a little bit longer. Hang around for another half hour. *Please.*'

She lost patience. 'I am not staying another second!'

'I need you to stay.'

'Well, tough,' she said. 'I don't need you. And I certainly don't need *this.*'

'You don't understand,' he said. 'If it isn't you, it'll be me. And I've got so much to offer.'

'You're right, I don't understand,' said Polly. 'And I don't think I want to.'

Robert's hands dropped to his sides, though she noticed he hadn't loosened his grip on the cutlery. 'You don't have to worry,' he said. 'Some are born posthumously. In the last resort, there is nothing but willpower.'

'Oh, stop wittering,' said Polly, and turned to pick up her bag. Something jabbed her in the back. She yelped, not from pain but surprise. She turned to see Robert tracing flamboyant trails through the air with his knife and fork.

'I. Want. You. To. *Stay,*' he said, punching invisible holes with every word.

'This is all wrong,' said Polly.

'He who does wrong to another has done the wrong to his own self,' said Robert. 'In other words, this is going to hurt me more than it hurts you.'

He prodded her with the fork again, this time in the ribs. The prongs barely made a dent in her jacket, but Polly felt goaded beyond endurance. She raised her hand to slap him, but before it connected there was a roar in her ears like the sound of an approaching juggernaut, and something hit her simultaneously in the face and chest with the force of a stampeding rhinoceros, and the world spun upside-down in a torrent of pain so powerful and all-consuming that at first she didn't recognize it as pain at all. The room turned red, and black, and red again, and then, just before it faded out altogether, she heard a voice coming to her across oceans, over mountains, soaring through time and space like an express parcel service, yelling, 'You want someone? Take *her*! Take *her* instead of me!'

She was woken by a hammering in her skull so hard it was as though someone were nailing her head to the floor. Sitting up was too daunting a task, so she had to make do with the view from where she was lying, although, even from a supine position, the effort of looking made her brain boil with agony.

Everything was veiled in a fine scarlet mist.

She heard a voice, but it sounded tinny, like someone on the other end of a long-distance telephone wire. 'You're OK. There's an ambulance on its way.'

Polly thought the first statement was cancelled out by the second, but didn't want to waste precious energy saying so. Her instinct connected the voice to a shape-less mass intruding into frame above her head. She thought it was probably a woman, and managed to wonder aloud where Robert had got to.

'Don't ask me,' the woman said. Polly tried to get her in focus, but there was something blocking her vision. She tried to move her head, but the muscles in her neck were refusing to obey commands from her brain, and each attempt ended in a fresh detonation of pain.

The shapeless mass loomed closer. Polly couldn't tell whether it had red hair, or whether the redness was due to the mist. The woman asked, 'Who *are* you?'

'Robert's girlfriend,' said Polly, realizing as she said it that this was no longer true. He'd hurt her badly, she didn't know exactly how, but now she would have no excuse not to leave him for ever.

The shapeless woman shook her head in a flurry of scarlet mist, and Polly heard her say, 'I'm afraid that's not possible. You see, *I'm* his girlfriend. Always have been.'

'I must have passed out again,' said Polly, 'because next thing I remember is waking up in hospital with my head wrapped in bandages. From the neck up, I looked like an Egyptian mummy. After two operations and a day and a half of dithering, someone finally broke it to me that they hadn't been able to save the eye.'

'What had he done?' I asked. 'Punched you?'

'Poked my eye out with his bloody fork,' said Polly.

I breathed in sharply at the thought of a cornea punctured by hard metal and popping like an overripe grape. My own eyes began to leak in sympathy. 'And where was Robert? What did the police say?'

'You want to know the final irony?' asked Polly. 'You want to know the best bit? I told everyone I'd done it myself. I said it was an accident, I'd sort of *dropped* the fork and – whoops – *fallen* on to it, though I don't think anyone believed me. The consensus was that I'd stabbed myself to get attention, but everyone was too polite to say so.'

This shocked me more than anything else I'd heard. 'But *why*? *Why* didn't you tell them the truth?'

Polly shuddered. 'I never wanted to see him again.'

'So you let him get away with it!'

Polly turned her sunglasses towards me. 'Not really. Three nights later, he was dead, and there didn't seem much point. He slit his throat, you know. Just like he'd seen in his bathroom mirror. He *said*.'

'Hallucinations?'

'Or some sort of premonition. Who knows?'

'You must have been relieved to hear he was dead.'

'*Relief* is not the right word,' she said. '*Relief* implies the threat has been removed.'

I asked uneasily, 'What do you mean?'

In a gesture that reminded me of my grandmother, Polly tapped the side of her head. 'He's still in here,' she said. She stopped tapping, but kept her forefinger jammed against her temple like the point of a pistol. 'He's still here, and I've had to live with it. And I live with it pretty well, considering.'

'You mean he follows you around,' I suggested helpfully, 'and you can't see him, but your friends keep asking who your shadowy companion is?'

'Don't be ridiculous,' she said. 'I mean I still look back over our relationship and make a mental list of the warning signs and berate myself for not having escaped while I was able to. I should have known better.

296

I *did* know better, but I was young, and when you're young you don't always do what's best for you.'

She fixed her shades on me. 'There's still life in this dead eye, you know. I can't wear the glass one they gave me, because I see things with it. It's enough to drive a girl crazy.'

Not for the first time, I wondered if Polly Wilson were crazy already. It was a ghastly tale, like an episode from a Gothic novel, but couldn't she have been exaggerating just a little? Things like that just didn't happen, not with Robert. Perhaps Polly had resented his talent. Perhaps she *had* put her own eye out, after all. There was something pent-up about her, something I sensed that made her a not altogether reliable witness.

I remembered to ask if Robert had left a suicide note.

'I don't know of one,' said Polly. 'You could always ask the other so-called girlfriend, of course. He might have addressed one to her. I couldn't bear to ask. I just wanted to put my life back together.'

'So he was two-timing you,' I pointed out unnecessarily.

'I think he was probably holding her in reserve,' said Polly. 'Maybe he had us stacked up, like jumbo-jets waiting to land at an airport. All I know is, if she hadn't arrived when she did, I would probably have bled to death. I never saw her again, and never asked after her, but I guess you could track her down if you wanted, the way you traced me.'

297

I wanted to stay and talk about Robert, but Polly had already lifted the curtain, and we passed beneath it, back into the shop.

'What was this other girl's name?' I asked as we wove our way towards the entrance.

'Ann-Marie something,' said Polly.

I stopped dead. 'You're kidding.'

'She did introduce herself at some point, but I wasn't in any condition to remember names.'

'I don't suppose it was Wilding, by any chance?'

'You know her?'

'Did she seem real to you?'

Polly laughed mirthlessly. 'Nothing seems real any more.'

I reached out to shake her hand, but she suddenly snatched her arm back as though I'd given her an electric shock. Her head was pointing like a gundog's, carried in a way that by now was all too familiar. She'd caught sight of something over my shoulder. I tried to follow the direction of her gaze, but all I could see was the gleam of the antique mirror on the far side of the shop.

'That made me jump too,' I said.

But now Polly was backing away from me, trying to put as many solid objects between us as possible. 'You brought him with you,' she hissed. 'You brought him with you, and you were trying to palm him off on me again.'

'No I wasn't,' I said. How could I explain that my own relationship with Robert was nothing like hers had been? That I was more than a match for him? That, for a start, I'd actually found his *Why do women have legs* joke quite funny.

'Get out,' she said.

'I'm on my way.'

'*Right now,*' she said.

The shadows had lengthened so that now I could hardly see her, but I could still hear her saying, 'Get out. Just get the fuck out of here.'

I didn't need any more telling. I knew when I wasn't wanted. I could take a hint.

SIX

GRAHAM AND I had patched things up after our tiff and were now seeing more of each other than ever. We had worked out quite a routine: we would start drinking in the Saddleback Arms at six or seven, adjourn to my flat at ten or eleven or whenever I couldn't see straight, have wild orgiastic sex, and pass out. I would open my eyes in the morning to find that Graham had already slipped off home, leaving his expiatory offering of chilled tea by my pillow. Maybe he just couldn't face me in the cold light of day, but I was glad he didn't hang around; being confronted with a face like Graham's was not exactly the best way to start the morning.

The fun did not come without great personal cost. I would wake up aching in every limb, with my head reverberating like the engine of a B-52 bomber. The hangovers were humungous and so frequent it was difficult to tell where one ended and another began. The diet of alcohol and pub food was also beginning to take its toll; there were permanent dark circles beneath my eyes, my skin was even blotchier than usual, and I felt podgier than ever. What I needed was a lazy holiday in the sun, but I'd left it too late in the year and besides, now I'd finally made it to west eleven, I found I really didn't want to go anywhere else.

I was left feeling unaccountably anxious, as though there were an express train hurtling up out of the dark towards me: I could sense its approach but couldn't work out which direction it would be coming from. I was so on edge that, in the market one Friday afternoon, when someone tapped me gently on the shoulder, I leapt in the air as though someone had poked me in the kidneys with a cattle prod.

I whirled round to find Sophie looking at me in amusement. She always seemed to be amused these days, as though she were getting a kick out of watching me slowly going to hell. I frowned back, trying to work out what was different about her; there were so many changes these days it wasn't easy to keep track. This time it was her hair – no longer blonde, but an extraordinary flame red which glinted wickedly in the sun.

'The stress must be getting to you,' she said, and suggested a drink to soothe my nerves. I thought it was a bit early to start drinking, but didn't say no; alcohol was probably just the thing to soften the pneumatic-drill pounding of my latest hangover.

'Stress? What stress?' I asked. I did indeed feel stressed, though I had no idea why. My career, though in its usual state of creative atrophy, was at least reasonably remunerative. My love life was plodding along nicely. But Sophie gave me a meaningful look, as though the two of us shared a dirty little secret. Something inside warned me not to pursue the topic, so instead I asked her what she'd done to her hair.

'Henna,' she said. 'I had it done this morning at Mane Event. Like it?'

I told her I thought it was very striking, but in truth I didn't care for it much. I didn't see the point; when you had hair like Sophie's natural wheaty blonde, I couldn't understand why you'd want to change it to some brassy hooker hue.

'What made you take the plunge?' I asked her.

'Don't know. Maybe I got tired of being tasteful. Maybe I just wanted to shock everyone. It's not as though it'll be like this for ever. It'll grow out.'

We bought drinks in Baldinger's and sat down at a quiet table near the back of the bar and she said, 'I've been meaning to talk to you for some time about this sleepwalking thing. It's rather embarrassing.'

I glanced sideways at her. She was staring down into her kir. 'That's all right,' I said. 'You don't have to explain. I didn't realise you were aware of it.'

Sophie did an almost imperceptible double-take, like a society lady checking to see if the tart sitting next to her was wearing the same frock. 'How could I not be aware of it?' she asked. 'Last night makes it three in a row. Last night you even got into bed with me.'

I said, 'I beg your pardon?'

'Don't you think you should see a doctor?'

'You think *I'm* walking in my sleep?' I asked, desperately backtracking.

'Why yes,' said Sophie. 'I thought you knew. Last night I woke you up, and you apologized and scuttled back upstairs.' She paused and lit a cigarette. 'I assumed you'd woken up, anyway. Maybe you just *seemed* awake. It's sometimes difficult to tell with you, Clare.'

'I don't remember *any* of this,' I said. 'Are you sure it's not the other way round? Are you sure it's not *you* walking in *your* sleep?'

Sophie sighed, 'Don't start that tit for tat thing again. What I want to know is how you got hold of my spare key.'

'I didn't even know I *had* your spare key,' I said, beginning to feel prickly and paranoid. I wouldn't have put it past Sophie to be playing some elaborate trick just to make me look stupid.

'Try your keyring,' she suggested.

I got out my keyring, and counted off the key to my flat in Hackney, the key to number nine, the key to flat number four. And stopped counting. There was one key left. I turned it this way and that.

'See what I mean?' asked Sophie. She held up her own key. The two matched perfectly. 'Nothing to worry about,' she said cheerily. 'Maybe it's your diet. You should stop stuffing yourself with junk food. If your GP can't help, I could always give you the name of my homeopath.'

I nodded, too stunned to reply. My head filled with a vision of Hampshire Place, after dark, coming alive as somnambulists wandered in and out of each other's flats, narrowly missing one another as they ambled up and down stairs with outstretched arms and unseeing eyes.

I tried to prise the extra key from its place on my ring, but only succeeded in breaking a nail. 'I have no idea how this came to be in my possession,' I said, and wondered whether to tell Sophie about the night I'd discovered her in my bathroom, but she seemed eager to change the subject.

'I'm sure it's not serious,' she said in a tone that suggested it was a symptom of terminal cancer, at the very least. 'Now, what are you wearing to Carolyn's bash?'

I was going to be wearing my new velvet jacket, but I didn't tell Sophie in case she accused me of playing copycat games again. The jacket had been acquired at terrible cost to my nerves as well as to my purse, but I wasn't about to share this information with her either. I wasn't sure I was capable of sharing it with anyone.

For years I'd been thinking velvet was hopelessly infra-dig, but now that Sophie had given it her seal of approval, it had rocketed to the top of my shopping-list. I had hunted through the head-shops and neo-psychedelia stores of Portobello Road, but the garments I found there all had folksy little touches such as smocking or embroidery. I had no intention of looking like a Norwegian goose-girl. I wanted something that could pass, in a dimmish light, for debonair.

It was a fine autumn day, cool but sufficiently bright to allow me to get away with wearing prescription sunglasses without feeling too pretentious. I felt stylish and in control of my life as I strolled through the market, despite having to elbow my way through the usual sightseers cluttering up the place. *West eleven belongs to me*, I thought, feeling sure the visiting rubes would perceive me instantly as one of the chosen few –

304

not just another face in the crowd, but a local, a Notting Hill *resident*.

Eventually I spotted what I was looking for on Portobello Green – a stall packed end to end with fifty-seven varieties of black velvet jacket, most of them unencumbered by unnecessary trimmings. The area beneath the Westway was wreathed in shadow, and I had to remove my sunglasses to ensure I was looking at black rather than bottle green or midnight blue. I found one I liked and slipped out of my tweed to try it on before stepping back to study myself in the full-length mirror propped up against the side of the stall.

'Suits you,' said the stallholder, a skinny youth with a wispy soul patch and single earring. He stared straight over my shoulder, and added, 'Doesn't it?'

I did up two buttons on the jacket and blinked, several times, eyes still adjusting to the gloom as I continued to gaze at myself in the mirror.

Time stood still. The only sound was the sound of my own breathing. I'd been looking, but only now did I *see*.

It was the first time I'd seen him.

It was his reflection I saw. He was standing just behind me, blending with the shadows, and it wasn't easy to pick him out against the background because he was dressed in black, just as Carolyn had said – like an undertaker, black coat and trousers and shirt, so that his face, by contrast, stood out a whiter shade of pale, whiter than a junkie's complexion, whiter than white bread, whiter than milk, whiter than white.

305

But then your skin would have been pale too if you'd been dead all those years.

He was noticeably taller than me, taller by at least a head, but he was stooping, shoulders hunched forward like a vulture's, as if to get a better view of what was in the mirror.

Which was me. It was my reflection he was looking at. He was trying to get a better view of *me*.

He was staring intently, staring with a hooded gaze that saw *everything*, even the things I had always tried to keep hidden. I could pretend what I liked, but he would always *know*. He would always *understand*.

In that instant, our eyes met and he smiled, and I wished, how I wished he hadn't, because it was a smile that was not in the least bit reassuring.

Still smiling, he drew his finger in a vicious sweeping gesture, from one side of his neck to the other. Like someone cutting his throat.

I registered all this in the time it took to blink once, blink twice, and then, without thinking, I turned my head to look back over my shoulder. Of course there was no one there.

There never had been anyone there.

The stallholder punctured the silence with his voice.

'Doesn't it?' he asked.

Time started to move forward again.

I turned back to the mirror, but the only figure reflected there was mine.

The stallholder rubbed his eyes. 'Sorry, love. Could've sworn you were with someone.'

STIFF LIPS

'You and the rest of the world,' I said, and, just as I was congratulating myself for having kept a cool front, I felt my knees beginning to buckle.

'Whoah,' said the stallholder, sliding a chair to catch me as I concertina-ed earthward. My mind flashed back with an incongruous feeling of triumph to the model couple I'd seen in Cinghiale; now I too had found myself a man to slide chairs beneath me as I sat down.

'You all right?' he asked.

'Thought I saw someone I knew.'

'Blimey,' he said. 'Take a look at your face.' He held up a small hand mirror, and I stared in awe. I'd turned almost as white as Robert Jamieson himself; my skin was the colour of tender baby veal that had never been exposed to daylight. I stood up, a little shakily. A million miles away on the Portobello Road, the crowds milled and murmured and went about their business in the crisp cool afternoon sunlight. I needed to get back there and mingle with the mass of living, breathing human beings. I needed to soak up some of their warmth.

'I'll be all right now,' I said to the stallholder.

And I honestly believed I was telling the truth.

For several days after that I tried to avoid looking in mirrors, but for someone as image-fixated as me it wasn't easy. *Where's the problem?* I asked myself. *You wanted to see him, didn't you? Well, you've seen him. Happy now?*

The trouble was, I wasn't happy at all. No matter how often I tried to persuade myself that Robert and I

307

were two of a kind, that we were made for each other – or that we would have been made for each other if only he hadn't been dead – I couldn't get the memory of that smile out of my head. I was prepared to do almost anything to ensure I wouldn't have to see it again, and if that meant going round all day with toothpaste down the front of my T-shirt or a bogey hanging out of my nostril, then that was the price I would have to pay.

But eventually, when it came to getting ready for Carolyn's birthday bash, personal vanity defeated all other considerations, and I confronted my reflection head-on. Lank hair, pale eyes blinking behind spectacle lenses: it was all disappointingly back to normal. How had I ever worked myself up into such a foolish panic? Robert Jamieson had been nothing more than a mirage. I'd been wanting to see him so badly I was ready to believe he'd finally shown himself.

It had been one of my life's ambitions to be invited upstairs at the Malabar, but now I was there I felt out of place, sandwiched between two groups of people, none of whom I recognized. All the more familiar faces – Sophie, Charlotte, Toby, Grenville, Isabella – were clustered on the opposite side of the room. Something, possibly pride, or perhaps the fear they would ignore me, prevented me from going across to talk to them, and naturally it never occurred to any of them to come over and talk to me. I was singing along beneath my breath to *The Girl from Ipanema*, telling myself I didn't *need* to socialize but was content to stand on one side and observe this peculiar sort of human being at play,

when I noticed Charlotte casting quick, almost flirtatious glances in my direction.

No, not at me. She was glancing at a spot somewhere
behind me, to my left.

But *of course* no one was bothering to cross the room
and talk to me. They could see I already had company.

He was here.

I felt my heart hammering so hard I thought it was
going to burst out of my chest like the horrible little
monster in *Alien*. But I had to get a grip. If I wanted
this relationship to go anywhere, I couldn't very well
fall to pieces every time my other half made his
presence felt.

I formed a mental picture in which I was a woman
made of steel, a bit like Margaret Thatcher in her prime
but younger, sexier, more compassionate. Then, feeling
more than capable of kicking a few men around the
room, I took a sip of champagne and murmured, 'I
didn't realize you were there.'

From somewhere to the northwest of my shoulder
blade there came a resounding silence.

'Nice to see you,' I said. 'Or not, as the case may be.'

I paused, giving him time to reply. When the silence
had stretched out into a minute, I looked round. And
of course there was no one there. What had I been
expecting? He hadn't revealed himself to me in company before, and he wasn't going to start doing it now.

But perhaps bang in the middle of a crowded party
was as good a situation as any to establish parameters.

'I'll be honest with you,' I said. 'I wasn't too happy
about that business with the fork.'

309

I glanced over to where Charlotte was still watching us intently. She whispered something to Grenville, who was standing next to her and whose arm, I noticed, had crept around her waist.

There were still things that needed saying. 'I don't like it when you play tricks,' I said. 'No more suddenly popping up like that, please. You know it makes me nervous.'

Charlotte nudged Sophie, who was on her other side. Sophie looked over in our direction and her mouth set in a bitter line. Now I understood why she'd usually steered clear of me when we'd been out drinking with the others. The sight of Robert and me – together – must have hit her where it hurt. For me, though, the sensation was one of sweet revenge for all the petty humiliations she had inflicted on me over the years. I wanted to make her suffer even more, so I tossed my head vivaciously, trying to make my hair bounce like it did on the models in hairspray commercials. I laughed and chatted animatedly to my invisible companion until Sophie and Charlotte grew bored with watching and returned to their conversations.

But I'd reckoned without Carolyn, who was studiously performing her duties as a hostess. She came up and kissed the air in front of my face and thanked me once again for the expensive scarf I'd given her – that wispy yet exquisite strip of silk I'd found stuffed into one of my pockets after the visit to Hyperbole.

'You all right?' she asked.

'Absolutely,' I assured her.

'I could introduce you to some people, if you like.'

'No need,' I said. 'Robert and I are fine.'

She looked a little perplexed. 'It's funny you should say that,' she said, 'because I was just wondering why you hadn't brought him along.'

It took me a few seconds to process this information, and then I had what I call a Tom and Jerry moment. This is when your jaw drops all the way down to the ground, your eyes pop out on stalks, your face turns the colours of the Italian flag, one after the other, and there's an orchestral chord so deafening it almost drowns out your bloodcurdling shriek of horror.

How could I have been so *blind*?

The look of genuine concern on Carolyn's face gave me heart; she hadn't been trying to catch me out. She gave no sign of having noticed my behaviour was any odder than usual.

'Robert's . . . not here,' I said haltingly.

'So I gathered,' said Carolyn.

Feeling like a fraud, I forced myself to ask if she'd bumped into him lately. 'Not for some time,' she said. 'Don't tell me you're not seeing him anymore.'

I burst out laughing. 'You could say that.'

'That's a shame,' said Carolyn. 'It's hard to find good-looking unattached heterosexual men these days.' She smiled warmly and started to move on. I clutched at her arm, not yet ready to let her go.

'Did you ever talk to him?'

'Of course,' she replied. 'You know I did.'

'May I ask what you talked about?'

Carolyn thought for a moment, eyes flickering back and forth. 'I can't really remember,' she said at last.

311

'But that's not to say he was boring. In fact, he was probably one of the most charming people I've ever met. What a shame you've split up.'

She patted me absent-mindedly on the shoulder and continued on her rounds, leaving me feeling more alone than ever. So now not even Robert sought my company. I looked wistfully across the room to where Sophie and the others were laughing and chattering in a cosy little huddle. My first instinct was to sneak home with a bottle of wine and ten packets of crisps, but I knew a binge like that would leave me feeling worse than ever. If that was how I was going to react, I might as well go back to Hackney *right now*.

The thought of having to return to the life I'd left behind fired me up. I was in Notting Hill, living a Notting Hill life among Notting Hill people, and if I couldn't hack it, then I might as well shrivel up and die.

So I took a deep breath and walked across the room and said, 'Hi.'

Grenville, now positioned a respectable distance from Charlotte, looked round and said, 'Hey there.'

There now, I thought. *That wasn't so bad now, was it?*

Sophie was a tougher nut to crack. I could tell she was trying not to snicker in my face. 'Been talking about anything interesting?' she asked breezily. 'Anything you'd like to share with the rest of us?'

'Oh, shut up,' said Charlotte. 'A girl can talk to herself if she wants to. Me, I do it all the time.'

This was a first. *Charlotte was sticking up for me.* I gazed at her as though she'd suddenly sprouted angels wings.

Sophie, on the other hand, was staring at her as though she'd made a bad smell.

It was a strange, disjointed evening, and, after that false start, I couldn't help feeling uneasy, even though the mirror in the ladies' lavatories reflected me and no one else.

But I couldn't keep my mind off Robert for long. I plucked up enough courage to ask Charlotte if they'd ever talked. She looked at me as though I were mad. 'Of course we talked,' she said. She recalled how once he'd asked if she fancied older men.

'Robert's right up your street, then,' I said. 'He's ... let me see ... He must be in his mid forties. That old enough for you?'

Charlotte tilted her head. 'He's getting there.'

'I sometimes feel like he's *already* there,' I said.

I asked the others about him too. Isabella, whose hobby was collecting celebrities, remembered how he'd once promised to introduce her to a member of the Rolling Stones. Toby cut in at this point and asked which one, and Isabella said Brian Jones, and Toby snorted derisively and said that wasn't possible, she must be confused, and Isabella said no she wasn't.

And then I made the mistake of asking Sophie. What had she and Robert talked about? She fixed me with a look that would have withered a plastic daffodil, raised her glass as if to propose a toast – and emptied its contents over my head with a heartfelt 'Fuck you' before stalking out of the room.

Funnily enough, my being drenched with champagne was the point at which the evening began to be a success. Everyone rallied round as I stood there with my shoulders gently fizzing. Carolyn used the scarf I'd given her to mop my face, declaring she'd never seen Sophie act like that before.

'I have,' said Grenville. 'She threw her drink over *me* once. Join the club.' He took out a large handerker-chief and began to wipe my jacket down, lingering over the front of it rather longer than was strictly necessary.

'What on earth did you say to her?' Charlotte asked me with a touch of admiration.

'Time of the month,' said Toby. 'Bound to be. Girls always get cranky around then.'

Marsha turned up late with her boring boyfriend in tow. I hadn't been aware she even knew Carolyn, but they exchanged warm greetings and Marsha presented her with a charming little Balinese knick-knack.

'Exactly how old *is* Carolyn?' Marsha asked me later.

I said I didn't know, but would guess roughly the same as Sophie, which meant roughly the same as me.

Marsha called us babies. 'It's my birthday next month,' she announced.

'So how old will *you* be?'

Marsha pursed her lips. 'It's the big one.'

'The big what?'

'My fortieth. The twenty-seventh of October.'

'Congratulations.'

'Just imagine,' she said with a shudder. '*Forty.*'

'You don't look forty,' I said, though I thought Marsha looked her age, no more and no less. I wondered what it would be like when I too reached that stage, the age when people said your life began, though it seemed to me to be the beginning of an inexorable slide into decay and death. Would I be married, with a family, or would I be unattached, unloved, a dried-up spinster squandering her talents on pictures of black-berry cobbler and key-lime pie? Not for the first time, I envied Marsha. Forty or not, she had a steady boyfriend, a job she adored, and, unless she was the world's most accomplished faker, she was happy with the hand she'd been dealt.

'The big four-oh,' she went on, shaking her head in disbelief. 'Only one thing to do in the circumstances.'

I dutifully asked, 'What's that?'

Marsha beamed. 'Throw a bloody enormous party. I'm going to throw the biggest fucking party I've ever had in my life.'

'Oh, good,' I said, looking forward to it already. I could see it now. Marsha would hire Cinghiale for the evening and pack it with *la crème de la crème* of west eleven society. We would swig champagne and nibble smoked salmon canapés and wiggle our hips to discreet jazz samba rhythms until some way past midnight, when we would link arms and stroll giggling back to the house, attracting envious glances from stray passers-by.

I was already planning what to wear.

'A Hallowe'en party,' added Marsha.

'I see,' I said, and suddenly it didn't sound like such a great idea after all. My gloriously sophisticated vision of smoked salmon and champagne evaporated – how could I ever have expected anything so stylish from a woman who wore *faux* snakeskin leggings – and was replaced by . . . what? Pumpkin pie? Barbecued shrimp? Shiny green apples a-bobbing in a barrel? Whatever refreshment Marsha came up with, it was bound to end in badly smeared lipstick and soggy *décolletage*.

'Why not have it on your birthday?' I urged. 'What's wrong with the twenty-seventh?'

Marsha explained patiently that whereas Hallowe'en was on Saturday, her birthday was on the Tuesday, and it wouldn't be practical to hold a party during the week. No one would come.

I told her *I* would.

'But you and Sophie work flexible hours. Most of my friends have nine-to-five jobs. They have to get up in the morning.'

'I suppose so,' I said.

'You don't sound terribly thrilled,' said Marsha. 'I thought you'd be really excited. It's about time you met my friends. You'll like them.'

I tried to look keen, but it was difficult to summon much enthusiasm at the prospect of being introduced to people with nine-to-five jobs. I wanted to meet people who did as they pleased. I wanted to meet artists and thinkers and minor aristocrats. I wanted to meet the sons and daughters of celebrities, and people on private incomes.

'It'll be fancy dress, of course,' said Marsha.

Of *course*. Anything less would have been unworthy of Marsha. I tried to imagine her dolled up as Dracula's daughter or the bride of Frankenstein, but it was impossible. She was more the *Annie Get Your Gun* type, more of a thigh-slapping principal boy in a cocked hat with a jaunty feather. I shuddered at the thought.

'With lots of that aerosol cobweb stuff,' Marsha went on, eyes misting over like someone revisiting a scene from her childhood, 'and blood running down the walls, and fluorescent skeletons and bats dangling from the ceiling.'

My once-pure vision of a tasteful society gathering had now degenerated into something distinctly low-rent. 'Do you really think Cinghiale will let you do all that?' I asked. I couldn't see blood meshing with all that tasteful Italian decor, unless of course the Mafia were somehow involved.

Marsha gaped at me. 'Clare, you've got to be kidding. I couldn't possibly hold a party at *Cinghiale*.'

I gaped back at her. 'Then where . . .?'

'Home, of course.'

'*Our house?*'

'Why not? There's loads of room. You and Sophie can invite your friends as well.' She clapped her hands with glee. 'We can convert the entire building into one big chamber of horrors.'

The idea gave me the shivers. Trying to sound as though I didn't care either way, I reminded Marsha that Hallowe'en had never been an auspicious occasion for former tenants of the house. 'Wasn't it then that Ann-Marie Wilding kept her appointment with the iron railings?'

'Who's Ann-Marie Wilding?'

'Never mind,' I said. 'But what about Robert Jamie-son? Didn't he cash in his chips on the thirty-first?'

317

A glimmer of understanding crept across Marsha's broad features. 'You're *superstitious*,' she said.

'I am not,' I said.

Marsha wrapped her arm around me and squeezed. 'Don't worry,' she said. 'I won't let the ghoulies get you.'

'I'm *not* superstitious,' I repeated. 'I just thought it might be easier to hire an outside venue, so we wouldn't have to worry about cleaning up, or things getting broken, or complaints from the neighbours.'

'But cleaning up's half the fun!' said Marsha, and I couldn't be sure she was joking. 'Look, it's no big deal. We'll keep it on the ground floor. I just thought it might have been fun to do things on a bigger scale, that's all.'

Had she looked crestfallen, I would have stuck to my guns, but no way was Marsha going to let her disappointment show, and it was the brave face that did it. I felt petty and mean-spirited, especially since she'd been the one who'd got me into my flat in the first place. I hastened to assure her that no, I didn't mind letting the party spread upstairs, in fact I insisted, there was hardly any furniture, *mia casa è sua casa* and so on, and I was sure Sophie would want to join in once she'd forgiven me for whatever I'd said to offend her.

I pondered my best course of action. Marsha could do what she liked with my flat, but I had no intention of being anywhere near Hampshire Place when midnight chimed on the thirty-first of October. I was going to get as far away as I could. The flat in Hackney was currently occupied by a globe-trotting Canadian friend of a friend, but perhaps it was time to pay one of my rare visits to my grandmother in St Albans.

Hallowe'en. As *if.* I had absolutely no intention of hanging around to see what crawled out of the woodwork. Do you think I'm *stupid*?

SEVEN

'JESUS!' I shouted, sitting straight up in bed.

'See what I mean,' said Sophie.

I'd been staring at my ceiling, wondering why all the little bumps and cracks had rearranged themselves during the night, when I realised with a cold shock of comprehension that it wasn't my ceiling at all.

On the other side of the bed, Sophie was propped up against a heap of pillows, lounging like a medium-sized odalisque except that instead of being nude she was wearing pale green silk pyjamas. What with the pyjamas and the red hair, she was glowing like a Technicolor goddess.

I asked what she was doing there. Then I corrected myself and asked what *I* was doing.

'You've been at it again,' Sophie said coldly. 'Now I'd like my bed back if you don't mind.'

Still a bit addled, I got up and padded over to the door, wishing I were wearing something more glamorous than the outsized T-shirt my grandmother had got free by sending off ten labels from cans of Pedigree Chum.

'How about returning my key?' Sophie called after me.

'I don't even know where *my* keys are.'

'Try the door,' said Sophie, 'where you left them.'

She was right. I retrieved my keys and wandered into Sophie's living-room to find something to jemmy hers off with. I didn't have my specs on, and so everything was in soft focus, the top of her worktable resembling a scene from the Arabian Nights, sprinkled with glimmering jewel colours and tantalizing scraps of treasure which on closer examination turned out to be Japanese pencils, translucent plastic rulers, and Italian-made sketchpads covered in mock-croc and nubuck.

I levered the key off with a pair of scissors and went back into the bedroom to return it to its rightful owner. 'I suppose you might as well stay for breakfast,' Sophie said ungraciously, and headed down to the kitchen, leaving me free to wander back into the living-room and take a closer look at something I'd glimpsed earlier.

The board on which Sophie had drawn her autumn garden was propped against the wall by the table.

From my standing position, and without spectacles, it looked innocuous, but I bent down apprehensively, half-expecting something to leap out and fasten on to my throat.

Close up, it still looked innocuous.

Perhaps *too* innocuous. There had to be a catch, but for the life of me, I couldn't work out what it might be. The scene was so autumnal, you could almost smell the dead wood and the toadstools. The flower beds blazed with red and yellow chrysanthemums. The leaves had turned crisp and golden; most had already fallen from the trees, and some had been swept into a pile, waiting only for a touch of flame to transform them into a roaring bonfire.

I scrutinized the picture for hints of something lurking in the undergrowth, for beady eyes gleaming, or warty snouts snuffling, or grotesque figures with limbs gnarled like the branches of trees. But there was nothing like that at all. Instead, two podgy-cheeked children clad in duffle-coats and mittens romped on the lawn with their golden-haired spaniel. And a jolly time was being had by all.

I nibbled at a ragged cuticle. The picture was horrible. It made me want to vomit.

It was obvious what had happened. Sophie had shaken off the dark influence and gone back to being normal.

It was weeks since anyone had seen Robert. I was beginning to wonder if he'd gone for good. Maybe thinking I'd seen his reflection in the mirror had been as good as an exorcism. It was a load off my mind, but at the same time I missed him. He still struck me as having most of the advantages of a real live man without many of the drawbacks.

Graham did his best, but he left a lot to be desired. Apart from the sex, that is, which was as wild and crazy as it had ever been; he turned into a beast between the sheets. I was even tempted to try it with a clear head, but on those rare occasions when we managed to stay sober, we never got beyond first base.

But at least my sex life was active, so when, later that week, Miles phoned and invited me out to lunch, I realized to my satisfaction that I wasn't as thrilled as I might once have been. With Graham catering for my physical needs, and Robert occupying the twilight zone of my fantasy life, the man who had started everything rolling in the first place had almost slipped my mind.

I wanted to go to Cinghiale, but Miles insisted on trying a place called Truffles which had recently opened in a cul-de-sac around the back of Westbourne Grove. The decor was wall-to-wall whitewash, the seats looked and felt as though they'd been welded out of scrap metal, and the menu was one long litany of tongues, knuckles and tripe. Miles let out a little whimper of pleasure and plumped for deep-fried pig's ear rolled in breadcrumbs and served in a mustardy vinaigrette with spiced red cabbage. All around us diners were tucking into loin roasts and fresh offal, and the juice was running down their necks. As I prodded my chitterling pancake with beans and sauerkraut, I began to feel nostalgic for the sort of rocket salad so minimalist that even Sophie might have hesitated to pass it off as a square meal.

I wasn't fool enough to believe Miles had invited me out because of my irresistible allure, and, sure enough, it didn't take him long to get to the point.

'Sophie said she was having a party.'

'She invited you?' I asked, vexed that he thought it was Sophie's party and dismayed to learn they were back on speaking terms. The news left me feeling slightly disoriented, as though I'd been guarding something of value, but had had my attention distracted at a crucial moment.

'So you'll be taking Ligia,' I said, sorry that I wouldn't be around to see Sophie come face to face with her nemesis. I was sorry too that I wouldn't be there to see Ligia for myself; in my head I'd built her up into a formidable opponent. Perhaps it was time to see what I was really up against.

'She won't be there,' said Miles, gazing lugubriously at his pig's ear. 'We split up. We weren't really compatible.'

'What a shame,' I said, trying to suppress the block-buster smile that was threatening to break out all over my face.

Miles fiddled with his fork. 'Actually I found she'd been shagging someone else all along.'

Miles had been shagging other women left, right and centre all the years he'd been living with Sophie, but I didn't remind him of that. Instead I said, 'Oh, bad luck. You must be feeling a bit depressed, then.'

Miles nodded. 'Suicidal. You know how it is. This party might be just the thing to cheer me up. I thought you might know who was going to be there. Which of Sophie's friends, I mean.'

Now I understood. He wanted Sophie back, and I was supposed to tell him if he had a clear run. Well, I wasn't going to roll over and play his game. It took me all of two seconds to postpone the proposed visit to my grandmother indefinitely.

'It's my party too,' I said.

'It is?' asked Miles, chomping away on a particularly stubborn piece of pigskin. 'Sophie said you'd be away.'

'I was toying with the idea. Nothing definite.'

'So. Who will *you* be inviting? Anyone I know?'

This, I knew, was Milespeak for, 'And who might *you* be shagging these days?' An image of Graham unfurled in my brain and hung there, undulating gently like a banner in the wind, but I made it go away. I didn't want Miles thinking I was *that* desperate. 'I'm sort of between men,' I said, peering at him over the top of my spectacles.

Miles looked pleased at the thought of there being at least one unattached female dancing attendance on him. He smiled a wicked smile that made my stomach do a back-flip. I considered the odds; they were big, fat and juicy. I would have an entire evening to work on him, and there would be no one to get in the way. Carolyn was ancient history; he wasn't about to retrace his steps with her. Charlotte had fancied him for ages, and I wouldn't have stood a chance against her in the normal run of things, but her style would be severely cramped by Toby, and perhaps by Grenville as well, though I still wasn't sure what was going on in that department.

I had no way of knowing whether or not Robert Jamieson was going to put in an appearance. Who was I kidding? It was the anniversary of his suicide; of *course* he was going to show up. But I would be surrounded by friends, and I had no intention of sleeping alone. I would have Miles in my sights and even if – heaven forbid – things didn't work out between us, there would always be Graham to fall back on.

The only other obvious contender for Miles' affections would be Sophie. This was a tough one. But she'd changed so much I wasn't sure he'd recognize her any

more, let alone fancy her. Maybe she was no longer his
type. Not that Miles had ever been fussy enough to *have*
a type.

But I had no intention of letting Sophie spoil things.
Not now. Not ever again.

EIGHT

O N THE MORNING of the party I got up early and
wolfed down a big bowl of muesli before tidying
the flat. There wasn't much tidying to do, but I
made sure that all the more embarrassing things –
such as the stash of Pop Tarts, the Madonna tapes,
and my *Bon Ton Guide to Chic Shopping* – were well
concealed, while items likely to impress – such as my
new Mont Blanc pen, the ashtray Marsha had got me
from Cinghiale, and a bottle of Extra Virgin Olive Oil
from the shop up the road – were occupying centre-
stage. On second thoughts, bearing in mind what Miles
had told me about his pen being snatched, I hid my
Mont Blanc and left the empty box on display in its
place.

Sophie and I had called a truce. After lunch I nipped
downstairs to ask if I could borrow some earrings and
she invited me in to take a look at her living-room. I
reeled in shock: the place had been transformed. The
white-with-a-soupçon-of-pistachio had been almost obli-
terated by black and purple nebulae, several galaxies'
worth of silver moons and stars, and a couple of
primitive rainbows. The windows had shed their fluttering buttermilk drapes and were now hung with ill-
fitting red velvet which looked suspiciously like the

curtains that had been up in my flat before I'd moved
in and torn them down.

'How are you going to get this stuff off?' I asked,
testing the surface of the nearest nebula with the tip of
a fingernail.

Sophie inclined her head and said, 'Maybe I want it
to stay.'

I was astonished and not a little discomfited. What
had happened to my friend's discerning eye for all that
was most refined in interior decoration? What about
her carefully worked-out colour schemes? Her eye for
subtle yet authentic detail? Either she was exercising a
zany sense of humour that had hitherto escaped my
notice, or she'd been infected with some rapid-acting
disease which had wiped out her taste receptors.

'When did you do all this . . *spraying*?'

'Oh, it wasn't me,' she giggled. 'I hired a couple of
tomcats.'

'Oh, what? You spotted them painting their names
on the side of a tube train?'

'No, I got Dirk and Lemmy to do it.'

'Dirk and Lemmy? *Dirk and Lemmy* have been here?'
I found it hard to believe she'd allowed Dirk and
Lemmy back within stippling range of her walls.

'They're down with Marsha right now,' said Sophie.
'They're really imaginative. Aren't you going to get
them to do something to your place?'

'They're here? *Now?*'

'Why don't we pop down and see how they're doing,'
said Sophie, taking me by the hand.

*

The door to Marsha's flat was propped open with a large metal Buddha, and the noise from an improperly tuned radio drifted out to greet us. The first thing I saw as I walked into her living-room was Dirk slopping a bucket of blood over the wall. The second thing was Lemmy sitting in the middle of the floor with a Rambo knife, hacking away at a pumpkin wedged between his thighs like an off-colour testicular swelling.

Lemmy's face lit up as he saw me. 'Clare!' he exclaimed. 'Silmarillion ornella muti!'

Dirk turned round, the front of his overalls an impressionistic study in scarlet. 'Clare!' he yelled, ditching the bucket and advancing towards me with arms outstretched. 'Where've you *been?*'

He smothered me in his bearlike embrace, leaving me smeared with so much red it looked as though I'd been attacked by a knife-wielding maniac.

'You're not mad at me?' I asked.

Lemmy and Dirk looked at each other like Bill and Ben wondering where on earth Little Weed had got to.

'Mad at you?' asked Dirk. 'Why? What have you done?' He adopted a schoolmasterly baritone. '*Have you been a bad girl, Clare?*'

'The Boar's Head,' I prompted him. 'Don't you remember?'

'Melissa stribling,' said Lemmy, shaking his head.

Dirk scratched his face, leaving a big red smear on his stubbly chin. 'Old bikers' pub,' he said. 'Lots of gays in there now. Not really your kind of place.'

'You mean you don't remember?'

'Remember what?'

329

I could have wept with relief. Dirk and Lemmy were so brain-dead they hadn't even *noticed* me running out on them. I couldn't understand how I'd got so worked up over it.

'I behaved rather badly,' I said.

Dirk and Lemmy sniggered. They thought they knew everything there was to know about bad behaviour.

'Do tell,' purred Sophie, who had stationed herself at my elbow.

'Impossible to misbehave in the Boar's Head,' said Dirk.

Lemmy nodded. 'Vetivert,' he said sagely. 'Nogbad.'

'You're telling me,' said Dirk. 'I mean, you should see what those gay bikers get up to on a Saturday night.'

As soon as Sophie realized there weren't going to be any true confessions, she lost interest in the conversation and wandered over to inspect Dirk's splatter effect. 'Looks like someone got chopped up with an axe in this very room,' she said.

'Noddy in toyland,' Lemmy said to her excitedly. 'Annabella salmonella.' He gestured towards the floor.

I was about to ask Dirk for a translation when Marsha came in from the kitchen, rattling her stainless steel cocktail shaker.

'I didn't know you were friends with Dirk and Lemmy,' I said, unable to keep the accusatory tone out of my voice.

Marsha looked at me in surprise. 'But *of course* I am. How could you live in west eleven for twenty years and *not* be friendly with *Dinsdale* and *Lionel*?'

'Dinsdale and Lionel?' I queried, having lost the plot. 'Who the hell are they?'

'Busted!' shouted Dirk.

Marsha collapsed into peals of mirth. 'For Heaven's sake, you don't think his dad christened him *Dirk*, do you?'

'Dirk Bogarde's father did,' said Sophie.

'Nah,' said Dirk. 'Dirk Bogarde was a Derek.'

Marsha told us she was making very dry Martinis and asked who wanted one. Dirk and Lemmy's hands shot into the air faster than the speed of light. Sophie said, *ooh yes*, and I followed her example, because even though I needed to keep my wits about me if I wanted the evening to proceed as planned, it seemed somehow supremely glamorous and Notting Hill-ish to be knocking back very dry Martinis at two in the afternoon.

'Clare wants her flat done too,' said Sophie. 'Don't you, Clare?'

'Is there enough time?' I asked.

'Pas de problem,' said Dirk. 'We work at warp speed.'

'Papageno,' said Lemmy.

'Just as soon as we've finished in here,' added Dirk.

I wasn't sure of Dirk and Lemmy's official standing in this company. Were they honoured guests or hired hands? Out of the corner of my mouth, I asked Sophie if anyone had issued them with a party invitation. Marsha overheard. 'Of *course* we invited them,' she boomed. 'How could you possibly have a party and *not* invite Lionel and Dinsdale?'

She tousled the top of Lemmy's head so affectionately that I wondered whether they'd ever been an item. Lemmy had a tendency to get romantically involved with the darnedest people. I'd always wondered how he'd managed to get as far as he did without Dirk there to translate for him.

'Down there down there down there,' rumbled Dirk as he applied another red stain to the wall and watched it trickle slowly down.

'Ah,' said Marsha. 'The Drunken Boats. They used to live in this house, you know.'

And Sophie whispered in my ear, 'They still do.'

As I climbed back upstairs, stomach comfortably lined with gin, I felt as though a great weight had been lifted from my shoulders. I felt liberated, carefree, and all those other words favoured by the makers of ads for sanitary towels. It was the best possible portent. Dirk and Lemmy were back, and it was as though they'd never been away. Miles was up for grabs. All was right with my world.

I'd even felt brave enough to talk to Sophie about Robert. I'd half expected her to tip her Martini over my head, but all she did was put her head on one side and give me a funny look. 'I thought he was with you,' she said.

'Not any more.'

Sophie looked exactly how I'd felt when Miles had told me about Ligia. 'What a pity. The two of you seemed to be getting along so well.'

'You saw him?' I asked her. 'All the time?'

Sophie looked smug. 'You mean you didn't?'

*

Dirk and Lemmy came up later to give my flat their specialist Hallowe'en treatment, and even though I'd forbidden the use of aerosols because I didn't want to have to paint the walls again, I had to admit they worked miracles. By the time they left, my living-room was looking every bit as spooky as the others. Dirk draped decorators' sheets over the furniture. Lemmy threaded severed chickens' claws on to lengths of long black thread and strung them across the ceiling like outlandish paper chains. I didn't ask where he'd found the claws. Some things it was better not to know.

I shaved my legs with a disposable razor, plastered my face with mudpack, and wallowed in the bath until the water cooled from balmy Aegean to icy Atlantic. I hadn't lingered so long in my bathroom for ages, but the ambience no longer seemed sinister, and besides, the mirror was safely misted up.

'Sorry, Robert,' I said, clambering out of the bath and wiping a small clearing in the foggy glass. 'I need someone who's going to be *there* for me. I'm afraid Miles is back in the picture.'

Wrapped in a towel, I went back into the living-room, slotted the Drunken Boats into my tape machine, and settled back into one of the decorator's sheets to coat my fingernails with black varnish. I hadn't played the Boats in ages. Only now did I realize how much I'd missed them; it was like being in the presence of old friends.

'Hello, Jeremy,' I said. 'Hello, Hugo, hello, Ralph, hello the other one whose name I can't remember.'

Down there down there down there

NINE

MY EVENING had been coasting along very nicely, thank you, until Graham dropped his bombshell. Up until then I'd been on a roll – for once in my life, scores of people seemed eager to talk to me, and I hadn't had a second to myself, let alone the time to entertain an unsettling thought.

And then Graham had gone and spoiled it all.

The epicentre of the party was turning out to be Marsha's flat, with Marsha herself apparently generating most of the vibrations as she lurched around the dance-floor in her stripy T-shirt, torn trousers, eye-patch and stilettos. Stapled to her shoulder was a stuffed parrot. She waved. I made myself wave back.

But the revelry was gradually percolating upwards. A few intrepid souls had already set up camp in Sophie's living-room, but so far the only explorers who had toiled even further up had taken one look around my draped, deserted nest and promptly fled back downstairs.

So when Graham turned up, and I took him upstairs to show him the chicken claws, we had the place to ourselves. I fetched my Cinghiale ashtray, and we sat on the edge of the draped table, and Graham produced a ready-rolled joint, which we smoked briskly, passing it back and forth in a businesslike fashion. I wasn't dead drunk, not as drunk as I normally was whenever Graham and I ended up in bed together, but I reckoned I was drunk enough, so I leant over and tried to kiss him.

He shrank back with a look of utter dismay.

I was taken aback. 'What's the matter?'

He muttered something about it not feeling right.

'What do you mean?' I demanded. '*I'm* the one who should be complaining about how it feels. Look at you – you haven't even bothered to shave.'

Graham explained that not shaving was part of his costume. It was only then that I realized why he was wearing furry gloves and what appeared to be some sort of toupee stuffed down the open neckline of his shirt.

'Oh, I see,' I said. 'You're supposed to be a werewolf.'

'Rrraaarrgh,' he roared, holding his hands up like claws. I roared back and tried to nuzzle him wolfishly, but he edged along the table, making nervous swatting motions as though I were a troublesome bluebottle.

'I'm sorry, Clare. I really like you, but I just don't think of you . . . *that* way.'

I leaned back and silently passed him the joint, blinking back the tears that were threatening to well up. When I was sure I wasn't going to embarrass myself, I asked, 'So what brought this on? Was it something I said?'

Graham inhaled deeply, giving himself time to devise a diplomatic reply. I watched him go cross-eyed as he tried to keep the tip of the joint in focus.

'You're one of my best friends,' he said at length. 'Let's leave it at that, shall we? Let's not spoil things.'

This was really too much. 'It's a bit late to talk about spoiling things, don't you think?'

Graham was picking at an obstinate shred of tobacco that had adhered to his tongue. 'What do you mean?'

'Excuse *me*,' I said, 'but what do *you* mean? We've been going at it like rabbits for months and now all of a sudden you're playing hard to get.'

Graham stared at me with a look of such absolute horror on his face that I wondered if I'd inadvertently cast aspersions on his manhood. He said something I didn't catch, or maybe I just hadn't *wanted* to catch it. I asked him to run it by me again, and leaned closer to make sure I didn't miss it again.

'No we haven't,' he said.

When I heard these words I leaned too far and had to stick out a hand to halt my slide. Graham, assuming it was another amorous advance, promptly launched himself clear of the table, well out of my reach, and started to back towards the door.

'That's right,' I said. 'Deny it.'

'Clare,' he said. 'You and I have never been to bed together. I'll admit we came perilously close to it once or twice, but we never went all the way.'

'This is ridiculous,' I said. 'What about all those cups of tea in the morning?'

'For Heaven's sake,' said Graham. 'I can't believe you get *that* drunk. The only time I ever stayed the night was when you passed out and I had to put you to bed, and even then I slept on the cushions in here.

Good God . . .' He'd come to the end of the joint and the filter was now giving off an acrid smell. 'You don't think I . . .'

His voice died away. By now he'd reached the doorway, and I was fighting off the urge to scream. 'Let me get this straight,' I said carefully, trying not to mangle the words. 'We never had sex? Not even once?'

Graham shook his head. 'I didn't realize it meant that much to you.' Now he was the one who looked as if he might burst into tears at any second.

'It doesn't,' I answered, now desperate to salvage a scrap of pride. 'It means *nothing*. When I said we'd had . . . *sex*, I was of course . . . joking.'

Graham looked only slightly less upset than I felt. 'You see,' he said, 'if I'd thought . . .'

'I know,' I said. 'It wasn't very funny, was it? I'm sorry, I've had way too much to drink.'

Or maybe not enough. Not *nearly* enough.

'I'd better get back downstairs,' said Graham, still anxious to put as much distance between us as possible. 'See you later, OK?'

'Later,' I said.

As soon as he'd gone, I retouched my lipstick and followed him down. I didn't dare spend any longer on my own. I needed food and drink. I needed company, and lots of it. I needed anything but the opportunity to stop and think. That was something I really didn't need.

I'd definitely been having sex with *someone*.

But if not with Graham, then with whom?

*

337

I operated for a while on automatic, sipping my wine as I watched the armies of the undead gathering in Marsha's living-room. The guests were dressed as vampires and ghouls, but quaffed Chardonnay instead of blood, and picked at roasted peanuts instead of tearing at ragged chunks of raw flesh. I thought I recognized a couple of the waiters from Cinghiale, but they failed to recognize me back.

Since company didn't appear to be forthcoming, I had to fall back on oral gratification. Food was the closest thing to hand. I hovered over the snack bowls and scoffed most of the cashews before graduating to the harder stuff – prawn vol-au-vents, bacon and mushroom quiche, and French sticks with salami and cheese.

I was feeding this food into my face as though there were no tomorrow when, as if in a dream, I noticed some sort of disturbance over by the door. A wraith-like creature detached itself from the scrum of kissy-kissing guests and came bowling across the room in slo-mo. Too late, I recognized Carolyn. In an uncharacteristically affectionate gesture, she flung her arms around my neck, trailing wisps of grey chiffon, and I was enveloped in a choking cloud of Miss Dior.

'There, there,' she soothed.

'What? Where?' I asked through a mouthful of French bread, trying to struggle free without getting my black satin shoulders smeared with her greasy white make-up.

'It's a bit *much*,' she said. 'Even when Miles and I were, you know, *seeing each other*, I would never have flaunted him in front of Sophie. I would never have *dreamed* of doing that. Not to a *friend*.'

'I'm sure you wouldn't,' I said, thinking that at any second Carolyn would say something that would cause this fuzzy conversation to snap into razor-sharp focus. I didn't have a clue as to what she was prattling on about, and was just starting to think that Lemmy's babbling was an infectious disease which Carolyn had caught, when we were joined by the Woman in Black. It was Charlotte, squeezed into a sexy black rubber sheath, with her natural shortish curly hair concealed beneath a straight black wig. Like me, she had made a half-hearted attempt to pass herself off as Morticia Addams, but she had an unfair advantage over me – she was thin.

I braced myself for a snide remark, but she merely looked me up and down and said, 'I see we share the same impeccable taste in old TV shows.'

I mulled over this sentence, trying to divine the hidden insult that indubitably lurked within. If I hadn't been on my guard before, my every nerve was now crouched in defensive mode. This was the second time Charlotte had taken my side. Carolyn was occasionally capable of random acts of niceness, but Charlotte had always been a Grade A, green-eyed, take-no-prisoners bitch. If both she and Carolyn were being friendly, then something was definitely up.

Was it a trap?

Had Graham been talking to them?

'Maybe she's trying to make Miles jealous,' suggested Charlotte.

The thought of Miles brought me back to earth. Miles was my mission. If I could land Miles, all this other stuff, the stuff I didn't want to think about, would fade quietly into the background where it could be buried and forgotten.

'We shouldn't pile *all* the blame on to Sophie,' said Carolyn. 'I mean, it's bad form on *his* part as well.'

'You mean on Miles's part?' I asked, still ten steps behind the rest of the world.

Carolyn and Charlotte turned to me and chorused, 'Not Miles. *Robert.*'

I continued to look at them with the same expression, but my skin felt as though it had suddenly taken on many of the characteristics of deep-frozen poultry. After a while I said, calm as you like, 'Robert's here now, is he?'

Carolyn and Charlotte exchanged jittery glances.

'You mean you haven't seen him?' asked Charlotte.

'Not as such,' I said.

'Don't tell me you didn't know,' said Carolyn.

'Of course I knew,' I said, though I knew nothing.

'You didn't know he was seeing *Sophie?*' asked Charlotte, hugging herself with the delicious melodrama of it all.

'You didn't realize he was *here* with Sophie?' asked Carolyn. 'Smooching with her, and in front of everyone? It's a bit much. I do think they should have been more considerate.'

I felt myself being tossed up and down on an emotional roller-coaster. Part of me was humiliated that Robert had turned his back on me and reattached himself to Sophie. Another part wanted to see for myself. Was this really the man I'd glimpsed in the mirror? Was he the one who'd been sharing my bed as well?

And yet another part of me, the most charitable part, the part that had been submerged for so long that I sometimes forgot it was there, wondered whether perhaps I shouldn't be warning Sophie to watch her back. Did she really know what kind of man she was dealing with here? Did she know he'd been unfaithful on a regular basis? Did she know about the fork? And if not, shouldn't I be telling her about it? God knows, we had our differences, and enough of them, but she was still my best friend after all.

I gulped down the rest of my drink and set the glass down on Marsha's mantelpiece. 'Will you excuse me,' I said, and left Carolyn and Charlotte staring after me, the grey lady side by side with the Goth. I was going to look for Sophie. I was going to see for myself.

It wasn't that easy, of course. It was like trying to pass through the enchanted thicket in the Sleeping Beauty story. I hadn't gone two yards before I was swooped on and snogged by a stocky sugar-plum fairy with chest hair. Toby was difficult to ignore at the best of times, but impossible to overlook when dressed in a spangly pink tutu.

He'd already formed some sort of alliance with Dirk and Lemmy, and was bantering away with them like someone who'd been awarded a Cambridge First in Lemmy-ese. The boys had been home to stock up on substances and change into costume, and had only just made it back. Dirk was swathed in toilet paper; strips of it dangled from his arms like semi-sloughed skin. 'Don't tell me,' I said. 'You're the Mummy.'

'Nah, 'said Dirk. 'I'm the *Andrex puppy*.'

I thought he looked more like a bullmastiff with a spongiform brain, but at least he'd tried harder than Lemmy, who appeared to be dressed as normal, apart from the ragged white sheet he'd draped over his shoulders.

'And you're a ghost,' I said.

'Ummagumma poseidon,' Lemmy gurgled trium-phantly, dropping to his knees and pulling the edge of the sheet down over his head so that I could see the blob of yellow duster material tacked to his back. There was a muffled comment from beneath the sheet.

'Pardon?'

'He's a fried egg,' Dirk explained.

'Of course he is,' I said. How could I have possibly failed to guess? 'And now if you'll excuse me,' I said, 'I have to go and find Sophie.'

I shouldered my way through wall-to-wall rollickers, none of whom seemed to give a fig about blocking the hallway and stairs. No sign of Sophie yet, but half-way up the first flight of steps I found my face jammed inches away from a head of sparse sandy hair with a faint sprinkling of dandruff. It was Graham – the last person in the world I wanted to run into. But he wasn't paying much attention to passers-by.

It was Isabella who spotted me. 'He's so cute,' she

squealed, disentangling herself from Graham's torrid embrace as I tried to squeeze past. 'He's so . . . *eengleesh.*'

And so utterly wet and a weed, I thought.

'And *zucchini,*' Isabella added mysteriously, slipping her arm around Graham's waist and squeezing hard. Graham gave the satisfied grunt of a merchant venturer whose ship had finally sailed into harbour laden with jewels and spices.

'I can't *wait* to take him home to Milano,' Isabella giggled. 'I can't *wait* to present him to my mamma, so she can fatten him up with some of her famous lasagne.'

I congratulated Graham as sarcastically as I could, though since Isabella had her tongue in his ear, I doubt that he heard. As I pushed on up the stairs, I felt my stomach being eaten away by a steady drip of acid jealousy, though I couldn't work out whether it was Isabella or Graham I was the more jealous of. If only I'd made more of an effort to be nice to our *amica* on her whirlwind stop-overs, I too might have found myself invited to the Giordano family villa to hobnob with Signor Giordano's mob connections and watch old Italian movies starring Isabella's glamorous mamma in her Euro-cutie days.

Going upstairs was turning into an epic journey. The landing outside Sophie's flat was packed with people queuing for the bathroom, another obstacle for me and a captive audience for Grenville, who was showing everyone the label of his Armani suit.

'I see *you* couldn't be bothered to get dressed up,' I said.

'But I *am* in fancy dress,' said Grenville. 'It's up to you to guess what it is.'

From somewhere behind me, a familiar, slightly bored voice said, 'Don Johnson in *Miami Vice*.' I twisted round and saw Miles, who didn't appear to be in costume either, though he somehow didn't stick out from the crowd the way Grenville did. A single lock of hair flopped fetchingly over his forehead. I was so relieved to see him that I flung my arms around his neck and tried to give him a kiss, but Miles jerked his head up so my lips grazed his chin. I remembered Graham doing something similar once, but the difference was that Miles, unlike Graham, had moved his head *on purpose*.

'Have I got lipstick on me?' he asked anxiously.

I fell back. This was not the scenario I'd planned. But before I could muster my resources for a second attempt, Grenville butted between us and fumed, 'I'm a *serial killer*. The whole point is that I look the *same* as everyone else.'

'But you don't look the same as everyone else,' said a queuing woman in a bloodstained ballgown. 'You're wearing a poncey designer suit, while everyone else is in costume.'

'*Miles* isn't in costume,' said Grenville, unable to keep the whine out of his voice.

'Shouldn't you at least be carrying an axe?' I asked, trying to revive my spirits by being nasty to Grenville.

'He nicked the idea from *American Psycho*,' Miles said.

Grenville looked even more annoyed. 'I did not.'

Miles ignored him and said to me, 'What's going on?'

I assumed he was wanting to be brought up to date. 'Graham and Isabella are in *love*,' I told him. 'Grenville and Charlotte are having an affair.'

'That's the most ridiculous thing I've heard in my life,' spluttered Grenville.

'I mean what's going on with *Sophie*?' said Miles.

Sophie. I remembered I was supposed to be going upstairs to warn her about the company she was keeping.

'I saw her with this guy,' said Miles.

'God knows where you got that idea from,' said Grenville. 'Charlotte and I are just good friends.'

'Who was it?' I asked Miles.

'Some guy dressed as a bodysnatcher. All in black.'

'Oh shit,' I said. 'Where?'

'I'm fond of her, of course,' said Grenville.

'Upstairs,' said Miles.

'Show me,' I said. Miles nodded and began to force his way through the bathroom queue.

'You haven't told Carolyn, have you?' asked Grenville.

'Of course not,' I said, trying to wriggle past him.

'It's nothing serious,' said Grenville, still blocking the way. Up ahead, I saw Miles's head bobbing for a few seconds before it was swallowed up by the crowd. I tried once again to start after him, but now Grenville was hanging on to my sleeve. 'Carolyn would kill me if she found out.'

I could have killed him myself. I was so desperate not to let Miles out of my sight that I said the first thing that came into my head. 'Why don't you ask Carolyn about her and Miles,' I said. 'Look, I've *got* to catch up with him.'

'Oh, *Miles*,' spat Grenville, as I finally managed to pull my sleeve out of his grasp. He was even more drunk than he looked. 'Everyone's trying to catch up with *Miles*.'

I left him fulminating there.

Sophie's living-room was full of people dancing like reanimated corpses, but Sophie herself was nowhere to be seen. I knew I had to keep searching, but I was short of breath, as though I'd just climbed a couple of hundred steps instead of a couple of dozen, and the thought of the laborious trek back down to Marsha's flat filled me with dread. The music was too loud, and I could feel the crowd pressing in all around me, so I put my head down and shoved my way through to a small breathing space on the opposite side of the room. I slumped against a wall, fanning my face with a paper napkin and trying not to have a full-blown panic attack. I wanted a drink so badly I was spitting feathers, and to cap it all, someone put on a tape of the Drunken Boats.

'Hot, isn't it?' I said to a nearby couple, a mad scientist with sticky-up hair and a gorgon wearing a wig made from a swimming cap and some rubber snakes. They stared at me as though I were barking mad.

'No, it's not,' said the scientist. 'It's not hot at all. As a matter of fact it's quite cool.' He and his companion lost no time in moving as far away from me as possible, leaving me with the young man who'd been quietly standing on his own behind them, wearing a sad, rather dreamy expression. Our eyes met. He quickly looked away.

'Don't I know you?' I asked him.

He shook his head and stared down at his hands. He seemed to me the sort of person who would have moist palms. I noticed he didn't have a drink and, reminded for the first time of my obligations as a hostess, asked if I could get him one. 'Yes, please,' he said, Adam's Apple bobbing as he nervously swallowed air.

I hadn't forgotten Sophie or Miles, but I knew that if I didn't have a drink soon I was going to pass out. I had just enough strength left to fight my way to the nearest filling station and collect two glasses of white wine. Weaving my way back through the zombie dancers, I took a good look at the man I was heading for. His haircut was short to the point of radical, and he held himself unnaturally straight, as though he had a broom-handle jammed down the back of his jacket. His face was plastered with pale make-up, and he wore an ill-fitting suit which made him look like either Gilbert or George, whichever was the ganglier.

I wasn't naive. I knew that when a man looked as square as this, the odds were that he would turn out to be incredibly avant-garde. I handed him his drink, and watched as he slurped at it inelegantly.

'Wine OK?' I asked.

'Lovely,' he said, wiping his mouth, and added, 'I don't normally drink wine.'

'Oh? And what do you normally drink?'

'Light ale, or stout.'

'I can get you some lager.'

'No, the wine is lovely,' he assured me.

Not exactly the world's most accomplished conversationalist, I thought, and decided he wasn't my type at all. I couldn't possibly go out with someone who described his wine as 'lovely'. But I persevered, trying to make small talk while scanning the room for traces of Sophie or Miles.

'Do you know many of the people here?' I asked him.

'Not a soul.'

I looked at him again. He was gulping his drink as though it were Horlicks, like an overgrown schoolboy with no social graces at all. He didn't even have the *nous* to pretend he was at ease. I felt a mixed sort of triumph; I'd actually stumbled across someone even more gauche than I was. I sipped at my drink, trying to think of something else to say.

'How many people do *you* know?' he asked boldly.

'Not many,' I admitted.

'I just moved here.'

'I've only been here a couple of months myself.'

'Are you Sophie?'

'No,' I said, 'I'm Clare.'

He shook my hand energetically. I'd been right about his palms. 'Clare, he repeated. 'Yes, I've heard about you.'

He looked at me with what seemed to be new respect.

I asked if he was a friend of Marsha's. He shook his

head so violently that the wine slopped against the side of his glass, almost spilling over. I realized he was a good deal more than just half-cut.

Not that I was feeling particularly sober myself.

'I don't know Marsha,' he said.

The desultory conversation dried up, so I decided it was now permissable to hit him with the Big One, the question I'd been dying to ask all along but had held back, out of propriety.

I asked him what he did.

His face brightened. I'd been expecting him to say he was a writer or performance artist, or perhaps a sous-chef or waiter, but instead he said, 'I just found a job, starting next week. But it'll mean moving to Balham.'

I felt a prickling sensation in my scalp.

'Don't tell me,' I said.

He looked straight at me, and I studied his face more carefully. It was a very sincere, slightly puzzled face. The signs were all there, laid out in front of me. I couldn't understand how I'd missed them.

'You're a butcher, aren't you,' I said.

He nodded, pathetically excited. 'One day I'll have a shop of my own.'

I'd noticed his skin was pale, but only now did I notice how *thoroughly* pale it was – a ghastly, shiny sort of pale. Almost translucent. He squirmed uncomfortably beneath my appalled gaze.

'What?' he demanded. 'What are you staring at?'

'You're not in fancy dress at all,' I said. 'And you're not wearing make-up, are you?'

His lips compressed into a prim line. 'Leave it

out,' he said, not so friendly now. 'What do you think I am?'

'Oh, I know what you are,' I said. 'But what I'd like to know is – what do *you* think you are?'

'Leave it out,' he said again, struggling to stop his voice turning high-pitched. 'I don't like that funny stuff.'

'I'm sorry,' I said. 'I'm sorry . . . *Arthur*, isn't it?'

'Yeah,' he said. 'Arthur. How did you know?'

'It's my party,' I said. 'It's my business to know. Tell me, Arthur, do you know someone called Ann-Marie?'

He blushed and cast his eyes down. 'She wouldn't have nothing to do with me,' he said. 'None of them like me. They all say I'm useless.'

He looked up, and there was a weird light in his eyes. 'But I'll show them,' he said. 'I'll show them I'm good for something.'

The light in his eyes frightened me so much that I quickly asked if he wanted another drink. He looked down at the empty glass he was holding as if wondering where the contents had gone.

'Don't mind if I do.'

'More of the same?'

'Yes, please. It's lovely, that wine is.'

I had no intention of providing Arthur with another drink. I just needed to put as much distance as I could between me and that corpselike complexion. I knocked back what remained of my own drink, and forced my way to the door, looking back only once. I'd half expected Arthur Mowbray to be gone, but he was still standing there, staring after me with his strange, yearning expression.

Sophie, I thought. I had to find Sophie. If Arthur Mowbray was here, who knew what other gatecrashers might be lying in wait for us? I checked her bedroom, but though there were several couples heavily engaged in necking manoeuvres, Sophie wasn't among them. I could feel one of my headaches coming on, but held it at bay long enough to fight my way back down to the first floor landing.

Maybe that last glass of wine hadn't been such a good idea after all. I found myself squashed against the banisters, gasping for air, and it was even stuffier here than it had been upstairs. Ogres and hunchbacks pressed in all around me. I needed to find another breathing space soon, or I was going to keel over. The down staircase was choked with laughing, chattering freaks, the noise of them sounding distant to my ears, like the echo in an indoor swimming-pool. I was about to plunge in and do the crawl when I caught sight of Carolyn and Charlotte and Grenville half-way down, their faces twisted in fury, all yelling at one another. The last thing I needed right now was to get caught up in a domestic brawl, so I turned and headed up to the second floor.

Maybe Sophie had come up here, I thought to myself. That would explain why I hadn't been able to find her. Maybe Miles had come up after her.

Maybe I would catch them at it.

The thought made me break out in goose-bumps. I no longer knew whether I was looking for Sophie to warn her, or to stop her from getting back with Miles. The two concerns had somehow merged in my head.

As I climbed the stairs, the crowd thinned out like oxygen on the upper slopes of a mountain. There were three stray guests in my kitchen, heads bent in earnest conspiracy. They glanced up guiltily as I passed and I wondered if they were taking drugs, but the smell coming out of there wasn't one of dope. It was more like food. More like tomato sauce.

But I kept going, leaving the last of the pleasure-seekers below me. My living-room turned out to be every bit as deserted as when I'd been up here with Graham. The cassette I'd left playing had long since come to an end; the only sounds were a low hum from the stalled tape deck, and the thump of the bass leaking up from Sophie's.

The chicken claws gave the room a rather forlorn aspect, as though a fox had slunk into a coop of hens and left their remains dangling from the ceiling as arrogant proof of his cunning. The sheets Dirk had draped so artistically over the furniture and which I had once considered so dramatic – so very *Interiors* – now made it look as though someone were in the middle of decorating and had left everything half-finished to go and make a cup of tea.

I began to feel sorry for myself. Half of Notting Hill was whooping it up down below, and not a single visitor could be bothered to climb a measly few stairs to see how *I* might be doing. I dug out my emergency stash of Silk Cut and sulkily lit one up. The air was so thick you could have sliced it with a knife; it couldn't possibly have been made any thicker by a few wisps of cigarette smoke, but I went across to open the windows anyway.

It was only when I got there that I found they were already open.

As I turned back into the room, my ears picked up a familiar rattle, like the sound of a throat being cleared.

And I saw one of the sheets ripple, not because someone was hiding underneath it but because the air had shifted as someone, somewhere, had opened and closed a door.

Now I knew what the noise had been. The rattle of the extractor fan. Someone had been in the bathroom.

I refused to look directly at the shadowy figure now framed in the doorway of my living-room. But I couldn't help hearing the muffled voice.

'Clare.'

I chanted a mantra to myself; I'd read somewhere it was what you were supposed to say if the film you were watching became too frightening. 'It's only a movie. Only a movie. Only a movie.' The trouble was, I knew this wasn't a movie. This was really happening. This was *real.*

I forced myself to hold my head up and look straight at him. After all, it couldn't be any worse than my worst imaginings. Could it? Would I see Arthur Mowbray, his hands dripping with entrails? Robert Jamieson with the edges of his cut throat flapping? Hugo Baudelaire with his crisp-fried skin? The headless drummer?

I saw none of these things.

What I saw was a glowing green skeleton.

TEN

'Y OU SCARED the shit out of me,' I said.

I felt like howling with laughter. Whatever I'd
been expecting, it hadn't been this pantomime Mr
Bones in a black Lycra body-suit with a luminous
skeleton design appliquéd on to the front. The voice
had been muffled because the face was covered by a
plastic skull mask, but even without the mask, I wouldn't
have been able to see who it was because he was holding
up a camcorder and was even now intent upon observing me through the viewfinder.

'Aren't you going to tell me who you are?'

Mr Bones exclaimed in surprise, as though only just
realizing he couldn't be seen properly, and pushed the
mask on to the top of his head.

'So that's where you got to,' I said.

Walter Cheeseman nodded. He seemed impatient to
get the pleasantries over with so he could start filming
again.

'So what are you doing back here?'

'Collecting rent,' said Walter.

I laughed. 'You're kidding.'

'Afraid not,' said Walter. 'Everyone pays rent.'

'Except me.' I laughed again. 'I'm here for free. No
one knows I live here, not even the landlord.'

I knew the words were a mistake before they were even out of my mouth.

Walter laughed too. 'But I *am* the landlord,' he said. 'And I think it's time you made a contribution.'

'I don't *mind* paying,' I said quickly. 'I wasn't trying to get out of it.'

'Of course not.'

'I can write you a cheque. Or if you'd rather have cash I could go to my hole in the wall.'

'Foolish girl,' said Walter. 'I don't mean *money*.'

I was feeling aggrieved. I'd honestly believed we'd had the makings of a firm friendship – romance, even. 'You've been lying to me all along,' I complained. 'And I thought you were different.'

'I wouldn't call it *lying*,' said Walter, giving me a flash of his famously humourless grin. 'But I *am* different. The difference is, I know what I'm doing.'

'How do you mean?'

Walter dipped his head modestly, as though responding to a tumultuous round of applause. 'I'm booking my ticket to the afterlife,' he said. 'And I intend to travel first class.'

I was back on that roller-coaster, and it was teetering on the brink of a drop so vertiginous that I couldn't see where it would end. All I could do was cling on for dear life, and pray.

'It's roughly a twelve year cycle,' Walter was explaining. 'Every twelve years or so, the house must have blood. Doesn't make any difference whether it's murder, or suicide, or an accident, but once the place has had its fill, it goes back into hibernation. Until the next time.'

We were sitting on the floor cushions, though I deliberately hadn't made myself too comfortable in case I was suddenly presented with the opportunity for a quick getaway. Occasionally Walter would point his camcorder at me, making me feel like a rat in a lab, but more often he would pan and scan around the room, even though there was nothing there to see. I kept telling myself to keep calm, but my stomach was lurching like a drunk on a cross-channel ferry. Walter Cheeseman was very definitely round the twist. I decided it was safest to humour him, at least until someone came upstairs to rescue me.

But who would want to rescue *me*?

'So what stage are we at now?' I asked.

Walter cocked an eyebrow in surprise. 'You hadn't guessed? We're approaching endgame.' He checked his watch. 'Always the end of October, always coming up to midnight. I'd say something should happen ... within the next ... hour.'

This was all I needed. 'Oh, that's *great*,' I said. 'Don't tell me. The house is going to burn down and we're all going to die. I knew I should have gone to Gran's.'

'We're not talking apocalypse, you know,' said Walter. 'Just one person will do.'

My voice sounded very small. 'Who did you have in mind?'

'I was hoping you could enlighten me on that score,' he said, stretching out his skeleton legs and elegantly crossing his skeleton ankles. The camcorder lens had swung once again in my direction. 'Have you seen anything . . . *unusual?*'

'You mean like Sophie and Ann-Marie?'

Walter's finger slipped off the button for a second. 'Ann-Marie?'

'The girl in your movie.'

Walter thought for a moment. 'Oh, *that* tart. What about her?'

'Sophie *saw* her. Even though she was dead.'

'Really?' Walter lowered the camcorder into his lap. 'And you've seen nothing like that? Nothing at all?'

'Nothing,' I said.

'Not even in the bathroom mirror?'

'*Especially* not in the bathroom mirror.'

'Your washbasin is definitely some kind of hot spot,' said Walter. 'The vibes are extraordinary. I suppose you know that's where Jamieson carved himself an extra mouth.' He leaned back and looked pensive. 'So, who's it to be? You, Sophie, or one of the others? It doesn't make much difference to me.'

I'd lost the thread. 'Who's what to be?'

Walter Cheeseman shook his head sorrowfully. 'How can I possibly make it any clearer? *Somebody's* got to die before the evening's over.'

It took a while for this to sink in. Walter made sure he had his camera trained on me when it finally did, of course.

'*Die?*'

'Look on it as a fascinating adventure.'

'I will *not*,' I said, struggling to my feet. I wasn't going to listen to any more of this sick nonsense.

'A voyage into the unknown,' Walter continued with a faraway glint in his eye. 'The idea of it fills me with awe.'

'Why don't *you* do the voyaging, then?' It was all I could do to stop myself bouncing off the walls. I began to pace up and down instead.

Walter became evasive. 'I shan't take that step until I'm ready.'

'Or perhaps, like every other film director who ever lived, you just prefer your victims to be young and female.'

He didn't hear me. 'Maybe in another twelve years I'll have it under control. That's why I bought this house in the first place, you know – I'd heard it had a history. Nicolas Wisley, you've heard of him? How about Bertram Van der Kleist? Maurice Defryss? Arthur Mowbray I *know* you've heard of, and the Boats. Of course it was dirt cheap back in those days. Property in the Piggeries wasn't quite so desirable back then.'

'So you acquired this place in the spirit of scientific research,' I said. The headache that had been sending out exploratory feelers for the past half hour was now launching a fullscale assault on my frontal lobes.

'I've been conducting the occasional experiment,' said Walter.

I thought back. 'The tapes in your wardrobe.'

'You've been sneaking around,' he said admiringly. 'I rather hoped you would.'

'So what are you telling me? You've captured the ghosts on film?'

'It wasn't always clear what I captured,' he said. 'I

missed it by a whisker when Jamieson jumped the gun. But this time I'm going to nail it. This time I'm going to be in the right place at the right time.'

'Let me get this straight,' I said. 'You're waiting for a ghost *so you can record it on film?* You're doing some sort of *supernatural snuff movie?*'

'Ghost is rather an old-fashioned term,' frowned Walter. 'Rather Victorian, don't you think? Perhaps we should change it to something less emotive, such as *immaterial essence.* Or *corporeally challenged entity.*' He yawned and scratched the back of his head. 'So who's it to be?'

My headache was getting worse by the second. 'Sophie's the front runner, isn't she?'

'Sophie does indeed appear to be the most suitable contender. Definitely the most sensitive and creative.'

I let that go. I was starting to realize that now was not the time to play the sensitive and creative card.

'And what if I warned her?'

'You wouldn't want to do that,' said Walter. 'Not unless you were prepared to take her place. But she fits. She's beautiful, talented, and she has a big streak of dark side.'

'Not as dark as all *that,*' I said.

'And,' said Walter, 'she's had sex with ghosts.'

I stopped pacing and turned to face him. '*What?*'

'She has, hasn't she? We know she's had carnal relations with at least one of them.'

'That's one of the requirements?'

'The single most important requirement,' said Walter. 'Though I believe there was a bit of a hiccup back in 1956 when Maurice Defryss exhibited a preference for young men, and the young man in question fumbled the baton, as it were. He fled, but too late. He still ended up back here.'

'That must have been Arthur,' I said. 'Who passed it on to Ann-Marie.'

Walter was looking thoughtful. 'You say Sophie saw Ann-Marie?'

I nodded. 'After she'd fallen out of the window.'

'But Ann-Marie didn't fall,' said Walter. 'You've seen my film. She took an overdose.'

Suddenly I understood, or thought I did. 'It wasn't a ghost she saw. It had nothing to do with Ann-Marie. It must have been a *premonition*.'

Walter nodded slowly, overcome by the wonder of it all. 'Past, present, future,' he marvelled. 'Like cable TV. Hundreds of channels. Something for all the family.'

'In that case,' I said, 'I'd better find Sophie and tell her to switch off *right now*.'

Walter looked amused, as though he'd just set a grand entertainment into motion. He was still filming me as I headed towards the door.

Half-way down I bumped into Lemmy, who'd shed his sheet and now seemed to be searching for somewhere to have a quiet smoke. 'Can't stop,' I panted. 'Got to find Sophie. It's really urgent.'

'Remember what the dormouse said,' said Lemmy. I kept going, but he shouted after me, 'You've got to hang in there, Clare.'

I skidded to a halt and looked back at him in

astonishment. 'I can understand you,' I said, retracing my steps. Sophie or no Sophie, this was a phenomenon that needed investigating.

'So you can,' said Lemmy. He didn't seem at all surprised.

'But why? Why now?'

Lemmy shrugged. 'Maybe you've never been this far out of your skull before.'

'I have to find Sophie. There's something wrong with this house.'

'I *never* liked it here,' said Lemmy. 'I don't like the way it feels, and I don't like the way it makes *me* feel. Even back in the old days I knew there was something wrong with it.'

That reminded me. 'You never told me you were in one of Walter Cheeseman's films.'

'Yes I did,' said Lemmy.

'And you've known Walter for years,' I added.

Lemmy made a ratlike face, as though he'd sunk sensitive teeth into cold ice-cream. 'If I were you I'd steer clear of that goon.'

'Why didn't you *warn* me?' I wailed.

'But I did,' said Lemmy. 'I told you dozens of times. I told you to go back to Hackney and stay there.'

I stopped wailing. Back to Hackney? There were limits. I preferred to take my chances. 'It's not that I'm *scared*,' I said. 'It's not that I'm in any *danger*.'

But Lemmy was looking me up and down, as though he'd only just seen what I was wearing. 'What are you supposed to be?'

'Morticia.'

Without warning, he dipped forward and plucked the spectacles from my face. 'Then you don't need *these*. They make you look like Nana Mouskouri.' I think he put them in his pocket, but I wasn't sure of anything any more, because my already hazy worldview had been reduced to a total blur.

'But I can't see.'

'It's time to go with the flow,' said Lemmy. 'Missa lingua pangolin. Lipatti lammermoor twingo bondarchuk.'

I groaned with frustration. 'You're talking rubbish again.'

Lemmy gave me a helpless shrug. 'Mukhadev capistrano binoche.'

I smiled weakly, and turned to grope my way downstairs.

'Frug with the slug,' Lemmy called after me.

Perhaps Lemmy had known what he was doing when he confiscated my spectacles, because I spotted Sophie as soon as I walked back into her living-room. It wasn't nearly as jam-packed as before, but she'd still managed to round up a small cluster of male admirers and was holding court, peering at their palms.

As far as I could see, there weren't any undertakers in the vicinity, but I moved in for a closer squint all the same. Sophie had gone completely native. She was dressed in a crinkly plum-coloured velvet skirt and white cheesecloth blouse through which nipples were clearly visible. As soon as she saw me she dropped the palm she was reading and rounded on me, hands on hips. 'Who the *hell* do you think you are, turning everyone against me? Carolyn and Charlotte aren't speaking to me.'

'Carolyn and Charlotte aren't speaking to each other,' I said, but Sophie pointedly turned her back on me and began to talk to one of her admirers. I was about to tap her on the shoulder and explain about Charlotte and Grenville when I caught sight of Mr Bones and his camcorder on the other side of the room.

He was pointing it straight at Sophie. No, *past* Sophie – towards the cluster of men slobbering in unison behind her: Frankenstein's Monster, a Killer Robot, a brace of Count Draculas, and a balding man in striped knee-breeches.

I placed my hand on her arm. 'Look, Soph,' I said quietly. 'Why don't we . . .'

'Oh, bugger off,' said Sophie, 'I'm dancing.' She grabbed one of the Draculas and whirled him around the room in a mutant hybrid of polka and pogo. I stood and stared helplessly as her skirt flew up and exposed her stocking-tops. I'd done my best. Could anyone have expected more?

The balding man shuffled up and offered me a glass of wine. 'You look like you need a drink, Tish.' His accent was unfeasibly posh, like a Conservative politician who'd been taking elocution lessons.

'My name's not Tish,' I said, but gladly accepted the wine and gulped a large mouthful of it down. The only way to handle all that was happening was to get a lot drunker than I was already. That much I knew.

I looked gratefully at the balding man, but couldn't help noticing that his few remaining strands of hair were scraped back into a naff ponytail, his frilly shirt failed to conceal the cantaloupe-sized paunch resting on his belt, and his shiny buckled shoes weren't half as shiny as his face, with its small piggy eyes sunk into the surrounding flesh.

He mistook my expression of revulsion for one of inquiry. 'I'm a Sadistic Hellfire Squire,' he said, drawing a bundle of woolly sausages from one of his pockets. 'And this is my wig.' He balanced the sausages on his head for all of two seconds before whipping them off and stuffing them back into his pocket. 'But it's too darn hot in here.'

'You're right there,' I said, thankful I had at last found someone who agreed with me about the temperature.

'Funny,' he said. 'I used to own this building. Years ago, when it was a bit of a slum. Pity I didn't hang on to the freehold. Property prices gone through the roof since then, haven't they? Even with the recession, they're still a lot higher than they were.'

'When was it you lived here?'

'End of the Sixties,' he said. 'Those were the days.'

I squinted at him afresh. 'You haven't by any chance heard of a rock group called the Drunken Boats?'

'*Heard* of them?' For a horrible moment I thought he was going to kiss me. 'My love, you are *talking* to one of them. Jeremy Idlewild, at your service.'

My heart stopped in mid-beat. I'd walked right into it. First Arthur Mowbray, now this. I took a step back, trying to ward him off. 'I *knew* you'd turn up. I just *knew* it.'

'I can't *believe* you've heard of us,' Jeremy Idlewild said in his poncey voice. 'You don't look old enough.'

I made myself count slowly to ten. For a dead person, he wasn't so very pale. Certainly not as pasty-faced as poor Arthur Mowbray. But then Jeremy Idlewild didn't look much like my idea of a pop star either. For a start, he looked at least forty-five.

Which is round about the age he would have been had he lived. I could have kicked myself.

'You're not a ghost at all, are you,' I said.

'Only in the metaphorical sense.'

'What about the others? *They're* dead, right?'

'Hey, we weren't *that* bad. We're all alive and kicking, except poor old Marky, who succumbed to the Big C last year.'

'So let me get this straight. You didn't die of an overdose? Hugo Baudelaire didn't cover himself in petrol and set light to it?'

'*Baudelaire?* Do you know, I'd quite forgotten Hughie used to call himself that.'

'Ralph Ergstrom wasn't decapitated in a car crash?'

Jeremy Idlewild tittered nervously. 'Is this some kind of joke? Because I'm not sure I find it funny.'

'I'm sorry,' I said. 'It's just that someone's been telling porky pies. Listen, did you know they've got your album here on tape?'

Jeremy Idlewild scuttled away from me and over to the tape deck with a haste that was positively hurtful.

*

I stood at the open windows with the Drunken Boats thudding against my back. Outside, the street was abnormally deserted for a Saturday night, as though everyone else had heard about an imminent nuclear attack and scarpered. As though this were destined to be the last party in the world. But I'd made it. It was past midnight, and nothing had happened. I was still here, and so was Sophie. Walter Cheeseman had got it wrong.

From somewhere behind me, there was a mighty shout of 'Apple bobbing!' and the sound of a minor stampede. I looked back to see the last of Sophie's fan club scurrying from the room. Sophie herself had stopped dancing and was now spoiling for a fight. She strode up to me and launched straight into it, without preamble.

'It's always the same, and I'm fed up with it. You suck up to my face, and slag me off behind my back.'

'That's not true,' I said, wondering what I'd done to deserve this latest outburst.

'I can't believe you're such a creep,' she said. 'Did it never occur to you that my friends only tolerate you as a favour to me? You must have realized that Miles always thought you were a joke.'

This was a malicious lie. I tried not to rise to the bait, but it was irresistible. 'Evidently not *that* much of a joke,' I said, 'or he would never have gone to bed with me as many times as he did.'

It was worth it. Sophie looked as though she'd been slapped in the face with a wet fish. I decided to ram my advantage home. 'He shagged Carolyn as well, did you know that? Miles would shag anything in a skirt.'

'You're such a . . .' said Sophie, but all of a sudden I noticed she wasn't giving me the hundred per cent attention I thought warranted by such disclosures. She was gazing past me, down into the street.

I followed her gaze, and found myself with that frozen chicken feeling all over again. Robert Jamieson was standing in the middle of the road, looking up at us and smiling the smile that was not at all reassuring. In the lamplight he cast a long shadow, one that stretched off into infinity.

'Oh no,' I said.

Even from this distance, and even though I wasn't wearing my glasses, I found I was able to read his lips. He was saying, *It's make your mind up time.* And he started to move towards the house – not walking, but drifting, like someone on an invisible walkway.

I could feel the blood draining out of my face.

'Oh my God,' I said. 'He's coming up.'

Sophie ignored me. She was still gazing over my shoulder – like Miles, like Carolyn, like *everyone* did when they spotted someone more interesting they wanted to talk to. Her eyes were shining, lips slightly parted, and I wondered if she'd seen Robert at all, or had simply gone into a drunken trance. I had to wave my hand in front of her face before she snapped out of it.

'He's on his way up,' I said. '*Robert Jamieson.*'

Sophie chose to hear only the second half of what

I'd said. 'That's typical,' she said. 'Just because I had a good thing going with Robert, you've got to pretend you're seeing him too. But he wasn't interested in you, and you know why? You have no class, Clare, you're a stone and a half overweight, and your sense of style is even worse than Marsha Carter-Brown's.'

She'd asked for it. I'd been saving the best till last. I said, 'At least *I'm* not going to die.'

That stopped her in her tracks. 'Who said anything about dying?'

'It wasn't a ghost you saw, Sophie, it was a *premonition*. You're going to fall out of those windows . . .' I looked at my watch. 'Any minute now.'

'I have absolutely no intention of falling anywhere,' said Sophie.

'Well, *something's* got to give. And I'm damned if it's going to be me.'

Sophie's expression shifted gear. She was looking past me again, but this time into the empty room.

Or perhaps it wasn't so empty after all.

'He's here, isn't he?' I whispered.

'I can't hear you above this frigging music.'

I shouted as loudly as I could, '*There's a dead man behind me.*' Now I understood. She'd been keeping me talking, giving Robert Jamieson a chance to sneak up while my attention was distracted. They'd been plotting it from the beginning. They were in it together.

Sophie's gaze hardly wavered. She was good, I had to give her that. 'There's nobody behind you, Clare,' she said, looking past me all the time. 'The only dead men are on the dance floor downstairs.'

'I'm not going to fall for it,' I said.

'You're really cracked,' said Sophie. 'First the sleep-walking, and now this. You should see a doctor.'

'It's *you* who should see the doctor,' I said.

'Oh, cut it out,' said Sophie. 'Get a life.'

I said, 'That's exactly what I intend to do.'

Which was when I felt myself moving. It was as if someone had positioned a giant magnet just outside the windows and I was being drawn towards it, inch by inch, my heels making squeaking sounds as I dug them in and they dragged against the floor. I tried to pull back, but it was no good – it was a tug of war, and I was on the losing side. My feet were on the point of losing contact with the ground altogether when I lashed out in a panic, trying to grab something – *anything* – that would put the brakes on my involuntary progress.

I'd drawn level with Sophie. 'What are you *doing*?' she squeaked, as I grabbed a fistful of her voluminous skirt. She tried to brush my fingers away, but I'd fastened on to the material with a grip like rigor mortis.

'You don't want to bother with me,' I said.

'You can say that again,' said Sophie.

'Sophie's got more talent in her little finger than I've got in my entire body.'

'I'm glad we've sorted that one out,' said Sophie.

'I'm fat and ugly and my fashion sense is even worse than Marsha Carter-Brown's.'

'Hear hear,' said Sophie.

And, miraculously, I felt the pressure ease off. I was able to step back from the windows and relax my grip on Sophie's skirt. She immediately stooped to

369

examine it, as though my fingers might have left a slimy deposit.

Why do women have legs?

He was no longer behind me.

Now it was my turn to look over Sophie's shoulder. Tit for tat, she would have called it. He was hovering behind her, little more than a shadow emerging from the background, but this time I didn't need a mirror to see him.

Sophie glanced up from her skirt, and she must have noticed something in my face because she said, '*What?*'

He looked straight at me, cocking an eyebrow, and I shook my head as violently as I could. It hurt for me to have to say it, but I didn't have a lot of choice.

'It's her you want,' I said. 'Not me.'

And he must have agreed, because he smiled and went for Sophie instead, and she was too startled to resist. He enfolded her in his arms and lifted her bodily off the ground – just as he would have lifted me, had I not been a stone and a half heavier. Then, like a spoilt brat smashing an unwanted birthday present, he hurled her back against the rickety iron balustrade. The railings uprooted from their concrete base as easily as palings being pulled out of soft earth. Sophie felt them give way, and scrabbled with both hands for a grip on the window frame, and for a moment or two it looked as though she'd checked her fall, but all she'd managed to get hold of was a fatigued scrap of velvet which crumbled to dust in her fingers, and she didn't get another grab at it because by then she'd lost all contact with the material world.

She was there.

And then she was gone.

Maybe I should have tried to help, but it all happened so fast. All I could do was stand and stare, and say the first thing which came into my head. Which was, 'Oops.'

Robert Jamieson turned round and smiled and gave a sort of mocking salute. I stared back at him, unable to move a muscle until he suddenly lunged for me with his hands hooked into vulture claws. I shrieked and covered my face, and when I looked up again there was no one in the room but me.

I forced myself to look out of the windows, being careful not to lean out too far. Down below it was like a stage set for the last act of a play. Sophie was sprawled in a circle of unnaturally bright light. She might have been leaning against the railings, maybe waiting for someone to come out of the basement, except that her head was twisted at an unnatural angle, and protruding from where her left eye should have been was the tip of an iron spear. Only her fingers moved; they were flexing, opening and closing on the night air.

Something dark and wet was pooling on the pavement.

Against my back, the music pounded.

Ker-chunk ker-chunk ker-chunk

But at least my headache was gone.

As I slowly backed away from the window, I glimpsed out of the corner of my eye a pinprick of red light that blinked on and off. I floated instinctively towards it, like a plant seeking the sun.

I wasn't alone after all. Walter Cheeseman, in his skeleton suit, was standing a few feet away, camcorder up against his face. After a decent interval, when he was sure he'd got everything there was to get, he lowered the camera and gave me a barefaced grin.

'Gotcha!' he said.

There was a silence which felt as though it might last for ever, and then Daisy said, 'Well, thank you, Clare, for sharing that with us.'

'I've never heard anything like it in my life,' said Luke. 'What a morbid imagination.'

'And not what you'd call a feelgood ending,' said Daisy.

'I warned you,' said Clare. She seemed on the verge of leaping up and storming out, but Miles placed a restraining hand on her shoulder.

'I shouldn't have let you do it,' he said. 'I thought it would be therapeutic, but now you're all upset.'

'I'm not upset!' snapped Clare. This time, he didn't try to stop her as she jumped up and stomped off towards the bathroom. Susie followed to make sure she was all right, and reported back that she'd heard muffled sobbing behind the locked door.

Suddenly everyone was talking all at once.

'So was Sophie pushed, or wasn't she?'

'What was on Walter Cheeseman's videotape?'

Miles had the grace to be embarrassed. 'The official verdict was accidental death.'

'But you don't think it was accidental,' I said.

Very quietly, almost inaudibly, Miles said no.

'So it was *murder*,' said Daisy. 'Clare *pushed* her.'

'I didn't say that,' said Miles. 'Look, she went through a really bad patch afterwards. Well, we all did, but Clare seemed to feel responsible. She spent some time in a ... I guess you could call it a hospital, this Sunnyfields place, but even then she insisted he was writing to her.'

'By *he*, you mean ...'

'Robert Jamieson,' said Miles.

'You're kidding,' said Daisy.

'But I bet Walter Cheeseman had some explaining to do,' said Susie.

Miles shrugged. 'Walter Cheeseman turned out to be a very on-the-level kind of guy. He just happened to be filming the party. I mean, he's a film director, so that was his job. And it just so happened he was pointing his camera at the right place at the right time. It was the video that let Clare off the hook, but for God's sake don't remind her of it. The only time we managed to watch it all the way through, she ended up having to be sedated.'

'But what was on it?'

'Incontrovertible proof that Sophie didn't fall – she was pushed.'

'But who did the pushing?' asked Daisy.

373

'You couldn't see his face,' said Miles. 'The guy was in fancy dress, for Heaven's sake. All in black, like an undertaker.'

Clare came back into the room, her face all pink and blotchy. Miles took her gently by the arm.

'Come on, pussycat,' he said. 'Time to go home.'

It was something of a relief when they'd gone. 'What a strange girl,' said Daisy, and we all knew exactly what she meant. 'Not unpleasant,' she went on, 'just a little peculiar. Not really comfortable in this type of social situation, is she? And the way she dresses is rather odd, too. Beige isn't exactly her colour, is it? Makes her look as though she's suffering from some form of liver malfunction.'

I recognized the reference to liver malfunction as one that Clare herself had made. Everyone except Susie giggled.

'You're not being fair,' she said.

'But you could tell there was something weird about her the moment she walked in,' said Luke. 'When Miles told us about the hospital, it all made sense.'

'I wouldn't underestimate Clare,' I said. 'She knew what she wanted, and she went ahead and got it.'

'What do you mean?' asked Susie.

Everyone was looking at me expectantly. I spun out the pause for as long as I dared.

'She got what she wanted,' I said again. '*She got the guy.*'

Daisy nodded thoughtfully. 'Miles is quite a catch,' she acknowledged. 'Or at least he used to be.'

'But she didn't look terribly happy,' said Susie. 'I bet you anything you like that he's cheating on her.'

'Maybe so,' I said, helping myself to the last of the wine. 'But it looks like a happy ending to me.'

All Pan Books are available at your local bookshop or newsagent, or can be ordered direct from the publisher. Indicate the number of copies required and fill in the form below.

Send to: Macmillan General Books C.S.
             Book Service By Post
             PO Box 29, Douglas I-O-M
             IM99 1BQ

or phone: 01624 675137, quoting title, author and credit card number.

or fax: 01624 670923, quoting title, author, and credit card number.

or Internet: http://www.bookpost.co.uk

Please enclose a remittance* to the value of the cover price plus 75 pence per book for post and packing. Overseas customers please allow £1.00 per copy for post and packing.

*Payment may be made in sterling by UK personal cheque, Eurocheque, postal order, sterling draft or international money order, made payable to Book Service By Post.

Alternatively by Access/Visa/MasterCard

Card No. `[ ][ ][ ][ ][ ][ ][ ][ ][ ][ ][ ][ ][ ][ ][ ][ ][ ][ ]`

Expiry Date `[ ][ ][ ][ ][ ][ ][ ][ ][ ][ ][ ][ ][ ][ ][ ][ ][ ][ ]`

Signature   _____

Applicable only in the UK and BFPO addresses.

While every effort is made to keep prices low, it is sometimes necessary to increase prices at short notice. Pan Books reserve the right to show on covers and charge new retail prices which may differ from those advertised in the text or elsewhere.

NAME AND ADDRESS IN BLOCK CAPITAL LETTERS PLEASE

Name _____

Address _____

_____

_____

_____

8/95

Please allow 28 days for delivery.
Please tick box if you do not wish to receive any additional information. ☐